A DREAM COME TRUE

He wasn't even trying to deny it anymore. He wanted her. His fingers tingled at the thought of caressing her.

Ruefully, he ran his hand through his hair. She trusted him enough to drift off to sleep with him beside her. Only a cad would take advantage of a situation like that.

She stirred, frowned, murmured something.

He couldn't help himself. He bent close to catch her words.

Her eyelids swept up. The expression in her eyes was peaceful, unaware. The eyes themselves were breathtaking—pale brown, with hints of green and gold around the pupil.

He should draw back and apologize. He was taking advantage just by leaning over her. She would come fully awake in the next minute and scream. Very slowly, as if he had come upon a small animal in a forest glade, he started to draw back.

Just as slowly, she smiled. Slowly, slowly, a soft blush rose in her cheeks. His skin prickled and his mouth suddenly went dry. He blinked rapidly. He was dreaming. He had to be.

She exhaled softly, making him aware that he, too, had been holding his breath. Her eyes scanned his face from forehead to chin, then they met his. If ever he had read a question in a woman's eyes, he read it now.

Inexorably, inevitably, he bent to put his lips to hers.

LOVING ENEMIES

Mona D. Sizer

ZEBRA BOOKS
KENSINGTON PUBLISHING CORP.

ZEBRA BOOKS are published by

Kensington Publishing Corp.
850 Third Avenue
New York, NY 10022

First Printing: October, 1996
10 9 8 7 6 5 4 3 2 1

Printed in the United States of America

With love to my cousin
Rexa Lee Pickett
and all the rest of Aunt Frank's family
who grew up with my family
in the hills of Arkansas.

One

The man in the thicket turned his head silently. Eyes closed, he listened for the call. Unconsciously, he clenched his fists in the pockets of his long blue coat. It was a call he dreaded, yet somehow had come to long for. Slowly, he released his breath. It whistled out between his bared teeth.

When he had heard the clop of the horse's hooves and the rattle of the wagon, he had known she was coming up the mountain. He had come out of his cabin and crossed the ridge to intercept the path she usually took. Now he crouched in the darkness, his heart pounding, his body sweating despite the cold.

He had to see her.

A halo of blue ice crystals encircled the full November moon. The very air glistened with frosty silver light. Esther's shadow bobbed ahead of her over the rough ground as she hiked swiftly after the snuffling pair of hounds. Despite her heavy boots, she made a minimum of sound. Her breathing was strong and even, her upper body relaxed from long practice.

Ahead of her, she could see Teet, her best black-and-tan coonhound, quartering around a thick stand of brush at the edge of the timber. The youngster she was training, a bluetick pup from down south in Johnson County, followed the older dog excitedly. She could hear his faint nervous whines, see him throw up his head jerkily as if he might find the scent on the still air. Once he stopped in his tracks to snuffle at the ground. He scampered away to the right.

"Don't touch! No! Don't touch!" Esther yelled.

Tail between his legs, head down, the pup returned to her side. The moonlight swam in his sorrowful eyes. Disgusted because he had struck the false trail, she nevertheless rubbed his throat and ears. When he stopped quivering, she patted his rump. "Take it. Go on, boy. Take it!"

He tossed an uncertain glance back over his shoulder at her, then with a loud whine he found Teet's trail and galloped away. Intent on the business of finding a raccoon, the seasoned black-and-tan had disappeared long ago in the darkness of the forest.

Esther hurried after them. Opening the door of her lantern, she lifted it high to pick a path through the wild grasses around the leafless blackberry brambles. She had no relish for the kinds of rips in her clothing and flesh that their thorns could inflict. Not even her homespun butternut trousers could withstand blackberry.

Once past the thicket, she closed off the light and paused to allow her eyes to accustom themselves again.

A deep, bugling call shivered the still air. The sound froze Esther to the spot in the midnight shadow of the Ozarks. She had heard it a thousand times and would hear it a thousand more, but she could never restrain the shiver of primal excitement that rippled over her skin and touched every nerve ending in her body. The deep bay of a hunting hound when it strikes the scent calls to man's most basic instincts.

In the shadows, the man hunkered down and peered beneath the branches. She was coming. He could hear the hounds draw-

ing closer. He had no fear they would turn from their path and tree him. The way she trained them, they would ignore everything except the scent she had set them on—raccoon, fox, or deer. He could watch her without her having the least suspicion.

Teet bugled again, his voice louder and more urgent, as if he had swung his proud head back in her direction.

At the second call, Esther sprang forward. Hanging the lantern on a nearby tree limb, she loped after the hounds. They were in full cry now. And just as she had done when she ran with her father for the first time, a skinny shirttail kid more than a dozen years ago, she felt the hair rise on the back of her neck.

Teet's deep, bugling call was a counterpoint to the youngster's higher, shriller notes. Straight on the trail Teet led, and the young hound followed. Through the forest they tore, signaling for Esther to come, come, come.

She came running as she always did—a slim figure in a shell jacket. Her features were shadowy beneath her gray slouch hat. He would never have recognized her face in broad daylight, but he knew her by her proud carriage. Shoulders back, breasts high, stride graceful and lithe, she ran as Diana the Huntress must have run across the hills of ancient Greece. The sight of her drew a shudder from him, tightened his loins, sent him a painful reminder that he was still male after all.

Eyes burning, he watched her race toward him, flash by his hiding place, and disappear into the night, her silvery hair in its long, thick braid twitching from side to side over her buttocks.

He had seen her. He should leave. Go back to the cabin. But the bay of the hounds was now almost a continuous cry. As one compelled, he turned to follow.

* * *

Esther stumbled when the ground rose under her feet. The raccoon was heading for the top of the ridge. A long stand of pine sprinkled with straight-trunked red oaks made the going fairly easy. Their thick branches overhead made the forest floor clean except for the needles that muffled the sounds of her feet.

The bay of the hounds rose ahead of her, too, as they bounded up the hill after the scampering raccoon. Her breathing quickened. She could feel the perspiration dampening her body.

The ecstatic calls veered to the right along the top of the ridge. As she pivoted, a low branch clawed at the top of her head, pulling off her gray slouch hat. Panting, she paused to rescue it and clap it on her head again and pull the bonnet string tight up under her chin.

At that moment she heard the calls separate. Teet's deep bay had turned down the valley while the bluetick's shriller call continued along the ridge. No longer travelling straight on the scent, the inexperienced pup was running on some trash trail.

She let out a mild curse. She had no choice but to go round the youngster up and return him to Teet. By that time her veteran would doubtless be frantically chopping at a coon's tree, his bay turned to a series of staccato barks. The youngster would join in, but without the experience of actually tracking the game. She would not be able to send for his owner to come and get him. She cursed again. She needed that money. Moreover, with winter coming fast, she didn't look forward to taking the pup out over and over to try to teach him to track.

Intent on her problems, she was out of the brush and onto a strip of slippery shale before she saw it. The soft rock crackled under foot as she dashed onto it. In the daylight she would have seen it through the trees. If she had been paying attention, even in the dark she would have known it was there when the trees stopped abruptly. Now she was struggling for balance as thousands of thin shards slid away beneath her.

She halted, alarmed by the shifting footing, and looked around her, but a huge thunderhead had rolled across the moon. In the cavernous darkness she realized she should have moved slower and carried her lantern rather than leaving it on the tree.

She took a hesitant step backward. The shale crackled like thin ice. Another slow, careful step back. Better a lost pup than a broken—

The whole ground cracked beneath her. In the grayness of the terrain, she had not spotted the narrow ravine cutting catercornered across her path. A muffled cry burst from her as she felt herself falling. Her arms clawed at the air in an attempt to throw herself backward. Her feet slipped out from under her. The small of her back struck the edge of the ravine, knocking the wind from her and paralyzing her usually quick reflexes. With a moan she toppled over the edge, sliding helplessly down, down. The slippery shale offered no handholds had she been able to grasp them.

One foot threaded between a rock and the rough trunk of a small tree. Gasping, she sought to halt her slide, but only succeeded in turning herself sideways. Struggling gamely, her body twisted and rolled over and over. Pain and panic wrenched a piercing scream from her.

Her foot broke free, uprooting the tree, but the damage was done. She had been trapped long enough for her plunging weight to twist the muscles and ligaments. Distracted from her efforts by the agony slashing up her leg, she could not prevent herself from tumbling headfirst into the darkness.

* * *

At the sound of her cry, the man halted in his tracks. She had hurt herself. He shivered. Ahead of him, he heard the sounds of her struggles, the clattering of pieces of shale, the rustle of dead leaves, the snapping of twigs. He lunged forward, but halted at the edge of the shadow. There he shivered again. He could not move into the open.

Instinctively, Esther threw her arms about her face and head to protect her eyes. The brush on the floor of the ravine slashed at her and only slightly cushioned her fall. Her head slammed brutally against the rocks until, boneless as a rag doll, her body finally came to a halt. More shale slid in and around her, rattling and hissing down the walls of the ravine.

She knew she didn't have a concussion. She hadn't lost consciousness. As she lay gasping, her body throbbing, her senses swimming, she kept telling herself how God had spared her, though her exercise in praising His intervention was little help against the fiery pangs that streaked upward from her foot and knee.

For a full minute, she lay on her stomach, her head clasped in her arms. When her mind at last sent commands to the muscles in her legs, nothing happened. For a sickening second she thought she was paralyzed. Galvanized by horror, she clenched her fists and flexed her feet inside the stout boots.

Thank You, O Lord!

Already she felt better. Gingerly, gritting her teeth and drawing her uninjured leg up, she rolled over. With a groan she pushed her arms down to her sides and stared upward at the icy moon. Its brilliant face swam and danced through her helpless tears.

Summoning a breath, she willed herself to draw up the injured leg. She gave a yell as the hideous pain smote her. Instantly, sweat popped out on her body, and her breathing quickened until she was panting like a hound that had been run hard.

With both hands she reached for her thigh and squeezed. The agony increased. Tendons must be torn loose. Sometimes an accident like that was worse than a break. If the leg had just gone ahead and broken, it could have been set and healed neatly. But if tendons and muscles were torn loose, they might never heal. She might have to drag a crippled leg around with her for the rest of her life. She might have—

One shaking hand let go of her thigh to swipe at the cold sweat on her forehead. She was going to put all that "might have" stuff right out of her mind. She had a problem right here and now that meant "might have" was going to have to wait its turn.

Now she was concerned with crawling back to the wagon. She stared upward at the narrow strip of sky. Before she crawled back to the wagon, she was going to have to climb out of the ravine. How deep it was or how far she had fallen, she couldn't tell.

Best call up Teet—if he was within hearing distance. She couldn't hear his bay nor the bay of the young hound that had caused this whole mess. The shale walls must be cutting off their sounds. Fighting a sense of hopelessness, she fumbled down the lanyard to find her whistle and blew three blasts with all the strength she could muster.

Prayerfully, she listened. If Teet had heard her, he would leave off his hunt and return to her, baying as he came.

The midnight forest lay silent around her.

With a groan of resignation, Esther levered herself up on one elbow. She must get to higher ground. Her head swam sickeningly, and searing pain knifed up her spine from the small of her back.

She groaned out a cussword she had heard her father use on only the most desperate occasions.

If she were any judge of her condition (and she prayed she was not), she would have to have a brace for her back as well as a splint for her leg. She might be permanently crippled. Her means of livelihood would be gone if she was unable to train the hounds. Gritting her teeth, she swallowed against the nausea welling up in her throat. The rocks beneath her body were sharp and cold. She began to shiver.

"Roll over on your belly and crawl out, Esther," she ordered through teeth that chattered. "No one's going to help you. You got yourself into this, and somehow you've got to get yourself out."

The man heard her. His keen ears picked up every word and took it as a condemnation. He clenched his fists; his body shuddered. She was strong. She ran through the woods at night. Accidents of this kind were bound to happen. She could climb out of the ravine by herself.

He'd better be on his way. Undoubtedly, her family and friends would be swarming all over this ridge in an hour or two. He hunched his shoulders and shifted his feet. Still, he stayed his ground.

Obeying her own orders, Esther rolled back over and pushed herself up on her hands. She drew her right leg up under her, hoisted her body—and balanced there unable to make the next move. Her left leg was too badly wrenched and consequently too painful to draw up under her.

She looked down her body in pure disgust. She would be forced to crawl and drag it along behind her like a dead weight. Except it was not dead. It lanced white fire up her thigh and along her spine.

No help for it. Muttering encouragement and castigation between her clenched teeth, she reached for the first handhold.

The man silently skirted the treacherous shale and walked to the edge of the ravine. Careful to stay in the shadow of the trees, he stared down. He could see nothing in the dark below him, but he could hear her moving, hear her groans. Every word of her self-directed monologue was intelligible in the still night air.

He thrust his fists deep into his pockets. She had chosen a dangerous business—running through the woods at night alone. Her breathing was coming in labored gasps now. She would be better off to stay still until someone came for her. He looked anxiously around him. If no one came for her in the morning, he would send some sort of word to someone—the storekeeper maybe, or the postmaster of the little town.

He would have to do so carefully. No one must know he was here. He looked down into the darkness. The shale clattered and rattled. He doubted she would be able to crawl out by herself. He hunkered down, his hands drooping helpless between his knees.

The sides of the ravine were steep, but at first Esther found convenient handholds in the small brush. Snaking upward on her stomach, dragging herself over the piles of sharp rocks, she managed the first ten or so feet. Then she could go no farther.

On hands and one knee, all but spread-eagled on the precipitous slope, sweat stinging her eyes, she searched the darkness in vain for another low bush. All around and above her was shale, slippery and crumbling.

Trembling with pain and exhaustion, she wrestled the whistle into her mouth again and blew.

The night was as silent as the grave—an uncomfortable thought given her present position. Teet must have tracked that coon halfway down the valley. As for the youngster, there was no telling where he had gone or what he had run after.

A particularly sharp twinge made her groan and shudder in agony. Her hand slipped on the branches to which she clung. The shale crackled and she slid backward several inches. Nowhere could she find the slightest purchase in the ancient sedimentary clay.

Unless she were very, very lucky, she was going to have to spend the night in this icy ravine. If she were only moderately unlucky, in the early morning someone might spot her wagon tied down on the dirt track. If her luck were running its usual course, she might get out of here if Carly Ord missed her when he came to clean out the kennels. No one else knew or cared about her. No one would miss her.

She blew the whistle again and again. The silence was unbroken. She opened her mouth to shout, then closed it. Better to save her breath. No one in his right mind would be out on this mountain at this time of night. She had been, she acknowledged grimly, and the good Lord knew she was not in her right mind.

The shale cracked menacingly, her good knee slipping down half a foot. She groaned and struggled to regain the purchase. Carly Ord was such a dunce he might have to miss her twice before he realized the hounds had not been fed. Every thought pushed the time of her rescue farther and farther away. If she were a weeping woman, she would never have a better excuse.

Almost afraid to move, she swung her head from side to side. Fortunately, the moon illuminated the cut on her side of the ravine. On her right rose the shale, slippery and barren as far as she could see.

On her left, she could see a few darker clumps of bushes and small trees thrusting up at acute angles. Her chance lay in that direction, she was sure. Groaning faintly with the effort, she awkwardly pivoted her body on her good right knee. The shale slipped, sliding her downward several hard-won inches.

Her bad leg bumped into an upthrusting rock. The pain left her without enough breath even to curse.

She raised her swimming eyes. Just a couple more yards across the barren slash. She slid her hand forward through the loose shale, searching for handholds, a buried root, an outcropping of some other stone, anything. One hand. Then the other. Then her knee. The shale crackled ominously beneath it, but held. She slid no farther.

Another foot and another. She dared not even wipe at the stinging sweat that ran into her eyes. The ground felt a little firmer. Perhaps she was getting out of the shale.

Another foot. The ravine was steeper here. She paused, balancing more carefully, leaning into the mountain. Her wrenched leg was a lead weight threatening to topple her over. The muscles in her limbs trembled from her effort.

Leaves rustled; stones rattled in the trees somewhere above her at the top of the ravine. Instantly, she reacted.

"Hi! Halloo! Hi up there! Help!"

The sound ceased.

Intently, she listened, but could hear nothing more. Her blood drummed in her ears. An animal, she counseled herself, an opossum or a raccoon. Or a trickle of water under the shale breaking up the surface by its pressure. Nothing. No one could help her but herself. A cold breeze wafted down the ravine, driving her into a fit of shivers. Still she tried again, her voice high and desperate. "Is anyone there?"

The man hunched his shoulders against the call. Lifting his foot with extreme care, he took a backward step and then another. Soft as a cat, he tested the ground with infinite slowness before resting his weight on it. He couldn't help her because he couldn't touch her, and he couldn't explain why he couldn't. He couldn't even talk to her. He had to leave her. He had to step back out of hearing. He had been hanging around so close that he could hear her panting and struggling. The desperate sounds were eating away at him. His palms were sweaty, his heart pounding.

Doggedly, Esther dragged herself along in the moonlight. With agonizing slowness, the distance narrowed to the clump of bushes. The sharp shale cut into her palms as she took her weight on first one hand and then the other. Her fingers hooked like claws into the shifting surface, desperate to secure a purchase.

The bush was almost within arm's reach. She gritted her teeth. Just a couple of feet. She only had to hoist herself forward and just a bit upward to catch on to the branches.

Suddenly, with an insidious hissing the shale began to slide from under her. Panicked, she reared back on her good leg and launched herself at the dark clump of vegetation. Her fingers raked through crackling leaves but found no limbs to clutch.

Her frustration changed to agony as her body pitched sideways onto her bad leg. Rolling down, helpless to stop herself, she bumped and twisted until she was brought up short, banging into a rock outcropping at least a dozen feet farther into the ravine.

The additional pain was nothing compared with the

agony of spirit she experienced. For several moments she could not move, could not even breathe. Arched back over a rock, her limbs sprawled in four different directions, she could not find the will to stop the helpless tears.

The cold stars whirled and swam overhead. Again she asked herself why she could not lose consciousness. Every part of her body throbbed with pain, yet her mind was crystal clear.

Suddenly, heavy boots crackled the shale at the top of the ravine. Chips and slivers of stone pelted her body. A dark shape came sliding down the steep side. She screamed as it came to a halt almost at her feet. Her eyes opened wide as a crouching silhouette blocked the moon and threw her own face into its shadow.

With a grunt the man straightened, coming to his full height. His fingers flexed and trembled. He still could not see her face from the depth of his shadow. He shivered, moving to the side. A stone turned under his foot, making him stumble. Then he could see her face for the first time. The moonlight drained it of color except for a dark scrape on her chin.

"Thank heavens," she breathed hoarsely. Her arm came up. Her trembling hand reached out for him. "I was so afraid—"

He dodged the hand, stumbled backward, and flung his arm wide to catch his balance against the slope. His mouth went suddenly dry. She mustn't touch him.

She heard the sound of his labored breathing. Her arm slumped back to her side. What was the matter with him? Had he somehow hurt himself sliding down the ravine? Was he crazy? Was he drunk? Both? She struggled up on her elbows. "Are you— Did you hurt yourself when you came down the slide?"

He froze. She expected an answer. He couldn't give it. He'd forgotten how. He threw his head back to stare up at the narrow sky. What was he doing down here? He couldn't help her. He couldn't even help himself.

Esther pushed herself up on her good right knee. Her effort to move her left leg sent a particularly violent twinge up her spine. Drunk or not, she had to have help. Again she extended her hand. Forcing herself to speak in a calm, soft voice, she said, "You'll have to help me."

He stared at the hand as if it held a gun.

She groaned more in disgust than pain. Her luck had run true to form again. She had been found by some sort of idiot. "Then forget it," she sighed. "You're standing in the way."

He pressed the heel of his hand hard against his forehead. Then with a sound almost like a sob, he dropped to his knees in front of her. Face-to-face, he was almost the same height, but she was so much slighter. He felt a sudden pity, then a mild surprise that he could feel anything for another human being. His rough glove touched her chin. Turning her face directly up to the moonlight, he pushed her hat back.

Esther closed her eyes. The pain from her myriad hurts, the demands she had made on her body, combined to leave her drained. With a sigh she surrendered her body to her rescuer. She could do no more.

Thinking she must be pretty badly hurt, he allowed her head to sink to his shoulder. Wisps of silky hair brushed his cheek, sending an unaccustomed frisson down his spine. Roughly, with a minimum of movement, he ran his hands down along her arms, arranging them at her sides. Next, he patted the sides of her torso as if checking to see that it was not twisted unnaturally. His movements made up in efficiency what they lacked in gentleness.

He could feel her right leg trembling beneath her weight. When his hands touched the left, she groaned. "C-careful."

His hands paused in their inspection, then continued with more care guided by her whimpers and gasps as to how to proceed.

By the time he had finished, Esther found herself wringing wet with sweat and light-headed from the pain. The shale crackled as her Samaritan stood up. She wearily turned her head trying to see his face, but the moon was still at his back. It shone full in her face and swam in her eyes, open wide, staring at him. She tried to speak, licked her dry lips. "Thank you—"

He did not acknowledge that she had spoken. Rather he looked from side to side. One hand swiped at his forehead and pushed his hat back on his head. No doubt the glove would come away wet with perspiration. He could feel the sweat soaking his shirt under his arms.

"I-I think I can walk," she whispered, "if you'll give me a hand."

He rubbed his hand across his face again, then stooped above her. Ignoring her offer, he thrust his hands under her shoulders and pulled her up to a stand.

The mere act of being straightened wrung another groan from her as her head tipped forward against his shoulder. "Wait. Just a minute—"

She put a tiny bit of weight on her left leg. Instantly, she stumbled in her effort to shift back to the right. Her full weight slumped against him—breast to breast, thigh to thigh. Her head fell backward. Her face was milk white and only inches from his own. The moonlight glittered along the path of her tears.

Wasting no time in fruitless sympathy, he set his hands at her waist and dropped down on one knee.

"You can't carry me," she whispered.

He shifted his grip to the backs of her legs. As she tilted forward, he rose beneath her, catching her waist under his shoulder.

Another strangled cry was jolted from her as her legs

left the ground and her abused body endured yet another wrench. And then for the second time in her life she fainted.

TWO

Esther could smell coffee. Not only could she smell it, but she could hear it bubbling along with the crackling of burning firewood. She had heard that people awakened from a faint unable to remember what had happened to them. Unfortunately, her mind was crystal clear. She had been rescued from a desperate situation by a stranger who had taken her . . . she knew not where. Opening her eyes, she inhaled the coffee. *Please,* she thought, *bring me a cup right now.*

She dared not try to get some for herself. The throbbing in her left leg would turn excruciating. By lying perfectly still and testing it gradually, she could take stock of the damage.

A sudden violent gust of rain struck the wall next to her shoulder. She shivered. The room had no real ceiling. Between the low two-by-fours that formed the rafters, she could see the points of nails sticking down through the bare wood of the roof. Another gust of rain, mixed with sleet by the sound of it, pelted the wall again. She was vaguely surprised that the shingles were doing their job so well. She closed her eyes and carefully flexed her knee.

More rain gusted again. With a shiver she remembered the ravine. Lord be praised she was not lying out there now. She would not have survived. In her shell jacket and wool trousers, she was too lightly clad to stand a night of this. She thought of Teet and the bluetick pup. They would be safe enough under the wagon if the poor old horses hadn't pulled themselves free and plodded back to the barn on their own.

Unless the storm had struck with unusual suddenness, she must have been unconscious a long time. Her benefactor would certainly have taken a long time to climb out of the ravine—no mean feat—and carry her here—wherever here was. He must be very strong. Where was he?

Iron clanked against iron. She had played possum long enough. Her situation wasn't going to change until she made a move. She lifted her head. "Thank you for rescuing me."

She could see him clearly for the first time, standing by a potbellied stove in a corner of the cabin. His dark eyes regarded her warily from beneath a thicket of wild black hair liberally strewn with white. It blended into a tangle of grizzled beard that concealed the lower half of his face.

He looked like a man who hadn't seen another human being in a long time. Stretching across large portions of Northern Arkansas and Southern Missouri, the Ozarks allowed such men to hide away in their deep valleys. Most were harmless enough.

Esther stared at her savior, trying to find a face behind the concealment. "Thank you," she said again.

He hunched his shoulders in what might have been a shrug.

The movement drew her attention to his garb. She stiffened. He had discarded the heavy coat that had billowed around him when he sprang down into the ravine. He wore no shirt, but stood in a shabby gray union suit. He had cast down the leather suspenders so they hung over his lean hips. Those things in themselves were not offensive. But running down the side of his light blue kersey trousers was a stripe of gold.

Her rescuer was a Yankee yellowleg.

The sight of the remnants of the uniform made her stomach turn. The war had been over five years now, but here in this corner of Arkansas it seemed as if it would never be over. As she watched, he wrapped a rag around the handle of the blackened enamel coffeepot and filled a cracked china mug. She could see the steam rise from it.

She closed her eyes and swallowed hard. She wanted that coffee as she wanted life itself, but the thought of taking it from a Yankee made her want to scream. As she lay there struggling for control, she heard his boots thud across the floor. The smell of coffee grew stronger. Then she felt a hand barely touch her shoulder.

Her eyes flew open. He held a mug out to her. The steam rose from it in a fragrant cloud. As she watched, he turned the vessel a little clumsily, so she could take it by the handle.

Her stomach triumphed over her pride. Esther pushed herself up on one elbow to take it.

He released it almost too soon. The mug dipped, and the coffee sloshed onto the floor.

"Sorry," she said.

He retreated silently to the stove.

Gritting her teeth against the pain, she tried to hitch herself up in the bed. The exercise was impossible given her incapacitated leg and the fear of pain. She settled for levering herself up on her elbow. The coffee cup trembled as she brought it to her mouth. The first swallow was hot, strong, and bitter. She wished for sugar, then forgot about it as the brew warmed her all the way to her stomach. She drank a second, longer swallow and waited impatiently for the stimulant to flood her system and steady her.

Maybe he wasn't a Yankee after all. Maybe he was a Southerner who had "captured" pieces of Federal uniforms to replace his own rags when they had worn out. All of them had had to do it before the war was over. A few had even been shot as spies after being taken prisoner in too many "captured" pieces.

She looked at him again, trying to find a clue to his identity, praying she would not be beholden to a Yankee. He had presented his back to her now. A long, straight back, with a narrow waist and hips. He wore boots that might once have been black. Officer's boots. Cavalryman's boots with split tops. She took heart in the knowledge that they could have been anybody's boots.

His silence along with the stiffness of his back and shoulders made her nervous. She glanced around the cabin. The only light came from a kerosene lantern smoking faintly on the plank table. Besides that and the stove, she could see the one bunk on which she lay, a locker, one chair, a wood box, and a tall cupboard. Without asking, she knew it was his home. What sort of man, particularly if he were a murdering, plundering Yankee, would live here like this so many years after the war was over? The speculation did nothing to reassure her. Her teeth clicked against the rim of the cup. Barely controlled shudders were spreading beneath her skin.

He turned in time to catch her drinking the last of her coffee. Still silent, he came across the room to pour more. She couldn't help but notice the way he moved— smoothly, with the posture of a military man. She would bet he'd never been wounded. No hitch or limp impaired his stride; no cant or stoop favored a shattered shoulder or a collapsed lung.

The rain slowed, but the wind increased, howling like a banshee and whistling through tiny chinks in the wall behind her. Suddenly, she was very cold. Her feet were like blocks of ice. When she wriggled her toes, she realized that she was still wearing her boots. Her rescuer had tucked her into bed, his only bunk, with her boots on. A glance down at herself and a little squirm told her she was wearing all her clothing. Only her slouch hat hung on the corner of the chair back.

The silence grew as she drank. He poured himself a cup and took a swallow, his dark eyes never leaving her face. They were hawk's eyes, black with gold around the pupils. Even as he drank his own coffee, he watched her like a wild creature.

She shifted uncomfortably. "Do you have any idea what happened to my hounds?"

He shrugged.

She realized he had not spoken a word. Steadily, she stared at the dark face, trying to penetrate the shadows. "I don't suppose I can do anything about them. I just thought you might have heard them."

He shifted his weight from one foot to the other. One hand passed across his chest and clasped the bicep of his arm tightly. He kept it there as he drank more coffee.

Setting her own cup in the corner of the bunk, she pushed herself to a sitting position, taking inventory as she went. All working parts above her hips seemed tender but not broken. She managed another wan smile. "Thank you for lugging me out. I don't think I could have made it to the top of the ridge."

Her silent savior nodded in assent.

She hesitated. Her head swam, and the pain in her left leg rose from a dull throbbing to piercing agony. Resting her shoulders against the wall of the cabin, she reached for her coffee. Yankee or no Yankee, beholden or not, she needed the brew's strength. She held the mug out to him. "Could I have a little more please?"

Obligingly, he filled it from the old speckled enamel coffeepot. She drank it in a single burning gulp and set the empty mug down. Then with a silent prayer she peeled back the quilts and swung her good leg over the side of the bunk.

She was conscious of his eyes on her. He was probably judging her. But he said nothing. Neither did he step forward to help her.

A man who wouldn't talk wouldn't help either, she thought. She sat on the edge of the bunk, her legs spraddled. Thank heaven he hadn't undressed her. Feeling the beads of perspiration start out on her lip, she clutched her thigh above the knee and drew her left leg up against her chest. When the knee bent, she could not bite back the keening cry. With hands that shook, she pushed down her thick socks and pulled up the butternut wool pant leg. Her ankle was badly swollen and dark red. She pressed it gingerly. It hurt no more or less from her fingers.

"I can't tell if it's broken or not," she gasped, "so I'll assume it's not. The leg smarts like the very devil, but it bends. It wouldn't bend if it was broken." She flexed the knee once carefully to demonstrate that she could move it. Tears stood in her eyes, and she sank back on the bed. Blackness threatened to overwhelm her, and she could feel the sweat break out over the rest of her body.

"M-more coffee." With only the barest of stammers he got the two words out before he handed her the mug.

So in need was she, Esther didn't realize that they were the first words he had spoken. With shaking hands she took the mug and swallowed gratefully.

For the first time he didn't retreat to the stove. Instead he loomed over her, blocking the light. She stared up into his shadowy face. Even with the light behind him, the hawk's eyes were the only source of light. "Better lie back."

Even hurting as she was, she was afraid of him. Any man so close, so powerful, was a threat. Especially when she was in such a weakened condition. She concentrated on stifling a groan as she lifted her left leg and set her foot on the floor. "I'm taking your bunk. It's late and you need to get to sleep. I need to get down the mountain."

The rain drummed steadily against the cabin.

He stepped back and let her come to her feet, supporting herself with her right leg. The pain of lowering her left leg to the floor had been terrible, but now even more blood forced its way through swollen tissues in the injured ankle and into her foot.

Esther clamped her teeth over her lower lip. Postponing the inevitable, she tugged out her father's pocket watch and snapped open the case. Somehow it had survived the fall. Now she read its face with a sinking heart. Two o'clock. Still hours till daylight. And the storm was far from over.

She looked from the watch face to the face of the watching man. He had carried her here. She couldn't guess her present location in relation to the dirt track she had driven in on. Common sense told her she could barely stand, let alone take a hike over rough terrain in the dark to find the wagon. Moreover, once she got there—if she got there—she might find her means of transportation gone. The old horses might have had enough and plodded home, taking Teet and the pup with them.

Still she had to make a try. She forced herself to take her weight on her left leg. The ankle buckled immediately, and she sprawled across the table. The pain did not subside for a full minute.

Her host set his coffee cup down and waited.

"I don't think I can walk just now," she gritted.

He nodded. "You took a bad fall. Don't act crazy now."

It was the longest speech he had made, and it put her on the defensive. She dropped into the straight chair. "I don't want to be a burden. You've done enough for me."

He waited.

He really wasn't very tall, she observed. Probably no more than an inch or two taller than she. Of course, she was tall for a woman. His shoulders beneath the underclothing were not abnormally broad or muscular. Instead, he looked thin, as if he ate irregularly. The thick beard grew from the hollows beneath his high cheekbones. "I'm sorry you had to carry me," she said at last. "I'm no lightweight."

"No," he agreed.

She made up her mind to try one more time. She pushed herself up, and willing her muscles to obey her, she put her weight on her left leg. The pain drained all the color from her face. Never had she felt anything so terrible. A few seconds only, then she dropped back down in the chair, clutching her thigh and rocking helplessly.

The man cleared his throat. "You can stay the night."

She nodded, looking around her. "I've got to, but you've only got the one bunk."

"I'll sleep on the floor by the stove." The words seemed to be coming more easily for him. She noticed his speech was clipped, without hint of Southern drawl or Texas twang.

Esther was sure he must be a Yankee. She closed her eyes against her disgust. Despite everything she could do, she was going to be beholden to one of the cussed yellowlegs. "Oh, no." She released her thigh and scrubbed her cheeks with her fingers. "I'll sleep on the floor. You saved me from spending the night in the ravine. I can't take your bed."

He regarded her silently.

Suddenly, she felt as if he were waiting for her to change her mind. Since time immemorial, males had been giving up their beds for the comfort of females. Southern women in particular made a practice of letting their men carry them around on silken cushions. But not Esther Woodson. The Yankees had taken the center of her life away from her. Bad enough she had to thank this one for carrying her out of the ravine and making coffee for her. She would never, never sleep in his bed.

Pushing herself up straight without a groan, she hopped a couple of steps toward the stove and sank down on her good side. With a tired wave of her hand, she said, "You take your bunk. Get the rest of your sleep. I'll try to find my way at daybreak. If you're awake to give directions, then I'll be much obliged." She pillowed her head on her folded arm and closed her eyes.

She heard the brush of clothing, the faint slap of leather. The brass buttons on the suspenders clicked against the floor. Her taciturn host must be taking his pants off. She pulled her head between her shoulders and settled down for the night.

The floor was hard. Her leg was injured. She was marooned in a one-room cabin with a damn Yankee taking off his clothes only a couple of steps away. She should have been uncomfortable, but instead she seemed to be floating. She didn't even know his name. And he hadn't asked hers. Names didn't matter. They were mortal enemies. Mortal enemies.

He was a killer. A destroyer.

Her thoughts were getting hazy. Exhaustion acted as a great anesthetizer. Within a minute her breathing evened and her limbs relaxed.

The glowing coals behind the grate of the potbellied stove limned Esther's huddled form. Lying in his bunk, York Phillip Bradburn, former captain with the 4th Pennsylvania Cavalry, volunteer on demand despite his father and his faith, stared at the woman's shape. The thick braid of pale hair lay like a skein of silk across the floor.

His starved eyes traced gently from the point of her
shoulder to the deep indentation of her waist to the generous rounding of her hips.

She was younger than he had imagined her, although
he had been away from women so long, he could not
really judge. Her skin was pale porcelain and fine-
grained. Her eyes, an unusual shade of brown, had surprised him the minute she had looked at him. They
looked him straight in the eye, as a man would.

He tucked his arm beneath his head, lifting it above
the curve of the pillow. From there he stared at her silhouette, his eyes wide and unblinking. Summoning up
memory he undressed her, imagining smooth skin beneath layers of clothing, white hips with gently curving
buttocks.

She stirred, moaned, breathed. Instantly, he closed his
eyes, feeling embarrassed heat rising in his cheeks. Her
presence changed the very air in the room where he had
been solitary so long.

He shuddered remembering the feel of her packed
over his shoulder. He had been able to smell her, to feel
her weight, to hear her breathing. He had not willingly
been that close to another human being in a long time.

He shuddered again, then congratulated himself. Perhaps he was getting better. Maybe this long isolation had
taken the edge off the painful memories. Moreover, he
didn't really mind her being here. She had made him
nervous at first, but he had been able to offer her coffee,
finally to speak a few words.

He had expected her to sleep in the bed, but she had
insisted on leaving it for him. When he had climbed in,
it had not been clammy and cold. He hunched his shoulder under the quilts. Once upon a time, he would never
have allowed a lady to surrender the smallest indulgence
to him. He would have been a perfect gentleman. But

the man he was now couldn't find the words to make the gallant gesture.

Through the grate he watched the flames begin to die. Before morning, his guest would be freezing if she slept on that floor without covers. He had an extra quilt in the locker. Experimentally, he framed the word. It came out in a whisper. "Miss—"

She hadn't heard him. He could barely see the top of her head above the collar turned up around her ears. Her good leg was drawn up, but the injured one lay stiff and straight along the floor. It would be even more painful by morning.

With a shrug he closed his eyes, pulling his own quilts around him. For a minute he lay still. Then his eyes opened. Reluctantly, almost angrily, he tossed back the covers. The room temperature was dropping fast. Padding across the bare boards, he could feel the chill through his thick wool socks. He opened the grate and thrust in another couple of lengths of hickory.

The woman on the rough plank floor lay dead to the world.

Opening the locker, he pulled out the extra quilt. With it across his arm, he paused fractionally, perplexed, glancing from quilt to woman and back again. He needed to wake her up to give it to her. But what if she was so deep in sleep that she could not be awakened?

Cold, damp air rose through the floor boards, and he curled his toes away from it. The action decided him.

He shook out the quilt and found its corners. Carelessly, he dropped it over her form, covering her head and shoulders, but leaving much of her back and the injured leg bare. Angrily, he stared at the unoffending cloth, disgusted with its behavior and his own ineptness.

Shaking his head, he dropped to his knees beside her. With only a momentary twinge, quickly mastered, he twitched the blanket over her. His fingers grazed her hip.

The long braid of hair, thick as his wrist, coiled away from her body like a tether. With the tips of his fingers, he nudged it over against her back. Finally, taking a deep breath, he purposefully tucked the edges of the quilt around her leg.

She stirred slightly; her weight shifted. Her hip pressed against his fingers. He froze. Was he sweating? Trembling?

She moaned and murmured unintelligibly.

He jerked his hand away as if it had touched the hot stove. Hastily, he retreated, edging backward until he encountered the low bunk. Climbing in, he pulled the covers back around him. For more than an hour, he watched her, his eyes burning in the darkness.

Every muscle tensed. The wind and the rain had stopped, but raindrops plunked steadily from the trees and from the eaves of the cabin. Morning creatures sounded their various familiar notes. But something was different.

He sat up, his hand ready to throw back the covers. The cold air rushed into his cocoon. A slight moan followed a sigh. How could he have forgotten? He had brought home an injured woman last night. Sliding back under the covers, he studied her by the gray light of dawn.

She had turned in her sleep so that she lay on her back. He stared at her profile, the high forehead, the straight, delicately shaped nose, the rounded lips. So still and so utterly lacking in color was she that her face might have been carved on a cameo. The shell effect was dispelled only by the pale, feathery lines of her eyebrows and eyelashes, the same color as the silvery hair that wisped around her face. Even her lips were colorless, as if pain and cold had driven all the blood deep within her body.

She shouldn't have been running through the forest at night. She'd almost gotten herself killed. Not that her life was any of his concern.

He sighed gustily and saw his breath fog in front of his face. His cabin was not much warmer than the Ozark hillside. Its singular advantage was that it was dry. Reaching under his pillow, he found his clothing. With practiced hands he pulled on his pants and socks. When he was more than half dressed, he turned back the covers a second time and reached for his boots.

Esther woke to the vibration of the plank floor under her ear. Her eyes opened blearily to the sight of a pair of worn, cracked boots less than a foot from her face. An instant of panic assailed her. Then she remembered. She had spent the night with a Yankee.

The grate in the woodstove creaked noisily as one boot shifted backward. She heard the thud of kindling being dropped in on top of the ashes. Soot sifted down from the grate onto her head and face. She took it in with her next breath and instantly began to cough. The ashes tickled her nose, and she gave a mighty sneeze. Its force jolted her awake in all parts of her body.

"And a good, good morning to you," she whispered to her leg as the aches and pains began.

The boots turned away and stalked out of her line of vision. She heard cutlery rattling against plate. Her host must be going about the business of preparing his breakfast.

The floor was as hard and cold as a slab in a meat locker, but she lay without moving for quite some time, marshalling her courage.

The boots came thudding back and stopped inches from her head.

Carefully she opened her eyes. His face hung above her, his eyes met hers. She read concern in them. He was leaning over, one hand holding the same cracked china mug, the other thrust deep in his pocket.

She took a deep breath and held it. Then in a single motion, she sat up. It was a mistake. Her head swam so nauseatingly that she had to catch it with both hands to keep from toppling over. With a heartfelt groan she drew her good leg up and rested one elbow on it.

Out of the corner of her eye, she saw the steaming mug held nearer, but she waved it away. Steeling herself, she gingerly bent her left knee. The much abused joint cracked loudly. When her heel took some of the weight of the leg, her ankle protested with a dull throbbing of its own. She shook her head. She had well and truly crippled herself, at least for the near future. Yet in the very near future, she was going to have to get down off the mountain.

Enough for now, she decided as she reached gratefully for the coffee. Despite the dark tangle of hair and beard, she could not mistake the expression of sympathy in the dark eyes. Taking a long drink of very hot coffee, she choked slightly. "I hope you shot the horse that dragged me."

The man didn't reply. If his mouth twitched into a smile, it was hidden behind the thick beard. Probably he had lived so long alone that he had forgotten how to make light of anything. He went back to the plank table and began to mix flour with water, condensed milk, baking powder, and lard.

Esther hitched herself to the chair, climbed it, and eased herself into the seat. Her leg might not be so bad once she had loosened it up. Moving it around would be the best thing for it. Grimly, she flexed it. The leg

hurt clear to the hip; but to get her back to her buck-board, it was going to have to do its duty. Soldiers could walk on broken legs. Hers was only sprained.

While she finished her coffee, she watched her host make biscuits. With sleeves pushed back, he worked the lard into the flour, added milk, and coaxed the mixture into a ball.

Esther watched fascinated. She had never seen a man's dark fingers coated with flour. Clearly, he thought noth-ing about the process. Instead of a rolling pin, he pinched off portions and shaped them in his palms. When the iron Dutch oven was lifted onto the stove top, the whole process had taken less than ten minutes.

In that ten minutes, she became aware of another problem. Pushing herself to her feet, she made her pain-ful way to the door. She kept her face averted, hoping that her host would not ask her any stupid questions. Mercifully, he said nothing. Nevertheless, her cheeks flushed bright red as she pushed open the cabin door and stepped out into a gray-and-white world.

The blast of air was so cold that her eyes watered. Last night's rain and sleet had left a steel blue sky. Ominous clouds, heavy with more rain, more sleet, and probable snow concealed the tops of the mountains. A slippery glaze coated the porch.

The trek around the corner of the cabin was unbeliev-ably hard. Every rock had a skin of ice. She dared not step away from the wall, for fear of a fall. When she had finished her business, Esther slumped against the side of the cabin and struggled to keep from bawling.

She could not travel under these conditions. She could not put a foot down without its threatening to slide out from under her. Back inside, the tiny cabin was over-heated by comparison. Cheerful flames leaped behind the stove grate. Coffee boiling beside the Dutch oven filled the cabin with its aroma.

Her host indicated the single chair.

Thankfully, she hopped across the floor and fell clumsily into it. When he thrust a cup of hot coffee at her, the hand she took it with was shaking. Her first gulp should have warned her, but she was so grateful for the hot drink that she didn't care about the taste. At the second, however, she grimaced. "What's in this?"

At first she thought he wasn't going to answer her. He had awakened her and fixed breakfast all without once opening his mouth. Finally, he bent and plucked a jug from behind the leg of the stove. Pulling out a corncob stopper, he poured a trickle of palest yellow liquid into his own cup. "Whiskey."

Esther raised her eyebrows. The Yankee had just told her how he managed to live in the Ozarks, a hotbed of Confederate sympathizers, fewer than a dozen miles from Pea Ridge. If she were a betting woman, she would bet any amount of money that he had a still somewhere close. From it he made and traded—she sniffed in the aroma—corn liquor.

He caught her staring at him over the rim of the cup. His eyes narrowed slightly, but he made no comment as he set the jug between them.

Eying it, Esther drank again. The alcohol warmed her. A slow, ironic smile quirked the corners of her mouth. Her father had enjoyed a snort now and again, but she had not drunk more than a couple of thimblefuls of whiskey in her life. Her mother's disapproval meant nothing to her now. Esther's sins had already damned her. What possible harm could a cup of coffee sweetened with whiskey be to her soul?

Her rescuer followed her stare to the jug, then back to her face. His expression was purely neutral. No embarrassment, no defiance, nothing. The brown, brown eyes were empty. He did not care what she thought.

Dropping a folded rag over the lid of the Dutch oven,

he lifted the lid to check the biscuits. Satisfied, he turned them out onto a tin plate, set it on the table, and glanced at her cup. "More coffee?"

She shook her head. "Still working on this cup. It's good stuff."

He did not acknowledge her compliment by so much as a flicker of a smile. He merely nodded shortly and turned his back to her. From somewhere in his cupboard, he produced a half-full jar of molasses.

Rebuffed, Esther set down her cup. At that moment a gust of wind laden with rain and sleet struck the cabin. The heavens had made good their threat. Her ankle gave a particularly vicious twinge in response. Leaning down, she began to massage her calf.

Her host cast a glance over his shoulder before tilting his head to listen. "More storms coming."

He dropped two knives onto the table between them and dragged around the end of the bed to sit down.

"Oh, no." Esther half rose, supporting herself on the table. "I'm taking your place."

He shook his head. Without ceremony, without invitation, he passed the tin plate of biscuits to her.

The patter of sleet increased to a steady drumming. Esther swallowed her coffee dismally. The hike to the wagon had become impossible. Surely, the old horses had pulled themselves free long ago. The reins had been knotted loosely to a small bush.

"Eat." Her host's voice interrupted her thoughts. He spooned molasses onto the plate, halved a biscuit neatly, and dunked it.

She followed his example, breaking and dunking the hot bread and carrying it to her mouth. Despite her worries, it tasted wonderful. Hot and light with a crusty bottom and top. She ate both halves and then drained the coffee cup.

He separated another with a knife and held the plate out to her. "Help yourself."

She shook her head. Thunder, unusual in a winter storm, rolled along the ridge and bounced across the valley. She shuddered convulsively.

In her mind's eye she could see a young bluetick hound, little more than a puppy, crouched shivering beneath a bush, thunder driving him to howl mournfully for help. Besides her pain for him was the fact that he was a very valuable animal. If he were lost or hurt—

She felt the tears start. Helpless, she sat as what began as a trickle swiftly turned to a flood. She wiped at them with her fingers but could not stop them.

Her host stopped his eating to stare at her. After a minute, he picked up her coffee cup and refilled it, again lacing it from the jug.

When he set it down before her, she clasped both hands around it, needing the warmth. Sick with embarrassment, she glanced up at him. "I—I'm sorry. I don't—I—"

Something was kindling in the depths of his dark eyes. Alarm? Surprise? Sympathy? He flexed his hands. Beneath the tangled beard, she saw his Adam's apple bob. "It's all right." His voice was different, less harsh, warmer, deeper. "You've been hurt. You—er—you let go."

She kept her head bowed. "I was thinking about my hounds," she whispered. "I'm trapped up here, but at least you've given me shelter and food for which I thank you from the bottom of my heart. But they've been left alone in the open. They're liable to freeze to death."

He waited silently, his face unmoving.

She shook her head, trying to cast away the terrible pictures. "Teet is just about the best. He's been my friend since I raised him from a pup. And the other one. He wasn't much more than a p-puppy."

Her host stared at her, a heavy frown drawing his black brows together. Her tears reminded him of civilities he had forgotten. She was crying for her dogs. Dumb animals. Her emotion surprised him. Had he really returned to a world where people had compassion for suffering? Where people were capable of love?

He stared at her pale face, her forehead deeply lined as pain wracked her. Her eyes were moist. He cleared his throat. "They'll probably be all right. If this Teet is as good as you say, he's probably already home and the pup with him."

She shook her head despondently. As a particularly hard gust shook the cabin, she hunched her shoulders. One hand sought her calf, massaging it gently.

Of his own accord, he supplied a piece of information. "I couldn't hear them any more when I was toting you home."

Esther pasted a wan smile on her face. Scraping back her chair, she pushed herself up with both palms flat on the table. "I apologize for crying. It's not a thing I do. I'm not silly like most females. And I thank you for breakfast, Mr.—"

Instantly, he was on guard. His eyes veiled their expression. His name was his business.

She saw and halted her speech. "Er—thanks. More than I can ever say for pulling me out of that shale last night. And for lugging me home. And for fixing breakfast. You make good biscuits. And the coffee warmed me right down to my toes."

She smiled to accompany her last remark and tested her weight on her bad leg. Her smile froze as the pain lanced upward. Drawing a steadying breath, she took her hands off the table to fasten her jacket. "Can you give me some idea of the direction of the dirt road that runs up behind Bas Boscomb's place? I tied my horses on it last night."

The man rose, too. His eyes scanned her up and down, noting the left leg bent at the knee, the toes touching the floor but taking no weight. He shook his head. "You'll never make it across the ridge."

"I have to."

"No," he insisted stolidly.

She put on her very best company manners. "I can't possibly impose on your hospitality any longer."

He looked around him. One corner of his mouth flicked upward. "Not much hospitality to impose on."

"My hounds—"

He shrugged. A bead of sweat trickled down his temple, but he set his jaw. "You can't find them. Whatever happened to them was over last night."

Her shoulders slumped in surrender. "I guess you're right."

With a nod he took up her coffee cup and put a spoonful of molasses in it. Steaming coffee followed while she watched with fascinated eyes, lips slightly parted. Last he poured a stiff tot of clear liquid into the cup and stirred the mixture.

"Drink this." He set it on the table within her reach. Then he flexed his shoulders. Despite a certain hollowness, he had strong shoulders and a broad chest. The cords stood out in his neck as if he were forcing the next words out. "Then you can get undressed and use the bed."

"Your bed," Esther gasped.

From a hook beside the door he took the long blue overcoat. Thrusting his arms through the sleeves, he did up the buttons. They were military and brass, although much in need of polishing. "I've got work to do. The bed's free. If you drink that—" he indicated the cup in front of her— "and lie down, you should be able to sleep."

For the first time in the entire wretched experience, she genuinely smiled. "I might never wake up."

Somewhere in the tangle of his beard, she thought she saw the flash of white teeth. "Oh, you'll wake up. You may have a headache, but your leg'll be rested."

She lifted the cup with both hands. "I don't drink. As a general rule."

He shrugged. "Play like you're snakebit. Believe me, you'll rest better."

He pulled a wool scarf from one of the deep pockets and wrapped it around his head, covering his ears and tying it under his chin. He did not touch the kepi that hung on a nail not far from the coat. Instead, he donned the hat next to it, a broad-brimmed officer's hat with gold braid around the crown. From the other pocket he pulled a pair of leather gloves.

Before she could protest, he was gone, closing the door behind him against the icy blast. Swaying slightly on her good leg, Esther looked around the cabin in bewilderment.

The full extent of her predicament struck her. The frisson that rippled along her spine had nothing to do with the vicious draft rolling across the cabin floor. She was lost, miles from her home, virtually stranded in an isolated cabin with a stranger who refused to give even his first name. He was most certainly a Yankee, probably a deserter, who made his living selling whiskey. Her mother would be horrified that her daughter had even spoken to such a man.

Desperately, she set her foot flat on the floor and eased her weight onto it. As the pain rose in a great paralyzing wave, she cursed weakly. She really had no choice.

She had been in worse predicaments before, she reminded herself. And survived them because she had not fought after the battle was lost. Teeth chattering, she pulled off her outer clothing and sat down on the bed.

Three swallows and she had drained the mug. She set it on the floor and lay back, pulling the covers up to her chin. The dizzying warmth of the alcohol spread to all parts of her body.

Her eyes burned as she stared at the door. She was every bit as evil as her mother had said. She was alone in a cabin with a Yankee who had told her to take off her pants and get into his bed.

And she had done it.

Three

He walked swiftly away, his breath crystallizing on his beard. The icy water dripped from the trees in heavy drops that struck without warning. He hunched his shoulders against the cold.

But he could not stay in the cabin. He needed to think, to turn over in his mind what her presence had come to mean. She should be driving him crazy by this time. His nerves should be screaming. But they weren't. Was he really getting better? Had the self-imposed isolation begun to heal him?

For the first time in five years, he could talk to another person without breaking out in a sweat. The conversation was far from normal, but at least he didn't stammer or cower or become so angry he wanted to smash someone's face. He shivered beneath his clothing as bitter memories assailed him. The rest of the world traded on other people's pain. They pried and probed and clucked with false sympathy. They exhorted him to be a man, to buck up, to forget. As if he ever could forget—

Of course, she wasn't really a hard test. She didn't know his past so she didn't ask questions. From the Ozark Mountains to the Missouri Breaks, a man's business was his own.

He stopped in the glade beside the leanto that covered the still. Pulling his gloved hands from his pockets, he stared down at them. Not a tremor. Neither was he nauseated. His stomach felt just as it should after a good breakfast. He believed he was improving.

He looked over his shoulder. Above the evergreens and the bright red oaks, he could see the thin trail of smoke rising from the cabin. At least he didn't wish that he had left her lying where she had fallen.

The rain had turned to pelting sleet by the time the cabin door flew open again in late afternoon. The weather's intensity had defeated even the heavy wool of the blue overcoat, the scarf, and the campaign hat. He dripped water from his hair, his beard, even his eyelashes and eyebrows.

Esther sat up and threw back the covers. Underneath them she was fully dressed except for her boots. "I put on some coffee," she said, a little breathlessly. "I thought you'd be glad to get it."

His body was going through the natural routine of shedding his garments. Without thinking, he said the correct words. "Thank you."

As she moved to fill his cup, he saw that she was getting around the cabin a bit more easily. "A little whiskey?"

He nodded as he rubbed his chapped knuckles briskly and blew on them. No question. The weather was killing cold. She would not have survived a night in the ravine, let alone made her way home today.

Esther poured a thimbleful from the jug into the coffee and passed the cup to him as he came to warm himself at the stove. He tasted it and frowned. Silently, he tipped more into it.

She clasped her hands and ducked her head. A slow flush rose in her cheeks. "Sorry."

He grunted.

He drank deep, then dropped into the chair to pull off his wet boots.

Hastily, she drew back to the bed and perched on the end, stretching out her bad leg. Besides being a Yankee, he might be a drunkard as well. He might drink himself into an ugly mood. She shivered. "I've heard the rain off and on all day."

He hesitated, framing an answer. "It'll freeze up solid tonight. By tomorrow afternoon it might begin to thaw."

She prayed he was right. "I'm sorry you're stuck with me. I've tried to walk around on the ankle today to keep it loose, but it's still in pretty bad shape."

His grunt was noncommittal as he pulled off the thick boot.

"It is," she hurried on, defending the injury. "I took a look at it and my knee, too. Red, blue, purple, every color but skin."

He paused momentarily at her description. Before his eyes flashed a picture of his own flesh over his ribs, across his belly, across the swollen expanse of his shattered shoulder. She was right. Red, blue, purple. Sympathetic pain wracked him.

The heavy boot thudded to the floor.

She saw him shudder, saw the stark withdrawal in his face, saw his dark eyes glaze. What had she said?

A faint sound reached her ears from outside. She glanced inquiringly at her host. With a faint smile at Esther, he rose and opened the cabin door some six inches.

A huge black cat with white boots and throat paused to test the air before picking his majestic way across the threshold.

Esther gasped. A dog, a partially tamed wild creature of some kind, she would have expected. Never a cat. What was such a creature doing so far from civilization? On he came toward the table on silent feet. Clearly an old tom, his head and shoulders were massive in comparison to the rest of his body. He might have been a miniature lion stalking through his kingdom.

She bent to keep the animal in view as he passed beneath the table. Her movement drew his attention. The creature crouched and spat a warning before springing sideways into the dimness under the stove.

"You're a stranger," the man said unnecessarily. His tone might have been accusing.

Esther leaned down from her seat to peer into the gloom. Eyes glittering, the cat hissed and laid back his ears. She straightened. "He looks mad enough to eat me alive."

"He'll calm down. It'll just take him a little while to get used to you."

She leaned over again and spoke as much to her host as the animal. "Easy, kitty-kitty. I'll be gone in a few hours and then you can have your cabin back."

The man blocked her view of the animal when he set his boots in front of the stove. Then he knelt to take inventory of his stores. From a box he pulled a slab of bacon, a can of peas, a couple of rutabagas and an onion. He regarded the meager provisions with a frown, then as an afterthought, he pulled out a sack of dried peaches.

Hardly fit food for a guest. He wished for fresh fruit, honey, whipping cream. Then he grinned at the direction of his thoughts. He had not entertained a guest in years. Indeed, he had not cared what he ate, only that he had something to eat when he felt hungry. Rescuing this woman might be the best thing that had happened to him in a long time.

"You keep the bed tonight." He was pleased that he had begun a conversation. Likewise, that he had thought to extend that courtesy to her.

"It's your bed. I couldn't keep you out of it."

Don't argue with me, he thought. *I can't stand it.* But he managed to sit still, his hands relaxed on his thighs. "I'll be fine."

She shook her head. "I can't take it. I feel bad enough about all this food. I can't impose anymore."

His nerves tightened. He pressed his palms more tightly against his thighs.

She sighed in exasperation, trying to think what to say that would make him change his mind. She had occupied the bed all day and all evening. She had had her turn. Beyond her sense of fairness was the uncomfortable feeling that she was sleeping in a man's bed while he slept just a few feet away. Pain and exhaustion had kept his presence from bothering her the night before. Now she was becoming aware of her rescuer's masculinity.

Her own fears were beginning to reassert themselves in little nervous shivers. She had not been close to a man in over five years. She never wanted to be again. What would she do? What could she do if he decided the use of the bed allowed him to take liberties with her person?

At that moment a distraction kept her from advancing a new argument. The black and white cat pulled himself from under the stove and stretched fore and aft. With a wide yawn he exposed gleaming sharp teeth and a curling tongue. Cautiously, he looked toward half of a leftover biscuit sopped in bacon grease. The man had set it on the floor beside the stove shortly after they had finished their meal.

Esther smiled as the black head bobbed in the air, catching the scent as it wafted along on the chilly currents near the floor. "Your cat isn't too sure about that biscuit."

"Big Boy?" Her host glanced over his shoulder and visibly relaxed. He could talk about the cat without arguing with her. "He's not my cat. He just stays here when the weather's bad. He's not anybody's cat. He belongs to himself."

Big Boy sat down on his haunches to regard each of the humans in turn. In particular his green eyes stared at Esther. His ears flattened and his chops peeled back, exposing glistening teeth.

When she made no threatening moves, his ears gradually lifted. At last convinced that the humans did not mean to attack him, he rose, squared his heavy shoulders, and stalked in the opposite direction of the food. His majestic strut was embellished by the stiff-legged limp off his right front leg.

"Oh, he's hurt himself." Esther's voice held a note of pity.

The cat froze in midstride, but the man did not so much as glance his way. "He got into a scrap with something a long time ago. Probably a big raccoon or a fox. He dragged himself in, torn to pieces. I don't see how he survived. But he did. One front leg was almost torn off. And that's not all."

Even as he spoke, Esther saw what else had befallen the animal. "He's lost his tail!"

"Came dragging it in behind him. It just fell off after a few days."

The cat circled the room, slipped under the bed, and finally came out. A yard from the food, he paused. Again he checked the position of the humans with exaggerated caution. Neither moved nor looked at the animal. Satisfied, Big Boy covered the last bit of floor and crouched in front of the plate.

"He won't take anything I offer to him," her host told her quietly. "He'll only eat something that he thinks has been dropped on the floor. He checks me over to be sure that I don't want it. Then he eats it. I've tried setting food down for him and calling him. He won't come."

"How strange."

"Not really. He just doesn't trust us. My guess is that he's had someone try to poison him. He won't eat anything from hand. Watch what he does next!"

Lapping at the food before actually taking a bite, the cat then ate half of the portion. Then he moved a yard away and settled down, tucking his paws neatly under him.

"He'll wait like that for a while," her host continued. "If it doesn't make him sick, he'll finish it."

Esther felt her heart turn over. So brave and defiant, yet so alone and afraid. She dared not glance at her host. "Poor thing," Esther whispered. "Poor, poor frightened creature."

The cabin was dark except for the lantern and the glow from the grate. Outside the wind had died and the temperature had dropped. Inside, the same problems confronted them. How could two mistrustful people be comfortable with only one bed in only one room? Esther poised on her good foot, using her left toe for balance. "I feel bad about all this," she said for at least the fifth time. "I've taken your bed all day."

"Don't let it bother you. I've slept out in worse than this." The man shook his head as he pulled on an extra shirt and pants. "I'll take the chair and prop my feet up on the end of the bed. I don't sleep much anyway."

She had forgotten that argument. "I don't either."

As if she had not spoken, he shoved another couple of hickory logs into the stove and turned down the lantern. Stolidly, he arranged himself in the chair and began to gather his covers around him.

Shaking her head, she capitulated. Taking care to avoid touching his feet, she crawled under the covers and turned her face to the wall. The bed was a hard box with corn shucks that rustled at the least movement; but she had plenty of covers, and the warmth eased her aching leg almost immediately. "I don't even know your name," she murmured.

A long time passed. "I don't know yours."

"My name's Esther Woodson," she volunteered.

This time he did not answer her. She waited in vain, chills prickling her spine. Fear gripped her. At her back sat a man who had been her enemy only a few years ago. He lived like an outlaw and would not tell her his name. She pressed her fist against her mouth. He might kill her when she tried to leave his hideout.

The hickory snapped and crackled behind the grate. Out of the darkness came his voice, deep and mellow. A gentleman's voice. "You don't need to be afraid of me."

"I don't know you." Her voice broke. She wanted to cry. The tears were very close to the surface.

"A country of strangers," he observed.

The bitterness in his voice made her raise her head.

"Go to sleep," he advised. "You don't have to worry."

She dropped her head back onto the pillow, but at the same time she felt compelled to speak. In the cold, quiet darkness things could be said that could never be said face-to-face. She cleared her throat. "I can't tell you how grateful I am. I'll owe you forever. There are no words."

His reply was bleak. "You don't owe me anything."

She raised her head again. He was in shadow, a black silhouette. She knew he could see her face in the glow from the stove. She shook her head positively. In that moment she wanted to make him understand the depth of her gratitude. "That's not true. As it's turned out, I would have died in that ravine. The norther would have blown in, and I'd have frozen to death."

"You don't know that," he scoffed. "I'm just the first person who heard you. Someone else would have come along in a little while. Forget about it or you'll start yourself crying again."

"Oh, I won't. My papa would have hoorawed me to death at the stunt I pulled last night."

He sat up alertly. "Will your papa be coming for you?"

She could feel tears prickling again. She swallowed them with an effort. "No. He's dead. No one will be worried about me. At least no one will be worried *enough* to come out in this weather."

He sat silent so long that she began to feel drowsy. She had actually drifted off to sleep when his voice came to her from a long way off. "You were crazy to come up here in the first place."

She acknowledged his scolding in a weak mumble. "I know. Seems crazy to me, too, now. It seemed the thing to do at the time."

He opened his eyes to acrid smoke punctuated with flashes of fire. Instantly, he closed them. He could not look at any more dead men. He could not.

His first breath was the all-to-familiar miasma of gunpowder and blood. He recognized another odor, the stench of human bodies torn apart. The bowels had disgorged their contents as well. On a battlefield, no man retained a shred of dignity.

He couldn't hear. He moved, shook his head to clear it. From a long way off he heard the sounds of battle. They were all around him on every side, shouts and screams and explosions, but far away as if he were on a promontory in the middle of it. The smoke. The smoke was so thick he couldn't see. He twisted his body and stood. Enemies were on all sides. He had to attack before he could be attacked.

Too slow. Too late. A mighty blow smashed into his shoulder. It lifted him off his feet and flung him backward. He landed on his back, breathless with pain. And with it more feeling. The metal beneath him burnt like a brand. He groaned, twitched, twisted, trying to stand. His efforts failed him, and before he had a chance to be alarmed, he was on his hands and knees, except that one arm wouldn't work. It stretched out in front of his eyes. It was bloody. He couldn't move it.

The yelling, cursing voices were coming closer. The explosions were louder. He would be blown to pieces. He had to crawl away. He panted like a dog as his mind ordered his hand to work, but that part of him was paralyzed. Like a dog he knew he could crawl away on three legs.

He began, but the first motion almost toppled him forward onto his face. Again. Again. Better. He was getting the hang of it. The ground was wet beneath his uninjured hand, spongy.

He opened his eyes again. Beneath his hand was a body, clad in a blue uniform. He had his hand on a man's thigh just above the knee. Instantly, he pulled back. A few inches and his hand slipped off into a pool of blood.

He screamed. And cannoned to his feet. And screamed again.

The scream of a man in mortal agony jerked Esther upright in her bed. Another scream more terrible than the first ended in a strangled sob. More sobbing followed and the sound of a heavy body stumbling toward her.

Disoriented by sleep, she tried to jump to her feet. Her stiff left leg caught and toppled her back against the cabin wall.

Another cry, this time for help.

She struggled to the edge of the bunk and stared frantically into the darkness. Except for the faintest of glows behind the grate of the potbellied stove, she could see nothing.

Clothing rustled. Fists thudded against wood.

"Damn! *Damn!*" The sobs became hoarse growls punctuated by words. Words she had never heard before— words whose meaning she did not know.

She pressed back against the rough wall of the one-room cabin. What had happened? Esther strained to see.

Had an intruder broken in without her knowing? Was her host locked in mortal battle?

The plank table went skidding across the floor and banged into the wall. The chair tipped over with a clatter. More thudding, clanging, banging. All were accompanied by the panting sobs and curses.

Esther hitched herself to the end of the bunk. Her host had hung her jacket on a nail near the door. She could slip it on and—

The din ceased abruptly. The cursing ceased, and the violent sobbing changed to quiet weeping. "Help. Please help. No. No. God!"

With a feeling of relief, she recognized the sounds of a nightmare. How many times had she herself wakened to find her pillow wet, the bedclothes on the floor? No intruder had entered the cabin. Her host must be lost in some horrible dream.

She hesitated. Should she go back to bed and say nothing?

"Please," came the whisper and then another sob. "Please—"

Guilt stabbed her. Because of her, he had volunteered to sit upright in a hard, straight-backed chair, his feet propped on the bed. She could not leave the man in such a state. The pain in his voice called to her. She had to offer what comfort she could to the man who had saved her life.

Light was the best thing to dispel the nightmares.

She edged her way along the wall, past the door, her destination the wood box. After fumbling for endless seconds while her host wept and pleaded, she emerged from behind the stove with a couple of hickory sticks.

Crouching low, she found the shiny handle on the first try and flung open the grate. Vigorously, she stirred the banked coals. Flames sprang up. By their light she saw her rescuer huddled on the floor. He had drawn himself into as tight a ball as possible. His hands were clasped around his head. He was moaning and sobbing.

Esther reached back for another stick and poked it into the heart of the fire. The light was minimal. The corners of the small cabin were still in shadows. Not expecting to find anything, she nevertheless peered about intently. As she had guessed, they were alone together in the cabin.

She thrust two more sticks into the flames.

"Doctor! Help! Here! Help! I didn't mean to do it. Doctor! Doctor! Help him, God damn you."

She went down on one knee and put her hands on his shoulder and side. "Wake up. Come on, Whatever-your-name-is, wake up."

At her touch his body seemed to lift off the floor in a movement of indescribable violence. It upset her precarious balance and sent her sprawling on her back. He was on her in a flash. His weight held her beneath him while his hands closed hard around her shoulders.

Her own startled cry of alarm was all but drowned by his voice yelling at her, still in the grip of some nightmare. "My fault!" he screamed. Not hers. "My fault. My fault. Don't let him die."

His eyes burned as he accused her, shaking her shoulders. The back of her head rapped against the floor. She bucked up to throw him off; but with only one leg in working order, she could not budge him.

His hands shifted, making for her throat.

Then she did scream, not a ladylike scream such as a fainting, vaporous heroine might have uttered, but a blood-curdling shriek pushed from the depths of her lungs. His hands closed about her neck, but not before she drew in a deep breath and screamed again. At the same time she stuffed both her fists in between his wrists and shoved them outward with all of her strength.

Her assailant stiffened. Then his grasp loosened, and

his hands fell away. The cursing ceased; the weight on her seemed slighter. She took instant advantage of the respite. Drawing back her left arm, she doubled up her fist and drove it into the center of the shadowy face above her. Her knuckles grazed his nose and smacked hard smashing his lips into teeth.

To her delighted surprise, the weight toppled off her.

Heedless of her injured leg, Esther rolled away. At the edge of the bed, the quilts drooped like a barrier, but she pushed herself through them, dragging them with her into the space under the bunk.

"What the hell!" The man's voice was muffled as though he held his hand to his injured mouth.

He struck a match. A minute more and the lantern shed its light on the scene. He stared around him, then down at his hand. His fingers had come away from his mouth with blood on them. He rocked back on his heels, the lantern swaying, making his shadow loom large on one wall and then the other.

He was trembling, and perspiration ran down into his eyes. He'd had one of his nightmares. He cursed bitterly. His torment never ceased. Pain might ease, wounds heal with hardly a scar, but the dreams went on forever.

He started toward his bed. Memory came rushing back. Where was the woman? He looked around him wildly taking in the overturned chair, the table pushed against the wall.

"Where are you?"

He glanced at the door, but the latch was still in place. She was here. He spun around in the center of the room, staring into all four corners. "Esther? Esther—er—Woodson? Where are you?"

* * *

Trembling in every limb, she hesitated to answer. He had probably been dreaming, but what if he were still not fully awake? At least here she had some protection until she could think what to do. He would have to move the bunk to strangle her.

Before the accident that dropped her here, she could probably have outrun him. Now her leg was killing her. If she made a break for the door, he would catch her in a couple of steps.

"Esther?" His voice sounded puzzled as he struggled with the state of the cabin and her absence. It also carried a note of fear. She held her breath, her hands furtively pushing down the entangling quilt.

"Esther. Where are you?" His legs came back to the middle of the room. He bent to right the chair. "Esther?" His tone changed to soft and gentle. Had he figured out where she was?

Suddenly, she felt very foolish. She was a woman grown, twenty-two years old for heaven's sake. Hiding under the bed was baby stuff. She went hot with embarrassment and anger at herself. At the first sign of danger, she had panicked. She should have picked up a length of hickory and knocked some sense into him. Failing that, she could have used the same hickory to knock his brains out. What fool would hide under the bed in a one-room cabin? What an idiot!

Unless he was crazy as a coot, a distinct possibility, he wouldn't need another minute to figure out where she was. Unless he'd been thrown off because he could never guess that anybody would be so stupid.

"Esther—"

She pressed her fist tight against her mouth and tasted blood on her scraped flesh. Whether hers or her host's she couldn't be sure. She hoped it was his. She took a deep breath. "Have you come to your senses?"

He swung round and dropped down on one knee. The

lantern clanked down beside him, sending its rays into the darkness. "Are you under the bed?"

She wiped at her cheeks with the edge of the quilt. "I certainly am. I don't intend to be murdered by a nightmare."

Her host sucked in his breath. Then his body seemed to collapse like a rag doll. "Murdered," he whispered. "By a nightmare? Did I attack you?"

From a warm bed she had plunged into a deep freeze. Now that the danger seemed to be over, her teeth began to chatter.

"Did you hit me?" he asked in a low voice.

She didn't want to tell him. Some men who were only moderately angry became furies when someone struck them.

"I guess you did." He didn't seem angry.

She swallowed. "Yes, I did. In the mouth. To keep you from murdering me. Are you bleeding?"

He touched his fingers to his smashed lips. "A drop or two."

"I'm sorry. I was so scared."

"You should have put me out of my misery." He rose and righted the chair. "It's all right," he murmured. "You can come out now."

She had already rolled over on her stomach. He sounded calm. One more reassurance and she would be out. "You're awake?"

"Yes." He turned the chair and sat down facing the bed.

She could see both feet, planted some distance apart, pointed toward her. She could also see the very tips of his fingers where his hands must be dangling between his knees.

"Esther." His voice was low and strained, completely different from his earlier tone. "Esther. Come out. I'm sorry. I— God knows, I— Please. I didn't mean to frighten you. I wouldn't hurt you. I've never hurt a woman in my life. I just didn't know."

She braced her good foot against the wall.

He listened hopefully to a scuffling movement. Finally, a white hand fluttered from under the bunk and slapped the floor. The fingers arched then curled round into a fist. He reached out to help her, then drew back. She probably wouldn't want him to touch her.

A shove with her good leg and her head and the quilts emerged from under the bunk. Trying to assume a competent air, she pushed until she was free from the waist up. Raising herself on her elbows, she gave him a wary look.

He leaned forward, his cheeks and forehead pale. A tiny smear of blood glistened on his moustache. A trickle ran over his lower lip and disappeared into his thick beard.

The sight doused every single bit of anger within her. It made her sick to her stomach. She had hit him hard enough to draw blood. When he was only having a bad dream.

For a minute they stared at each other; then he leaned forward a bit hesitantly. "May I help you?"

"No, thanks." Sick as she was with pity, she still didn't want him to come anywhere near her. He was a soldier after all. The enemy. Soldiers stole and destroyed and raped and killed.

She scrambled ungracefully out from under the bunk. The dust of she couldn't imagine how long clung to her front. She tottered to her feet, wrinkling her nose and wiping at her clothing.

"I'm sorry." He bowed his head.

She shivered. The memories of the danger and fear welled up inside her. He had flung her down and thrown himself on her. Where his hard hands had clutched, her shoulders and her throat throbbed. "You scared me to death," she said in a voice harder than she intended. "I thought you were fighting with someone. I thought you needed help."

He tucked his head down between his shoulders. He was swiftly becoming aware of the sweat soaking his clothes, the pounding of his heart. His stomach clenched painfully. He could not rejoin the human race. He had endured another of his damned nightmares and frightened his guest almost to death. A drop of blood fell on the back of one of his limp hands. The blow that she had dealt him in self-defense, the blow that had awakened him from the horror, had split his lip. Wearily, he touched his fingers to it. It was only a tiny cut, unworthy of his attention. "Are you hurt? Did I do any damage?"

She dropped down on the bunk and stared at him. "Damage?" The word surprised her. He had aroused the fears that she thought she had suppressed forever. Yes, he had damaged her. But she wouldn't, couldn't tell him about them.

"No. Not really. You just about scared me to death. But you didn't really hurt me." Her voice quieted. After all, a soldier could be expected to have terrible dreams. She would change the tone of the conversation. "But you could have been very sorry for what you did."

He waited, not understanding what was coming, but accepting whatever it was.

"If I'd run outside and gotten wet and caught pneumonia and died—" She glanced around her meaningfully. "Then you'd never have gotten rid of me. I'd have haunted this cabin forever."

He did not smile at her attempt at levity. Face grim, he stared at her while she bent to draw up her injured knee and massage her calf. Thank God she had not run off into the night.

Gathering courage, she shot him an accusing look. "I thought you were being murdered."

"No great loss if I had been." He shook his head in disgust.

She sneezed and brushed more dust from the front of her shirt. "Doesn't look like you've ever cleaned under there."

He didn't seem to hear her. His black, self-castigating thoughts were driving him deeper and deeper inside himself. When he spoke, his apology had nothing to do with housecleaning. "I'm sorry," he muttered bitterly. "I'm sorry. I just hope I didn't hurt you."

She let go of her knee and stared at him. He was really sorry. The last of her anger evaporated. She hastened to reassure him. "It's all right. I accept your apology. I'm fine. No harm done."

He hadn't really been talking to her, so he paid little attention to her words. The images of the dream, flashes of horror, clawed at the edges of his mind. With glazed eyes he stared at nothing, his face bleak.

Esther's tender heart responded to the picture of despair. She put her hand on his knee. "It's all right!"

He shuddered.

She waved her hand in front of his face. "It's all right. It's all right. Listen to me."

He blinked, then shook his head. "No. It's not all right. I had a nightmare. Another damned nightmare. Damn it all to hell."

She pushed herself up from the bunk. "I'll tell you what you need." She limped across to the stove. "You need some coffee. The fire's going again. I'll make some."

He shuddered. His fists clenched, then relaxed.

She rummaged through his box of stores and emerged with a delighted cry. "No. Not coffee. Look here." She turned around with false heartiness to display a blue package. "I'll make us some hot chocolate. That will make us both feel better."

When he still did not respond, she waved it in front of him, forcing him to look at it. From frightened victim she had changed to mother protector. "Baker's chocolate. My father used to fix it for me. Why don't you lie down while I fix you some? You probably had a nightmare when you fell off your chair. I shouldn't have let you give me the bed. It was your bed and you needed to sleep in it."

He did not move at first, but she reached across him. Her hand went by his face, the index finger pointing toward the bunk. "Go on. Get in."

He flinched, then slowly rose and scuffled across the floor. Instead of stretching out on the bunk, however, he sat on the end, propping his shoulders against the wall.

Between melting the chocolate in the water and adding sugar, she glanced at him. Though he sat back with eyes closed, his posture screamed his tension. His feet rested squarely on the floor, his hands lay at his sides ready to push himself erect at the first threat or emergency.

Her spoon scraped the side of the pan. His eyes flew open, shooting her a frantic look before finding the source of the noise and relaxing slightly.

"I'm just like a kid about hot chocolate," she informed him with a bright smile. The homely activity had gone a long way to restoring her own emotional balance. Homely chatter might be just the ticket for her tormented host.

Also, despite some initial pain, her leg had loosened up remarkably. She tested it and found that it could at least keep her balance without a twinge. "My father and grandfather used to take me and my brother camping. We'd run the hounds, and then we'd gather round the camp fire and follow the recipe on the Baker's chocolate package. Just like this. Daniel and I would race to find the firewood, so the water would get to boiling. I drink coffee in the morning, but hot chocolate is the drink for evening. And for when you wake up in the middle of the night."

She stirred the mixture on the stovetop, talking calmly, gauging his reaction. So far she had seen no sign that he was paying any attention. She glanced at her watch. At least a good four hours till morning. She heaved a depressed sigh. The sooner she could get home, the better.

The heat was beginning to build up in the cabin. The warmth from the stove felt good to her sore leg. She rummaged again in the box and found another can of condensed milk.

"Almost done," she called in a falsely cheerful voice. "Would you like me to put some extra sweetening in it? Might help to settle you down for the rest of the night."

At last he met her eyes. "Yes, please."

She reached behind the stove for the jug and started to uncork it.

"Bring it here."

"Now wait a minute." The last thing she needed was to spend the rest of this eternal night with a drunk.

"Bring it here." His dark eyes were steady in his face. His voice hardened. "I won't hurt you. I can promise you that. Just bring your chocolate and the goddamned whiskey."

He had destroyed her peace with the cussword. She had a wild impulse to fling the jug at his head and run for her life. Drunken men were as dangerous as rattlers, and they didn't care who they hurt.

Four

Esther took a step backward and then another. She didn't realize she was shaking her head.

He held out his hand wearily, palm down. Not reaching for her, not tacitly begging her to put her hand in his. "Look, I've said I won't hurt you. I've been through this before. I don't have the strength to hurt anybody after one of these things."

She could feel the heat of the stove against her legs. Another step and she would collide with it. "This could be the first time."

With his other hand he pressed his thumb and third finger tight over the bridge of his nose. He shouldn't be surprised. Any woman would be advised to run from a madman. And he knew he was mad.

His dark eyes were pools of misery as he looked up at her. "I don't think so. I'm tired enough to pass out where I'm sitting. And I'm sick because I scared you. I need a drink."

She stood poised, her injured leg taking part of her weight. She was ready to run if he made a false move.

"Please."

Her face seemed to relax a little. After a terrible few seconds, she limped toward him.

He sat up and reached for the jug. She withheld it until she had handed him his chocolate. He grabbed it impatiently and took a drink. It was hot and sweet and good. Once upon a time, it would have been enough and more. Now he longed for the whiskey and the oblivion it would bring for a few hours. Grimly, he pulled the stopper and poured fire down his throat.

She retreated to the chair, but he called her back. Where the words were coming from, he didn't know. He hadn't had enough alcohol to loosen his tongue. "Why don't you sit down on the other end of the bed and cover yourself up? I won't sit here but a minute. When something like this happens, I have to get out of the cabin. I'll go walk it off."

"It's below freezing out there," she reminded him.

"Doesn't make any difference." He subsided against the wall, the jug on his thigh.

She stared at him, one hand on her hip, the other around the mug of cocoa. The chair was hard and straight-backed, made of ancient oak. No chance to rest in that. And she wanted her leg to feel the same or better in the morning. "All right. But don't you for one minute try anything."

His eyes narrowed and then slid past her to the orange flames leaping in behind the grate. "No chance. I told you. I've done this before. In a few minutes what I dreamed will hit me and I'll be out of here like a light."

"How can I trust you?"

He shrugged as alcoholic warmth pervaded his limbs. "Don't trust me, then. I just think you'll be more comfortable. If I'd wanted to hurt you, I'd have done it before I dozed off and fell out the chair. If you don't trust me, you can stay awake and wake me if I start pitching around again."

She stared long and hard at the chair before giving in. It didn't even have a cane bottom. Picking up the quilts, she dropped one at his side and took the other for herself.

"Thanks, but you don't need to—"

"It's your quilt. Maybe you got too cold and it gave you a nightmare."

He drained the cocoa. How he wished it were something that simple. "Cold didn't give me a nightmare."

Through half-closed eyes, he watched her drape the quilt across her shoulders and sit down. She doubled her right leg at the knee. Then with exquisite care and much biting of her lower lip, she managed to get the left leg propped on top of it. Then she arranged the quilt to cover her entire body.

Once she was covered, she settled back. "Nightmares can be funny things. Sometimes too much pepper will give you a tummy ache. Or eating just before you go to bed."

"No." He took a long drink off the jug.

She finished her hot chocolate. A draft of frigid air slipped between the logs of the cabin and set her shivering. She pulled up the pillow to block it. "I hate the night myself. I don't sleep if I don't have to. At home I prowl for hours."

Her confession surprised him. He rolled his head to look at her. "You do? Why?"

Her mouth tightened. She pulled her head down into the quilt like a turtle retreating into its shell. "The war."

He snorted. "You don't know what war is."

She snapped her head around. The hatred in her eyes made him suck in his breath. "I know."

Just those two words, uttered low, fell like lead between them. If she had been a wolf, he would have drawn back a bleeding hand.

He ran his hand around the jug and suddenly thought of the yellow stripe down the side of his pants. Awareness dawned. He was a Yankee, and she, a native of the Ozarks, had seen war as no others in the state of Arkansas had. Only a few miles from here, the armies had fought at Pea Ridge. He thought about asking her about it. Then he changed his mind. "Have a swig. It's guaranteed to drive the horrors away."

She shook her head. "Or bring them on."

He brought the jug back to his thigh. "Suit yourself, but I'll guarantee it'll help for a while."

They sat for several minutes in strained silence. Inside the stove the wood hissed and crackled. The little cabin creaked from the weight of the ice and snow on its roof.

"You know you really shouldn't blame yourself for nightmares," Esther said finally. "I used to have terrible nightmares myself. And I couldn't do a thing about them."

He was too wise to snort at her confession, but his expression was one of disbelief.

She nodded. Her fingers curled around the mug. She tilted it and looked into its depths. "As a child I had them," she continued. "I sort of grew up with them."

"What does a kid have nightmares about? Stomach-aches from too much apple pie." He settled more comfortably on his end of the bed. At any minute his nerves would set up their infernal jangling, and he would have to run away. For a little while longer he could listen to her story.

"I had nightmares about hell and the devil."

This time he couldn't keep back his deprecating snort. "I still have them. Sometimes every night."

The look she turned on him made him a little uncomfortable. It was pity and certainty combined. "I'll bet you don't. I used to dream about going to hell and burning forever. I was so bad that I knew I was going there. And the thought of it scared me. I didn't want to go."

"Little kids don't go to hell. Where'd you get such crazy ideas?"

"From church."

"Church?"

"The sermon was always on how the devil takes the

people who do bad things. And since I was always doing bad things—"

"Not little children, for heaven's sake." This whole thing was upsetting him, but not in the way he was usually upset.

"Even little children," she insisted. "If they don't mind, the devil will take them away from their good mothers and fathers."

He sat up straighter and turned to her. His voice held a combination of outrage and incredulity. "What kind of a church was that?"

She pushed herself off the bed and limped to the stove as if his attitude made her uncomfortable. A little bit of chocolate remained in the pan. She poured it into her mug. "A good church."

He shrugged. He should have known. If the woman believed such nonsense enough to have nightmares about it, she would certainly defend the church that taught it to her. It was like the damned war, he thought. More battles fought, more men killed in the name of peace on earth.

Her eyes wide and brown now, she stared at him over the rim of the mug. "It was a big part of my life."

He searched the long unused store of knowledge that was once his pride. "No child should be taught religion until he's old enough to reject it."

She gasped and seemed to shrink back, although she never moved. "You're very sure?"

The question brought him up short. He wanted to cry and laugh. What a fool he was! He was sitting here spouting atheism to an innocent believer. And throwing out more words than he had spoken in the past year, feeling more passion than he had felt in five. He swung the jug around to his mouth and drank. "I'm not sure of anything."

She came back and sat down on the side of the bed,

her back straight, her eyes filled with what? Hope? Fear? Pain? He could not tell. "What makes you doubt everything?"

Now that was a question he could answer. "The same thing that makes you believe everything. Experience."

"Oh, I didn't say I believed everything. In fact, I don't believe all that stuff anymore."

He looked pointedly from the jug to her.

She flushed. Defiantly, she held out her mug. "Sweeten that up for me."

He put his hand over the mouth. "Not unless you really want it. You don't drink with me to prove a point."

"I guess you're right." She took the mug back. Climbing into the bed again, she rested it on her stomach.

The flames had subsided to an occasional blue tongue flickering out of the heart of dark red coals. Freezing cold was already penetrating through the wall at his back. He wasn't nearly drunk enough. And his nerves remained remarkably quiet.

He lifted the jug, but set it back down again without drinking. It was still half-full. He could take it a little slower. "How'd you come to be running after dogs in the middle of the night?"

Instantly, she corrected him. "Hounds. Don't call them dogs. They're hounds. Coonhounds to be specific."

"Okay. How'd you come to be running after hounds in the middle of the night?"

"That's the way I make my living. I own a kennel." Her voice radiated pride. "My hounds are descended from George Washington's pack of English foxhounds. Their ancestors came with mine from Virginia through Kentucky and then south through Tennessee."

He looked at her erect posture with renewed interest. "And you train them?"

"I raise them and train them and sell them, and train pups for other people. They pay me to."

Some of his skepticism must have shown in his face.

"They're very valuable animals," she explained. "They're killers of varmints that kill poultry and destroy crops. They used to hunt foxes for gentlemen's sport. Now they hunt raccoon and possum and fox, too. Whatever the farmers want them to. But they have to be properly trained." She tossed back her braid. Her voice was excited. "My hounds will hunt and kill whatever you want them to."

He could feel a smile tickling the corners of his mouth. She was serious about this. Even though she was a big girl, she was still much too frail to be doing this sort of thing by herself. He hazarded a guess. "With your husband?"

He might have stabbed her in the heart. All the bright enthusiasm went out of her face. Her head went down. She pulled the edges of the quilt tightly around her. "I don't have a husband."

"Brother? Father?"

"No one." Her voice was muffled. "*I* raise and train the hounds. *I* own the kennel. It belonged to my grandfather and my father before him. And now it belongs to me."

He thought about her answer. A hickory knot popped and sprayed sparks. The lantern flame sank to a blue halo. He didn't have any more coal oil until he made a trip to buy some. When that light went out, they would be in darkness. He should leave the bed to her, but he didn't want to. For the first time in more than five years, he felt human. He wanted to hang on to the feeling. He searched his mind for something to say.

Her voice came out of the quilts. "Of course, if something's happened to my best hound, I'll be in a hole it'll take me a long time to climb out of."

"He's probably better off than you are." He did not know whether the animal had survived or not, but he wanted to give her hope. He wished he hadn't mentioned a husband. He took another drink. "Tell me more about your kennel."

She turned over on her side to face him. Carefully she eased her injured leg out straight along the edge of the bunk. Her foot was only a couple of inches from his thigh. He wondered that he didn't feel compelled to move away from her.

As if she told him a bedtime story, she began to speak. "My grandfather came into Arkansas with the Peels of Kentucky. They were followers of Daniel Boone. Pawpaw brought his black-and-tan hound and two bitches." She chuckled softly. "And that was all it took."

"And when was that?"

"Around 1820. His hounds were famous. Teet's descended from their long line. He's wonderful. Smart as a person. Big. With a voice like a bugle. When he calls, you have to follow. I raised him myself. Pawpaw picked him out of the litter when he was just a week old and said he was mine."

Something began to stir inside him. She had really loved her grandfather. Love. He had forgotten about it. "Was your grandfather the one who took you to church?"

"Oh, no." Her voice was growing sleepy. The words were slurring. "He was the one who took me out of the church—for a while."

He took another swig on the jug and set it on the floor. He spread the quilt she had dropped between them and wrapped it around his shoulders. He wouldn't be able to sit here much longer. His nerves would drive him out into the night. But so long as he was here, he might as well keep the cold off his back.

He looked over at his guest. Her head was snuggled down between her shoulders, her right leg drawn almost against her chest. He listened. Her breathing had evened out. One pale white hand lay on the bed between them.

"Your grandfather sounds like a smart man," he whispered to his guest.

His own hand moved as if with a will of its own. His fingers touched hers, slid beneath them until they lay across his palm. Warm and smooth. Not exactly smooth perhaps. But a woman's calluses were different from a man's, just as a woman's hand was different.

In another lifetime he had held a woman's hand, caressed it, put his mouth to it. A woman had kissed him and wept when he rode away. For a time letters written on vellum stationery in an elegant flowing script had come to him.

But he had been wounded, believed dead. And when he came back, his father had told him she had become engaged to someone else. He had never tried to see her. He lowered his head until his mouth almost, but not quite, touched the pale hand he cradled. Another inch—

He sat back abruptly. He was acting like a complete idiot. The woman beside him would be gone tomorrow. He would lead her away from the cabin back to the road by blazing a trail. Unless she were Daniel Boone or David Crockett, she wouldn't be able to find her way back. When she came running her hounds through the mountains, she might call to him a few times, but he would never answer.

He should have returned to the chair; but he had made his nest, and the alcohol had relaxed him. He wrapped another quilt around his legs and propped them up on the chair. Another drink, the last from the jug, and he set it on the floor. He would think of something pleasant, but as he sank back he found he had no need to think of anything.

* * *

The man opened one eye slowly. The variety of torments occurring inside his skull forbade a sudden flood of light. His temples throbbed excruciatingly. The eyelid grated like sandpaper on the eyeball. Each separate tooth ached vaguely whenever his coated tongue touched it.

A sound had awakened him. Still half asleep he wondered irritably about its source. If he were not in such pain, he might be able to doze off again. He closed his eye, trying to ignore the discomfort that a hangover created. For the troubled of the world, the price of oblivion always took a high toll on the body. At least he manufactured his own poison rather than buying it in a saloon.

He tried to roll over onto his back, but found himself backed up against the wall of the cabin. To roll over on his stomach was also impossible. A body was pressed warmly against him.

He opened both eyes in stunned realization. His arm was thrown over a woman. His hand was nestled delightfully between her thighs. Unfortunately, she was turned the wrong way. The curve of her buttocks fit the space beneath his chin. Her shoulder was pressed against his groin. Her cheek rested on his thigh.

For over five years he had not spent a night with another human being. He had wandered from place to place. Gradually, he had realized that he could not stand to be around people. He left the towns entirely and slept where he could until he had found this cabin in the Ozarks.

Then Esther Woodson had fallen into his life.

He hoisted himself up on his elbow and stared in disbelief at his bedmate. How had she managed to get so close to him? Of course, the nightmare had occurred and he had gotten drunk, but not too drunk.

Curiously, he tested his reactions. Where was the nausea? the sweating? the tension coiling in his gut? the mounting anxiety? He felt relaxed, even rested, except for the hangover. A thrill of excitement went through him. Perhaps—

But would he feel this way if he had stayed sober last night? His fingers rubbed the inside of her thigh. Beneath the butternut wool of her men's trousers was the first woman he had touched intimately in years. A pulsing, faint but definite, began in his groin. He flattened his palm against her, feeling the heat. If he slid his hand back only a couple of inches, he would press against—

Her eyes flew open. Disorientation, warmth at her back, breathing, pressure. Beneath her cheek a hard-muscled thigh flexed. And a hand between her legs. Flashes of memory, pain, disgust, shame.

"No-o-o-o!" She flung herself off the bed. Hitting the floor on her back, she rolled and came up in a crouch. Primal ferocity wrung a snarl from her. If her injury pained her, she didn't feel it.

No man was ever going to take her against her will again. She would kill him with her bare hands or die at his, but no man would ever violate her body and walk away to brag about it.

"Stay away!" she warned him, doubling up her fists like a man. "I'll scratch your eyes out. I swear I will."

A shamed flush burned on his cheekbones. He had violated her trust in the worst possible way. The hand he put out to beg for peace trembled slightly. "I'm sorry. I apologize. It was all a mistake." He made his voice soothing. "We fell asleep."

"Yankee!" She spat the poisonous word at him. "Yankee trash. Murdering. Raping. Robbing. Trash."

He flinched. "The war's over."

"Not in the Arkansas Ozarks," she swore. "Not in my lifetime. Not by a long shot."

He could not argue with her fury. Like a hot wave,

the nerves that had been quiet for two whole days set up their jangling. Clumsily, for he was shaking from head to toe, he managed to push himself up from the bed and reeled to the door. His head pounded from the hangover and with the violent emotions as well.

"I'll leave," he groaned. "I'll get out."

"Just let me out of here!" she screamed.

"No." He jerked the blue coat off the nail and swung it around his shoulders. "No. Stay here. I won't come back until it's warmed up enough for you to leave."

"I'll leave now," she insisted. She stooped for her boots. She would rather run out of the cabin in her sock feet than chance his anger. He was still feeling the effects of the whiskey. When the fumes cleared out, he would be angry.

He caught her by the shoulders when she made a dive for the door. "No."

"Oh, don't," she begged. She twisted out of his hands and sprang back. "Don't you touch me."

"I won't. I won't. Just calm down. I'll leave. You don't need to be afraid." He took a deep breath. His shoulders barred her way to the door. "Think a minute. You don't know the way back."

"I'll take my chances."

He swallowed. "Just stay here. I didn't mean to do what I did. I know it was wrong." He seemed to be searching for a word. "Unforgivable. I was asleep. I haven't been able to sleep—I haven't slept with anyone in five years. I— Can you understand that?"

"So you thought you'd take advantage of me?" She could dimly see what he was talking about. But he could be lying.

"No. I never. I was still half asleep."

They were both panting hard, shaking their heads for different reasons, their emotions riding them hard.

"Don't go. You could wander around the mountain

half the day." He pulled the wool scarf from the nail. "I'll leave. When I come back, I'll take you home."

An impatient yowl came from the other side of the door. It broke the tension between them.

"He wants in," the man said. "It must be below freezing out there."

Without another word, he opened the door and slipped out. He could not force her to stay. She was free to go if she chose. He could only hope that she would calm down and think about what had happened.

The bluish sun hit his eyes like a bolt. He closed them momentarily, then dropped off the porch and headed into the grove. Great lungfuls of fresh, cold air eased his headache almost miraculously and cleared his brain of the cobwebs.

He hunched his shoulders. Esther Woodson had every right to be frightened and furious. She had screamed at him in her anger. And he had violated her privacy, if nothing else. How could it have happened? How had their bodies huddled together without his knowing about it?

He closed his eyes again, remembering the feeling of her body against his, the warmth. He lifted the hand that had lain between her thighs and rubbed his thumb over the tips of the fingers. Was there a hope of his recovery?

Back on the porch, the black cat sat on the step, his green eyes accusing. Then he yowled again, louder, more demanding than before.

Behind him the door swung open. Esther's voice reached the man's ears. "Come on in, and be quick about it."

Big Boy looked up at her, then back at the man. His eyes closed as if in thought. Then with insolent slowness he rose and arched his spine before pacing with measured tread across the threshold.

The minute the door closed, the cat loped across the

floor and ducked beneath the stove. Esther began a sys-
tematic pacing, forcing the leg to perform, putting her
weight on it, driving the blood through it. As she walked,
she muttered to herself. She should leave immediately.
Except she couldn't. She was his prisoner. She didn't
have any idea where she was.

At length she realized the cabin was stone cold. She
moved to the stove to poke up the fire and add logs.
From the semidarkness beneath came a hiss of warning.

"Big Boy?" Esther pressed her fist against her forehead. She needed to get a hold on herself and settle
down. She dropped into the chair and bent to peer at
the black shadow huddled against the cabin wall. "Come
on, pretty kitty. Don't you be scared. I couldn't hurt a
cricket, much less a big old fella like you."

Accompanied by a fierce hiss, the tom bared his fangs.

"Good old Big Boy," she crooned. "Good kitty. Come
here, Big Boy. Come on." She held out her hand palm
up.

The shadow did not move.

"Come here, kitty-kitty."

The shadow edged forward. One white boot and then
the other emerged from beneath the stove. The cat settled down with head and shoulders in the open, his yel-
low-green eyes regarding her steadily.

Esther sat back up. "Good kitty. How'd you lose your
tail? Humm? Did you tangle with an ol' rackety coon? I
bet he looks worse than you do."

The cat allowed his eyes to close to mere slits and
tucked his paws away under his body.

Esther held down her hand, palm open.

He froze, regarding her reproachfully.

"Come on," she coaxed, her voice crooning. "Come
on, big kitty. You can come out in the open. I won't hurt
you."

He hesitated, green eyes staring balefully. At last, his

decision made, the cat that nobody could touch moved with majestic deliberation under her outstretched palm. His eyes closed. He arched his head, so she could stroke the length of his back.

"Sweet kitty," she crooned, stroking the hard black back over and over again, feeling the scars from a hundred claws beneath the thick fur. Up close his black coat was liberally sprinkled with white hairs.

It reminded her of her host's black beard and hair, salted with gray. Even as she stiffened her resistance to pity, she realized she had forgiven the man the intrusion. Her head had been on his thigh as well.

The cat began a deep-throated purr of contentment and acquiescence.

"Why, you're an old fellow, aren't you? You're getting like an old grizzly bear. How'd you lose your tail? Poor thing. Why, you like to be petted, don't you? Yes, you do. You do. Sweet kitty." She scratched behind his ears and beneath his chin. Instantly, he arched and threw back his head, exposing his throat to follow her fingers.

She grinned. "I'll just bet if I hung around here and petted you long enough, you'd get to where you liked it. Pretty kitty."

The new fire logs caught, and the cabin began to warm. Esther pushed herself up and began her circuit again. This time the cat did not retreat, but his slitted eyes never left her limping figure.

Esther had lain down for a rest and dozed off when her host stomped up onto the porch. The noise brought her off the bed to stand beside it, fists clenched at her sides, ready to flee or fight.

He entered in a breath of fresh, cold air and made directly for the stove. Pulling off his gloves, he spread his hands before the grate. His cheeks above the beard were pink, his eyes clear.

After a minute, he turned and regarded her warily.

"I waited," Esther said at last.

He nodded. "Good. The sun's been too weak to burn off the clouds, so the temperature's just gone above freezing."

"Then I can leave." She would need all afternoon to get home. She would still have a long way to walk once she got to the road.

He nodded slowly. "Yes. I'll take you down the ridge."

Esther fastened her jacket. "You don't need to trouble yourself. If you'll give me directions, I'll be gone before you know it."

"I'll take you down to the road." His firm statement allowed for no argument.

She nodded, expecting nothing else. He was a hermit after all. She knew more about his cat than she knew about him. Good manners reasserted themselves. She must not forget all the things he had done for her, not the least of which was probably saving her life. "I don't know how to thank you for all the trouble you've been to on my account. I've eaten your stores; I've used your supply of wood and coal oil." She spread her hands. "I don't have any money—"

He cut her off abruptly. "I don't want any money."

She shrugged, then held out her hand like a boy who had been prompted to do the right thing. "I'll always be beholden to you. I would have died out there."

"Probably not." He looked at the hand extended to him as if he had forgotten what she might have thrust it out for. It was the same one he had touched last night before he went to sleep. Another violation of her person, that one on purpose. He thrust his own hands behind him and cleared his throat.

"I think so," she insisted. "I think you saved my life."

Not looking at her, he pulled his gloves from the pocket. "I'll get my hatchet and cut a hickory for you to use as a walking stick."

As the door closed behind him, Esther sank onto the chair. The fear of him had disappeared completely. Oddly she did not feel elated about going home. Her sense of obligation lay like a burden on her. He had saved her life. She looked around the rude, barren cabin. How sad to live like this. The tragedy in his past must be so terrible that she couldn't conceive of it. Certainly, the anger and pain that had boiled out in that nightmare had been more than she had ever seen.

Big Boy came from beneath the stove to wind his body around the leg of the chair. Unconsciously, she dropped her hand onto his head and stroked him.

Her host's boots stomped on the porch, and the door swung open again. The man's eyes opened wide in surprise at the sight of the cat accepting her petting. "Got your stick," he said curtly. "Are you ready?"

She took the hickory crutch. He had evidently looked for some time to find just the right shape. It had a right-angle fork at the top and a crook in the middle where her hand would grip it. She tested it the length of the cabin and back. "Perfect. Might have been grown to order for me."

Her host looked pleased. Then he remembered the experiences of numbers of wounded men and added a word of caution. "Just don't forget to lean your weight on your hand and arm, not your armpit."

"Is that right?" She tried to do as he told her and tottered a step. When she put out her hand to steady herself against the wall, he put one hand lightly in the small of her back to support her.

His touch lasted only a moment; but she threw a quick alarmed glance over her shoulder, and he let his hand drop immediately. His frown deepened until it was almost a scowl.

But she smiled her appreciation before she hastily looked away. "Well, let's go," she said heartily. "If you'll point me in the right direction, I can find my way down. Down is always easier than up."

He opened the door for her. "I'll take you down."

She made a wry face at him as she limped through. "It's not necessary. I've taken too much of your time already."

"I don't have anything else to do," he muttered as he helped her down the steps.

"I left my wagon on the third logging trail east of Bas Boscomb's place." She squinted in the blue sunlight.

"I know."

She stared at him. "You know?"

He looked away across the ridge at the limitless expanse of green, orange, and red trees. Here and there patches of mist or low-hanging clouds still covered them. Not a leaf stirred. The forest was silent around them. "I've watched you come into the woods for a long time now."

Not looking at her, he stepped back up to close the door. Before he could shut it, the black cat streaked through and leaped from the top of the porch.

Stunned by her host's confession, Esther watched the tom bound into the brush at the clearing's edge. "So long, Big Boy."

By the time he had gotten her down the steep slope beneath the ridge, Esther was panting and white from negotiating the outcroppings and patches of ice. Her leg was hurting from ankle to groin, her foot swelling in her boot. At the base of the steepest part, they paused for her to sit on a rock and ease the strain on her arm and shoulder. Teeth set, she stripped off her glove to examine the blisters on her palm.

His face grave, her companion peered intently over her shoulder. His index finger hovered over the dime-sized water blister on the heel of her hand. "I should have wrapped that thing for you."

She pulled it away and plunged it back into the glove. "You cut the crutch for me." She stood up. "I couldn't have made it without it. Besides, they're not bad. I'd probably have gotten them anyway no matter how heavily padded the stick was."

He rose beside her and pointed. "We're almost there."

The road was empty. Esther's relief that at least two of her animals had returned to the stable was tempered by the knowledge that she had at least a mile to walk. Nevertheless, she faced her host. "I'll be fine now. It's just a short walk down the road to Bas's. He'll take me home."

Her rescuer stepped back, a doubtful expression on his face. "Are you sure?"

She nodded with a wave of her free hand. "The place is just around the bend. I can't thank you enough. Words won't—"

He shrugged dismissively. "Then don't say them. Take care of yourself."

She held out her hand. He hesitated only fractionally before clasping it. "Good luck."

"Same to you." A brief, hard squeeze and he pulled away, thrusting his hands into his pocket.

"And thank you."

"You're welcome."

She paused, reluctant now to say goodbye. A bond had been formed between them. It might be tenuous, but it was there nevertheless. More was required. "And—er—you're welcome to come to my place anytime. That is, I wish you'd come to visit me. Let me show you my appreciation. Let me fix you dinner." She bowed her head. "None of this is coming out right."

"I'm much obliged for the invitation."

With a half smile she looked at him resignedly. "I mean it."

He took a step back. "Thank you."

She looked at him steadily. "I don't even know your name."

He hesitated. "It's York."

"York?"

"Goodbye, Esther. Take care of that leg." He turned on his heel and started back up the mountain.

She watched him for less than a minute, so swiftly did he disappear into the brush.

Five

"Home safe and sound, Esther." Bas gave her a snaggle-toothed smile. His withered cheeks were red with cold. "Don't you be runnin' them woods again without tellin' me. Thataway, I can come and fetch you if you get in trouble."

"I won't do it again, Bas." For the third time she listened politely to his fatherly lecture. He had known her grandfather and grandmother. He attended her mother's church, although not regularly. While he had never been interested in her as a child, he had been a friend of her father's. She was sure Bas felt obliged to give her advice for Noah's sake.

"Just see that you don't."

She climbed down from his wagon. Her leg was killing her, and all the blisters on her hand had broken; but she climbed the six steps to her front door in record time. "Goodbye," she called to him, "and thanks again."

Inside the door, she staggered to the settee and dropped onto it. Her leg throbbed rhythmically. Both ankle and knee had swollen from overuse. She lifted the injured member up on the cushions and stretched out.

After a minute of blessed stillness, she lifted her head to stare out the window at the kennels. Teet. The bluetick pup. She should—

No. She paid Carly Ord to come in to clean out the runs and take care of the horses in the stable. His instructions were to feed and water the animals if she hadn't already done so. She would just have to depend on his having been faithful. The well of her physical strength was about run dry. Whatever she could do tonight had to be done for herself.

Her first task would be to light the fires in the kitchen and bedroom. Thank heaven she had laid them before she went out. Had it only been two nights ago? She felt a hundred years old.

The big wood stove in the kitchen began to radiate heat almost immediately. She sometimes believed that it was alive in some slow-moving way, or perhaps it had been used so many years that an eternal warmth lay just beneath the skin of the iron so that only a tongue of flame would bring it to the surface.

Immediately, she set water to boiling in two kettles and the big iron pot. She was going to have a bath before she crawled between the sheets to sleep for a week.

Had anyone missed her? She stared across the back lawn to the kennels.

Beyond and below, the road circled into the little town of Cutter's Knob. She knew its location only by the curls of smoke rising from the chimneys and flues. Its rooftops to a one were overtopped by tall trees. Some wore the fall colors of scarlet, umber, and gold. Some were dark green pines and spruces. She had craved this remoteness when she had moved into her grandfather's house. Now, shivering with cold, fatigue, and pain, she wished fervently for someone to welcome her home.

Esther pulled the bathtub in front of the cookstove and filled it with hot water. With the oven door open, she soaked her abused body until she could feel almost human again. By the time she emerged an hour later, wrinkled but eased, her bedroom was warm. She had only to fill her hot water bottle and fall into her bed.

Huddling on her side, the blankets around her ears, she stared through the window at the mountainside. Outside, the bleak afternoon had given way to a chill, windy dusk as another norther, this time a dry one, blustered around the house. Listening to its miserable moaning, she wondered about the man named York in his drafty cabin somewhere in the distant darkness.

"Me and my boys come to make a withdrawal." Eyes blinking wildly, a grin on his handsome face, Jesse James poked his .44 double-action revolver between the bars of the Bank of Mt. Vernon. The teller stared cross-eyed into the muzzle and nodded furiously.

Behind his desk the banker's eyes narrowed. From beneath his brows he surveyed the scene in his otherwise empty bank. Three masked men had ranged themselves around the lobby of the bank. One pulled the shade down on the door and locked it. One trained his gun on the banker himself. The third came behind the counter and held open an ordinary sugar sack.

Jesse James's .44 never wavered. "Fill 'er up."

The banker considered palming his own .44 from the cash drawer beneath his desk, but it was a single-action. They would hear the click when he cocked it. Reluctantly, he nodded. The teller was already emptying his drawer.

In less than a minute, the teller and the banker were lying facedown on the floor. "Preacher" George White came trotting up with the horses when he saw the shade go up and down. Pulling their masks off their faces, the robbers walked out of the bank and climbed aboard.

"Thank you kindly," Jesse called from the door. "Be sure and tell the army you were robbed by Jesse James and his gang. Sure wouldn't want anybody else to have

to take the blame. Or get the credit." He gave a hoot
of laughter and slipped out. His horse was already par-
allel to the sidewalk. He leaped into the saddle, and he
and Frank galloped away through the dust raised by
Preacher George and Cole and Jim Younger.

The rattle of Carly's old wagon awakened Esther as it
circled past the stable and down toward the kennels. She
groaned as yesterday's strained muscles protested despite
the long, delicious soaking.

She heard the old man throw out the weight, heard
the wagon creak as he climbed down. Heard him wheeze
and cough. He had come to work at ten o'clock, just as
she had hoped. At least he had been faithful. The
hounds had not suffered from her enforced absence.

Teet!

She pushed herself up and limped to the closet. She
couldn't wait any longer to find out if her favorite hunter
had made his way home. If he had, she would rejoice
and count her blessings. If he hadn't, she would go back
to the mountain with her whistle to find him. Teet was
resourceful. He would still be alive up there, unless he
had tangled with an animal bigger than he was.

She would not expect to find the pup returned. A raw
youngster, never away from home more than a couple of
times in his life, had no chance. She shook her head at
her reflection in the mirror. How could one misstep have
cost her so much?

"Mornin', Esther girl." Carly's drawling twang dis-
torted every word to incredible length as well as assigning
vowels the unique sounds of the mountain people of the
Ozarks. Hands thrust in the pockets of his overalls, he

noted the crutch as she limped across the yard. "Did y' hurt y'rself?"

"Morning, Carly. I'm afraid so." He was a sweet old man in the twilight of his years. She could not fault his faithfulness. But his lack of curiosity or concern could have cost her her life.

"Took a fall, did y'?"

"A bad one. I fell into a ravine night before last and twisted my knee."

" 'S that so. Well, don't that beat all? That's why y' didn't unhitch the horse t'other day."

She gritted her teeth and made a mental note to start looking for someone to replace him. Surely someone younger and more able-bodied must need some money badly enough to work for her, despite her reputation. She crossed her fingers before she asked the next question. "Did Teet come home?"

The old man nodded slowly. "Yep. Found him lyin' close up next t' his fence yesterday mornin'. Young 'un with him."

Esther slumped against the hickory crutch. "I'm luckier than I have a right to be," she breathed. "I was afraid I'd lost them both."

"Might have," he agreed. "Lots of ice a couple a nights ago. Hard on man 'n' beast out on the mountain. We're goin' t' have a bad 'un." His long face with its wire-rimmed glasses was a mass of vertical and horizontal lines. His aged shoulders hunched against the biting wind. Carly Ord was of her grandfather's generation. If her grandfather had lived, he would have been seventy-eight years old in September.

"Don't I know it." She smiled wanly. After all, Carly had done what she paid him for, unhitched and stabled the horse as well as fed and cared for all the animals. They had not suffered along with her. "Thank you for taking care of the hounds for the last few days."

"Just doin' my job." He pulled one hand from his pocket and touched the brim of his old felt hat. "Vard 'n' me was pals fer a long time. Thought a heap o' Vard."

The mention of her grandfather brought unaccountable tears to her eyes. She must be weaker than she thought. Hastily, she bent to open the gate of Teet's run. The hound bounded out and thrust his head under her hand. While his tail whipped back and forth in delight, she patted his head and rubbed her thumb over the mahogany crescents above his eyebrows. Steadying herself against the fence, she leaned over to hug him hard. "Teet, you made it, old fellow. And brought the pup back with you. You're the best. The very best in the world. I'm so glad you made it back, old fellow."

Under her gentle attention, the hound made a low crooning sound deep in his throat.

"When did you miss me?" she wondered softly. "Did you come hunting for me? I'll bet you did." She inspected the velvet ears, found a burr hidden deep in a soft fold, and plucked it out. The hound's hindquarters feathered ecstatically against her, jostling her against the fence. His muzzle brushed against her hand, and his tongue slid out to lap once against her palm. The gesture moved her almost to tears. It was a measure of Teet's great affection and loyalty for her, for hounds did not lick their owners. They were neither pets nor friends. They were trained for one thing and one thing only—the chase and ultimately the kill.

Carly's false teeth clicked as he maneuvered them around in his mouth. "Heard tell of some ruckus 'cross the Missouri border, Esther girl."

She looked up in alarm. "Ruckus?" Instantly on the alert, she gave the rangy hound a final pat. "Get back, Teet."

Carly closed the gate to the run for her. His old eyes

watched her keenly. "Yep. Didn't hear what 'xactly, but might o' been some of yore kin."

Her stomach clenched. The skin on her arms pebbled in alarm. "Where'd you hear it?"

He hunched his shoulders. "Elmo Stamford."

She used the hickory crutch to steady herself. Sarcasm riddled her voice. "Our sheriff's been thinking and hoping that for years. I think he just tells people that so they'll let him keep his job."

"Y' shore could be right about that. Gotta be some reason why he keeps gettin' elected." Carly chuckled and wheezed. "Y' want me to hitch up the wagon fer y'?"

She shook her head. "Thanks just the same, but I'll ride."

The village of Cutter's Knob had grown up at a crossroads. The general store was on one corner. A man could stand on its porch and look four ways at once. The longest street, the one that led over the mountain to Bentonville, boasted the boardinghouse and the dressmaker. At the very end on the hill from which the town got its name stood the church. On the opposite end of town from the church was the one-room school.

On the crossroad was the feed store and the courthouse with the jail in back. Across the street was the doctor's office with its hand-painted sign swinging on the gate.

The other end of that street was occupied by the blacksmith's forge, the tailor shop, a wheelwright, and a livery stable. Clustered next to and in back of all these businesses were the houses of the owners.

Esther had tied her sack of provisions onto Babe's saddle horn and swung into the saddle when Sheriff Elmo Stamford caught hold of the cheek strap of the mare's bridle.

"Been gone somewhere, Esther?" The bay mare shied, but the big man hauled the horse down. Despite his pendulous stomach and huge thighs, he could move with surprising swiftness without getting out of breath. His efforts to catch and control her horse had cost him nothing. Now his bulging eyes slid over her body, stripping her, searching for weapons and for weakness.

Esther liked to think that no matter how rudely people treated her, she could live side by side with everyone in Cutter's Knob. In the case of Elmo Stamford, she knew she lied to herself. Like coals of fire, her animosity toward him burned.

"No," she replied shortly, her eyes straight ahead. "I've been minding my own business."

"Try again," he insisted. His other hand came to rest on the pommel, a couple of inches from her thigh. The short fingers looked all the stumpier because each nail had a half-moon of filth beneath it. The swollen knuckles, too, were grimy.

"I haven't been anywhere," she replied. "I got stuck up on the mountain for two nights when I was training my hounds, but—"

"All them dogs was in the kennel," Stamford interrupted her.

Inwardly, she was shaking with anger, made all the more potent because it was helpless. He had prowled around at her place. He had gone in amongst her hounds. Perhaps he had even opened her door, walked through her living room, gone into her bedroom. She could feel acid spurting into her stomach. She set her teeth to keep from cursing him.

Counted among the citizens of Cutter's Knob, but not accepted by them, she had made a peaceable trip into town for groceries. Even though the women refused to speak to her, the storekeepers took her money readily enough. Now with one gunnysack of foodstuffs tied to the saddle horn and another to the cantle, she was ready to ride away.

But Stamford stood in her way. He had no right to be asking her these questions. Unfortunately, the silver star, the only clean thing on his body, had turned the town bully into a monster. The citizenry despised him, but they kept him because he was a vicious brawler. They could count on him to give a very unpleasant welcome to any undesirable who rode into town.

While she was harmless enough, many unwelcome travellers were not. Northwestern Arkansas had long been a safe route west for the deserters from both armies of the Blue and the Gray. The people who lived there trusted no one, for more than likely a stranger might be an outlaw.

"Heard tell your cousins are headed this way," Stamford went on. He put his hand deliberately on her knee.

She didn't pretend not to know which cousins he was talking about. She tensed, eyes searching the short, sunlit street. It was empty, but even if it were full, she had no hope of help. "I wouldn't know. I haven't seen my cousins since the war was over. If they came through here, I doubt if I'd hear from them."

Teeth bared like a snarling dog, he squeezed hard. His thumb and third finger dug in under the kneecap.

"Stop it!" She jerked the reins hard to the right and drove her heel into the mare's side. Babe surged forward and buck-jumped sideways, but Stamford still kept his grip on the cheek strap.

The sheriff sniggered. "Knee sorta tender?"

"Damn you! Let go of my horse!"

"Right bad language. Yore mammy'd sure be unhappy if she heard it." Deliberately, he crowded the bay against the side of the general store, trapping Esther's right leg on the other side. He closed his hand around her left knee again. "Now you tell me where you been. What's the weather like in Missouri?"

"Missouri! I don't have the least notion. I haven't been anywhere." Anger and fear swept over her in waves. Wasn't anyone going to help her? Across the street a couple of farmers came out of the seed and feed store. She recognized one of them as a man whose hound she had trained. They looked at the scene curiously. Were they just going to stand there?

Stamford squeezed again. At the same time he threw his weight against the mare's shoulder.

Red rage stained Esther's vision. The reins were in her hand. Devil take the consequences. She whipped them across the sheriff's face, aiming for his sneering mouth and eyes.

He yelled, ducking back from the mare's side.

"Gid-dup!" Esther yelled. She slashed at her tormentor again, and he released the bridle to protect his eyes. With all the power in her abused legs she clapped her heels into the mare's sides. Babe bolted forward as only a quarter horse could do.

Stamford yelled at Esther to stop, but she put her face against the black mane and tore out of town. Only when the horse had run her quarter mile did Esther allow her to drop to a gallop and then to a lope.

When she could think, she shook her head. Her cousins were headed this way, Stamford had said. What difference did that make? She never thought about them. And she was equally certain they never thought about her. She shivered as terrible memories came flooding back.

The war with all of its destruction had been hundreds of miles away in states like Mississippi, Alabama, Georgia and Virginia. Apart from the unimportant battle up at Pea Ridge, the fighting had not touched Arkansas. Not until her cousins had come riding down the valley. They

were running from the horror they had perpetrated at
Lawrence, Kansas, begging favors from their blood kin.

She and her father had welcomed them and their
friends—handsome devils, wild as the wind. And her life
had never been the same. If she had it to do over again,
she would have stood on the porch and shot them dead
as Frank and Jesse James galloped up the road.

A black, piano-box buggy drawn by a dapple gray gelding came round the side of the house and into the yard
in front of the stable. Esther stared in disbelief. Five
years. Five long years had passed since that buggy had
rolled into her yard. She let the hayfork fall from her
fingers. A trembling began in the pit of her stomach and
spread to her limbs. Tears choked her throat. She had
to swallow rapidly to push them down.

Her mother, Rebecca Ruth Blessing, alighted and lifted
her clear, unlined face to the cool breeze of the mountain. She was dressed in unrelieved black, as the widow
of not one, but two good and noble men. But her suit
was no sackcloth and ashes. It was the best grade of wool
serge trimmed in silk soutache braid. The hip-length
black cape had an astrakhan collar and a silk satin lining.
She lifted her black-gloved hand to wave to her daughter.
The gesture was not a greeting but a summons.

Esther closed her eyes briefly. What was Rebecca doing
here? She had seen her mother rarely and then only
from afar for the last five years. Once she had humiliated
herself so far as to confront the minister at her church,
but two of the deacons had pushed Esther out the door
before she could exchange so much as a word with her
mother.

Self-consciously, Esther smoothed the soiled and faded
work shirt and straightened the shell jacket. Her hair was
untidy, her hands were dirty, and probably her face was

as well. She shrugged. She was at work in the kennels.
She couldn't be scolded for being improperly dressed.
Served her mother right for coming out unannounced.
Glancing at the crutch leaning against the fence, she
walked slowly by it, striving to conceal her limp. Better
not show weakness. Setting her face in calm, placid lines,
she approached with tension making her nerves hum.

Rebecca held out her arms lovingly. "Esther Elizabeth."

"M-mother?" Esther faltered. Without quite knowing
how, she went into her mother's arms, to be enveloped
in softness and the fragrance of Apple Blossom *eau de
toilette*. Her eyes filled with tears. Her throat clogged with
them. Her mother held her. The beloved parent, who
had sent her into exile, had returned. "Mother," Esther
whispered again. "You're here."

"Of course I'm here, dearest. At long, long last."

"Mother," Esther repeated, hugging her mother hard.
"I'm so glad to see you and hear your voice. I didn't
think you'd ever speak to me again."

Rebecca held her daughter for a moment, then
stepped back to the length of her arms. "You look just
the same, Esther. A little thinner perhaps. But still the
same sweet smile."

Embarrassed, Esther ducked her head. "Thank you,
Mother. You look lovely, too." She meant the compliment. Rebecca looked nothing like a woman of her age
might expect to look after living all her life in the Ozarks.
Indeed, she looked little older than Esther. Fifty she
might be: but her complexion was blooming, and her
figure remained slender. What once had been blond hair
the color of cornsilk had silvered to a pale white-gold. It
looked much the same as Esther's.

Rebecca dropped her arms and looked around. She
laughed a little and spread her hands. "Everything looks
very much the same."

Esther stared at the older woman. What was her mother here for? She slipped her arm through her mother's to lead her up the path. "Will you come in the house? I'll make some tea."

Rebecca looked up at the house. A gentle smile played round her full pink mouth. Only the faintest wavery lines drooped down from its corners. "You've done something to the front." Her tone was faintly chiding.

"Yes, I've added a rail along the porch. And in the back I've made a sun porch. In the spring I get out pots and fill them full of ferns and flowers."

"It looks different. Not like your father's house at all."

Esther tightened her lips on an irritated reply. Somehow Rebecca had taken longer steps than her daughter, so that she reached the front door first. Without hesitation she opened the door and stepped inside, leaving Esther to trail behind her into her own house.

Rebecca took a complete inventory as her gaze swept the room. She scanned the shabby settee and chairs, the old rag rug, the pendulum clock swinging and ticking on the wall. Then she seemed to relax. She closed her eyes and drew in a long breath. "It smells exactly the same. Lavender—and apples. I can remember when your father first brought me here, Mother Woodson had a big bowl of apples sitting right here on the table."

"I have a bowl in the kitchen," Esther told her. "Would you like to sit here while I make the tea?"

"Oh, no." Rebecca caught her wrist and turned her daughter to face her. If she had taken an inventory of the room, she now took a close inspection of Esther from the muddy brogans on her feet to the old slouch hat on her head. By the deepening of the lines around her mother's mouth, Esther knew she was displeased. With a faint sigh, she walked out, leaving her daughter staring at her. "I'll go with you into the kitchen," she called.

"After all, I came to see you. We do have so much to catch up on."

In the hall between the living room and kitchen, Esther realized that Rebecca was doing more than leading. She was looking for something. "The bedrooms," she said. "I just want to see if they're the same."

Leaving Esther, she flung open the doors one by one. What was Rebecca looking for? Carly's words and Elmo Stamford's harassment held the answer. Esther folded her arms. Let her search till doomsday, but she wouldn't find Jesse James. Esther's mouth set in a hard line, but her mother returned with a pleased smile on her face.

Rebecca sat at the table and ran her hand across the rippling oak grain. Half a century of meals had been served on it. It was good for half a century more. Esther stoked the fire and moved the teakettle from the back of the stove. When it began to whistle, she poured hot water through the tea leaves flavored with dried apples and cinnamon. All the time she could feel her nerves prickling along her spine. Her mother was checking on her. But why now? After all these years?

Hands moving mechanically, Esther pulled down china cups and saucers that had come from Virginia in a covered wagon, then opened a drawer that held old silver that needed polishing rather badly. She straightened her spine. This was Woodson land, not Blessing. Rebecca was not going to make her run from her home.

She poured tea for the both of them and sat down opposite her mother. The woman had come here on some kind of errand. Determined to make her speak first, Esther waited.

"I heard you were hurt," Rebecca said at last.

Esther glanced up sharply. From whom had she heard it? Their glances collided.

Rebecca's slipped away. She stirred her tea, tasted it

carefully, then set the cup down. "You shouldn't be living out here alone."

The melodious voice had been a prelude to some of the worst moments in Esther's life. What would happen, she wondered, if she simply walked out the back door and left her mother sitting alone with a startled look on her face? Eventually Rebecca would have to go away.

The silence grew between them as they sipped their tea. At first Rebecca remained serene, her eyes roving the kitchen, recognizing old things with which she herself had kept house when her daughter was a baby. When she finished her cup, Esther refilled it, even though her mother shook her head.

Shortly, a frown line appeared between Rebecca's brows. "I miss ginger cookies," she said at last.

"Ginger cookies." Esther nodded. "Mammaw did make good ones. I haven't thought about them in years. It hardly seems worthwhile to make when I'm living out here all alone."

Rebecca smiled. "You don't have to be alone anymore."

Esther tilted her head to one side. "Have you thought of a way to restore my virginity and free my soul from shame?"

Rebecca colored. "Esther!"

"Your words, not mine, Mother." Her hands were cold, her mouth dry. She took a fortifying drink of tea, suddenly wishing for some of the Yankee's whiskey to bolster her courage. "What did you come for?"

Rebecca leaned across the table and put her gloved hand over her daughter's bare one. The contrast between butter-soft black kid and wind-chapped, work-roughened skin did not escape either woman. "Esther, you can be welcomed back into the fold again."

Esther moved her hand out from under her mother's. "What do I have to do to get back into the fold again?"

Her mother's voice turned unctuous and ministerial. "Only be sorry for your sins and vow to live a good life from now on."

Esther shook her head. Crossing her arms, she rocked back in her chair, balancing on the hind legs. "I was sorry for my sin, as you called it, five years ago."

Rebecca looked annoyed. "The sin was fresh in the mind of everyone—"

At that moment a hound bayed. Esther recognized Juniper's voice from the far end of the kennel. Anxious to break off the conversation, she started up, but her mother caught her by the wrist. "Sit down, Esther, and drink your tea." Her mother's voice carried just the right note of firmness. "It's probably nothing but a rabbit."

Esther sank back, only just managing to keep from saying, "Yes, Mother." Instead, she said, "My hounds don't bay at rabbits."

Rebecca set the teacup down so hard it rattled in the saucer. "Will you stop this obstinacy? You always were a stubborn, willful child. I would have thought your recent experiences had taught you something."

Her remarks were the last straw. She was twenty-two years old, no longer simple sixteen. Right now with her sore knee and her weariness, plus the shock from the encounter with Stamford, she felt more like fifty. She couldn't play the role of minister's daughter and virgin acolyte any longer, no matter how much she wanted to. She rose. "Say what you came to say, Mother."

Rebecca clasped her hands in front of her. "Your daughter needs a mother."

The mention of Sarah was a pain so sharp, it made her startled gasp spread through every vital part of her body. She wrapped her arms tight around her. "She does," Esther snapped. "She always did. That's why what you did was so horrible."

Rebecca's face lost some of its color. "I did what was best."

"You punished me for something that wasn't my fault."

"When will you understand that the woman is always at fault? It is her duty to be the guardian of the morals."

"In wartime, Mother?"

The older woman rose and pushed back her chair. With a swish of her black skirts, she walked out of the kitchen. Esther followed her and watched silently while her mother settled the black cape around her shoulders. "People can forgive what happened five years ago, Esther Elizabeth, but hear me and know that I'm speaking the truth. They cannot forgive the life you are leading out here alone."

Again Esther thought of Elmo Stamford. What poison had he been pouring into her mother's ears? Even though she knew she would never be able to justify herself to Rebecca, she stretched out her hands in supplication. "Mother, I'm not doing a thing out here but earning a living."

"You're a woman. It's not your place to earn a living, particularly not with those dogs." Rebecca's eyes flashed, and her voice rose and fell as if she were exhorting a congregation of sinners rather than one errant daughter. "What you're doing is man's work. They'll blame you for it. They'll make trouble for you. You must give this place up and come to me. You can marry, and Sarah can have what she has never had—a mother and a father."

Esther threw up her head. Now she thought she understood the reason for the visit. "Who have you picked out for my husband, Mother?"

Rebecca had the grace to blush. She swallowed and stammered, "The conference is sending a new assistant minister."

Esther crossed her arms again. She might have known. Rebecca saw lives as pieces to be moved around at what she interpreted as God's will. "I'm not going to marry. Ever. I remember what you told me. No man will ever accept me. I'm ruined forever."

"I'm sure that Tom Pennebaker would make a union with you if I sanctioned it."

"Mother!" Shaking with anger and tears, Esther clenched her fists. "Is that what you want for me? A 'sanctioned' marriage to a man I've never met?"

Rebecca's eyebrows rose. With a sorrowful expression, she reached out to touch her daughter. "Esther, this is your only chance. You know that. It's the only way for you to come back to the fold."

Teeth clenched against a scream of rage, Esther flung open the door. "You'll have to hurry, Mother, if you want to get back to town before anyone misses you. It wouldn't do for anyone to know that you've been out here talking to the Whore of Babylon."

Rebecca stopped on the threshold. As the November wind lifted skirts, she tucked her gloved hands inside her cape. She had on her loving and forgiving face. "Just come for Thanksgiving, Esther. Come and see her and how happy we all are, and how happy you can be. Tom won't be there. He's coming the first of the year. You can come home gently with all your family around you. Come on Thanksgiving Day. You can gather round the table with us in love and harmony."

The temptation to yield was overwhelming. For five long years she had been alone every holiday. Now here was her mother, once the most beloved person in her life, opening her arms. But the price was too great. Esther searched her mind for a plausible excuse. The Yankee on the mountain. He was as lonely as she. The words came out in a burst of inspiration. "I have a guest coming for Thanksgiving."

"Who?" Rebecca's beatific smile dimmed slightly. Her

eyes narrowed, and she frowned. "You don't know anyone."

Esther flinched. "I know a few people."

"I warn you, Esther."

"Goodbye, Mother." Esther moved into the doorway, forcing her mother to step back. "It was good to see you again after all this time."

Rebecca recovered her smile. "Come anyway and bring your guest. She—" She paused and looked expectantly at Esther, who neither nodded nor shook her head. "Your guest is welcome to come with you. Everyone is welcome at Thanksgiving."

Esther closed the door gently and leaned against it. She heard her mother's footsteps on the porch. Heard the buggy roll away. The silent tears flowing down her cheeks turned to heartbroken sobs.

Six

The longer Esther sat, the angrier she became. She clenched and unclenched her hands as her leg throbbed painfully along every nerve ending in her body.

She was stupid. Stupid! Half-sick with pain and exposure. Bullied by Elmo Stamford. And she had gone right into her mother's arms, forgetting how Rebecca never did anything that was not part of her grand plan. All the love in the world, all the love she professed for others, was offered as a bribe or withheld as a punishment.

Esther choked over the swelling pain in her throat. Poor, poor Sarah.

Rebecca was using Esther's daughter as a hostage. Her message was clear. "Give up everything that is yours—your home that came to you from your father, your livelihood, your freedom—and in exchange, I will love you and allow you to love me and your daughter."

Angrily, Esther pulled up the pant leg of her father's old overalls. Her leg was alarming to look at, she could tell it was on the way to healing. She wasn't crippled. She would be able to run free through the clean darkness of the Ozarks again. She could follow the clear bugles of the hounds. And even if she couldn't, she wouldn't give up her work.

What had Rebecca said? That it made men angry. If it did, then that was just too bad. She refused to believe that most of her customers were angry and resentful.

Most seemed nice enough. Her accident had left her in pain, but it was only physical. It was nothing compared to the emotional and spiritual pain her mother's visit had cost her.

Her mother had reopened wounds long ago scarred over. One of the worst was the pain of not being perfect—and being constantly and lovingly chastised for it. Just the thought of seeing her mother every day and enduring those sweet, sad looks made her a little sick at her stomach. If Tom What-ever-his-name-was was anything like Rebecca, she would go mad within the first year.

No one could live and keep sane among people who pointed out faults in the mildest of tones. She shuddered.

No. She no longer belonged body and soul to Rebecca Ruth Blessing. She couldn't live constantly striving for a state attained only by angels.

Her whirling thoughts were making her ill. They were the sorts of thoughts her mother had set her to meditating on when she was very young. Why should she continue to do her mother's bidding? Rebecca had been gone almost an hour. Why was Esther still crouched here rubbing her knee like some wounded animal in a hole?

She had made up her mind and declared herself. She would not come to Thanksgiving dinner.

What if her mother came for her again with some of her deacons to drag her to the feast? Esther knew she was too weak to fight them alone. They might just come in the buggy and take her away on Thanksgiving Day. They might bring Sarah to beg her to come.

The thought made her bury her face in her hands. That alone would make her give in. No one had the kind of strength to deny the plea of her own child.

Sarah. Oh, Sarah. Are you happy as an angel on earth?

"Damn!" The word exploded into the still room, echoing in her own ears, making her feel guilty.

She needed a savior. And just this week a savior had come into her life. All she had to do was go get him. She shoved herself violently out of the rocker and limped to the door.

At the pace Jesse and his gang were travelling west, they would have crossed over into Indian Territory the next day if the sheriff of Lawrence County hadn't known the town marshal of Neosho, Missouri.

At the Newton County line, Rich Worland and his deputies met them with a hail of gunfire. Riding some of the best horseflesh in the state, Jesse led his gang south, outdistancing Worland. When the gang crossed into McDonald County, they slowed down and turned west again.

At a crossroads Worland and his men ambushed them again. The Indian Territory was out of the question. In hot pursuit, Worland and his deputies chased the gang due south toward the state of Arkansas.

Again the better and faster horses carried them out of sight. With their horses staggering and blowing under them, Jesse held up his hand. As they slowed, he began to cuss the sheriff of Neosho.

"We could go back and ambush him," Cole suggested sourly. "Drill a hole clean through him. He sure won't be expecting that."

"Leave it be," Frank advised. "We'll cross into Arkansas and take the fork for Siloam Springs."

Their saddlebags jingling pleasantly, they loped over the border. The local marshal, an old buffalo hunter, climbed down and set up his buffalo gun.

As the gang rode down the valley, his first shot knocked off Cole Younger's hat and notched his ear. His second creased the point of Brother Jim's shoulder. His

third from the distance of nearly half a mile lodged a
spent ball under Frank James's shoulder blade.

Bleeding and scared, the outlaws rode on. Alternately
galloping and walking their horses, they couldn't think
of anything except putting as much distance as they
could between them and their pursuers.

When they camped for the night, Jesse took a pocket-
knife to the lead ball in Frank's back. Frank promptly
fainted. With his brother unconscious, Jesse managed to
pry the thing out, but he had torn up the wound considerably.

"We've got to take him somewhere quiet. He's got to
rest," Jesse said.

"He ain't the only one," Jim Younger muttered. The
bleeding had stopped, but his shoulder ached so badly
he couldn't sit upright in the saddle.

"We're all just about worn slick," Cole agreed. He fin-
gered the top of his ear gingerly. "We're going to freeze
to death if we don't find somewhere to sleep."

They were miles from Indian Territory now and deep
in the Ozarks.

"Climb up." Jesse boosted Frank into the saddle, and
put his arm around him. Frank's wound was shallow, but
if it got infected or if he got pneumonia from the
weather, he might die.

Supporting his fainting brother, Jesse led the way
southeast deeper into Benton County. He had vowed
never to visit his Woodson kinfolk again. The thought of
Noah Woodson made him sick. And he hated to go near
his cousin Esther, but Frank was feverish.

One by one, the five riders eased their horses up the
logging track. The woods concealed them from anyone
riding along the road that looped the mountain and
passed through Cutter's Knob on the way to Fayetteville.

* * *

Esther guided Babe up the mountainside at an angle. At the top of the ridge she soon lost her way in the trees just as she had expected to. Even as hurt as she was, she had known that the Yankee was keeping her walking until she could never find her way back to his cabin.

She dismounted and limped gingerly into a glade a few yards away from the horse. Standing in the middle of it, the sun dappling the rocks and grasses around her, she blew three sharp blasts on her whistle. Three sharp blasts. Wait half a minute. Three more. Wait.

For two minutes she kept up her noise, with a silent prayer that Bas and his family had gone into Cutter's Knob. She would hate for the old man to hear and be alarmed that she might have hurt herself again. Three more blasts.

A good-sized limestone ledge made a handy chair. She settled herself on it and blew three more. She shut her mind to the idea that she was doing something stupid. Instead she concentrated on what she would say to the mountain man when she saw him.

Three more blasts, then she cleared her throat and shouted. "York! Halloo! York!"

"York!" Her voice echoed back to her from the mountain to the east.

When the echo died, she shouted again.

Again the echo answered.

She was beginning to feel distinctly foolish. She blew again and called again. Nothing. Except she had probably frightened every animal within a mile. She looked around her doubtfully. Perhaps she should have gone back to the slate canyon and tried to call him from there.

But she had no idea which direction he lived from there. She didn't even know which side of the canyon he had carried her out on. And even if he heard her, he might not answer. She looked around her sharply.

Was he hiding in the woods somewhere watching her, his eyes burning beneath his tangled hair?

She shouted again, then rose from her seat and limped back to the edge of the glade. There she leaned against a tree and hung her head. She had started her leg hurting again, and she felt like crying. That was all she seemed to be doing today. Crying.

Gripping her thigh tightly, she faced the fact that he had acted anxious to get rid of her when he brought her down the mountain in such haste. Probably she had climbed the ridge for nothing. She shivered as the cold wind penetrated her jacket. A band of clouds was moving in from the northwest.

Pushing herself wearily off the tree, she took two steps, then gasped.

One minute she was alone; the next he stepped out of the brush onto a lichen-encrusted boulder. Hands on hips, face stern, mouth tight beneath the edges of his curly black beard, he made her think of a particularly fierce king of the mountain. Except that his knee-length blue coat, boots, and campaign hat made her think of General Ulysses S. Grant.

Of course, he was taller and much handsomer than Grant, even with his unkempt locks. The coat was open and swept back behind him, making his shoulders look exceptionally broad while his waist and hips tapered. She felt a spurt of excitement somewhat more than nervousness.

They stared at each other. Then she smiled. "Hello."

"What do you want?"

The hostility in his voice drove the smile from her face and rocked her back against the tree. If she had not told her mother she was having a dinner guest, she would have left him. She had had enough rudeness to last a lifetime.

Unfortunately, she wanted this man to do her a favor.

She plastered a weak smile on her face. "Oh, you really scared me. I wish you hadn't sneaked up on me like that. I didn't think you were anywhere within miles, and then you suddenly appear out of nowhere. You might give me warning. Call my name. Whistle. Something."

His mouth compressed even tighter. "I don't answer until I'm certain who's calling me."

She looked around, wondering how close to his cabin she might have been. "Have you been hearing my whistles and shouts all along?"

"I'm not deaf." He jumped down off the ledge and came toward her with long, swinging strides. The edges of the blue coat flared out. She was struck by how beautifully he moved. Straight-backed, graceful, with an even stride. His horseman's thighs stretched the blue trousers tightly.

"No, of course not." Conscious that she was staring at him, she transferred her gaze to the mountain behind. Only a few feet from her, he stopped and folded his arms, his expression forbidding.

She swallowed. A show of appreciation was as good a way as any to begin a conversation. "Er—thank you for saving me and taking care of me."

"You're welcome."

Now that she had found him, she felt strange about extending her invitation to him. Strange and a little frightened. What did she know about him really? He might come down the mountain to her home, knock her in the head, and take her money.

"How's your leg?" He interrupted her thoughts.

"Good. Fine. The hickory staff is working just fine, too. It's back on the mare's saddle." She tossed a look in the direction of the horse. "I can get around fine for short distances. After the first couple of days, I went right on with my chores. I can ride if I don't try to put my left leg in the stirrup."

He nodded without answering.

She hurried on. "I hope I didn't put you out too much, or eat up too much of your food, or anything."

"You didn't."

She paused.

Cawing noisily, a crow flapped from a red oak tree. York's eyes shifted to follow its flight.

Clearly, he was bored by her presence. She drew a deep breath. Then lost her nerve. She couldn't find the courage to ask this man to dinner. She had never asked anyone to dinner before. She had never even entertained anyone for dinner. "Well, goodbye then." Her face flamed with embarrassment and frustration as she turned back down the mountain. "I just wanted to say thank you."

She made her way to the horse before he caught up with her. The hardest part was mounting, taking her weight on her left leg in the stirrup. He put his hands on her waist and lifted.

"I don't need your help," she hissed. "I've been riding all my life."

He nodded silently, but he did not let go of her. "Ready?"

"Yes."

She shot up as if she were lighter than air. So surprised was she by the ease with which he lifted her that she almost forgot to throw her leg over the saddle. When she was settled, she looked away in embarrassment. "I really could have made it myself."

He stepped back. His teeth flashed for one brief instant through the tangle of his beard. "No sense hurting if you don't have to."

She leaned over to pull Babe's rein free from the tree limb, but he was there before her. He handed it up to her.

"Thank you." She gathered the reins. Her mouth was formed to click her tongue to Babe and move out.

He cleared his throat. "What'd you come up for?"

She shook her head. "Nothing important. That is, to thank you."

He reached up to put his hand on the horn. Unlike Elmo Stamford, he didn't lay his hand on her arm or leg. She liked that. She looked down and saw his hand was clean.

His mouth quirked up at the corners. She might have imagined that he smiled. "Come on. You rode all the way up here. You might as well tell me what you came for."

His eyes were not flat brown in daylight. Gold flecks radiated through the irises and swam as the lowering sun of late afternoon shone in his face. The pupils contracted in the sun, but his gaze was steady, as if he was used to its light.

Amazed, she felt an unaccountable heating of her stomach muscles. Her mouth went suddenly dry. She stared at a spot between the horse's ears while the blush rose in her cheeks.

He dropped his hand and stepped back. "Well, I guess I better be going. Can't spend all day standing around."

"If you must know, I came to invite you to have Thanksgiving dinner with me." The instant she blurted the words out, she was sorry. Her face flamed again. "I just thought you might be hungry for some fresh vegetables and a hen and corn bread dressing," she added lamely. "It was probably a stupid idea. But you're welcome. You're most welcome. Come when you want to Thanksgiving morning."

Without glancing in his direction, she reined the horse around in a circle, ducked under a tree limb and started back the way she had come.

* * *

York glided out of the sunlit glade into the thicket. A hundred yards to the east was a bluff. The side of the mountain had fallen off, leaving an open vista where it had broken away. Tall pines still held their place to the very edge. Against one straight trunk, he threw up an arm and leaned his forehead against it. From that post he could watch his visitor's progress into the valley.

Sometimes Esther disappeared completely to emerge farther on. Sometimes he could see only a part of her as she rode through scrub vegetation. Sometimes she would guide the mare down through a bare rocky channel or across a ridge where he could see all of her. She rode straight-backed, her slouch hat pulled over her eyes. That tantalizing braid swung back and forth with the horse's movement. She was a feast for his starved eyes.

For almost a minute, he had watched her sitting on the rock, blowing her whistle and calling to him. How long had it been since someone had called to him? How long had it been since someone had wanted him? He had savored that minute, not wondering what it meant to him, and only when she began to look discouraged, had he stepped out into the open.

She was beautiful. With her hat on the rock beside her, her face lifted to the warm sun, she had sent a warm surge of desire through him. The shell jacket had fit snug against the generous curves of her breasts. Her legs clad in the butternut wool were long and slim. They would be strong. And beneath the trousers her belly would be flat. He shuddered at the path his thoughts were leading him down.

When she disappeared for the last time, he thrust his hands deep into his pockets and tramped back toward his cabin. He walked head down, his thoughts whirling, his nerves humming with strain.

She had come to invite him to dinner. Of course, he couldn't go. Her house would be full of family and friends. Children would stare at him and run away and hide. Kindly, well-meaning women would probe and pat and want him to tell his story, so they could tell him what to do. Bluff middle-aged men who knew absolutely nothing about war would tell him to buck up.

He had gotten away from all that and sworn never to return.

A hen. She'd said they would have a hen, roasted and basted with its own juices. He could picture the bird, steam rising from its brown and glistening breast. With corn bread dressing. And yams, that popular southern form of potato, baked with pecans and brown sugar.

She would probably have apple pie. Most people in the Ozarks had at least a couple of apple trees in their yards. The scent of cinnamon and nutmeg and baking apples would fill the house. His mouth began to water.

Suddenly, he wanted more than anything in the world to go to her feast. Pain began like a rat in his stomach and gnawed its way into his heart and mind. He could smell that food cooking, could see that table with the steam rising from the hen's breast, could hear the laughter and exclamations of delight and anticipation from her family.

In that minute he made up his mind to accept her invitation. Even though he was a Yankee and she wore castoffs from the Confederate army, she had invited him. Maybe they were symbols. They were going to be celebrating an American Thanksgiving together.

A slow smile turned up the corners of his mouth. Light of heart, he bounded up the steps of his cabin. He shed the coat and hat and drove his fingers into his hair. There he froze.

Slowly, slowly, he pulled a lock of hair down in front of his face. *Good Lord! It reached all the way to his chin.* He pushed it back and clutched at his beard. *A double handful.* He must look more like a bear than a man.

A panicky feeling gripped him. He couldn't go as he was. He would have to make preparations. His heart stepped up its beat.

He needed to find out when Thanksgiving was. He remembered it was celebrated on a Thursday in November, but which Thursday? He didn't keep a calendar. He didn't even know what week it was, let alone what day.

He went down on his knees beside the stove. With the poker, he pried up a floorboard and pulled out a pair of saddlebags. From one he drew a handful of bills. Peeling off a couple of twenties, he stuffed the rest back into the bags and returned them to their hiding place.

Imbued with a sense of urgency, he hurried from the cabin. He had a great deal to do before Thanksgiving, and he didn't know how much time he had to do it in.

"Something is going on. And I don't like it. Esther Elizabeth looked different." Rebecca Blessing sat in her favorite seat—a brown leather wing chair. It rose a full foot above her head and wrapped liked the armor of authority around her slender shoulders.

Before the war it had belonged to a judge of the circuit court in Ft. Smith. It had been stolen by carpetbaggers and brought through Cutter's Knob on a wagon loaded with goods. Sheriff Elmo Stamford had confiscated the wagon and distributed their goods as he saw fit.

From it Rebecca met with members of her ministry and her church.

"Of course she'd look different. It's been years since you've laid eyes on her." Daniel Blessing leaned forward in his own chair, a ladderback with a cane bottom. He sat across the desk from his mother when he sat at all. Usually, he stood and got instructions.

Rebecca looked more annoyed than ever. "It may have been years since I've actually seen her, but I've had regular reports. Always the same. She was living a useful, repentant life. She was truly sorry for what she had done. Suddenly, she isn't repentant anymore. And she's doing something she shouldn't be. She spent two nights away from the house. Two nights. And when she came home, she was limping. She had the audacity to run her horse over the sheriff yesterday and then gallop out of town."

Daniel looked down at his hands. They were white and smooth, the hands of a gentleman. With them he soothed and patted and ministered to the needs of the congregation. He was twenty years old and had never had sexual relations with a woman. He could not suppress the hot spurt of resentment that he felt toward his sister. She had succumbed to temptation at the age of sixteen, and here she was falling into sin again. He didn't dare tell his mother that he was jealous.

"I want you to go out and talk to her, Daniel. Daniel!" Rebecca had spoken to him twice.

He raised his head. "I don't think—"

"You're her brother. She'll be overjoyed to see you. She needs to know that we all want her to come back into the family. You'll be able to convince her where I can't."

He sincerely doubted that. He rose and stood awkwardly in front of his mother. "I haven't spoken to her in five years. If she didn't listen to you, she won't listen to me."

Rebecca frowned. "You must make her listen. Tell her how wonderful your life has been. Tell her about the joy you've found. Tell her about Sarah and how much she needs a mother."

The subject of their conversation did need a mother. And a father and a good spanking. Sarah Susannah was a double handful who was fast becoming unmanageable. For the first time Daniel saw some advantage to his sister's coming back. She would take over the child.

He smiled at his mother. "I'll go talk to her, if you want me to."

"I do." Rebecca leaned forward, her hands clasped. "And, Daniel, do your very best on this. Make her see reason. She's created enough scandal in this family."

The old homeplace looked just the same, maybe a little older, but only a little. Daniel was surprised to see it in such good condition. Evidently, his sister had been making some money out here with their father's kennels. Again he felt the angry resentment. They were his kennels, too.

But his mother had taken him away.

Instead of knocking on the front door, he had walked around the side of the house and down the backyard. There were more runs than he remembered. More of everything than he remembered. She was making a living. She could live out here alone not having to fetch and carry and be at the beck and call of anyone.

His face contorted. His mother was a fool if she thought Esther had been repenting all these years. She had been living alone and enjoying herself.

The big black-and-tan whose run was nearest suddenly scrambled to his feet. He had caught Daniel's scent on the breeze and was instantly on the alert. He lifted his head and bayed loudly. Behind him another called and another.

His sister appeared from somewhere in the maze. When she caught sight of him, she let fall the watering can she was carrying. She drew in the deepest breath he had ever seen a person take, and then her eyes took on a wary look.

"Daniel?"

"Hello, big sister." He smiled and held out his arms. A wave of nostalgia overtook him. She had been a good

sister, all things considered. She had read stories to him
and taken a few scoldings for him. Sometimes when he'd
made mistakes, she'd taken the blame so he wouldn't be
punished. He could feel a stinging at the back of his
eyes.

"Daniel?" She couldn't believe her eyes. "Daniel?"

"It's me," he said. His mouth worked. He frowned
fiercely to keep the tears from falling. Then he grabbed
her awkwardly. "It's me, big sister."

"Oh, Daniel." She clamped her arms around him in
a death grip and hugged him hard. "I can't believe it.
Oh, this is too much." Her brother. Her only brother.
Handsome, smiling, beautiful as a Christmas angel. His
wavy blond hair the same color as hers brushed the back
of his collar. Five years had not aged him at all. At twenty
he looked just as she remembered him. Only his body
was a little taller. They had been the same height five
years ago. With her arms around him, she found he was
a little heavier, a little broader in the shoulders.

"Big sister. Esther." His voice was deeper, with a man's
timbre.

"Daniel." She buried her head in his shoulder and
held on tight. For a moment he reminded her of their
father, Noah Woodson.

At last they drew apart, their cheeks wet. Her arm slid
round his waist to draw him into the house. Once inside
they hugged again and again.

At last she stepped back and pulled a handkerchief
from her pocket. "I can't believe it," she murmured, snif-
fling. "If I'd made a list of people I expected to come
to see me, your name wouldn't have been on it."

His smile faded as the color of shame flooded his
cheeks. He clasped her shoulder and pulled her against
him again. "I'm sorry about that, big sister. I should have
come before."

Her smile, too, disappeared. She shook her head as

she put the handkerchief away and motioned him toward
the settee. "Yes, you should have. But I guess Mother
wouldn't let you until now."

His ears were burning as he dropped down on the seat
and ducked his head. Like hers, his fair complexion revealed every emotion. "I—I—Mother took me with her
and—"

"Don't let's talk about that." She cleared her throat.
"Shall I make us some tea? I don't have any coffee."

"That's all right. I don't need anything." He looked
around him curiously. The house where he had lived for
fifteen years was little changed, but he knew he was a
stranger. Pieces of furniture that he thought he recognized looked different somehow. And they were all arranged differently. He ran his hand over the top of the
library table behind the couch. It was satin smooth, the
fine grain showing clearly through the varnish. "I
thought this was black."

"It was. And gummy."

She sat down on the other end of the settee to face
him. The silence grew between them. After the first
heady rush of emotion, she felt only a leaden unhappi-
ness. She was sure he had not come of his own free will.
Calmly, she folded her hands in her lap. "Little brother,
you're the second person in the last two days who's come
to see me after five years of avoiding me as if I had the
plague. I know you didn't come here to look at the old
furniture. Would you like to get to the point?"

He could not meet her eyes. Instead, he concentrated
on making his fingertips trace the grain of the library
table. "I—I guess that would be best."

"I think it would be."

He reached into his breast pocket and drew out a rec-
tangle of heavy cardboard. Silently, he handed it to her.

A little girl's solemn face stared up at her. She sat sideways in a chair, her face turned toward the photographer.

She was dressed in white lace, her blouse tucked, her waist encircled by a wide sash tied with a huge bow whose ends hung off the chair. Her hair was styled in long curls that spilled down her back from an identical bow at the crown of her head. In her hand she held a little book.

Her beauty, her solemnity, almost broke Esther's heart.

She gasped for air and thrust the picture back at him. "Take that thing away. Monster! How could you? My God, you call yourself a kind man. How could you hurt me like that?"

"Esther—"

She flung herself across the room. Braced against the front door, she threw out a hand to ward him off. "Stay away from me. Did Mother tell you to show me that?"

His face white, he rose, fumbling the picture back into his pocket. "No. I just thought you'd like to see a picture. I swear—"

Sucking in a deep breath, she willed the pain to turn to fury. "Liar! You're all determined to drag me into your circle. Every single one of you. And you don't fight fair. You don't fight fair at all."

Daniel came toward her, reaching for her hands. "Esther, I'm sorry. I had no idea you'd be so hurt."

"Oh, no? And how did you think I'd feel?" Her face was white except for the gray, pinched look around her lips. "How would you feel if she were your baby, and you'd never been allowed to see her?"

Seven

Esther burst through the front door and stumbled across the porch. Throwing both arms around the pillar, she pressed her cheek against its smooth wood. Her eyes were dry, and the pain was subsiding. She had no tears to shed for what Daniel had done to her. The cold November wind struck her full in the face and served to soothe her wounded feelings.

Still, she flinched when she felt his hand on her shoulder.

"Come on back in and sit down before you faint. I've put it away." He looked at her with some concern. "You're not going to faint, are you?"

She shook her head, her cheek rolling against the pillar. "I'm not going to faint. You're not dealing with some weeping, grief-stricken parishioner. I've been through more than you even imagine. Nothing you're capable of doing can make me faint."

He pulled his hand away. Leaning out over the porch rail, he tried to face her. "I said I was sorry. There's no need to get mad at me. I was just showing you a picture."

"Leave."

"What?" He drew back.

She pointed to his saddle mount hitched to the post beside the walk. "Leave. Leave right now."

He backed away from her until he was standing on the threshold. His hands made ineffectual motions. She stared at them contemptuously. She could not imagine that they would soothe anyone who was angry or upset.

Daniel's face reddened. His eyes could not meet hers for more than a second before sliding away. Moreover, he looked guilty and ashamed.

"I—I apologize for upsetting you," he stammered. "Come back in out of the cold. We can still have a visit. I haven't seen you in five years. What have you been—"

"Daniel." She swung her arm wide, showing him the way into the yard. "Just leave."

He backed hastily into the living room. "No. Not until I say what I came to say."

Her hold on her temper snapped. She strode past him into the house and forced him to turn to face her. Her blood was roaring in her ears. She had to clench her fists tight at her sides to keep from striking her brother. "Then say it, damn you, and get the hell out."

He flushed at her language. "If you'll just calm down."

With an exaggerated sigh she dropped into the old rocking chair next to the fireplace. "I'm calm. Now say what Mother told you to say."

He flushed even brighter. His blond hair and eyebrows appeared paler than ever by contrast. "You're going to cause more talk."

She laughed. "So what!"

He shook his head sorrowfully. "Mother's right. She says you're not sorry anymore for what you did."

Esther glanced down at her hands lying along the rocker's curved walnut arms. They remained relaxed. The last of the awful anguish, the helpless regret, had vanished. "Tell her she's still half-right. I'll be forever sorry for what happened to me." Her eyes locked with her brother's and made him drop his accusing stare. "But I've stopped believing that it was my fault."

"You bore a bastard child!" Daniel's voice rose and

cracked with righteous outrage. "You brought shame upon the family."

Esther nodded. "And nothing will ever change that. So why does the family want me to come back to them?"

He wavered. She could see he didn't understand that himself. He cleared his throat and mumbled something about forgiveness.

She waved his remark aside, her lips tight. "I might have been ready to be forgiven a few years back when I was seventeen or eighteen and practically starving to death out here alone. Every woman in town was against me, and not a single man held out a hand to help. My family left me. The only friendly face I saw was Teet's."

He couldn't look away. Her words pounded around his shoulders. He had been old enough to have sneaked out here and brought her food. He should have. Instead, he'd worked every day that he wasn't in school in his mother's church. He hadn't thought about his sister at all. "I couldn't. Mother—"

She lifted her chin. "It's always Mother now for you. And she always will be. On your way out, Daniel, look around you. Do you think I really need forgiveness?"

He had seen the kennels only briefly, but he had heard hunters and farmers in Cutter's Knob and in the surrounding county talk about her hounds. His jealousy kindled again. Struggling to tamp down resentful feelings, he tried one more time. "You have to come and join us." His voice dropped into its preaching timbre. "Sarah needs you. Your daughter needs a mother."

"Get out!" She came out of the chair like a fury. Her face contorted as she slammed her fists into his shoulders. "Get out! Get out! Get out!"

He gave way before her, but he wouldn't stop talking. "She's turning into a terror. She behaves just like you're doing now. She screams and throws these awful temper fits when she can't get her way."

"Get out!" She shoved him out onto the porch. "Get off this property!"

"I see what's wrong with her now. Like mother, like daughter is right, I guess. Mother can't do a thing with her." He reeled back against the hitching post. The horse whinnied in alarm and shied. "If you won't come for yourself, think of your child. You need to come and get her."

"Damn you, Daniel Woodson!" she screamed at him from the porch. "Damn you! Damn you!"

Face pale, he jerked the reins free and swung into the saddle. "I'll tell Mother what you said."

"Good! Tell her and be damned!" She lunged back into the house and slammed the door.

Esther stretched out on the settee, her leg propped up on pillows. She still wore her gown and robe. Her hair, still uncombed, was hitched over one shoulder, raveling untidily from its night braid.

A gray day stretched ahead of her. On her stomach lay a worn copy of *Pride and Prejudice,* but even Jane Austen could not pull her into the sweet forgetfulness of fiction. In midmorning on Thanksgiving Day, she lay in a bored stupor, too lethargic even to fix a bite of breakfast for herself.

Heaving a deep sigh, she rolled over on her side and let Jane slide to the floor. She stuck out her left foot and wriggled her bare toes. At least the discomfort was mostly gone. A new red scratch decorated her ankle. She pulled up her knee to examine the red line running from instep to the hem of her wrinkled flannel gown.

When had that happened? she wondered. Receiving no answer and finding herself in no danger of blood poisoning, she straightened that leg and drew up the other one for a cursory inspection.

Someone knocked on the door. She jumped and twisted around so abruptly that she almost fell from the settee. Had they come for her? Oh, God. She didn't want another confrontation with her family. She wouldn't answer the door.

The knock came again.

"No matter what they say, I won't go with them," she promised herself. "They can see I'm not dressed." She flung the door open wide. "You're wasting your time—"

She stared at a perfect stranger. A tall, black-haired man stood on the porch. His black winged eyebrows accented his deep-set dark eyes. The face was a sculptor's dream with high cheekbones and square jaw marked by a cleft in the chin. But the singularity of the face was its tan forehead and cheeks that made a marked contrast to the pallor of the jaw and chin. A faint flush of color stained those cheekbones.

Esther looked past his broad shoulder, but saw no black buggy or saddle mount at the hitching post. She returned to her visitor, obviously a gentleman, who shifted from one polished boot to the other a bit uneasily. His suit was dark tan corduroy, his trousers thrust into the tops of his boots. Beneath the coat he wore a vest of black leather and a clean white shirt beneath. He stood unsmiling on the front step, a gunnysack folded into a bundle in the crook of his left arm.

Recognition came in a flash.

"Er—York?"

He nodded shortly.

One hand flew to her hair, the other to the front of her robe as she frantically scrambled to draw the edges together. She swung the door partially shut and leaned round it. "York!"

He looked wonderful. So handsome that she could feel little thrills of excitement running through her veins. At the same time she flushed scarlet with embarrassment.

She had invited a man to dinner and had made no preparations. She wanted to die.

His mouth twisted as he took in her clothes and loosened hair. The whole skein, a waterfall of silver and gold, swayed almost to the floor in the open doorway. It was the most beautiful thing he had seen in years. She looked young and adorable. And embarrassed.

She hadn't expected him to come. Disgusted with himself, he shifted his weight to drop back down a step. Somehow he should have let her know he accepted her invitation. Unfortunately, he had forgotten so many of the social amenities. The simple courtesies and how to perform them came flooding back. The country people on whom he depended for his trade would have been glad to post a letter for him. But writing had not occurred to him in such a long time. He wondered if he still knew how.

Instead he had spent a week fretting about whether to go or not to go. Moreover, when he had finally decided on a course of action, he had been hard put to get ready. Months and years of neglect of clothing and person could not be washed away in a single tub of water and the stroke of a razor.

Two days ago he had hung back across the street from the barbershop in Bentonville. When the place was empty, he had entered and sat sweating while the barber worked over him. Face, hair, nails, all had been in desperate need of attention. As an added fillip, he had removed his wrecked boots, and the barber had carried them to the shoe-shine boy in the saloon. The enterprising fellow had charged him a quarter instead of the usual dime because of the extraordinary amount of work they required.

All day yesterday, as he pressed his clothes and finished his preparations, he had worried that he was making a mistake. A part of him had watched in amazement as he had walked down the trail, a frown between his brows, his mouth set in a hard line. Likewise, that part of him had jeered when he wiped his damp palm on his trouser leg before he knocked on the front door.

And now he had done it all wrong. Ruined it. He frowned heavily and set his jaw to hide his disappointment.

Obviously, she had not expected him for dinner today. She had probably forgotten that she had asked him. She was undoubtedly going somewhere else.

Esther swept her hair back out of the door. "Oh, York, I wasn't—that is—" Her other hand pulled the skirt of her robe tight across her thighs. She was decently, if inappropriately, covered from neck to toe. "Do come in," she invited graciously. With a brilliant smile she flung the door wide again. "You're early."

He had forgotten many things, but he had not forgotten how a social lie sounded. Mouth curling in self-contempt, he thrust the sack into her hands. "Here. I'd better leave."

"York!" The sack was heavier than it looked. She had to catch it a second time as it threatened to slip through her hands. "Oh, York! No. Wait."

He pivoted off the step and strode away, his eyes wintry, his mouth a thin, straight line.

She set the sack down on the porch and ran after him barefooted, her hair flying wildly. "York! Wait. Stop a minute."

His long strides had carried him halfway across the frosty lawn when she caught up to him, grabbing his elbow in both hands. "Please stay. Oh, please."

He shot an angry look at the pale, clutching hands.

She saw it, but she didn't let go. "Please," she begged. She pulled a face the like he had not seen since childhood. Then she smiled, trying to get him to smile, too. "I know I've scared you nearly to death. I do look a wreck, but believe me, I clean up pretty well. Please come back and give me a chance.''

Suddenly he realized she was out in the front yard in her gown with her robe flapping open to mid-thigh. Embarrassed, he glanced quickly around to see if anyone was looking, then jerked at his arm, but she clung, hopping a couple of steps.

"Stop. Oo-oo-oo." The last was a moan.

He looked down at the whitest, littlest feet he had seen in years. She had curled her toes under in the ice-covered grass. "Good Lord," he groaned. "Haven't you got any sense? You'll catch cold out here without shoes. You're in your—er—nightgown.''

She linked her hands at his elbow and smiled up at him with her very best smile. "Come back in with me, York, and wait while I get dressed. I'm so glad you came. I really am. You don't know just how glad.''

Reluctantly, he allowed her to drag him back across the lawn and in through the open door. The warm, welcoming air caressed his face. He had put a snug, well-built house out of his mind. In his cabin the wind blew between the planks of the floor, and cold damp seeped through the walls. Two steps inside and his feet felt the unaccustomed softness of rugs.

"Come on in." Esther kept a firm pull on his arm. "Here. Sit here." She all but pushed him into the rocking chair.

He lowered himself a little gingerly. It tilted back to a comfortable angle. A fire blazed. Perhaps he would wait just until she got dressed. After all, he should apologize for embarrassing her and for all the rest of it.

Throwing her hair back over her shoulder, Esther darted to a bookcase built into the wall beside the fireplace. Her index finger ran along the spines until she found the one she sought. "Here." She thrust a leather-bound book into his hand. "Read this while I get dressed.''

"But—"

"I really do beg your pardon for sleeping late this morning. Why don't you just settle down and give me a few minutes?" She whisked the empty cup and saucer off the coffee table and padded swiftly from the room.

With the book cradled in his hand, he stared about him. The bright warm colors in the room bedazzled him. A crocheted afghan glowed from the settee. The rag rug beneath his feet was a sunburst of concentric circles running from a yellow center to a black edge. The ruby lamp reflected the leaping firelight. Everything was warm and glowing. He squinched his eyes shut, then opened them cautiously. After the dull gray and brown of his cabin, he needed to take things slowly.

He turned the book over. She had handed him *The Sketchbook of Geoffrey Crayon* by Washington Irving. His hand shook slightly as he opened it. How long had it been since he had read "The Legend of Sleepy Hollow"? So long that he could believe another man might have read it.

With his hand palm down on the opening page of the story, he looked round the room again. The table behind the settee held an arrangement of autumn leaves and spikes of orange bittersweet. Like water to a man who had been lost in a desert, he drank in the colors and the welcoming warmth.

He swallowed hard and pinched the bridge of his nose. Long dormant emotions threatened to overflow. He tilted his head back and drew a deep, calming breath, then slowly released it. The fire crackled in the hearth. He opened the book.

When Esther returned, he was deep in the story of Ichabod Crane. "Did you find something you wanted to read?"

He closed the volume, but kept his finger in the place as he rose. "It brings back memories," he admitted.

She had twisted her hair into a loose knot on the back of her neck. In place of the wrinkled flannel gown she now wore a bibbed and tucked white blouse and a long skirt of brown and black houndstooth check belted at her narrow waist by a wide brown belt. On her feet were brown kid shoes. She had darkened her eyelashes and eyebrows and pinched her cheeks to heighten the color.

The sight of her cut through his vitals like a dagger. She went together with the room and the book. He ate her with his eyes.

She stared at him, too, taking in the sheer physical beauty of him. She had never seen a man so well dressed, so well mannered, so breathtakingly handsome. She had never had a man rise when she entered the room. She blinked and cleared her throat nervously.

"Please, do sit down." She dropped onto the settee, and he resumed his seat. "I'm sorry you had to wait for me to get dressed," she began. "I just didn't—that is—I slept late—"

"I'd better be going," he muttered again with a side-long glance at the open fire. The heat from the fireplace was turning his muscles to water. He was enjoying the rocking chair, too. Just the angle that it tilted his body was soothing.

Esther smiled. Her eyes crinkled at the edges, and her mouth softened. The expression was so infectious that he felt himself smiling back involuntarily.

"Do you want to? Really?"

Frowning, he dropped his eyes to the pages. "I should have told you I was coming."

"Yes, you should have," she agreed. "You would have been spared the sight of me dressed in a tatty old bath-robe and flannel gown with my hair flying every which way like a mare's nest. But since you didn't exactly high-tail it into the hills, I suppose you've weathered the shock."

He glanced at her hair, then hastily away. One reason he had strode away so rapidly was the almost painful surge of desire he had felt at the sight of that hair. Her little bare feet in the icy grass had made his hands itch to sweep her up in his arms. He cleared his throat and crossed one leg over the other. "You looked fine. Comfortable."

"Oh, I was. Also nursing a bad case of self-pity. I'm so glad you came. I really wanted you to." She was silent for a moment. Her eyes searched his face, trying to see if she had convinced him of her sincerity.

At last he relaxed. A hesitant answering smile widened his mouth and transformed his whole face. For the second time that morning, she realized that York was far and away the handsomest man she had ever seen.

"If you're sure—" he began.

"I'm positive."

He stared at her in silence for a moment as though trying to catch a flicker of deceit. At last he seemed satisfied. "Then I'm glad I came."

Suddenly conscious that she had been holding her breath, she caught up the sack left alone by the door. "What did you bring me?"

He clutched the book. "Oh, just a little something for the meal. Some walnuts and some—er—some—something to drink."

She drew out the small earthenware jug and pulled the cork. "Smells powerful."

He raised his eyes to the ceiling in an expression of innocence. "I know you said you don't drink much, but I thought for the holidays—a small libation wouldn't go amiss."

With each speech, his conversation seemed to come more easily. Obviously, he was a well-educated man with perfect manners. She smiled gamely. "We'll have it with the mincemeat pie." She unwrapped a Mason jar. "More?"

He shrugged. "It's a quart of apple brandy. You can cook with it if you want to."

She held the pale gold liquid up to the light. It really was pretty. "You make brandy, too? I thought—"

"I make lots of brandies. Blackberry. Apple. Peach." He could not keep a measure of pride from creeping into his voice. "They've kind of become my specialty. There's quite a demand. Among friends, you understand."

She could see that several of his liquid dollars had been spent on a shave and haircut. She wondered if the suit were new and the boots. She set the jar on the table with a smile. "Well, then, Mr. York, I'm glad to be included among your friends."

"Just York, please."

He smiled. His eyes no longer looked flat and opaque. Light glowed in their dark depths. The warmth from the fireplace had colored his cheeks. She felt the stirrings of something old and long forgotten. Except it was different from a girl's youthful sexual responses. These were the undeniable attractions of a woman for a man. She could feel a blush rising as she sternly reprimanded herself. The very last thing she needed was a lustful yearning for a Yankee.

Still her pulses were singing with joy. He had come after all, and together they were going to have a wonderful Thanksgiving dinner. "Why don't you sit there in front of the fire and enjoy your book?" she invited. "I'll get dinner started."

His eyes flicked to the open book in his lap. He would have liked nothing better, but he shook his head. "Let me help you fix dinner," he suggested. "No sense in you doing all the work. I can read later."

She hesitated. She could tell that he really wanted to

read, but she had been alone so long that she hated to forego a minute of time with any sort of company. Likewise, she had never heard of a man helping in the kitchen. According to her mother, the menfolk should relax at their ease, even eat their full dinners before the women even sat down. All this had been reinforced with appropriate scriptures. Having York in the house was an act of rebellion. Having him actually in the kitchen with her would be tantamount to heresy.

She smiled. "I'd be glad of the help."

Her guest laid down the book and reached for the buttons on his suit coat. "You lead the way," he said seriously. "I'm not sure what a real kitchen looks like, but I'm willing to follow orders."

She could have hugged him. Instead, she impulsively put out her hand and caught his. His eyes flickered, but he didn't pull back.

"Come through here. I've been living alone so long that fixing for two people will be something new."

He looked startled. "Isn't your family coming for dinner?"

She donned her shell jacket and picked up a basket by the back door. "I don't have any family. Before you take off your coat, you can help me catch a hen and bring milk and eggs from the spring house."

In only a little over three hours, they sat down to dinner. The lighthearted conversation during the preparation continued throughout the meal itself. She told him stories about her hounds and their trials. He told her nothing at all. He could not remember a single thing from his past life worth telling.

To York each bite tasted better than the last. After living so long on canned and dried stuffs and wild game, he had almost forgotten the taste of fresh domesticated fowl and homegrown food. After his second piece of apple pie splashed with apple brandy and topped with clotted cream, he turned his chair away from the table and clutched his stomach in mock protest. "Lord, woman. You'll burst me."

She went so far as to prod his shoulder. "You ate it all yourself. I didn't urge you."

"It's all your fault, though, for being such a good cook," he groaned.

"My grandmother taught me," she acknowledged happily.

"Don't try to shift the blame onto your poor old grandmother. She didn't bake the corn bread dressing and make the giblet gravy."

"She actually did plant the asparagus from roots she brought from Virginia," Esther said softly. The thought of family dimmed her joy, but only for a few seconds. "You peeled the apples and grated the nutmeg," she reminded him. "And whipped the cream and made the coffee and made the brandy to lace it with."

"I can't believe I did all that to myself," he mused.

"You even licked the bowl after you finished whipping the cream."

"I did, didn't I?" He smiled reminiscently. "I don't think I've done that since I was a little boy."

They sat silent then, neither knowing what to say, afraid to speak for fear of destroying the peace with bitter memories. At last she pushed back from the table. "Go on in the living room with your coffee," she instructed. "I'll wash the dishes and join you in a few minutes."

"No." He rose steadfastly. "You wash the dishes and I'll dry them. Then we can go into the living room together."

"Oh, no," she objected. "I think that would be rude of me. You're the guest. To help me cook is one thing; to wash dishes would be wrong."

He was already at the sink, pumping water into an iron pot to heat. "I'd feel silly sitting in the living room all by myself letting you wait on me. I might get the idea that I was an invalid or something." He replaced the cover on the half-eaten pie and gathered up the silverware.

"But—"

"We'll get this done a lot faster if you work, too," he kidded softly. Then he stared at her when she laughed. He had actually made a joke. He had made someone else laugh. She was very, very pretty when she laughed. He would like to see her laugh more often.

"Would you like to see my hounds? You've shown me your brandy and your whiskey. Maybe you'd like to see what put the food on the table here. I have to go out and feed them anyway." She looked at him diffidently. When he glanced through the curtains at the gray day, she quickly stepped away. "Of course, it's cold and damp out there. You don't have to come with me. Just stay here by the fire and read."

Although he wanted nothing so much as to sprawl out on her couch and take a nap, the walk would do him good. "I'd like a good walk." He congratulated himself on being able to tell a social lie. "I'll be glad to help if I can."

She took her shell jacket from its hook beside the door. When she would have shrugged into it, he took it from her and held it. He had made the gesture without any particular thought. It had seemed natural to him. Then he became aware that his hands had rested a bit long on her shoulders. She looked up at him inquiringly. Instantly, he drew back and went for his own coat.

He matched his steps to hers as they walked down the hill to the kennels. Several of the hounds raised their heads alertly, eying her approach, their muzzles lifted to catch the breeze. The big hound in the first kennel scrambled to his feet with a low whine.

Esther entered a small shed and came out with a tow sack. "Beef jerky. I fed them early this morning, but they like a little bit more." She dropped a double handful of bite-sized pieces into the big hound's feeding dish. "This is the famous Teet. You remember how concerned I was about him. He's the best. I got him when I was twelve. He's getting a bit old, but he's the leader of the pack."

She leaned over the wire fence and touched her fingers to the hound's dark head. In response, he whined again and lifted his muzzle for her to scratch under his chin. She looked at her guest to see how the hound was impressing him.

He smiled back at her. "He looks like he's had the best."

She blushed with pleasure and led him to the next cage. "This is Marth." She patted the head of a raw-boned bitch. "Her pups have the clearest bugle you ever heard. I've bred her successfully to Teet seven times. I've got orders from hunters over the border in Missouri for their pups." The hound crooned low in her throat before wolfing down the food. "Sweet lady."

York mentally counted the number of runs and estimated the number of hounds. "What's the market for animals like these?"

She looked surprised. "The best market in the world. Farmers need them to keep down varmints. Sportsmen want them to hunt. They'll all pay well because I train the hounds right. They always take what I tell them to. They won't run on trash trails."

Down the line she took him, explaining about each one of the hounds as they passed. As she went, she petted and talked to them as if they were her children while they leaned against the mesh to touch her legs and raised their heads for her caress.

She showed him Birdsong and her new litter of six. Trigg, the only remaining pup from Marth's last litter, was being picked up the first of December. Annie was pregnant by Juniper, the stocky male at the opposite end of the row from Teet.

It took her more than half an hour to feed the animals. "There's a lot of work here for one woman."

She returned the tow sack and latched the shed. "I don't think of it that way. I really love the hounds. They make me enough money to live on. And they're such great company—loyal, brave, dependable, smart." She led the way back to the house. "What more could anyone want?"

They carried their coffee, liberally laced with brandy, to the living room, where Esther slid down onto the settee on her spine. "I don't intend to move for a while," she announced. "If you want to read, go right ahead. Any book in the library is yours."

"You're sure?"

She stretched out her legs in front of her and crossed her ankles. "You're my guest."

He went back to "The Legend of Sleepy Hollow." For several minutes neither moved except to sip reflectively at the steaming cups. At last Brom Bones threw the pumpkin at Ichabod's head and rode away into the night. York closed the book reverently and rolled his head in her direction. "I had forgotten."

Not pretending she didn't understand, Esther smiled at him. "It's wonderful, isn't it?"

He stroked Washington Irving lovingly before he set the book aside. Then he turned to her, laying his hand along the back of the settee. "That was the best dinner I can ever remember."

"I'm glad you came."

A log collapsed, and a shower of sparks drew their eyes to the hearth. His voice was soft as he admitted, "I almost didn't. It took a lot of nerve for me to knock on your door. When you weren't dressed, I was so disappointed."

"Were you really? You ran away awfully fast."

"Embarrassment."

"What did you have to be embarrassed about? I was the one who was caught in my nightgown."

He chuckled at the memory. "I'm glad you don't live on a crowded street in Philadelphia."

"Then you're glad I chased you across the icy yard in my bare feet?"

He patted his stomach lovingly. "Lord, yes."

"I'm glad I did, too." She finished her coffee and set the empty cup and saucer on the table. With a faint moan she leaned back against the settee and closed her eyes. Almost immediately her even breathing told him she had nodded off to sleep.

He watched her. Who was this woman with whom he'd eaten dinner? He supposed both North and South had their share of young women trying to make a living when their brothers or husbands had failed to return. He was glad she didn't seem to blame him for his part in it.

He wanted her. He wasn't even trying to deny it anymore. His fingers tingled at the thought of caressing her.

Ruefully, he ran his hand through his hair. What should he do now? Waking up with his hand between her legs and her head on his thigh had served to remind him of what he was missing. Now staring down at her, those feelings came raging back.

She had invited him into her house and trusted him enough to drift off to sleep with him beside her. Only a cad would take advantage of a situation like that. He wouldn't betray her trust. He couldn't.

She stirred, frowned, murmured something.

He couldn't help himself. He bent close to catch her words.

Her eyelids swept up. The expression in her eyes was peaceful, unaware. The eyes themselves were breathtaking—pale brown, with hints of green and gold around the pupil.

He should draw back and apologize. He was taking advantage just by leaning over her. She would come fully awake in the next minute and scream the way she had the night in the cabin. He couldn't bear to spoil this moment. Very slowly, as if he had come upon a small animal in a forest glade, he started to draw back.

Just as slowly she smiled. Slowly, slowly, a soft blush rose in her cheeks. Her eyelids swept down, hiding the breathtaking eyes, then swept up again. His skin prickled, and his mouth went suddenly dry. He blinked rapidly. He was dreaming. He had to be.

She exhaled softly, making him aware that he, too, had been holding his breath. Her eyes scanned his face from forehead to chin, then they met his. If ever he had read a question in a woman's eyes, he read it now. His body stirred powerfully.

Inexorably, inevitably, he bent to put his lips to hers.

Eight

His kiss was a revelation to her.

No one had touched her lips like that. Certainly never with the feather-light brushing that sent chills prickling over her body. She gasped.

Instantly, he pulled back an inch. No more. And she moaned with the sense of loss. His lips returned firmer this time, incredibly warm. At the same time gentle fingertips caressed the side of her cheek. They slid across her skin, ruffling the tiny invisible hairs.

She sighed and their breaths comingled. Brandy and cream and their own special taste. She closed her eyes with the headiness of it.

He kissed her again, longer, his lips caressing hers, opening to touch his tongue to the seam, begging entrance into her mouth. Almost involuntarily, she drew him closer. Her lips parted for his tongue, welcomed him. From the depths of her throat came a small sound of delight at the satiny feel of him.

His arms went round her and drew her close. Her breast flattened against his chest. Her body moved when he moved.

Her heart began to pound. His muscles tensed.

The pounding came again.

Reluctantly, he released her. His voice was hoarse. "Someone's at the door."

She tore out of his embrace like a wild thing, her head

snapping round, her eyes searching. Her mind worked furiously. Was it her mother or brother or both? Thanksgiving Day was over, and she had disappointed them. They had come to take her by force.

The pounding came again. A woman's voice called, "Esther! Esther!"

Her stomach clenched. Slowly, she pressed her palm against her abdomen, willing her caller to go away.

His question was uttered in a flat voice. "Want me to hide?"

She snapped her attention back to him. Yes, she wanted him to hide. The last thing she wanted or needed was for her mother to discover that she had entertained a man. A stranger and a Yankee alone in her home on Thanksgiving. *Hide!* her mind screamed. *Disappear! Don't let yourself be seen.*

Then a curious defiance asserted itself. She had hidden from the world too long, wearing the mantle of shame, scorned and looked down on.

"No. Keep your seat."

Drawing a long breath, she rose and moved around the settee, favoring her left leg. She was conscious that York had risen, too, and stood waiting, his stance alert.

She opened the door in the middle of another series of knocks. "Yes?"

" 'Bout time you got here, Esther." A heavyset woman with a bright red face filled the doorway. Without preamble she began to scold. Then she gasped.

Esther locked her arms tightly around her chest. She could feel her stomach shuddering with nerves. "What's wrong, Martha Virginia?"

Carly Ord's spinster daughter moved to the right to get a clearer view of York. Her eyes were wide, her mouth forming a perfect O.

"Martha Virginia?" Esther prompted.

"What?" With difficulty the woman tore her eyes away

from the handsome man standing in the middle of Esther Woodson's living room. "What?" she asked again of Esther.

"What did you come for?"

"Oh? Oh, yes." She let out her breath in a rush. "Pawpaw done took with a real bad sinking spell, Esther."

"I'm so sorry to hear that." Esther's effort to offer sympathy went unacknowledged.

The woman rushed on with her tale, telling it in a whining voice that seemed to say the burden and the pain were all hers while Carly was an inconsiderate old fool. "He was feeling poorly, and then he just sort of keeled over at the dinner table after I'd gone and fixed this big meal with all the trimmings. I put him to bed and we sent for the doctor. While we was a-waiting, Pawpaw made me promise that I'd run up here and tell you that he couldn't come for a spell."

"I'm so sorry." Esther hated the thought of Carly's being sick and of what his illness might mean to her. He was the only one who had come on the place for so long. She hesitated, phrasing the question reluctantly. "Will he be coming back at all, do you think?"

The woman's voice wobbled. She clasped her pudgy hands tight to her protruding bosom. "I kindly sort of doubt it. But Pawpaw's tough as a hickory knot. He could be up and frisky as a jaybird in a couple of days. Or he could just lie there for a spell."

Not knowing what to say, Esther prayed that Carly had fallen over rather than eat the monstrous dinner that Martha Virginia had cooked, but she very much feared that the old man might not be back at all. Seventy-eight was very, very old. Carly Ord had been born the last year that George Washington was president of the United States.

In the silence Martha Virginia bobbed her head in York's direction. "I see you're entertaining a friend, Esther."

"Oh, yes." Esther rolled her eyes. No help for it now. "Martha Virginia, this is a friend—er—of my brother's." She stepped aside.

York came to the door. "The name's York," he said softly. "I'm sorry to hear about your father."

Martha Virginia actually smiled. Her fingers kneaded her bosom as if her heart were pounding. Esther would have been amused if Martha Virginia had not been one of the worst gossips in Cutter's Knob. Daniel would hear by noon tomorrow that a friend of his had been in Esther's house on Thanksgiving evening.

"Thank you for coming all this way to tell me." Esther stepped between the older woman and York. "Tell your father to hurry and get well. And tell him he can have his job back the minute he's able to do it."

Martha Virginia blinked as if she had suddenly remembered what she had come for. Her mouth quirked. She licked her thick lower lip. "That's real good of you, Esther. I'll sure tell him."

Esther waited. Martha Virginia waited. Finally, the older woman nodded. "Well, I'd better be going."

"Good night."

Martha Virginia stared hard at York, memorizing his features. "Good night."

"Thank you for coming and bringing the message. It was very kind of you." Esther closed the door in the woman's face.

With a sigh she walked back to the settee. Sorry as she was for Carly's "spell," she could not help but breathe a tiny sigh of gratitude. Should her mother and brother come to take her away before Christmas, she could say she could not leave her hounds. "No cloud so black . . . ," she murmured.

"Problems?" York came after her and was watching her closely.

"Our visitor was Martha Virginia Ord. Her father Carly

works for me, but as you heard he won't be back for some time." She shook her head. "Probably never."

"I'm sorry."

"I'm sorry, too. He was a friend of my grandfather's. He deserves to rest, but he's worked all his life. I don't suppose he'll be very happy lying in bed."

Esther slumped down on the settee, more depressed than she cared to admit. She was going to miss Carly. He had never faltered in his friendship and support. So completely had she been scorned by the town that for weeks on end he was the only person who came on the place.

Her first guest in five years sat down beside her. His dark eyes searched her face. "What did he do for you?"

She shrugged. "Oh, he fed the hounds when I wasn't around, cleaned out the kennels, fixed things that needed to be fixed."

"He sounds indispensable."

"I'll miss him." She laughed a little. "I certainly can't spend two days and two nights in a mountain cabin at the drop of a hat."

York smiled in his turn, infected by her ability to laugh. Those two days she had spent in his cabin, he now regarded as rounding a bend in his life. He had followed her around it, and now he felt different about himself.

Suddenly, she remembered what they had been doing when the knock came. Nervous, she sprang up. "How about some more coffee? Another piece of pie?"

He shook his head. Surprised at his own perception, he knew that she remembered and was alarmed. Where would those two kisses have led? He was very much afraid that once aroused his body would have been very difficult to control. He stood up, too. "I'd better go. I've been forgetting my manners all day. I've way outstayed my welcome."

The lamps and the fire made the room cozy. Outside

the windows was a wall of darkness. The light mist that
had drifted down all day was turning to an icy drizzle. It
was very much like the night she had fallen into the
ravine. She shivered. When he left, she would be alone
again, perhaps for months. She felt the contradictions
within her own body. One part knew he should go and
quickly. Another weaker part wanted him to stay. "It's
too late for you to walk home tonight. You did walk,
didn't you?"

He nodded with a shrug. "On my own two feet. And
I can go home the same way."

"But it's dark." Why didn't she keep her mouth shut?

"Not for me. Remember, I'm the one who walks
around in the dark. I can find my way back without eyes."
Was she about to invite him to stay the night? It was the
height of temptation. The cabin had never seemed farther away or more forbidding. He strode to the closet
and found his coat.

Esther came after him. She clasped her hands and
swallowed hard. A blush burned in her cheeks. "You're
perfectly welcome to spend the night. The settee is long
enough, and I've got plenty of quilts and pillows. I'll send
you on your way with a hot breakfast in the morning."
She sounded as if she were issuing an improper invitation. Moreover, she was begging. Stunned at her own te-
merity, she caught her lower lip between her teeth.

Frowning blackly, he shrugged into his jacket, his back
to her.

She moved back, hugging herself, gooseflesh prickling
on her upper arms. "I—I didn't mean to say the wrong
thing."

He lowered his head to fit the button through the but-
tonhole with careful attention. "You didn't."

"I think I did."

He finished his task and shifted his shoulders under
the material. "What you did was offer me a place to

spend the night. You're a fine, decent person. You'd offer the same to anyone rather than have them walk away in the rain and the dark. You're a lady, ma'am. And now you feel guilty because—I'm—what I am."

He did not guess the turmoil that was going on in her mind. He did not know her shameful past. He was the first person who had called her a lady in five years. "I really wish you'd stay." She tried to make her voice matter-of-fact as her grandfather or her father would have. "It would be the worst breech of hospitality to send you out on a dark road to walk miles up the mountain to an icy cabin."

He went still, as if listening alertly to her. "I don't want to intrude."

"I stayed for a couple of nights with you," she reminded him. "I really owe you a bed and breakfast."

For a moment he looked tempted, then shook his head. "I'd better go."

She drew a deep breath. Her eyes dropped. He was leaving, and she would probably never see him again. "All right."

He paused. A soft groan escaped him. He turned back. In a couple of short steps he crossed the room. His hands closed over her upper arms. Her head snapped up as her eyes flew wide in surprise. As her lips parted, his mouth came down hard on hers. His tongue lanced into the opening, flicking over her teeth, touching her tongue, drinking the taste of her.

She gasped for breath as he transferred his grip. One hand splayed, to press against her spine and bring her body into contact with his. The other hand slid over her shoulder and around her neck, keeping her from drawing back. She was effectively caught, unable to move while he gave full play to his desires.

He was rough, demanding, desperate almost as he drew the response from her. As if he tasted what he did not want to taste, touched her in spite of himself, he shuddered deeply.

Added to the sweet taste of her was the feel of her soft breasts against his chest while the bones of her hips fit tightly against his own. Her breathing increased its rhythm to breathless gasps. He tore his mouth from hers. Still holding her immobile as a kitten by the scruff of its neck, he slid his lips across her cheek. Her smooth skin smelled of spices and apples and woman.

Esther closed her eyes, giving herself to the power of his embrace. Even with his very genuine male hunger came the sense that he had himself under control. It was a totally different experience from the painful nightmare in which she had conceived Sarah. Starved for human contact, she responded with her whole body. Her hands clutched at his waist, digging her fingertips into the hard rows of muscle along his back. Her own lips moved against his cheek. Her chest heaved as she felt him draw in a harsh, shuddering breath.

As suddenly as he had begun the embrace, he thrust her from him. They stumbled apart. He fell back against the door, cursing softly, not looking at her.

Her eyes never left his face as she caught herself on the edge of the library table. The feel of his mouth and the imprint of his hard body on hers drove all reason from her mind. Only desire remained, like a fire storm, like a fleshquake. She shook with it. The female parts of her, awakened and expanded in sweet pain at the base of her belly. Gasping, blind, she wrapped her arms around her waist and hung her head.

"I'm sorry," he said, a very real pain gripping his body.

Esther felt the pain in the sound. He was the man who lived alone by choice in the woods. She was the woman who lived alone in the valley, outcast by kin and kind. Only a few years ago, they had been mortal enemies. A kind of insanity had gripped them both.

"I'm sorry, too." Her voice quivered. Mortally ashamed of her need and what it revealed about her, she spun away, crossing her hands miserably across her chest. Her breasts were hard, their nipples tingling. Her loins felt swollen, bathed in hot wetness. Her mother was right after all. She was a shame and a disgrace. A harlot like Mary Magdalene. "I don't know what happened to me." She was lying. She knew exactly what had happened to her. "I haven't—I don't—"

He straightened and wiped the sweat from his forehead. "I've got to get out of here."

She hunched her shoulders as she heard him pull open the door. Did he hesitate? Did he open his mouth to speak but change his mind?

The door closed firmly. She heard his footsteps across the porch and then across the frozen grass.

The silence grew in the room. She sank to her knees, her forehead dropping to rest on them. If he had gutted her with a knife, he could have hurt her no more. How she wished she had not done what she had done! He was right to run from her. What man would not?

Praying for death, she huddled there, desperately ashamed, yet burning with passion unaneled.

York plunged down the road from Esther's house as if her hounds bayed at his heels. He ran to cool the heat that their kiss had aroused. He ran to put as much distance as he possibly could between them so it would be impossible for him to stay the night.

He ran to escape the demons that howled in his brain. And those he could not get away from.

At the Y at Bas Boscomb's, he thudded to a halt. His chest heaved with the effort. His blood pounded in his ears. His hands braced on his knees, he bent over from the hips in a coughing fit.

While he was in that position, a rider loped up behind him and pulled his horse to a halt. Prickles of fear slid down York's spine. The horse stamped and snorted. The tack jingled, and the saddle creaked as the rider dismounted.

"You shore do run, boy," came the nasal voice behind him. "I ain't never seen the like."

York spun around.

Fully six feet tall and nearly four feet broad, the figure advancing on him was gargantuan. York braced himself for a confrontation that was sure to be unpleasant. By the light of the three-quarter moon, he could see a silver sheriff's badge gleaming dully on the black frock coat.

"What you runnin' from?"

York stepped back, searching himself for control. He might be able to answer one or two questions without dissolving into blind panic. Even winded, he could outrun the fat man. By the time the sheriff climbed back on the horse, he would be in the brush on the side of the mountain. No one could catch him then.

"I said, 'What you runnin' from?'"

York swallowed. Could he remember how to stall, how to lie so someone would believe him? "Just hurrying to get on home before it gets nasty."

"Uh-huh." The man slipped his left hand under his lapel and pushed the badge forward. "See this here, boy?"

"Yes." York took another step back, and another.

The sheriff advanced. His other hand swept his coat aside and pulled his revolver from its holster. "Well, it says that I get the truth told to every question I ask. And if I don't think you're tellin' the truth, I'll just use this to ask you again."

York could feel the trembling begin in his belly. Yet his mind registered the irony of the situation. Was he going to survive the war and its horrors to be shot in the middle of a country road by a jackleg sheriff from Arkansas?

"Now," the man went on, separating each syllable for emphasis. "What you run-nin' from?" He waddled closer, swinging his body weight over first one leg and then the other. He was taller than York and clearly used to his size intimidating everyone.

York balled his hands into fists, and his teeth clicked together as he clenched his jaw. He couldn't endure this. He absolutely refused to be intimidated by anyone anymore. He had retreated to the cabin in the mountains to escape from people much more kindly and tolerant than this.

"You hear me, boy?" The sheriff stabbed the muzzle of his revolver against York's breastbone.

Stamford might as well have touched a match to a barrel of gunpowder. York exploded. His right arm swept the Colt aside. He drove his fist into the pendulous belly swinging in front of him. A malodorous gust of air whooshed into his face as the sheriff bent over. York stepped back and straightened the man with a right to the jaw.

The round face contorted; the prominent eyes bulged. The sheriff dropped to one knee, clutching his middle. His mouth moved, gaped, tried to pull in air.

York didn't wait to see whether the man could recover. He bent and twisted the sheriff's Colt from his hand. The man howled like a wounded bull when York flung the weapon as far back down the road as his strength would allow. Then he spun and ran.

Ice sheened every plane of gray shale, thousands of crystal pinpoints setting the whole ridge a-glitter. To York's hot eyes, it was a foreign surface, dangerous, alien, unwelcoming.

Boldly, he set his feet upon it, uncaring when the tiny crystal towers shattered and the soft rock beneath them cracked ominously. From his first step, he staggered drunkenly. The ice offered no purchase for the soles of his boots. Time and again he went down, caught himself on outstretched fingertips, rose, and went on.

Halfway across, the whole surface disintegrated. One foot slewed forward; the other, back. He fell hard, in a painful split, slamming one knee into the icy rock and tearing the muscle at the back of his opposite thigh. The pain drove a cry from him.

In another breath the shrill cry changed to a primal scream. The actual pain was nothing. He had endured much worse and survived. His scream was for the agony of his soul. He had struck down a lawman in the performance of his duty. A man running for dear life down a country road in the middle of the night was cause for alarm.

He could have been a robber or a murderer or both. He could be insane. He could be a danger to himself and the rest of the countryside. The sheriff had been right to be suspicious. He had pulled his gun when York had evaded his question, and York had attacked him.

He wasn't fit to walk among civilized human beings. He surely wasn't fit to form a relationship with a kind woman like Esther Woodson.

Rolling over on the ice, he dragged his injured legs together. Resting on his forearm, he looked around him at the midnight wall of trees. The moon lighted the entire scene in silver, picking him out, exposing him to the ghosts of old enemies who watched in the darkness. Old enemies and old friends. The old friends were the worst. They observed him uncaring of his panic and his pain.

He had no right to live a good life when they were dead. They sneered and tormented him, destroying him little by little, gauging how much of him remained. They had missed him tonight at Esther's. But they had come back full force when the sheriff had threatened him.

They had destroyed his reason, sent him into a blind panic. Ghosts they might be, but they were always there.

He pushed himself up onto the undamaged knee. "God damn you. God damn you all," he whispered. With a litany he condemned them. The ugly words poured from his mouth.

The shale crackled and slid enough to throw him off balance again. It silenced him as if the earth herself sent warning that other gods heard and noted what he said. He caught himself with both hands. Then silently, like an animal, he crouched, three-legged, the cold seeping upward through his veins. The ice crystals blinded him. The darkness dared him.

Tears began to trickle down his cheeks. He could feel their hot paths on his icy skin. He was alone. Alone. He could feel even the ghosts withdrawing until only MacKenzie remained.

MacKenzie. "Go away. Stay the hell away from me! MacKenzie!!!"

He didn't realize he had bellowed until the echo answered from the bluff.

From the canyon.

From the mountain.

An alien sound in a gentle forest, it rang through the silent Ozarks.

At length he pulled himself across the ice to the ebony trees. Hand over hand, he climbed up a rough trunk until he stood against it, head tipped back, sweat beading his forehead.

A tiny breeze ruffled his hair, but could not cool the heat of his emotion. Fury, fear, despair held him in their sway.

He thought he might have lost consciousness for a minute. When he opened his eyes, he had gained some measure of control. His head fell forward on his chest. He was such a self-pitying bastard. For a moment there he had been insane. Screaming and cursing at nothing. At ghosts. He had attacked a lawman—for God's sake—like a dangerous felon and then run. He ought to be locked up.

And he had no reason to behave as he did. He had spent a good day, a pleasant day, with a civilized person. He had kissed her.

She had returned his kiss with warm eagerness.

He felt an agonizing twinge in his groin. With a gasp he covered it with his hand. Another layer of sweat broke out on his forehead which had not yet cooled from the last. Thunder of guns, flashes of fire, burning pain, screams of his dying comrades. He had not been killed. He lived and tasted and felt and desired a woman again. And they never could.

Every muscle, every nerve shuddered beneath the power of guilt.

With a groan he clutched at himself. Arms locked in a tight circle around his knees, back to the tree, he prepared to face the terrors of the rest of the night.

Martha Virginia's story spread through Cutter's Knob in the middle of the morning after Thanksgiving. A man, a young man, had been standing in the middle of Esther Woodson's living room, just as bold as brass. His name was York or Stork or maybe Stark. Martha Virginia wasn't sure about that.

But he wasn't from around here. Where had he come from? she wanted to know. She wondered if he might have taken up with Esther. Or maybe Esther had taken up with him?

The women in the general store put their heads together, hissing and spitting like a nest of vipers. Around the stove the old men cackled at their wives' resentment and partly at the idea that someone in this dull little corner of the world might be having a little fun on the side.

The gossip held that he was part of the James gang. Esther's cousins were in the neighborhood. Everybody knew they had robbed a bank in Missouri and the sheriff of Neosho had chased them into Arkansas. Frank James was known to have been wounded. Maybe they were all hiding out at the Woodson place. Was Martha Virginia sure it wasn't Jesse that had been standing there?

She wasn't sure because she'd never seen Jesse James. But the man said his name was Stork. She was sure about that. "And he was young and real clean-favored. Course, handsome is as handsome does, but he wasn't no old man."

Elmo Stamford was absolutely fit to be tied. He had like to never found his gun. By the time he'd found it, the outlaw was long gone. He thought about going back to the Woodson place and scaring Esther into giving up his name. He would have, too, but he didn't want anyone to know that some wild-eyed idiot running down the road in the middle of the night had pulled his gun right out of his hand and thrown it away.

He was scowling so fiercely that a little girl hid her face in her mother's skirt as he walked past. That made him feel a little better. He puffed out his chest and strode into his office.

Two men waited for him. One sat in the chair behind his desk; the other turned from the window where he had been watching the sheriff's progress up the street.

Stamford made a motion toward his gun, then froze. He couldn't cover them both, split up the way they were. He thrust out his chin and his belly. "What the hell you doing in here?"

Neither one of his intruders looked as if he ever

smiled. Lean and bristly as lobos, they rested their hands on their gunbutts. The one behind the desk rose slowly, his rheumy eyes locked with the sheriff's. "Just come by for a little information."

Stamford relaxed a fraction. All kinds of people wanted information. Lawmen, private citizens, the army. Bounty hunters. "Uh-huh."

"Heard tell that Jesse James and his gang are heading this way," the one at the window said.

Stamford grinned. His eyebrows pulled together above his bulging eyes. "I've heard about him, too."

They waited.

"Course, I ain't actually seen Jesse James, but he's got kin out west of town. If anyone'd know where he is, it'd be her."

"Her?"

"Yep. His cousin. Name's Woodson. She'd know because she's put him up before. Come to think of it, there was a fellow coming out of her place last night. Young fellow. Stranger around here." He eyed them carefully; each word seemed to act like a goad to them.

Their hands twitched on their gunbutts. "How do we get there?"

Rebecca clasped her hands together and prayed hard. For all she knew, that man Stark that Martha Virginia Ord was telling everybody about might have been in the house the day she was there. She had seen the living room and the kitchen, and the bedrooms. He might have been hiding in the closet. She prayed even harder for the strength to turn away the righteous wrath boiling inside her.

She had had doubts lately about her daughter. Doubts about her own unforgiving nature. She had taken the first step, held out the hand of friendship, but it had been rejected. She had sent her son to make the offer again with a photographic likeness of Sarah. Surely, the sight of that blessed face should have softened Esther's obdurate heart.

Daniel had reported that Esther had driven him off the place.

Now she saw the reason. Esther was living in sin—in mortal sin—committing all sorts of transgressions including fornication. Rebecca slipped to her knees beside her desk and bowed her head. Tears of anger and betrayal slipped between her eyelids. The sin of her daughter could so easily reflect on herself.

A good half hour passed before she rose up. Her hands cold as ice, she washed her face to remove all traces of tears, put on her bonnet and cloak and walked with determined strides to the sheriff's office.

Elmo Stamford might lack a gentlemanly demeanor, but not all the Lord's tools looked like angels.

Teet leaped to his feet, head thrust forward, muscles a-quiver. His keen nose picked up a familiar scent, and his tail wagged once.

Esther turned from the run to see York striding across the lawn toward her. Surprise made her clutch the two-by-four at the top of the fence. She had tried to put her Thanksgiving visitor out of her mind and go on with her life. Now she felt a surge of excitement at the sight of him. "Why, hello, there." She smiled her best welcoming smile. "Fancy seeing you so bright and early in the morning."

Her caller scowled as if she had said something unwelcome. He halted several feet from her, hands thrust into the pockets of the familiar shabby army pants. He had left the blue coat at home, substituting a rough army-issue blanket with a hole cut in the middle. Uneasily, he shifted his feet. His boots, so carefully polished for his Thanksgiving appearance, were scuffed and muddy again. His jaw was covered with four day's growth of black stubble.

She hesitated, uncertain. Had he come to thank her for dinner? Was he paying a social call? An uncomfortable silence stretched between them. Finally, she asked, "What can I do for you?"

He cleared his throat. "I remembered your man got sick."

"Carly Ord? Yes. I went to see him yesterday." In fact Carly had not known she was there. He lay on his side, his face to the wall, barely breathing. His stooped body had hunched until his legs were drawn up against his chest. He might have been a child lying there. "He's very low. I don't imagine he'll be back."

"I thought maybe you'd need—that is, you have a job that needs doing."

"Do you mean you want to work for me?" She came out of the run.

Teet thrust his head in the open gate and slithered out at her heels. He lowered his head and snuffled along the ground until he found York's tracks. Tail whipping back and forth, he followed them out for several yards and then back.

Neither human looked the other in the eye. They both watched the hound. Finally, York said, "That's right. I thought you might give me the job, just until he gets back on his feet."

She hesitated. "But I can't pay you. I mean I *can* pay you, but just what I paid Carly, a couple of dollars a month. He really came over, I think, to keep an eye on me, for my grandfather's sake."

He brushed her argument aside. "I don't need much. I can work for the experience."

"Experience? Cleaning out kennels!"

"I don't know anything about dogs—er—hounds. I could learn while I'm here. You could teach me." His scowled lightened. The corners of his mouth flicked upward in what was almost a grin.

"There's not much to be learned about cleaning out kennels. How to wield a shovel is about the size of it."

"I've always liked dogs—er—"

"You can call them dogs if you like," she interrupted. "Most people do anyway. Even people who know better. But they're correctly called hounds."

At that he did grin. "I'll do my best to remember. Hounds."

She looked over her shoulder at the double row of runs and houses. They required many hours a day. When she had finished that, account books had to be kept and breeding papers filled out. And then there was always the work within the house. Without him she would fall farther and farther behind. "You're sure about this?"

"Positive."

She tilted her head to one side. Teet had returned to her side and dropped down on his haunches. He opened his jaws in a wide doggy yawn accompanied by a sharp whine. Evidently he had found nothing to be alarmed about in his inspection. She really needed this man to work for her, but her curiosity wouldn't allow her to accept him without knowing one thing. "Would it be too much to ask your full name?"

He kicked at a red rock that thrust its sharp nose out of the surrounding clay and scowled so fiercely that she thought he was going to turn and walk away. Still not looking at her, he shrugged. "Captain York Bradburn, ma'am." Unconsciously, his shoulders went back; his head came up. "Fourth Pennsylvania Cavalry, 64th Volunteers."

She dropped her eyes to hide the surge of cold anger his name, rank, and unit resurrected. Not that she felt like a traitor to the Cause. She had never known what the Cause was. But she could never forget what they had done to her father and to herself.

He was watching her closely. "I'd better leave."

"No." Her head came up. Her eyes were shining with tears. "The war's over. You all won. And we lost. I have to get over it."

He wondered what she could have needed to get over. She would have been a child when the battle of Pea Ridge was fought. Probably like so many, she had lost a brother or a father. "I'll get some more pants," he offered. "The war's over. I don't need the uniform anymore."

She smiled a watery half smile. "If you're willing to do that, then I guess I can declare a truce. Pleased to meet you, Mr. Bradburn."

"York is good enough. In fact, I wish you would call me York. I'll call you Esther." He managed to smile. "I think we've come too far to go back to formalities."

She had a wild impulse to thrust out her hand, but somehow she could not bring herself to do that. Maybe later when she got used to the idea that she had hired a former enemy to take care of her father's hounds, she could shake his hand. Instead, she nodded. "You're right. Come and meet the pack."

Nine

Sleet pelted Esther's yellow slicker. Though she raised her shoulder against it, the stinging pellets struck her cheek and stung her eyes. She could feel them melting through the crocheted scarf wrapped around her head and throat.

Ahead of her, York trundled a wheelbarrow full of clean straw, the bedding for the last two hounds in the kennels. In a voice that carried the stern tone of command, he had ordered Esther back to the house. And in her own stubborn manner, she had continued to plod along behind him, opening the cages for him. His scowl was thunderous each time she held an animal that liked the weather no better than its mistress did and might be inclined to snap at a man it still considered a stranger.

Finally, when the last hound was bedded down and made as comfortable as possible against the freezing weather, Esther caught York's hand, and together they slipped and slid up the hill to the house.

With a cry of relief, Esther burst into the kitchen. The warmth from the cookstove enveloped her like a blanket. Not satisfied to wait, she pulled open the oven door and held out her gloved hands to the heat.

Behind her York halted, but she motioned him over. "Get good and warm," she advised him. "Pawpaw always said that the best way to keep from getting a bad cold was to get really warm."

"I don't need to get warm," her hired man protested. "I've got to go out in the cold again."

She swung around. "You'll do nothing of the sort. The sleet is already sticking. It's mixed with snow. You can't walk miles up the side of the mountain in this stuff. You'll never make it."

He shuffled his feet and scowled out the window. Under his blanket cape, he had to admit he was chilled to the bone, but he couldn't stay here. Not with her. He should have left the instant the first grains began to fall, but half the hounds would have been without bedding. They had picked the wrong day to change it.

"Come on." Esther moved to the sink. She pumped water into the coffeepot and added grounds. "Get up close to the oven," she urged. "You're probably colder than I was. And I was frozen."

With poor grace, he capitulated. His much worn military gauntlets were soaked through. When he pulled them off, his hands were blue and wrinkled. They would get a bad case of frostbite during a walk back to the cabin. He stretched them to the oven and set his teeth to keep from moaning.

Sensing that she had won the argument, Esther said no more. Instead, she set herself to stretching the meager supper she had planned. A pan of corn bread would make the beans go farther. She had plenty of bacon. Apples could be baked with the bread, and she had plenty of cream to pour over them.

At last, York closed the oven door and stepped back. He opened his mouth to protest, then closed it with a snap.

"I can make up the bed in Pawpaw's old room."

"No!" The word was uttered with more force than necessary.

She shrugged. "You don't want to sleep in the other bedroom. I'll make up a bed for you on the settee."

Again he shook his head. "I'll sleep on the floor in here."

She faced him, plainly annoyed. "If that'll make you feel better, you go right ahead. All the same, I might point out that since the bedrooms are also in the back of the house, the kitchen floor is closer to my bed than the settee in the living room."

He shot her an angry look. She was treading perilously close to saying what was better left unsaid, namely, that they were aware of each other. "I'm only thinking of you."

"I know you are, York, and I appreciate it. You've been a perfect gentleman and the best hired hand a woman could ever have, but tonight you can't help yourself. You're going to have to stay the night. Just forget that I'm a woman and relax."

He was in the act of unwrapping his scarf, so his face was hidden from her. When he pulled the material down, he had a suggestion of a smile on his face. "Esther Woodson is not a woman. Esther Woodson is a man." He looked her up and down in a manner that made her blush. "Have you ever tried to *forget* anything, Woody, my man? You can try to remember. But if you try to forget, you just naturally remember."

Chuckling, he shrugged out of his coat and hung it on a peg by the door. It seemed such a natural thing to do as if he belonged here. She grinned at his back. Her father would have liked him. Infrequently, she caught a glimpse of the man he once had been—a keen thinker with a sense of humor. She didn't doubt that she was bringing him around. To do so pleased her at the same time it made her uneasy.

She tried to push the dangerous feeling away. As he moved around the kitchen, scooping coffee beans from the sack, putting them in the grinder, she was becoming increasingly aware of how at home he seemed. And how attractive he was. His hands were so graceful, so sure of every movement.

York handed her the box of ground coffee before going back to the table and sitting down in the chair closest to the stove. The big kitchen suddenly seemed a bit crowded. Esther would have to pass within inches of him whenever she put anything on the stove. Her braid swung gently across her buttocks as she went about preparing corn bread. Unable to take his eyes off it, he shifted in his chair and crossed his legs. No doubt about it. In order to avoid the cold, he was going to have to endure the heat of a mighty uncomfortable night.

Pellets of ice sticking to his eyebrows and eyelashes, Cole Younger urged his horse abreast of Jesse's. "If you've got any kin in these parts, now's the time to trot 'em out."

Jesse nodded. The gang were freezing in their saddles. Between fits of coughing Frank rode hunched over in the saddle, his arms crossed over the horn. Instead of scabbing over and healing, his wound kept oozing. In his weakened condition, he was bound to catch pneumonia if they didn't find shelter.

Jesse turned in the saddle. The rest of his men, strung out on the trail, were not much better off than his brother. Snow and sleet lay thick on the brims of their hats and filled in their horses' prints as fast as they appeared. Cole was right.

It was a long shot. He wouldn't blame Esther if she shot him dead the minute she laid eyes on him. But maybe she'd take care of Frank. With a low but heartfelt curse, he headed for Cutter's Knob.

York lay on his back staring upward into the semidarkness. One arm was tucked beneath the feather pillow;

the other lay relaxed across his chest. The room was warm. The pallet, a feather mattress and a couple of thick winter quilts, was much more comfortable than the bunk on which he would have slept.

Except that he couldn't sleep. Above his head the kitchen clock ticked. On the half hour it chimed, and on the hour it struck. The sounds did not bother him. What bothered him was the presence of Esther Elizabeth Woodson. All evening long, he had watched her stoop and reach and toss her head as she prepared their simple supper. He had watched her braid twist and writhe like a live thing, the shape of her buttocks clearly displayed in a tight pair of what had once been her brother's overalls.

Worse, he knew how she looked in a nightgown and robe. He had seen her with that damnable braid coming loose around her shoulders. A man could lose his soul because of her hair. It must be a yard long. Or longer. He could bury his hands in it and pull her to him. He could hold her captive while he kissed her—

He groaned.

The clock struck two.

Spending the night had been a bad idea. He had known it. He had warned her. He should have walked right out of the door before she ever bent over to poke more wood into the old black stove. Hell! He should never have come in. Outside the pelting sleet had changed to shushing snow. An awful thought struck him. Suppose the snow were so deep that he couldn't get home tomorrow. Suppose he were trapped here for a day or two with her body just a few yards from him. He cursed himself to the warm darkness.

He could visualize her lying in her bed. Although he had never been in her bedroom, he could imagine how it would be. She loved and preserved old things. The bed would have come from Virginia. Or perhaps from England. It would be walnut or oak or cherry with a crocheted bedspread over handmade quilts. The mattress would be full of feathers. A man could bring a woman to ecstasy in comfort.

He rolled over and pulled the pillow over his head.

Much more of this and he'd have to go out and roll in the snow.

Esther kept time to the ticking of the clock on the nightstand. The snow filled the room with extraordinary light. Her bed was warm and, oh, so comfortable. As tired as she was, she should have been able to drift off to sleep. She certainly had worked hard enough.

But her hired hand had worked much harder than she. The difference between him and old Carly Ord was no surprise. What was different was the way he took more work than his share. Scowling blackly, he would gently move her aside and take over any task he deemed unsuitable for her. Indeed, he scowled so constantly that the expression no longer held any terrors. She wondered what he would do if she stuck her tongue out at him and then went over and hugged him. Would he smile, curving that usually stern mouth, and put his arms around her? How would her body react when the heat and hardness of his body was pressed to hers? She sighed in the darkness. He was becoming very familiar, almost necessary to her life.

She flounced over in bed so hard the ropes creaked. She should be ashamed of her thoughts. He was nothing but a hired hand. She paid him a tiny sum of money and fed him his lunch. He lived in a cabin in the mountains. Truth to tell, he was probably a little crazy from the war.

The thing never to be forgotten was that York Bradburn was the enemy. That her father, beaten and bloody, had been supported between two bluecoats while another slipped a noose around his neck and—

She moaned. If only she could go into the kitchen and fix herself some hot milk. Except the cause of all this sleeplessness lay on the floor. She should have insisted that he sleep on the settee. She turned over and snuggled down in her favorite position. She would do as her mother had instructed her to do to fall asleep. She would recite a few Bible verses. She would close her eyes and force her body to relax.

Forcing her body to relax, she realized, was like trying to forget. Force made the body tense, as trying to forget caused the mind to remember. She could see York smiling at his own joke. He had a nice smile. His teeth were even and white. So many men chewed tobacco or smoked pipes. Not only were their teeth an ugly brown, but the juice ran into the corners of their mouths and down the grooves to their chins as well.

York Bradburn was the most handsome man she had ever seen. In another day in another time, a young Esther Woodson would have fallen head over heels in love with him. She would have scandalized her mother and her dear father and probably flung herself at his head.

From the kitchen came the faintest chime of the kitchen clock. One— Two— She opened her mouth wide in an imitation of a yawn trying to fool her body into believing she was sleepy.

Someone banged on the front door. Not just a polite knock, it was the metallic thudding of a gunbutt. Esther bolted up in bed and reached for her robe. Fear shot through her, and then remembered horror all but paralyzed her. In just such a manner and on just such a night six years ago, Jesse James had pounded on the door.

Her father had let him in and—

At the kitchen door she met York. His hands closed over her shoulders. Without thought she put her palms against his chest and leaned against him, accepting his protection. His presence was warm and comforting. They stood together for a moment, adjusting to being roused from their beds, marshalling their forces.

"Expecting company?"

"No." She shook her head. She was shivering. Her teeth were chattering. "I don't know—"

"Have you got a gun?"

She nodded. Taking his hand, she led him into the living room. From the drawer in the library table, she handed him an old army pistol. "It's single-action," she whispered. "You have to pull the hammer back."

"I know," he replied dryly. He checked to see that it was loaded and then cocked it. "I had one of these."

"Sorry."

The pounding came again.

Esther whimpered. Terror poured ice into her veins, setting her to shivering. The Yankees had knocked on the door just like that, the night they had dragged her father out onto the porch. They hadn't left until he was swinging lifeless from a rafter.

And when she had tried to fight them, they had beaten her into unconsciousness. For years she had avoided men and hidden from any Yankee soldiers that chanced to ride through Cutter's Knob.

Now a Yankee stepped close and put his arm around her. He could feel her trembling and hear her teeth clicking despite her clenched jaw. He hugged her reassuringly, but he wasn't really aware of her. The old military readiness was returning. A certain calculating coldness was settling over his body. It left him unafraid, detached from his body, his spirit impervious to any form of shot and shell. If they came through the door shooting, he would kill them all. "Get away from me now," he whispered. "If they shoot, you might get hit by a stray bullet."

"What are we going to do?"

"Open it for them."

She shuddered, then reluctantly stepped forward. He caught her arm. His mouth brushed her ear.

"No, not like that. They'll be expecting that. They could shoot through the door." He took a step to the right. "Now. Down on your hands and knees. Crawl to the left side of the door. Left side. Left side. Not behind the door. Head down. Way down. That's right."

She was shaking like a leaf and so glad he was here. If not for him, she would have barged right up and opened the front door and made a perfect target for whoever waited there.

Neither one of them would be in the direct line of fire when the door opened. The pounding came again.

"Now, reach up and open it. Keep your head down as low as you can. When the door opens, fall flat on the floor."

She did as he ordered. The key was icy cold in her fingers and difficult to turn, but she managed it. Then the china knob. She pulled back until the door was free. Slowly it swung open.

"Esther—"

She recognized his voice. After all these years, she would have known it anywhere. Not given to profanity, she still let fly with a good one as she climbed to her feet. "God damn you, Jesse James. You scared us half to death with all that pounding."

The young outlaw lowered his gun. He called to the waiting riders. "Come on in, boys. We found the right place."

"No." Esther climbed to her feet and caught the door-jambs with both hands, barring his way. "You can't come in here. I won't have you. Never."

"Esther—" Jesse placed his icy glove over her hand and pried her fingers away from the door. "Frank's hurt, and we're about frozen." Still she resisted. "Esther, Clell's dead. He got shot down more than three years ago."

Jesse was going to come in. She looked into his diamond-hard eyes and knew that a protest was a waste of breath. She stepped back. "All right. But you leave just the minute this storm breaks."

Two of them came up on the porch, supporting Frank between them. A fourth took the reins and led their horses away in the direction of the stable.

"Howdy, Miss Esther." The biggest of them nodded familiarly. "It's mighty good of you to put us up. We wouldn't put you out, but we're about froze to our saddles."

Esther's voice fairly seethed with anger and resentment. "I'm a fool, Cole Younger. I should have shot Jesse and then you."

He chuckled and shook his head as he and his brother Jim helped Frank James onto the settee. Esther struck a match and lighted the ruby lamp. As she replaced the chimney and adjusted the wick, Jesse drew in a hissing breath. He had discovered the silent man with the business end of a Colt revolver trained on them. Cole and Jim spotted him at the same time. Instantly, they scrambled back into the shadows in different corners of the room, putting pieces of furniture between York and them.

Jesse's hand found his gunbutt, but he didn't draw. A wicked smile curled his mouth. "Who's your friend, Cousin Esther?"

Cold fear gripped Esther. Jesse was as dangerous as a poison rattlesnake. Many had not feared him because he was young and handsome and the son of a Methodist preacher. Many had suffered, and some had even died.

Not waiting for her answer, Jesse sauntered to the fireplace and bent to poke up the flames from the bank of coals. Beneath his black hat, his steel blue eyes never left the silent man who followed him with the barrel of the gun.

"Yellowleg!" As the fire blazed up, Jesse spat the word into it. In the semidarkness, the hammer on Cole's gun clicked back. Jesse started for his own gun. "What's he doing here?"

"Put it away, Cole! Leave him alone, Jesse!" Esther stepped in front of York. "He works for me. The war's over. Or hadn't you heard?"

Her cousin glared at her, his eyes hooded and as cold as death. "It's sure and certain over for Noah, ain't it?"

She sucked in her breath at her cousin's cruelty and gave back as good as she got. "And whose fault was that?"

"It sure wasn't mine. I didn't drag Cousin Noah out of his house and hang him from the rafters on the porch. And all because a bunch of Missouri boys hid out in his barn." Jesse looked over her shoulder at York. "Hear that, yellowleg? That's what you did to this girl's pappy."

Esther threw a glance over her shoulder. York's expression never changed. Likewise, the gun was steady as a rock. She knew a thrill of fear. Would he shoot through her to get to Jesse? Looking into the glinting eyes, she was sure that her cousin wouldn't hold his fire just because she was in the way.

And as for Cole Younger—the story was that he had once killed three Yankee prisoners with one bullet, he had tied them all together and fired one shot into them to test the power of a new rifle. Her legs were shaking so badly, she could hardly stand.

"I heard tell what they did to Cousin Esther, too," Jesse went on, each word erupting from his lips like the bullets from his gun. "They beat her until she was near dead and left her lying there underneath Noah's body." His blue eyes blinked furiously. "Whatever the hell me and the boys are, we don't make war on women and children."

They all stood frozen in silence. Each plunged back into his own private hell. Each one of them achingly young and forced to live beyond horrors.

Suddenly, Jesse smiled, completely transforming his face. Esther remembered that when her cousin smiled, he could charm the birds off the trees. His hand slipped off his gunbutt. In the shadows, Cole Younger eased his hammer down. Jesse knelt in front of Frank, who lay in a sort of stupor on the settee. "Hey. You're right. The war's over. Forgive and forget. Right?"

Slowly, she stepped back out of the line of fire. And as she did, three things happened simultaneously. The front door swung open and George White stomped into the middle of the scene. York swung halfway around to cover him, and Jesse James lunged past her and drove his head into the pit of York's belly. Esther screamed when Cole Younger grabbed her and dragged her into his corner out of the way.

Brother Jim stepped forward with practiced ease to finish the job Jesse had started. Drawing his pistol, he brought the long barrel crashing down on the side of York's head. The Yankee crumpled.

"Good job, Preacher," Jesse called to George. Climbing to his feet, he dusted his hands and strutted over to Esther.

She was so angry she could not speak. If York was badly hurt, she promised herself then and there to kill them all, one by one, starting with her cousins. Cole's big hands slowly released her arms. When Jesse came within arm's length, she swung at him with all her might. Her fist caught him on the point of the cheek, just below his eye.

He howled and staggered back.

Cole laughed and ducked as she swung round at him. "Hey, not me. Jim's the one who knocked out the yellowleg."

"You—you—" She could not think of anything bad

enough to call them. Her vocabulary of swear words was too limited.

Jesse had recovered and was scowling. Jim was laughing because Cole laughed, and the Preacher was looking from one to the other, trying to see the joke.

"Esther. Esther, gal." From the settee, Frank spoke, his hoarse voice deeper than usual. "I could sure use some hot coffee. If you wouldn't mind making us some, I'd be much obliged." When she hesitated, he held up a weak hand. "We don't aim to hurt nobody. On my honor." His words ended in a coughing fit.

Frank did look like death and sounded worse. Esther liked Frank well enough. He didn't frighten her as Jesse did. Esther patted him as she passed the settee and knelt beside York. His eyelids were already flickering as he tried to struggle back to consciousness. She lifted his head and felt the temple. A lump the size of a guinea egg stood out from it. From a scratch in the center of it a thin line of blood crept into his black hair. His hand twitched, and his body jerked as he tried to lift the gun.

She wanted to cry, to hug him to her breast, to curse her cousins and their kin.

Jim Younger stooped over her and retrieved the Colt from York's grasp. Barely twenty years old, he was sincerely sorry, not for hitting York, but for distressing her. "I didn't hit him real hard, Esther. He'll be all right in a few minutes. I wouldn't have hit him at all if I'd knowed he was somebody you was sweet on."

The gang with the exception of Frank hemmed her in. On her knees, she faced them with York's head in her lap. "Don't try to make me glad you're here. You're bad. All of you. You're bank robbers. You robbed a bank up in Missouri and the Neosho sheriff chased you into Arkansas."

"Now, Esther," Jesse began, "you know Confederate dollars ain't worth a Chinaman's whisker."

"You've had five years to earn Yankee dollars, Jesse James. Don't use that old excuse with me." She was so angry she was shaking. "You can't stay here. Not because I don't want you, but because everyone knows about you. People have been looking at me like I'm one of your gang for weeks. The local sheriff tried to push me around because you're my cousins."

She glanced down at York. His eyes were open. A deep line of pain creased his forehead, but she could feel the muscles tensing. She laid a restraining hand on his shoulder. "You're not welcome in Arkansas, boys. I know how you got shot, Frank. And you, Jim. Cole, is your ear notched permanently? But if I asked you to leave, you wouldn't."

They lounged around the room, sullen and guilty, but unmoving.

"So as long as you're here, I'll feed you, but you have to promise not to hurt York."

Like bullies in a school yard, they scowled at the Yankee. He pushed himself up on his elbows and put a hand to his temple. The blood was still sticky.

"Best stay down, yellowleg," Cole growled.

"He will not," Esther exclaimed. She climbed to her feet, assisted by Jim, who seemed truly contrite. In her turn, she helped York to his feet and supported him until he steadied. Male hostility filled the living room. Jesse was mad as hell, his eyes blinking furiously.

Frank spoke from the couch. "As long as you're up, why don't you go on in the kitchen, Esther. I'll be much obliged for anything you can spare. Just a cup of coffee'll do just fine."

She shot her older cousin a grateful look. "It may take a while to fix. The fire's probably out. Come with me, York."

"He stays in here," Jesse snarled.

"No." She kept her hand wrapped around York's arm. "He comes with me. I need him to help me."

"I'll be more than glad to help you." Cole came up on her other side, his big body so close she could feel how cold his clothing was.

"Let her alone," Frank commanded. Obviously in pain, he rolled his head on the back of the settee. "For God's sake. We're putting her out enough. Both of you settle down."

Chin up, she led York through them and into the kitchen, conscious that both Jesse and Cole were following her. Damn this bad weather. York would never have stayed over and been in such danger. Jesse and Frank would never have ridden in on her. She offered up a silent prayer that she could get through this night without someone getting killed.

Jesse took in the pallet on the floor. "Making yourself right to home, ain't you?"

Ignoring her cousin, Esther pushed York down on the chair and started her preparations. The coals still had enough fire to catch the new wood almost immediately. Coffee was boiling in quick time. Esther pulled out a tin of soda crackers. Prying the lid off a quart jar of tomatoes, she poured the contents into a bowl in front of the two men. "Help yourself."

"Not much for a hungry man, Esther." Jesse looked truly hurt.

"It'll hold you until I can get some stuff cooked. Why don't you two carry it in to Frank and Jim?"

Jesse exchanged glances with his cousin, who nodded. Cole picked up the things and walked out of the kitchen. Jesse dropped down at the table across from York. He regarded the other man through narrowed eyes as Esther began to prepare another meal.

* * *

Prowling through the pantry, Cole found the jugs that York had brought for Esther's Thanksgiving. With a triumphant laugh, he snatched them up and bore them out into the living room, pulling out one of the corncobs with his teeth.

Jesse hooted with pleasure as he pulled the jug out of Cole's hand and turned it up. "Man, oh, man. That's the real stuff. Where'd you get this, Cousin Esther?"

York was slumped on a rolled-up rug beside the fireplace. Alert to what the drinking signalled, he forced himself to sit up straight. Passing the jugs around amongst themselves, drinking his whiskey and brandy straight, the boys would be drunk in a hurry. They might all pass out, in which case, he and Esther would be safe for hours.

Unfortunately, their unwelcome guests might turn mean. Given the light in Jesse's wildly blinking eyes, he could well imagine the situation would get very nasty before too much longer.

Esther also saw the danger. She had refused to go to bed and leave York alone. "If you're going to drink, you have to get out of here," she called loudly. "None of my folk ever held with drinking, and yours didn't either. Frank, you're a good Methodist. Tell Cole Younger to put those jugs back where he found them."

Frank let the brandy run down his throat before he answered her. "This is just some medicine, Esther. Don't you worry none. Nothing's going to happen."

York motioned to her to sit down beside him.

Within half an hour Frank was asleep, and Jim and George were nodding where they sat. Only Jesse and Cole remained awake, passing the fiery whiskey back and forth between them—a pair of lobos, their eyes glowing in the firelight.

York's eyes burned from the shadows. Esther had given up to her exhaustion and nervousness so far as to rest against his side. At last her head tilted onto his shoulder, and her breathing evened out.

Jesse regarded the pair with speculative eyes. "Don't that look sweet, Cole?"

At twenty-seven, the oldest of the gang, Cole cast a bleary eye in their direction. "Sweet as a sugar tit." He slurred his words until the last syllable which dribbled off his chin. "Sweet as— Sweet as—"

"Where'd you get prime stuff like this?" Jesse pushed himself out of his chair and strutted over to stand before them.

"Quiet," York murmured. He should have shot Jesse the minute the outlaw identified himself. But hindsight was always perfect vision. "She's passed out. You've kept her up practically all night."

Esther jerked awake to see Jesse leering down at York. "How long you been playing house with her?"

York tensed, calculating his chances of jumping Jesse, wrestling the gun away from him, and shooting both him and Cole before Cole Younger drilled him and probably Esther, too. Reluctantly, he forced himself to relax. "I work for her," he said evenly. "The storm caught us unawares. She insisted that I stay the night rather than walking home after dark."

Jesse looked at Esther. "That true?"

"Yes."

"How long you worked for her?"

Esther bridled. She would take personal questions with implied scoldings from her mother, but her outlaw cousin was another matter. "That's none of your business, Jesse. What difference does it make what I do with the rest of my life? Since you and Clell Miller got through with my family, I don't have a shred of reputation left."

Jesse grimaced and strode back to the fire. Snatching up a jug, he drank liberally. Then he looked over his shoulder at her. "I guess I owe you for that, don't I?"

Esther pushed herself to her feet. Long suppressed rage roiled within her. Since Jesse had asked the question, she would give him the answer. "Yes, you do. And you'll never be able to pay me back for what you've taken from me. Never." Heedless of danger, she met him toe-to-toe. "That night with Clell Miller took every hope and dream that I ever had away from me and left me with a baby. When the Yankees killed Papa, I wish they'd killed me, too. My mother took the baby away, and she and my brother disowned me. No woman in this town will speak to me. I'll never have a husband or a family or—"

She choked. Anger, exhaustion, and years of suppressed grief clogged her throat and threatened to overflow her brimming eyes. She snapped her head away, hiding her face with her hand.

Jesse stepped back, his face blank. He reeled around searching for Cole, who shrugged. His eyes blinked furiously at one and then the other. He was breathing hard, a kind of wrath threatening to explode at any second. Then suddenly, he chuckled. He took another drink, then set the jug down with a thud. "Go get Preacher."

Esther snapped her head back around to stare at her cousin. What was going on in the twisted mind of Jesse Woodson James?

Cole rose with alcoholic dignity and paced out of the room. York braced his legs against the wall and pushed himself up. Before he'd let Esther be hurt further, he'd get her tormentor.

Esther stepped back to come between them. In a hoarse voice she asked, "What do you think you're going to do?"

"Do?" Jesse ran a hand over his shaggy brown locks. "Why, Cousin Esther, it may be five years too late, but I'm going to do what I should have done with you and Clell. I'm going to see that you and this yellowleg get married."

Ten

"You can't!" Esther's mind whirled.

"Don't see why not." Jesse lounged at his ease, grinning. "It's plain as pikestaff he's a-living here with you."

"He's not."

"I'm not." York's protest covered up hers. "Listen here—"

The Navy Colt with the double-action cap-and-ball seemed to appear magically in Jesse's hand. High color flooded his cheeks. He looked like a man ready to kill something. "I've listened, yellowleg. And I've seen. And I know what I know. You've been playing house with my cousin here, bringing her whiskey and sleeping over. She's out here all alone with no one to speak up for her."

"Jesse." Esther tried to get his attention, but he had made up his mind and saw clearly his course of action. Her father had been used to saying that no one was as bull-headed as a James.

Cole returned with "Preacher." George White yawned a face-splitting yawn and looked from one to the other.

"You're crazy." York put his arm around Esther and moved her firmly aside. "Your cousin was kind enough to give me a job. We've told you the truth."

"Listen to him, Jesse. He lives up on the mountain. He got me out of a tight spot one night when I was trailing some hounds."

Jesse was laughing now, almost hysterical with excitement. He waved the Colt in George's direction. "Hear that, Cole. They've been meeting up on the mountain. Just until he got up enough nerve to come down here and move in with her."

"Jesse! It wasn't like that." Esther wrung her hands. This couldn't be happening. It couldn't be. She must be lying in her bed dreaming every bit of this.

Ignoring her, Jesse motioned George forward. "Now listen here, both of you. George here is a Baptist preacher. He got the calling after the war. He preaches a real good sermon most Sundays."

"And robs banks on weekdays," Esther added, her words bitter with sarcasm.

"The Yankees robbed us," Jesse told her stubbornly. "We're just taking what's due us."

"That's a bunch of—"

York put his arms around her. "It's all right," he whispered in her ear. "It's all right. It's not legal."

"It's as legal as damn near anything else in this part of the country," Jesse averred. "How's about I get me a shotgun off of Jim's saddle? Will that make it legal enough for you?"

"I should have shot you on the porch, Jesse Woodson James." Esther sobbed.

York turned her head into his chest and smoothed her hair. To Jesse, he said, "Let's get on with it."

The outlaw grinned. "I always did like a man who stepped right up and took his medicine."

Esther's head was reeling. Keeping up with Jesse was like keeping up with a will-o'-the-wisp. He constantly changed shape. Now he was looking at York as if the enemy were his friend. "How can you even think about marrying me to a damn Yankee?"

The grin never faltered. "If you don't get along with him, I can always kill him and it's no great loss."

She stared into her cousin's face. He meant what he said.

York took her hand. "Go ahead with it, Preacher, or whatever you are. At least when we're married, she'll have someone to take care of her."

She whirled, trying to twist out of his grasp. "What are you talking about? You don't want to marry me. And I don't need anyone to take care of me."

He caught her other hand, so they were face-to-face. "Listen. I don't want to get married, but not because of you. I don't think I'm fit to marry, but as long as Jesse James is providing the preacher—" He nodded ironically to each in turn. "If I have to do it, then there's no one I'd rather marry than you."

George pulled a small, worn book from his vest pocket. "The Lord be with us and turn the light of His countenance upon us—" His voice was surprisingly deep. With the Good Book in his hand, George White was suddenly a different man. His body straightened. The travesty took on an air of dignity.

Esther smothered a sob as she looked down at her old faded robe. Beneath it her feet thrust out in two pairs of socks for warmth. Her hair had come loose from its night braid and hung over her shoulders. She had never really lost the dream of a white dress with a veil in church.

"Just a minute." York turned to face his bride. His face was stern. As if he knew what she was thinking, he pulled the lapels of the robe together so they were straight about her body. He smoothed her hair back from her temples and pushed it back over her shoulders where it hung behind her like a veil. "It will be all right," he assured her, "Everything will be all right."

Eyes stinging with tears, she faced the men. Jesse and Cole, Preacher White, and her former enemy and future husband the damn Yankee York Bradburn. "Bullies."

With terrible swiftness they were married.

Cole Younger passed the jug to York. "I ain't her cousin," he informed the Yankee, "but I've knowed her since she was little. She's a handful."

Furiously Esther snarled at the outlaw, who grinned as if she were a pet kitten that had spat at him. They were all grinning. Every last man jack of them was acting pleased with himself. Even York acted like it was the most natural thing in the world for outlaws to force decent people into marriage. He lifted the jug to his mouth. She saw his throat work.

Damn them! Damn them all!

No longer afraid of hell or the devil, she wrested her gun from Jesse's belt and brandished it round the room. They all fell back before her. "I'm going to bed," she announced. "Alone! All of you just stay away. The first one who sticks his head in my door gets it blown off."

She stomped out without waiting to hear their reaction.

Jesse went through the next day with a smile on his face. That night he pointed his gun at York and drove him into Esther's bedroom. "She ain't had nobody in five years, so take it kind of easy on her."

"You crazy son-of-a-bitch." York cursed him even in the face of the gun. "Do you think she's a whore who'll take just anybody? My God, man. She's a decent woman. I hardly know her. She hardly knows me."

Jesse laughed. "No better place to get to know a woman than in the bedroom. They go all soft and weepy. She's been alone so long, she's turning into a bitter old hag."

York pictured Esther's bright hair, her smooth, clear skin, her lush figure. He wondered what kind of women Jesse was used to that he could call Esther a hag.

Jesse heaved a sigh. "It's bad for a woman to be alone, 'specially after she's had a taste for it. Clell was a son-of-a-bitch. But he thought he was God's gift to women. I swear I didn't know what he was up to until it was too late. Then I beat him up."

"You should have killed him."

Jesse shrugged. "He was a good man otherwise." He dropped his hand to the Navy Colt. "Tell her I threatened to shoot you. That's what I'm doing right now. Tell her I was going to plug you dead center if you didn't get in there with her. I'm going to check on you later, so you'd better get the job done."

"You cold-hearted bastard."

Jesse nodded. "You just about got me pegged. Just make her come out with a smile on her face in the morning."

Esther lay stiff as a ramrod in the bed. With hands clenched in tight fists, she clutched the covers up to her chin.

"You needn't worry," York promised her. "I won't touch you. But I'd better get in bed. Your cousin is a very determined man." He lowered his suspenders and sat down on the edge of the bed to pull off his boots.

Esther clenched her teeth as the bed sagged under his weight. She felt her body tip slightly. Oh, this was going to be an effort.

Turning his back, York unbuttoned his shirt and then his pants. In one quick movement, he slipped beneath the covers. For the second time they were forced by circumstances to climb into bed together. The first time had been an act of nature. This time it was Jesse James

They lay side by side staring at the ceiling. The room was light as only a moon reflecting off clean, sparkling snow can make it.

Used to sleeping alone, she could feel him breathing, feel the warmth from his big body seeping between the sheets, creeping closer, enveloping her. It was delicious, and she hated him because it was.

He cleared his throat and put his hand up to his face to scratch his cheek. The scratching reminded her that she needed to scratch a much more intimate part of her anatomy. She squirmed in an effort to relieve the urge. The bed ropes creaked. Instantly, she was still.

He yawned and turned over on his side away from her. "Good night."

He had a good idea there. She turned over on her side away from him. "Good night."

The kitchen clock chimed faintly. Gradually, Esther began to relax. More than half-asleep, she burrowed more deeply into the covers. Her hips wiggled nearer to the source of warmth.

On his side of the bed, York lay conscious of his blood pumping, his breath a little faster than usual. When her hips touched his back, he tensed, listening. Her breathing was heavy and even. Reaching behind him, his hand slid over her body at the curve of her waist. To his despair, his fertile imagination filled in the rest of the details.

Keeping time with his imagination, his manhood hardened. He set his teeth to suppress the moan of desire so acute that it was pain in every muscle of his body. Cursing Jesse James, he thought of throwing himself out the window into a bank of snow.

So hot and raw was he that he would probably melt it.

Just then, his bed partner, his wife, sighed. Turning in her sleep, she pressed against him, clasping him with breasts and belly and warm thighs. Sound asleep she clung to his warmth, sinking deep and deeper into boneless peace.

He could turn and take her in her sleep. Even as the

tempting idea formed, it repulsed him. No matter how desperate his situation, he would not take a defenseless, unwilling woman.

But was she really unwilling? She was certainly hanging onto him as if he were her hope of heaven. She might protest as she opened her body to him. She might weep for form's sake afterward, but— He discarded those ideas, too. They were the common excuses all rapists made.

He set his teeth and pulled his hand away. She stirred and murmured something. He closed his eyes and listened for the clock.

As quickly as the snow had fallen, it began to melt. Warm Gulf winds, carried up the mighty Mississippi and the wild Arkansas, came blowing into the Ozarks two days later.

Frank James looked like a new man after almost forty-eight hours of sleep. Jesse and Cole had finished the jugs and recovered from their hangovers. With many thanks and a jaunty salute, the James gang galloped away.

Esther and York walked out to the runs. The hounds came out of their kennels shaking themselves and stretching. Almost all immediately flopped down sideways to the east and let their black saddles absorb the sun's rays.

York lifted his eyes to the mountain. "I guess I'd better go, too."

Esther said nothing.

"I can't come back."

She leaned over the fence. Teet rose to thrust his head under her hand. She stroked his ears in silence.

York felt a clenching in his gut. What a surprise to find that he didn't want to leave either the farm or her. Likewise, what a surprise to find that for almost three whole days without interruption, he had functioned as a human being! He should have had nightmares and cold sweats when faced with constant exposure to enemies like crazy Jesse and the ever-menacing Cole Younger.

Instead, he had remained in control. He had focused on protecting Esther and taking as much of the work off her as he could. He had brought in the wood to keep the fires going. He had helped her do the cooking and the endless dishwashing.

When Jesse had tried to give Esther money, she had thrown it in his face. York had met him outside and taken it and asked for more. Jesse had scowled before handing it over anyway.

"It's damned hard for her," York had explained bluntly. "She doesn't have anything except what little she makes from the hounds. It's taken a lot of what she can't afford to feed you Jayhawks."

Remembering the conversation, he shrugged. Jesse's money was in the kitchen drawer with the knives where she couldn't help but find it. Shoving his hands into his pockets, he started off.

He was off the property and on the lane when she came running over to him. "Wait," she panted. She caught up with him and floundered, her hand to her throat. "Come back, York. Come back tomorrow and work for me. We'll just forget what happened."

He looked at her sternly. "I can't forget what happened." He set his hands on her shoulders. "I'm not made of steel, Esther. I've slept in your house for four nights and in your bed for two. I haven't touched you in any way but as a brother or a father. I can't do that anymore. If I come back, then I make you my wife."

She shivered at the depths those words stirred in her. A slow flush stained her cheeks. She scanned his face, reading there all sorts of secrets and desires. So the fork in the road had been reached before she'd even had time to think or to analyze her feelings. Damn Jesse James! That was always the way in life.

Did she want York Bradburn? As a husband? She could have all of him, or she could have none of him. Winter stretched long and empty before her as it had done for the last five years. And no one was going to come riding up this road except her mother and her brother.

This man, this all-but-stranger, offered her so much she had never thought to have. He was handsome, well-educated, clean about his person. He had always treated her with unfailing politeness. He could give her children that she could rear for herself. She had little doubt that she could come to love him.

She rose on tiptoe and set her lips to his. "Come back early," she begged him. "We'll talk—before we go to bed."

His arms went round her, and he hugged her hard, kissing her again and again. She could believe that he was as starved for affection as she was, because she returned every kiss, met it, matched it. They stood in the middle of the snowy lane under a blue-gray sky for a long time.

"May I come in?"

Esther couldn't believe her eyes. She had answered the door to find her mother standing on the front porch. Rebecca Blessing looked more determined and at the same time less sure than when she had come to fetch Esther last month.

Esther's mind raced. Why had Rebecca come again? When Esther had ordered Daniel out of the house, she had half expected never to see either of them again. For just a second, she considered closing the door in Rebecca's face. Today of all days, she didn't want to think about her mother or anything connected with the church in Cutter's Knob.

After York had strode away promising to return and make her his wife, Esther had decided to cast all doubts about her shotgun marriage aside. The house was full of the scent of apple cobbler. As a sort of commitment to York, to begin as she meant to continue, Esther had decided to fix her very best supper.

The sight of her mother brought all the old shame flooding back. Every muscle tightened; her breath caught in her throat. Probably Daniel had come, too. Esther scanned the yard beyond her mother's shoulder.

"I came alone."

Although the last person she wanted to see was her mother, Southern laws of hospitality decreed that she be welcomed as any other traveller on a cold day. "All right."

In the living room the two women faced each other without allies and without the sentimentality of reunion and welcoming. An awkward silence fell between them. Esther was determined not to speak first. Rebecca had come knowing how her daughter must feel. Let Rebecca say what was on her mind.

Esther studied her. Rebecca wore a different coat from the one she had worn the month before. A navy blue wool duster, it fairly swept the floor. Instead of a bonnet, she wore a feminine version of the military Hardee hat, its black brim pinned up on one side, an ostrich plume curling back from her face. The hand she put out to Esther was gloved in butter-soft black kid.

With a surge of acute resentment, Esther realized the garments were more valuable than the sum total of her poor closet. She shifted her feet in their three-year-old boots. Beneath her worn overalls, her legs were encased in raggedy long johns. She had knitted her own sweater from gray wool unraveled from her father's sweater. It had a snag in the sleeve.

Rebecca made a move to unbutton her coat, then stopped. She shifted her feet beneath the marked scrutiny. "May I sit down?"

Still staring at the clothing, Esther motioned to her grandfather's chair beside the fireplace. "Of course. Would you like some tea?"

"Only if I can come in the kitchen while you make it."

Esther froze. The last thing she wanted was her mother gazing sharp-eyed around the kitchen. The empty jugs were still on the board. The plates and cups from the James gang's visit were still to put up. "The kitchen's a mess."

Rebecca slowly slipped out of her coat, revealing a navy gabardine suit ornamented elaborately with silk satin revers. She held the coat out to her daughter, who bent pointedly to poke up the fire. The sparks flew. When Esther finally straightened, she found her mother draping the coat over the back of the couch. Hiding her annoyance, Rebecca spread her mouth in a hearty smile. "Oh, I don't mind. I've seen messy kitchens before."

Esther straightened. "But not for a long time."

Nonplussed, Rebecca sat down and folded her gloved hands in an attitude of quiet resignation. "I suppose I don't need any tea." She reached out and patted the settee arranged at a right angle to the chair. "Do sit down, Esther Elizabeth, and don't spoil your pretty face with a scowl."

Mouth curving in exasperation, Esther sat down on the other end of the settee from her mother. "What brought you here, Mother? Why don't you say whatever is on your mind. The afternoon is wearing on. You don't want to be caught out on the road after dark."

Rebecca smiled her most loving pastoral smile. "I was hoping you'd come home with me."

Esther crossed her arms over her chest. "Why were you hoping that?"

"Because you would want to. After what I have to tell you." She drew in a deep breath. "The truth is I need you. I came to talk seriously to you. You have to come back. I need you beside me."

Esther ducked her head and pressed her hand hard to her forehead. She was going to have a headache before this visit was over. With regret she thought how excited she had been only a few minutes before. Orphans were really lucky folk. "Mother, I haven't changed my mind since November. I told you then I wouldn't be coming back."

"Your daughter needs you."

Guilt was a knife in the heart stabbing deep, but she rubbed her hand back across her slightly mussed hair and looked her mother squarely in the face. Tears stung her eyes and threatened to spill over, but she stubbornly dashed them away. "Then bring her to me."

The angelic mask slipped a little. Rebecca looked truly surprised that her daughter had made such a request. "Esther Elizabeth, that's just not possible."

"Why not?" The minute that she asked the question, Esther wished she had not. It opened the door to her mother dragging out all the old arguments of shame and scandal. "Never mind. Don't tell me."

Rebecca pursed her lips. "I'm sure you know all the reasons. If she came to you, she wouldn't be brought up in a decent home."

The words hurt, as Rebecca had intended. Esther rose and thrust her hands in her pockets. With the scuffed toe of her boot, she rubbed at a spot of soot on the hearth. "Then I don't see what you're here for except to hurt me. You've come before. You've sent Daniel. And

you've both hurt me by dangling my daughter in front
of me like a carrot. If you only knew how many times
I've dreamed about her, thought about her."

"And come to sit across the street to catch sight of
her," Rebecca said gently.

With those words Rebecca damned herself. Esther
could feel hot rage boiling up in her. Her hands came
out of her pockets in fists. "You knew? You knew!"

"Of course I knew." Rebecca reached out her gloved
hand. "Calm yourself, Esther. That's why I'm here."

The anger turned cold. Esther eyed her mother speculatively. "You need me for something. Or you need something from me."

"I only want to end this long exile and bring you
back."

"But why now?" Esther studied her mother's face carefully, but found nothing there to read. "Daniel told me
she's behaving very badly. He said you couldn't control
her. But I know that's not true. You can control anyone
you want to."

Rebecca drew back her hand and buried it in her lap.
Her smile dimmed. "Daniel said that."

"He did."

The smile returned full force. "Well, there you have
it. From your brother's own lips."

Esther shook her head. Sensing she was on the verge
of some discovery, she regarded her mother steadily.
"But that's not it."

"Your daughter needs you."

Esther walked away to the window. Pulling aside the
curtain, she looked out. The snow was almost gone, so
quickly had the weather changed. She let the curtain fall
back. Something dire had brought Rebecca here. She
needed Esther so badly that she offered Sarah as a sacrifice. "Sarah needed me desperately before she came to
think of you as her mother. Maybe when she was one or

two or even three, she might have loved and accepted me."

Esther choked, but swallowed and kept on. She shook her head. "But not now. Be honest, Mother. You told Sarah I was dead, didn't you? You've forbidden anyone to mention me, so she has no idea that I exist. If I came back with you today, you wouldn't want to tell Sarah that I was her mother. You might let me take care of her, like some sort of nurse, but you're her mother. Am I right?"

"Of course we would tell her you're her mother," Rebecca declared. Then when Esther's eyebrows rose, she shifted ground. "We wouldn't lie to the dear child. However, I do think that a period of getting to know you might be best before we told her."

"And then she could hate me because I hadn't been with her all these years." Esther knew she was right when her mother dropped her eyes and squirmed in the rocker. Exhausted with emotion, Esther leaned against the wall and moved the curtain aside again. She wished York were here. She wished she could see him coming up the road with his long, marching stride. She was very, very tired.

"Esther!" For the first time Rebecca's voice was sharp. "You must see reason. It's not proper for you to live out here any longer."

"It's never been proper, Mother." Esther thought she couldn't bear to look at the beautiful face again. She wished her mother would just quietly leave. "But it's too late for me to give it up now. Sarah, my dearest daughter, will have to grow up with you as her mother. Maybe she'll be luckier than I was. Surely, we won't have another war for a while."

Rebecca rose and clasped her hands in front of her. Her mouth set in a tight line. "Esther, those remarks show bitterness. We are supposed to forgive even our enemies."

"But not too soon." Esther had forgiven her enemy, but she was very sure that her mother would be shocked when she found out about the extent of her daughter's forgiveness. Another moment and her mother would begin to preach at her. She would not stand for it anymore. Esther dropped the curtain and walked to the door. "Mother, I'm going to have to ask you to leave."

Rebecca gasped. She did not exactly clutch her throat, but one hand pressed hard against her chest. Esther could imagine that her mother had never been asked to leave a place in her life. Rebecca was the one who ordered the comings and goings of her flock and of her family. Her face turned white and then red. "Esther Elizabeth Woodson! Are you dead to everything that is decent and good?"

Esther opened the door. The cold air rushed into the room. A feeling of frustration gripped her. Suppose her mother refused to leave. She could not take her by the shoulders and throw her out bodily.

"I'm sorry to ask you to leave, but—" one side of her mouth quirked in a wry smile— "you did come uninvited. And I've got supper to fix—for my husband."

The announcement staggered the older woman. She stumbled across the room to clasp Esther's shoulders. "Married?" she croaked. "Married! You!"

Once she had announced her marriage, she felt a flood of guilty joy. She had taken control of her life. For the first time in twenty-two years she had done something untinged by her mother's manipulation. She knew she was being petty, but the sight of her mother's face was rich reward. By that act she had gone beyond her mother's power. At that minute if Jesse James had been there, she would have thanked him. Reluctantly, of course, but she would have done it.

Rebecca's face looked positively haggard. "Who?"

"A man."

Rebecca slapped her daughter.

The slap was a match to the tinder. Esther caught her mother's wrist before she could raise it again. Whirling, she caught up Rebecca's beautiful coat from the settee and dragged her mother out onto the porch. "Go!" Esther flung the garment at her. "Put on your coat so you won't freeze and go. And don't come back."

Rebecca let it fall. Her face was ugly red. Her mouth was contorted. "Who is he?"

"If I told you his name, you wouldn't know it. It wouldn't mean anything to you because he's not from around here."

Rebecca's fingers curved like talons. Trampling on the coat, she reached for Esther again, but her daughter fended her off. "The James gang! Those robbing, thieving heathen have been through here, and you've married one of them. That Clell. The one who ruined you."

Esther shook her head. "He's dead, Mother. He died a long time ago."

Rebecca's eyes widened. "How did you know that?"

The cool lie flowed smoothly over her lips. "I read his name in the paper years ago."

Rebecca was practically frothing at the mouth. She brandished her fists in her daughter's face. "It's someone else in Jesse's gang. Is it that horrible Cole Younger? He's a murderer, a fornicator—"

"Leave." Esther backed toward the door. Her heel touched the threshold. "You can't do anything about it. I'm married. He's a good man." She sincerely hoped he was. "He works hard and he's well-spoken. He's handsome and kind. Very kind," she added. "He goes out of his way to help people. He's generous. He's brave. He wants to take care of me."

She had not realized until she began to enumerate his good qualities, how many York had. While she knew little if anything about his past or his family, she knew a great deal about him. From the moment he'd dropped down into that ravine to rescue her, he'd been showing her what kind of man he was.

She had a smile on her face by the time she had finished describing him, and her mother had calmed somewhat, although she wasn't pleased. "You've lost your mind," she accused. "You've lived out here by yourself until you don't know a good man."

Thoroughly disgusted, Esther turned on her heel and stalked back into the house, intending to leave her mother standing on the porch.

Rebecca refused to be left. Voice hoarse with rage, she followed on her daughter's heels. "I warn you. I don't intend to let this matter rest. You don't know what you're doing. He probably married you for your land. I knew I should have sold this place after your father was murdered."

Esther anchored herself to the door. "Goodbye, Mother. We've both said much too much."

Rebecca drew in a long, controlling breath and let it out slowly. Her voice sounded almost normal. "The sheriff will take care of this."

Esther froze.

Rebecca's smile was ugly. "Elmo Stamford will take care of him. He's kept an eye on everything for me. He'll take care of him."

A sharp rapping on the back door startled them both.

Eleven

York's smile disappeared when Esther opened the back door. He had never seen her look so drained. Even in his cabin, wracked by pain and at the mercy of a sinister-looking stranger, she had maintained her self-possession. Today that seemed to have deserted her utterly. Her face was so pale that he put his hand on her arm to steady her. "What's wrong?"

"Nothing. Everything."

Her enigmatic reply struck him hard. Had she changed her mind? He could feel his stomach knotting. He put down the two jugs he had brought back from the cabin. "What's happened?" When she hesitated, he reached out to take her hand. It was clammy. "Did Jesse come back?"

"No. Worse." Succumbing to the pull of his hand, she blundered down the steps and into his chest.

His arms closed round her, and for an instant he bore her whole weight. It alarmed him. "What's wrong? Are you sick?"

"No." Her voice was muffled. Her forehead rested for a moment against his collarbone. She was trembling.

"What's the problem?"

She raised her head and looked back over her shoulder. Before he could ask again, an older woman appeared in the open door, a woman who might have been an older version of Esther, except her face was twisted with malevolence. He knew in a minute that she must be his mother-in-law. And she was furious. Her striking blue eyes lanced at him and at Esther as well. York felt her animosity like a blow. He stiffened. His eyes narrowed, and his jaw set as his hands clutched protectively at Esther's back. He pressed his lips to his wife's hair. "Lucky I came back as soon as I could."

She looked up into his face. Her eyes were tear-filled. Her mouth trembled. "Yes."

The older woman posed like a statue of judgment in the doorway. Her icy stare looked him up and down, peeling the clothes off his body, peeling back the skin and layers of flesh. He had the feeling she was slicing him to death with her eyes.

Once upon a time he had known her kind well. In Philadelphia among his mother's friends were women who were the heart of the oldest families in America. They were the self-appointed guardians of heritage, the arbiters of taste and culture, the dictators of morality. They believed in a place for everyone and everyone in the place they had shoved him into. They expected perfection. When he had not returned with the proper triumphant attitude, when he had not behaved as he should, they ruthlessly and lovingly pointed out his deficiencies.

Esther turned within the circle of his arms. Her shoulder and hip pressed against him, her weight still partially supported by him. "Mother, may I present my husband, Captain York Bradburn?" She tilted her head back to look up into his face. "York, this is my mother, Rebecca Ruth Blessing."

"Mr. Bradburn." Rebecca's face might have been carved from stone by a sculptor who wanted to portray disapproval. The woman's expression was forbidding. *Take your hands off my daughter,* it seemed to say. Her eyes skimmed over him as critically as ever an officer inspected his command. Her mouth curled at the sight of the jugs with their corncob stoppers. The yellow stripe on his pants struck fire from her eyes.

"Mrs. Blessing." He was not surprised that she disapproved of him. She would not be a good mother if she were pleased that her daughter had married someone she had never met. Likewise, no woman wanted her daughter married to a man who brought in jugs of whiskey. And finally, he was a Yankee, one of the army who had hanged her husband, Esther's father, if he remembered Jesse James correctly.

No, he could not be angry at her for her antipathy toward him. But he was angry because she had upset his wife. His wife. How quickly the instincts of possession and protection had asserted themselves in him. Esther had brought him back to the world with a vengeance that was almost beyond belief. His blood was racing, his woman was safe in his arms, and he felt much like his old self.

He broke the contact with the older woman to glance down at Esther, willing his gaze to communicate his sympathy and support.

Like figures in a tableau they stood frozen, each uncertain how to begin, whom to attack and whom to defend.

Rebecca spoke first. "You were in the Yankee army, I see."

He nodded. "Yes, ma'am. Six years ago. A long time ago. I was wounded and didn't even make it through to the end."

Esther could feel herself relaxing slightly. Her mother hadn't actually charged down the steps and leaped for York's throat. She shifted her weight onto her own feet.

"You seem in good health now." Rebecca's tone was sneering, implying that his wound must have been of no consequence. "And what have you been doing in the last six years? Recovering?"

York gazed at her thoughtfully. If she had been sympathetic, he would have praised Esther to her. But this woman wasn't sympathetic. Bitterness fairly emanated from her.

When he did not speak, Rebecca's mouth tightened into a thin line. She had been given nothing to attack. "Esther! May I have a final word with you before I leave?"

York squeezed his wife's cold hand as Esther left the circle of his arms and mounted the back steps. Determined not to let her face this dragon alone, he followed her, keeping his hand in the small of her back.

At the door Rebecca tried to bar his way. "May I speak with my daughter alone?"

He didn't hesitate. He could imagine all sorts of hateful things she would say. Esther didn't need to face this harpy alone. "She's my wife. I think we both need to hear whatever advice you can give us."

His mother-in-law's lips thinned. Eyes blazing, she was forced to step aside and allow them to enter their own kitchen. In strained silence, Esther filled the teakettle and set it on the range. York took off his coat and faced his adversary.

To their surprise, she seemed to surrender. In a cool manner, she said her goodbyes, extorting a promise that they come to church soon. They followed her through to the front. There she flushed an angry red at the sight of her coat flung on the boards.

York stooped to pick it up and attempted to brush it off.

With poor grace she jerked it out of his hands. In haughty silence she tossed it on the seat of the buggy and climbed in. Without looking at either of them, she drove away.

"There goes the army in retreat," York murmured in Esther's ear.

"Unfortunately, she'll be back," came the low response.

"Big trouble?"

"I'm not sure. Some, but how much, I d-don't know." Esther had begun to tremble again. Her teeth were chattering by the time she got the last words out. He put his hands around her shoulders and guided her back into the house. Pushing her down on the settee, he threw another couple of logs on the fire.

"Relatives are the worst," he observed at last.

"My mother is worse than most."

He glanced at her. Silent tears were coursing down her cheeks. "Hey . . ."

"Never mind." She tried to fend him off, but he would not be deterred. He sat down beside her and put his arms around her. Giving comfort wasn't something he had thought of in a long time, but his wife needed help. He tipped her head onto his shoulder and held her while she wept softly.

At last, she gave him a watery smile as she counted her blessings. For the first time she did not have to endure the hurt alone. She allowed herself to snuggle against him with his warmth wrapped around her. She could feel his big hand slowly rubbing her back.

They held that pose for several minutes until the room began to warm. At last he pulled away. "I think I'd better get some new pants."

She chuckled. "I think you're right."

In the kitchen she set a cup of steaming hot chocolate in front of him.

He glanced up at her with a ghost of a smile. "Haven't we done this before?"

Managing her own faint smile, she went out onto the porch and returned with the jugs. Pulling the stopper from one, she poured a generous splash into his cup. "I believe so."

He warmed his hands around the cup as she poured whiskey into her own. They drank together. The warm, sweet drink slid smoothly down her throat. She could see why people came to like it.

"This is good," he murmured.

"Nothing like it." She drained the cup and waited. Gradually, the alcohol calmed her so she stopped shaking. "I'm sorry. My mother said terrible things to you."

"Actually, she didn't say much. And it was water off a duck's back, believe me. I've heard much, much worse. You wouldn't want to hear my father when he gets going."

"But there's no excuse for what she said. I'm truly sorry."

"I'm sorry, too. She must have really torn into you." His dark eyes were deeply sympathetic.

Feeling disgusted, Esther sank back, staring into the chocolate cup. "If you didn't already hate what Jesse made you do, you'll hate it now. You must think my whole family is bad."

He took another sip of his drink. "I don't think anything of the sort. Why don't we just forget the whole thing?"

She wished with all her heart they could. But Rebecca's threat had frightened her terribly. Elmo Stamford was a law unto himself. He liked to frighten and hurt people. She couldn't doubt that he could do almost anything to them, and no one in Cutter's Knob would say a word. "There's something you have to know."

He motioned her to take her seat across the table from him. She did so, feeling frightened. He was in danger for the second time from her family. She hated to tell him, but he reached out and nudged her hand. "Give me the bad news."

Esther could not meet his eyes. "She's been having me watched."

He grunted. "She's probably not the only one."

His lack of concern surprised her. "Why do you say that?"

"You're Jesse James's cousin. Everybody knows it. They also know he hides out with relatives. You've probably got every law officer in this corner of the state riding by every so often, not to mention bounty hunters and a Pinkerton man or two."

She couldn't believe her ears. She who had lived in virtual isolation for five years had been watched. "I haven't seen anybody."

"They've probably been around and spoken to you. Maybe they came to buy a dog or have you train one."

She slumped back in her chair, amazed, her mind remembering time after time when strange men had appeared out of nowhere. She had thought nothing of their questions, except sometimes to wonder at their ignorance about the hounds they seemed so interested in buying. "I can't believe it. Five years. You must be mistaken. They've wasted so much time."

The side of his mouth quirked up. "Maybe not. I think Jesse knew enough to stay away. He didn't bring his gang in until the worst night of the year. And then when the snow melted they left before dawn. He knew better than to ride in here on a bright warm day to stay a spell. He might have been shot off the front porch or on his way to the outhouse.

She reached for the jug again. It was enough to drive a woman to drink.

He grinned as he held out his cup for a refill. "What else did you want to tell me?"

"My mother. My mother is going to tell the sheriff. He's a horrible man. Everybody in the county is afraid of him." She started to tell York about the incident in town, but decided against doing so. He had stood up to Cole and Jesse for her. He had held her in the face of Mother's blackest looks. If he knew Elmo Stamford had grabbed her horse and pushed her against a building, he might be angry enough to do something dangerous.

She frowned, trying to pick her words carefully. "He'll do what she says. He might come out here. I don't know exactly what he could do. We're married after all. We're not doing anything wrong, and we're minding our own business."

York listened philosophically. If the man hadn't yet come galloping out to put him under arrest for assault, he probably wouldn't. Most small town sheriffs were unequipped to handle more than an occasional drunk on Saturday night, and Stamford wouldn't want anyone to know that York had thrown his gun away. Still, he didn't want to make light of the danger. "A lot of good people weren't doing anything wrong just before they got killed."

She closed her eyes, remembering her father's shock. As Jesse said, he was just letting some boys sleep in his barn. Jesse and the boys were much worse now, wanted everywhere, killers. If Elmo Stamford could prove they had spent the night here—

She heard the chair scrape back, heard York come around the table, felt his touch on her hair. Almost lazily, he closed his hand around the braid where it was thickest. Tugging on it gently, he tipped her head back and bent to kiss her lips. She opened her eyes.

"This was what first attracted me to you," he told her. "I'd hear you coming, and I'd run to see you. The hounds would run right by me. And I'd hide in the bushes and see you coming. You'd run on by and I'd see this—" he pulled it playfully — "bouncing and switching over your backside. I'd think that I couldn't stand to see anything so beautiful and not do something about it."

She shuddered. Hot liquid seemed to melt her bones. Her mouth opened. She wanted him to kiss her, invited him with her eyes, her mouth. Her hands clasped round the arm he braced on the table. The mixture of emotions she had endured for the past seventy-two hours had left her raw. And now she was hearing things no one had ever said to her before. She had never known such heat, such desire, as shot through her body now. She strained upward to meet his lips.

He put one arm across her back, the other under her knees, and swept her up in his arms. "I'm not sure I remember how to do this."

She shuddered with desire. One kiss and her body flamed response. "I never learned. Teach me."

In her virginal bedroom with its lace curtains and handmade quilts, they stripped off their clothing. She pushed aside the spread and pillows and then hesitated.

On the other side of the bed, York also hesitated. "Doubts?"

"Yes." She looked at him, embarrassed as he let his eyes roam over her. The gray light of late afternoon exposed her completely, all the secrets of her body that no man had ever seen before.

He had never seen skin so white, or hair so silvery gold. Her small nipples were pale pink. It took all his strength of will to step away from the bed.

"No. No." She put one knee on the mattress, reaching across to him. "The doubts are not what you think. I'm just afraid. I've never made love with any man but the one time. He was a boy, the same age as I was. Sixteen. It was pretty painful. But I've grown up a lot since then. And I've read a lot. I want you." Her voice quavered. "But I don't know what to do."

Her innocent confession aroused his protective instincts at the same time it enflamed him. While he ached to possess her, he would have to be extra careful. He would have to remember things he'd all but forgotten. The first step was the easiest. He smiled what he hoped was a reassuring smile. "Just lie down and relax."

She did so, closing her eyes tightly. She felt the bed give under his weight. Warm skin rubbed against her. His fingers touched her cheek.

"Don't close your eyes," he murmured. "The eyes are part of the senses, too. The fingers. The ears. The nose." He kissed each one in turn. "The tongue." He brought his lips down on hers and ran his tongue across her lips.

Clell had never said a word. He had moved silently and in darkness. He had been fast and rough and had hurt her badly. She shivered, not so much at York's sensual touch as at the sound of his voice. Clearly this was going to be different. She put her arms around his back.

He quivered and drew back. "Don't do that. I don't think I can stand that."

Instantly, she pulled them back above her head. "I'm sorry."

"Don't be." He kissed her again. "It's just that I haven't had a woman in a long time. A very long time for a man. It's hard to control myself. I know how beautiful you look to me, and I know how good you'll feel. It's hard to wait."

Her own eyes were liquid with desire. "Don't," she whispered. "Don't wait."

At her bidding, his hands began to move. They stroked down the undersides of her arms and across her white breasts. He had forgotten so much. The look of a woman's skin, the scent of her body, not completely disguised by perfumes.

A frisson of desire prickled the skin under his fingertips. Her body stiffened on the bed, her heels digging in, her chest arching as he circled her nipple with his fingers. Her eyes flew open.

He was smiling above her. "Is that good?"

Why did she feel like weeping as she stared at him? "Yes."

He kissed her nipple. Then his fingers continued down over her ribs, her belly, to the fine silver-blond curls.

She gasped and shrank back against the bed.

He smiled. "Don't be shy. Let me touch you there. You'll like it. I promise."

"But there?" she protested. Before she realized what had happened, he had slid down in the bed and pressed his mouth to her mound. She gasped and raised her head. "Are you sure you're supposed to do that?"

With his lips moving against her and his breath heating her, he asked, "Do you like the way I make you feel?"

She sighed. "Yes."

"Then I'm supposed to do that." His fingers gentle, he parted the soft hair, the fragile lips. The nerves throbbed in the soft folds of pink flesh. He touched it delicately with the tip of his tongue.

At the instant of contact, she cried out. Her whole body shuddered. Her knees contracted, pushing against his chest. But at the same time her hands grasped his head, pushing him down. His mouth laved her as she gasped and writhed.

The touch of his tongue was like pulling a trigger. She climaxed with a speed and intensity that astounded him. She had said she had been alone five years. He reveled in satisfying needs she did not know she had.

His own body was shuddering, ready to explode. He clenched his teeth. Hot blood pulsed through his entire length. Rearing up, he parted her, found her wet and hot.

Eyes wide and wary, she spread her legs wide. He

guided himself to her opening and slid in with one heart-stopping stroke.

She cried out with pleasure and surprise. Her thighs clamped his sides, her hot velvet sheath clutched him, and his climax began. With a groan he drove deeper and deeper. His head whirled; his heart and breath stopped together. He was nothing but his own force emptying himself into her body. He never even had a chance to pull back.

In the eye of the storm, he gathered her tightly in his arms and glued his mouth to hers. Her arms and legs closed round his shoulders and waist, locking him to her. From dreading another human being's touch, he had gone to wanting her to hold him forever.

They lay as one animal joined together, their breaths mingling. Then, slowly, she began to rock him in the cradle of her body. Her quiet breathing was a song in his ear. Her fingers skipped along the bones of his spine.

His muscles went limp; his very bones seemed formless. He felt so good. So good. Except that his eyes were burning. Suddenly, he realized why. He was weeping.

The last of the weak December light streamed in across their bodies. The gray hills beyond the window stood in clouds to their shoulders.

Esther woke to the touch of a man's hand. Her eyes opened lazily. She turned her head. Her silver-blond hair sifting from York's fingers made a veil between their bodies. As it fell to the bed, York's hand lifted it again and again, letting it fall between him and the light. He had never touched individual silk threads, but he imagined that they were rather like this.

"Are you hungry?" he asked suddenly.

"No." Hypnotized, she watched the fingers with their short-cut nails as they slid down between her legs and

trailed across her inner thigh. She sighed at the feel of
their rough, callused tips. Her hair rose on the back of
her neck at the exquisite delicacy of the sensations.

They were naked together. Wondering, she saw a man's
body in the light of day and saw her own body in a new
way. Colors were muted. Her eyes moved over fawn-
colored planes and hollows.

"Sure?" He rose and walked calmly across the room
to put more wood on the fire. He seemed not to care
that she could see his buttocks and thighs. She pushed
herself up on her elbows. Deep within, her own body
began to ache pleasurably with need. She felt a flush rise
in her cheeks. He was so nude, so hairy, so firm.

When he turned, his penis erected at the sight of her
breasts, their nipples hard and swollen. He needed her
again. Instantly. He padded toward her, his jaw set as he
struggled to control himself again.

For the first time, she noticed the mass of silver scars
on his shoulder. He had been wounded. And she must
kiss it and make it well. She welcomed him as he slid
beneath the covers.

The fingers of York's hand trembled ever so slightly.
Like feathers and like fire, his fingers traced the contour
of her cheekbone. With torturous slowness, they brushed
the velvety surface alongside her ear. Her eyes closed involuntarily as her whole being vibrated. Her teeth clicked
together in painful ecstasy.

"What are you doing?"

"Learning you," he murmured. "Learning what pleases
you. A good musician has to learn his instrument. A lover
has to learn his beloved."

While she could still think, she thought about what he
had said. Her own education had been much better than
most. She had read the Bible from cover to cover, including the "Song of Solomon." She had read all the
books on her father's shelf and the newspapers when she

could get them. The men she knew were almost without exception illiterate. Only her cousin Frank James actually read the classics and enjoyed them.

- This man was far superior to Frank. She wondered about him. Had he gone to the university? Had he studied for the law? For medicine?

All four fingers slid down the side of her neck to find the throbbing pulse beat while his thumb rubbed against her earlobe.

"You have a hole in your ear," he whispered.

"Yes. I have a hole in the other one, too."

He put his mouth to her earlobe and sucked on it. She twisted and raised her shoulder to push his mouth away.

"What happened to your jewelry?" he asked.

"I hid it. It's in a safe place."

He sent a shiver down her spine at the same time that her pulse leaped under his fingers. "Why don't you get it and put it on?"

"Now?" She didn't know whether she could get up in front of him. She was sure she couldn't stroll across the room the way he did and kneel before the cedar chest.

"Yes."

As if she were in a dream, she pushed back the covers and moved on tiptoe to the chest. Lifting the lid, she found herself kneeling as easily as she had knelt to pray and quickly found the box in the bottom. In it were her grandmother's gold hoops and garnet earbobs.

Gold or garnets? She chose the gold hoops. With trembling hands she used the mirror in the lid of the chest to insert them, and then she rose.

He was leaning up on his elbow, watching her, a smile of pleasure on his face. His eyes dwelt on and caressed what had been the high firm breasts, the slight rounding of her belly with its silver markings where the baby had stretched her. Beneath it her legs were long and power-

ful. Her strength made their lovemaking unique. He
pulled her in and gathered the cover around them. His
lips found the gold ring and tugged at it gently.

She lay on her back, her head on his arm, his warmth
enveloping her. The words of King Solomon to his beloved echoed in her mind. *Behold thou art fair, my love.*
And the bride's answer. *I am my beloved's; and his desire is
toward me.* Her breath sighed out between her clenched
teeth as she realized dimly that she had been holding it.
"Do you care about me?"

He was silent. She heard him draw a deep breath that
shuddered as he inhaled.

She clutched the edge of the covers and stared at the
ceiling. "I haven't the right to ask that question," she
admitted distantly, "but I'd like to know where I stand.
An honest answer might hurt a little now, but a dishonest
one will hurt terribly in the long run."

He left off his kissing and rolled onto his back. Though
his arm still bore her weight, the covering warmth had
gone. "I wish I could say yes, but I don't know myself.
The way I feel right now is not the way I've been feeling
for the last few years. All I can say is that I want to love
you. But I can't make a declaration yet. Do you mind?"

"I don't mind. I don't mind at all." She rolled over
on her side. Her eyes searched his closed face, trying to
read its terrible secrets. She put her mouth to the scarred
shoulder beneath his cheek. The glimpse of hell she saw
in his scars was only the tiniest part of what he had lived
through. Would he be able to tell her more? And was
she strong enough to hear it?

His eyes closed. He controlled his breathing with difficulty.

A wave of tenderness swept her, to be overwhelmed by
another of uncontrollable desire. Too long alone, too
torn with her own guilt, the lovemaking had released
her. Suddenly, she felt she balanced on the razor's edge

of hysteria. In a roil of emotions she began to kiss and
caress him. Her lips and teeth and tongue caressed his
throat on their way to his nipple.

It was his turn to gasp. He raised his head and turned
her face back up to his. In it he read the desire—the
flushed cheeks and the liquid eyes, the trembling mouth.
He groaned helplessly. "We may have to feed the hounds
in the dark."

Slowly, they strolled back up the path, stopping at
cages as they went. The night was unusually warm for
December. The moon bright. The shortest day of the
year was almost upon them.

The hounds were eating now, wolfing their food. They
paid no attention to their mistress.

Only Teet met them and leaned against the heavy wire.
Esther reached over the top of his run and rubbed his
ears. The big hound crooned softly. His tongue lolled
out, and he licked the back of her hand just once.

"Parents never leave off giving advice," York observed.
"Everybody's parents are about the same."

"This is much worse than that. Much, much worse. My
mother doesn't even try to give advice. She just does
what she thinks is best for me." The thought of Elmo
Stamford riding by her place every so often made her
so angry she wanted to kick and break things. Unable to
do that, she could not get control of her tears. All that
loving in the afternoon must have made her weak. Impatiently, she scrubbed the sleeve of her jacket across her
eyes. "Damn! Damn! Damn!"

He patted her shoulder reassuringly. "Let it all out."
She turned into his arms.

With only an infinitesimal pause, his patting continued. The top of her head ducked under his chin as she
tried to hide the tears that would not stop. Her familiar

scent filled his head. He liked the idea that he would live with this scent for the rest of his life.

Her hands were tight fists curled under her chin as the sobs grew heavier.

She was breaking down completely in his arms. Letting go. Terrible pain flowed out of her. That he could empathize with. He could feel it. He pressed his cheek—and then his mouth—against the top of her hair.

"Come on," he whispered. "Let's get you back to the house."

The sobs were unceasing, as if they had been dammed inside of her for years. She couldn't answer him. He felt her head nod slightly against his neck.

Gently, he turned her and helped her to stumble up the hill.

Once inside the house, he guided her to a chair and pulled one opposite her. Dropping into it, he sat holding her hands.

The minutes rolled by on the small digital clock above the sink.

Finally, she shuddered once and pulled her hand away to reach in her pocket for a handkerchief. "Sorry," she mumbled.

"It's all right."

"I couldn't bear it a minute longer. I just couldn't." She dabbed at her eyes and wiped her nose.

"There's no way to fight them," he said. "Whatever they do is always for your own good or with your best interests at heart." He could not keep the bitterness from his voice.

She smiled a watery smile. "They're so sure."

He rose and fetched her another handkerchief. "Nothing can be worth those tears."

She tossed back her braid. "You don't know."

"I know pain and frustration."

"But you haven't committed mortal sins," she whispered.

His eyes darkened; his hands clenched. His voice was just as soft as hers when he said, "Oh, but I have."

Their eyes locked, the pain leaping between them. She reached for him, and he caught her hands and drew her up into his arms. They clung together, his arms hugging her until he could feel her heart beating through the layers of cotton and wool.

They were two gently bred people whom circumstances had turned into orphans of the war. Still they did not dare to speak, did not dare to share their secrets. For the moment they took comfort in the warm presence of someone to share their pain.

"Rest," he whispered. "Rest. Tomorrow we'll go into town and face these people and get it over with." As he spoke, he thought of the night he had met the sheriff of Cutter's Knob. He wasn't looking forward to their next meeting, but it had to happen. He was Esther's husband now. He kissed her smooth forehead. "It'll be the beginning of the rest of our lives."

Twelve

The wagon had passed the farm's eastern boundary line when they heard a horseman coming up fast behind them. York looked over his shoulder in time to see the big man on the Roman-nosed gelding pulling alongside the wagon.

Esther sucked in a frightened breath. "It's the sheriff."

York felt a prickling up his spine and considered whipping up the horses.

"Pull up there!" Stamford bellowed.

York shrugged. To drive on was foolish. They would have to stop when they rolled into Cutter's Knob. And then the sheriff would deliver his message on the streets. Perhaps that might be the best place, but York doubted that Stamford would tone it down or soften his words.

The road was a little wider in front of Bas Boscomb's place. There York pulled the team to a halt and looped the reins around the brake.

Stamford sawed on his reins. The gelding sidled and backed but finally stood for its rider to climb down. The sheriff's face was red from the wind and from his exertions. He was not a good rider. Galloping a horse hurt his innards and made him walk spraddle-legged for a week. Consequently, he was furious when he stepped down out of the saddle.

His temper did not improve when he looked up into the face of the wagon driver and recognized the man who had thrown his pistol away. His red face turned puce. "You!" he thundered. "Get the hell down here."

As York started to obey, Esther grabbed her husband's arm. "Don't do it. Stay up here with me."

Stamford's goggle eyes rolled in her direction. "You stay out of this, Esther, or you'll get more than you bargained for. You've still got a lesson coming to you. Remember. I'm just doing my duty as sheriff of this county."

York regarded him steadily. He knew the type. Stamford was like at least half the sergeants he had known. Petty tyrants. Bullies. And big and beefy enough to enforce their tyranny with fists. He heaved a sigh. He did not want to fight in front of Esther.

Stamford caught him with one foot on the wheel and the other in the wagon. He pitched to the ground, barely managing to turn his body. Instead of his face, he lit in the muddy ditch on his shoulder.

"Damn you!" Her husband—hers!—had been attacked. Red fury blinded Esther. She threw herself out of the wagon, clawing for Stamford's face. Her upper body slammed into his chest. Her nails raked his cheeks. Howling, he toppled backward into the ditch.

Besides a couple of inches of slushy water, the sides of the ditch were slippery from the thaw runoff. Stamford's feet were still in the roadbed. His hands could not get a hold in the greasy clay. But what kept him howling was Esther, who sat on his chest, beating him with her fists and yelling.

York pushed himself back and climbed to his feet. He could not keep from grinning as he lifted his wife off the sheriff.

"Are you all right?" she cried, when he had set her on her feet. She threw her arms around him. "Oh, York, are you all right?"

Even knowing that they were in serious trouble could not suppress the warm feelings of something very like

happiness that coursed through him as he held her. She
pulled a handkerchief from her pocket and tried to mop
the mud from his face. She felt his shoulder where he
had fallen. "Does this hurt? Does this?"

In the meantime Elmo Stamford managed to roll over
in the ditch and climb to his feet. His whole backside
was soaked and covered with mud. Even his face was
splattered. Esther had knocked his hat off. The brim dab-
bled in the water. His face was white with rage.

He would have been a joke if he had not been as
angry as a razorback and twice as dangerous. He drew
his gun, an ancient Savage Navy revolver, and aimed it
straight at Esther's back. Without thought York hauled
her up against him and swung around, presenting his
back and shielding her with his own body.

She screamed and began to struggle. "Don't shoot!
Don't shoot. My mother never told you to shoot anybody!
Don't shoot!"

Behind him York heard the hammer click back on the
single-action revolver. He swallowed and braced himself—

The click came again. The sheriff had pulled the trigger, and the ancient weapon had misfired. While Stamford cursed and fumbled, York pushed Esther back
against the side of the wagon and spun. Diving beneath
the gun, he drove his shoulder into the man's paunch
and sent him flying back into the ditch.

The sheriff howled as if he were dying. The explosion
of his revolver drowned out his cry and echoed off the
mountains. Esther screamed again. "Run! Run, York!"

The sheriff floundered in the ditch, trying to train his
pistol on them.

"What's a-goin' on here?"

Stamford threw a look over his shoulder. Bas Boscomb
came loping down the hill from his house. He looked

harmless enough except for the double-barrel shotgun cradled in the crook of his arm.

"Shoot him!" the sheriff bawled. "Shoot the gol-darned son-of-a-bitch!"

York put his hands on Esther's waist and lifted her bodily into the wagon.

"No. No. Put me down."

"Get out of here." He pulled the reins free of the brake.

"Hold your horses, young fella," Boscomb called.

The sheriff was on his knees cursing. He had dunked his gun in the ditch water and now his powder was wet. He clicked it and clicked it again futilely. "Shoot him, damn you."

"Don't see no reason to do that," Boscomb replied laconically. "He ain't doing nothin', and she ain't goin' nowheres without him."

Stamford pulled his portly body upright and stood swaying, his face so red that Esther wondered fleetingly if he would burst a blood vessel and fall over dead. "He's under arrest," the sheriff yelled. "He resisted arrest. Shoot him."

"Didn't do no such thing," Boscomb contradicted. "I seen the whole thing. He was gettin' down from the wagon. She's the one who jumped you and knocked you in the ditch." He cocked his eye up at Esther standing in the wagon box, the whip in her hand. "Mornin', Esther."

"Bas, I could hug you, but I'm so dirty you wouldn't want me."

He grinned, showing a couple of missing spaces between his teeth. "Well, I'll just wait on that until you get all cleaned up. But I'm holdin' you to it."

Stamford's legs were too short and his body too heavy to allow him to leap the ditch and get back on the road-bed. He was forced to wade across, slipping and cursing, face purple with humiliation. "This man's a criminal. I'll arrest you, too, Boscomb. You're helping him escape."

Boscomb winked at Esther. "Say, that sounds like a good idee. Whyn't you climb up there by her, young fella, and go on to town. The sheriff's goin' up to the house with me and get cleaned up and get his temper cooled down." When the man continued to curse, Boscomb cocked a disapproving eye. "Maybe Maybelle'll fix y' a cuppa coffee if y' sweeten up that talk."

York glanced up at Esther, who nodded and held out her hand. He tipped his hat to their neighbor. "Much obliged."

Leaving the sheriff fairly dancing up and down with rage, they drove away.

Esther felt decidedly uncomfortable as the wagon rumbled down the dusty street. In her imagination she could hear buzzing and humming coming from behind every window they drove past. The people of Cutter's Knob were looking at her. Shameless hussy. Fallen woman. Blot on the face of town. She and a man—a Yankee—bold as brass—daring to show their faces. She could imagine the citizens who had shunned her for five long years pointing at the yellow stripe running down York's pant leg and hissing.

Her cheeks were burning and her palms were damp when York hitched the team to the rail in front of Carolan's general store. He held up his hands to her, but instead of letting him lift her down, Esther put her hand in his, climbed out onto the wheel and jumped down like a man. "You don't have to treat me so carefully," she told him. She hated that her voice quavered. "I've taken care of myself for a long time."

He looked at her sharply and squeezed her hand before he let it go. "I know. That's why you need a bit of spoiling. Don't worry. It'll be all right."

Together they entered the store. Bertha Carolan and her two customers stopped talking to gape. As Esther led York toward the dry goods table, the ladies could clearly see the yellow stripe on his pants. At the back of the store, the spit-and-whittle oldsters one by one turned their white heads to stare.

Ed Carolan, the storekeeper, exchanged a tight look with his wife before he hurried out from behind the grocery counter. Once in the aisle, he swelled out his chest and hooked his thumbs in his waistband. "We don't have anything to sell to a Yankee."

"But you sell to me," Esther said smoothly, "and I'm the one who's buying. We need a pair of pants." She looked at York. "No, two. One for work and one for dress."

"One's enough," he told her under his breath.

"And a couple of shirts." Playing like she hadn't heard him, she smiled at Ed. "And then we'll fill the grocery list. And we need a few other things. We might have to spend about five dollars in here."

"Five dollars?" Carolan glanced at his wife, who stopped her head in midshake.

York tried again. "I don't need so much, Esther."

"I guess all them clothes would come nigh to five dollars." The storekeeper nodded. With a pleading glance at his wife, he led the way back to dry goods. Her eyes widened even as an angry flush stained her cheeks. Oh, how she hated to sell to them. Her mouth pinched tight as a penny purse, she waved them past her.

"By the way, Mr. Carolan, I'd like you to meet my husband, York Bradburn. York, this is Ed Carolan He's owned this general store since before the war. He knew my daddy. Didn't you, Mr. Carolan?"

"Husband!" Carolan blinked. "Did you say 'husband'?"

"Pleased to meet you." York thrust out his hand.

The rumble and scratch of ancient men's voices came from around the potbellied stove. At the dry goods table, the ladies gasped and whispered. The storekeeper looked uncomfortably across at his wife. Her face was nearly purple with suppressed emotion, but five dollars was five dollars. Sometimes they didn't take in that much all week. "Mr. Bradburn."

The men shook hands stiffly and got down to the business of selecting York's clothes.

Her part done, Esther wandered down the aisle, aware of the hostile silence of the three women. She had reached the last glass case in the row when the doorbell jingled. Bertha left her customers to greet the newcomer. "Land's sakes," she exclaimed. "What are you doing here?"

The newcomer made no answer. Paying no attention, Esther stooped to peer through the glass at a small tray of men's pocket watches.

"Are you my mother?"

The voice was high and piping—and angry.

Esther's heart missed a beat, then pounded so hard it shook her chest. She whirled around and steadied herself on the edge of the case. Staring up at her was a skinny little girl with long cornsilk hair, straight as a string and hanging in her eyes. Between the strands of hair, dark brown eyes shone bright and accusing. "Are you my mother?"

Esther felt a knife twist in her stomach. "I—" Her voice failed her. She cleared her throat before she tried again. "I guess I am. Are you Sarah Susannah Blessing?"

"No one calls me Sarah Susannah," the little girl stated flatly. "I'm Sarysue Woodson. And I'm a female bastard 'cause you didn't marry my paw."

"Dear Lord." Esther went down on her knees in front of the child. "What are you saying?"

"Just what everybody else says," came the rejoinder. "Except they don't say it where Grandmother can hear them. She'd be mad as fire."

Esther put out her hand.

Bertha Carolan came down the aisle. "Sarysue, you'd better scat."

"No." The look Esther threw at the storekeeper's wife could have consumed her where she stood. "Sarah, I—" She couldn't think of anything to say. Her eyes drank in the thin neck and the thin little hands. Sarah wore a badly damaged sky blue wool coat, with a matching silk velvet collar and cuffs. Velvet trimmed the pocket, too, but it hung down in a corner tear. Food spots left a trail down the front, and the hem was muddy. One of her white cotton stockings sagged over the top of her high-button shoes. The other stocking was out at the knee. Both knees were scabbed.

Sarah might have been a poor child who had been clothed out of the church ragbag except that the garments were very expensive and fit her perfectly.

"What're you staring at?" Sarah put her hands on her hips. "It's not nice to stare. In fact, it's rude. I tell everybody that, but they do it anyway."

Esther's body sagged until she was sitting on her heels. "Do they stare at you often?"

"All the time. All the kids do. And they whisper. That's rude, too." She tossed her head, and the straight, flyaway hair went in every direction. When some of it strung down in front of her face, she stuck out her lower lip and blew upward. The hair lifted but fell back.

Esther reached out for it, but her daughter stepped back.

"She stares," she announced loudly, jerking her head

in Bertha Carolan's direction. "And she whispers. And she looks at me like I've got something wrong with me."

Esther vowed then and there never to give Bertha Carolan another penny's worth of business. If they had to drive clear to Springdale for their clothing and extra groceries, they would just have to make the trip.

Sarah was interested in something more than the shopkeeper's wife. "Do you live out on the edge of town with Jesse James?"

Esther rose to her feet and glared at Bertha, who retreated hastily. "No. I do not. Jesse James was your grandfather's sister's son, so he and I are cousins; but he lives in Missouri."

"He robs banks," Sarah informed her. Then she raised her voice defiantly. Her eyes sparked fire. "When I grow up, I'm going to be bad like Jesse. I'll be even worse than Jesse."

Esther could feel tears burning her eyes. They were overflowing, and she couldn't stop them. She could think of nothing to say to this angry little girl. And she needed to say so many things. "I don't think I'd want to be like Jesse. He steals money that other people have worked very hard to save." She was striving to sound off-handed. "I happen to know that Jesse has a very hard life. He's hunted and shot at. Sometimes he's wounded and hurt. Someday he'll be killed."

"What're you crying for?"

Esther dropped to her knees again. She was trying so hard not to get upset, but the pain was so terrible. "I'm crying because I love you. I've loved you since you were a baby. And I've never seen you. And you're so beautiful."

The little girl stared at her. Her scowl was monstrous. "I'm not beautiful."

Esther shook her. "You're very, very beautiful."

Sarah stuck out her lower lip and blew the hair out of

her eyes. "Grandmother says I'm beautiful, but Daniel says pretty is as pretty does. And since I'm bad and getting badder, I'm the ugliest girl in this town. I may be uglier than some of the boys. But they're awful bad."

"Esther."

York's voice reminded her of where they were. "Here, York." She smiled through her tears. "I'd like you to meet someone," she said to Sarah.

"Who?"

"Here he comes."

"What do you think of the way these fit?" York came down the aisle with Ed Carolan following, a tape measure round his neck. Both men stopped at the sight of the two. The storekeeper gaped, then cast frantic eyes at his wife, who shrugged as if to say she had nothing to do with this. York came to stand beside Esther and rest his hand on her shoulder. As he loomed over her, Sarah backed away until the doorknob prodded her in the back.

York's voice was soft. "Is this someone special, Esther?"

"Yes, York, this is my daughter Sarah. She's been living with her grandmother."

The little girl looked at them both. Her face twisted as if she might cry, but she didn't. Instead, she stuck out her tongue and screamed. Then she flung herself out of the door and ran screaming down the street.

Esther burst into tears, and York pulled her up and hid her face against his chest.

"That child," Ed Carolan said. "She's a slap in the face of everything that's decent in this town."

Esther rounded on him, her own scream not unlike Sarah's. "She is not! I'm the one! I'm the one! I—"

York hauled her in again and held her while she sobbed helplessly.

The storekeeper, with the danger of five dollars disappearing out the door, hastened to send his wife to the

back of the store to make a cup of tea. He motioned to
York to guide Esther to the curtained alcove his customers used to try on his clothing. He brought a chair for
her to sit down in. Then he left them alone while he
wrapped up the packages and filled the rest of Esther's
shopping list.

When his wife made the tea, he brought it to Esther
himself.

Esther could feel herself calming down. The tears were
gone; the cold truth remained. York had his arms crossed
over his chest, waiting patiently, his handsome face im-
passive. She stared at the cup of steaming tea, not wanting it, yet knowing that she needed something to put a
little heart in her. "That was my daughter."

"Yes, sweetheart. She looks just like you."

She snapped her head up. "Do you think so? Oh, do
you?"

"Peas in a pod."

"She's mortally unhappy." Esther looked hopelessly at
the tea, then set it on the floor. "She wants to be like
Jesse James."

York rolled his eyes. "Don't you people have anything
else to talk about? There's a whole country full of people,
and all I've heard since I came down off the mountain
is Jesse James."

Esther did not answer. She kept thinking of the things
Sarah had said. The words "female bastard" dinned in
her ears. The magnitude of her sin bore down upon her.
She had to get this child away from her grandmother
and protect her from the yammering tongues of the
townspeople. The tears threatened to start again. She
tilted her head back and kept them from spilling over.

York squatted down in front of her. "What do you want
to do now?"

She shook her head. "I can't think. Let's pay and go
home. I want my daughter. Now that I'm married, I think

I can get her. My brother Daniel doesn't want her around anymore. Maybe he can help me. But I'll have to think about exactly what to say and how to say it."

He picked up the tea. "Drink this. Even if you don't want it, drink it anyway. It'll get you warmed up a little for the drive home."

In the street outside, Elmo Stamford was waiting for them when they started for the wagon. The mud had caked and begun to crumble off his clothing; but his face was still smeared, and his hands were filthy. Men came out of the feed store two doors down and leaned out of the porch of the boardinghouse. One man came out of the door of the courthouse and walked out into the street.

The sheriff looked around him and pitched his voice so everyone could hear. "Jesse James's been spotted in the neighborhood. He and his brother and Cole Younger robbed a bank over in Missouri and got chased into Arkansas. He wouldn't've come here except that he's got kin where he can hide out."

York took Esther by the arm. "Climb in."

"I'm thinkin' that I got me one of the James gang right here in the street." He looked around him, trying to gauge the attitude of the listeners. "I'm thinkin' that this here fella that she *says* she's married is the fella she's been messin' round with all these years."

"No." Esther pulled her arm out of York's grasp. "He's got nothing to do with the James gang. I haven't seen Jesse in years."

York caught up to her. "Get in the wagon. He's not going to do anything."

Esther looked around her. Ed Carolan had come out on the porch of his store with their packages. As if nothing out of the ordinary were happening, he loaded them in the back of the wagon. Then he came up to York and held out his hand. "Mighty glad to make your acquaintance, Mr. Bradburn. Esther's *husband*"—he raised his voice—"is always welcome here." Leaning forward, he lowered his voice. "Come in soon and often. We'll talk about opening an account."

York shook his hand. "Much obliged." He took his wife's arm. "We'd better get started, Esther. It's getting late."

He helped her into the wagon and climbed in beside her. Slapping the reins on the horses' backs, he drove out of town past the silent men.

"How far away does my mother live, Daniel?"

Daniel looked speculatively at his niece. "Quite a ride."

The little girl sat on the floor tearing a doll's dress to rags. It was practically a new doll, one ordered from a department store in New Orleans. Since the store belonged to an importer, Daniel did not doubt it came from France. From there it had come up the Mississippi and then on the Arkansas to Fort Smith. Three of its delicate fingers were already broken off. Its wig made of real hair was a rat's nest.

He swallowed. His niece was the most unhappy person he had ever known. He knew his mother knew she was, but Rebecca refused to admit that anything was wrong, just as she pretended she knew nothing of the terrible names that people called her granddaughter.

"A long ride?"

"Yes."

Rip! The skirt came away from the waist. Suddenly, his niece wadded the doll's dress up into a tight ball and threw it at him. The doll followed. He caught it and laid it on the floor under his chair.

His niece had her fists dug into her hips. She stuck out her tongue at him. Instead of making him furious as her behavior usually did, it made him sad. He merely shook his head.

With a scream of rage, Sarah ran from the room.

All the way home Esther was silent. Her mind whirled. *I'm a female bastard 'cause you wouldn't marry my paw.*

She choked back a sob. Nothing could be more terrible than the sight of that little face. Like a sleepwalker she went about her chores. Finally, at the supper table, she broke her silence. "She was so thin."

York leaned forward and took his wife's hand. "She was as healthy as a young goat."

Esther started. "What are you saying?"

"That child looked as if she were tough enough to chew nails and spit out the pieces."

"You don't know what you're saying."

He shrugged. "Maybe not, but I say she was thin because she runs off everything she eats."

Esther started to protest, then closed her mouth. Not uncommon in the Ozarks were healthy children who ran wild in the hills. Esther had been one herself now that she remembered. She had run so fast and played so hard some days that her body had jerked and twitched all night long. Her legs had pumped until Daniel refused to sleep with her.

"She's a brave little thing," York went on. "Did she come in the store by herself?"

"Yes."

"Probably to find you." He walked to the stove and poured himself another cup of coffee. His own nerves were jumping and twitching. He had to warn Esther before they went to bed that he might have another nightmare. When the sheriff had thrown him into the ditch, he was pretty sure that he wouldn't have been able to get up if **Esther hadn't** jumped on the sheriff and ridden him down.

His wife had certainly saved him from a bad beating if not from being shot. He had to thank her with all his heart, but right now she couldn't think of anything except her daughter.

"But how would she even know who I am?" Esther pressed the heels of her hands to her throbbing temples. She had been torn apart and put back together so many times today that she was sick. Red flushed her cheekbones, and her face felt as if she had a fever.

"Someone told her."

"She said people were rude to her. She said they stared and they whispered." Esther hated to tell York those things. She could not bring herself to tell him what Sarah called herself.

York leaned back in his chair. "I can sympathize with her. That's why I left Philadelphia. People stared at me and whispered behind my back until I couldn't stand it. Sometimes they'd just walk right up and insult me. And you know the hell of it? They'd think they were doing me a favor. They were doing it for my own good."

"Oh, God." Esther let her head rest on her folded arms.

He reached over and patted her shoulder. "Want some whiskey?"

She shook her head. "No. I need it too badly."

He slid his hand over her neck, massaging the tense muscles. "One drink isn't going to turn you into a drunkard."

She looked up at him. "I don't know how many more nights of this I'll have to face. All I know is I have to have my daughter. And I don't know how to get her except over my mother's dead body."

* * *

"Just hold it right there, Jayhawk!"

York froze. A burly man with a grizzled beard stood framed in the doorway of the stable. More shocking than his presence was the double-barrel shotgun he had trained on York's chest.

He motioned with the barrel for York to move in the direction of the kennels. "You took your own sweet time about coming out of that house this morning," he complained. "I been waiting since afore sunup."

York considered leaping to the side, but a shotgun blast would tear a hole through the stable walls, and if that didn't get him, he had nowhere to run but an open field.

"Get on." The man pushed the barrels into the small of his back. "Walk ahead of me."

"Listen, I ain't no Jayhawk." York imitated Bas Boscomb's twang to the life. "Name's Carly Ord. Born and reared in these hills."

"Save it." The barrels prodded him again. "In a few minutes Jesse James is going to come walking out of that house, and I'm going to get myself a reward."

"Jesse James!" York's irritation was unfeigned. He was fed up with people taking him for a member of the James gang. "Gol-darn it! That no-good scalawag better not show his face 'round here. He'll get his damn-fool head blowed off."

"Get on back of them kennels." The man poked him again. He was a professional all right. But York had little doubt he would be shot along with Jesse and Frank and brought back in a wagon to claim the bounty. The fact that they would get no bounty for him would be considered bad luck.

The two men walked between the rows of runs. Hounds on each side of them sprang to their feet, low growls issuing from their throats. Teet reared up on his hind legs. His big jaws snapped. Nervous froth dripped from his muzzle. The man stepped sideways away from the big hound, but his shotgun remained trained on York. "Maybe if you lie down on your face and keep your mouth shut, I'll just look the other way if me and my pard get Jesse and Frank both."

"York!"

Both men turned at once to see Esther spring off the back step and dash down toward them.

"Dammit, I didn't figure on no woman." The man swung the shotgun toward her, then hastily swept it back. Most men, even bounty hunters, stuck at making war on a female.

"Esther, go back."

"York!" She skidded to a stop.

"Son-of-a-bitch!" The shotgun poked again. The man closed his hand over York's shoulder. "Listen, lady," he shouted. "If you want this fella alive, you'd better—"

York's control broke. He drove his elbow into the man's midriff. His captor grunted but did not give up his control.

"You want to get rough, I can get rough." He slammed the shotgun across York's neck and dropped him to his knees.

As York hooked his fingers into the mesh of Juniper's run, he saw a horseman leading a couple of mounts emerging from the trees at the back of the place.

"York!" Esther screamed once more and ran toward them.

"Women," the man with the shotgun muttered. He gave one despairing look at the house, then loped away toward the rider.

Esther reached the first run. She fumbled with the latch, flung the gate wide. "Teet!" she screamed. "Teet! Take! Take him!"

"Oh, Jesus!" The bounty hunter flung a glance over

his shoulder as the big black-and-tan bounded out of the gate and threw up his muzzle, seeking a scent on the air.

The hound quartered back and forth down the aisle. He snuffled at York's shoulder, then dropped his nose to the ground to drink in the bounty hunter's scent. Then like a bloodhound he threw up his nose and bugled.

Esther hurried after him, throwing open the runs of her best hunters. "Birdsong! Take! Boone! Take! Juniper! Take!"

Led by Teet, the pack streamed out across the lawn. Esther ran after them. They were coonhounds trained to hunt and kill raccoons. What they would do against men, she could not imagine. She doubted whether they would even recognize the bounty hunters as prey, but the sight of the four big animals charging in relentless full cry was the only weapon she had.

"Jesus!" The man with the shotgun broke into a dead run as his partner on horseback pulled up. The pack was gaining on him. They would reach him before he could reach the horses. Terrified by the din and the oncoming pack, the horses reared and plunged.

"Teet! Kill it!" Esther screamed. "Kill it!"

The big black-and-tan bugled like the last trumpet. His stride lengthened. His mouth drank the wind. Saliva dripped from his fangs and his lolling tongue. In that instant he looked exactly what he was, one of man's oldest friends, bred to hunt down and kill whatever he was ordered to. His call changed to a growl.

The horseman let go of the leading rein. With a panicky curse, he wheeled his horse and clapped spurs to its sides. He would have hit the lane at a dead run, abandoning his partner to his fate, but he spurred his mount into the two other mounts. The three horses whinnied, curvetting, bucking. And then the hounds were among them, nipping at their ankles, baying, growling.

The man with the shotgun leaped for the saddle. Teet's

jaws slashed viciously into his thigh. The man screamed and chopped down with the barrel of the shotgun at the black head. At the same time he got a leg across the saddle. The blow loosened Teet's hold. The other horseman managed to rein his horse into the clear and gallop away. The other two horses followed, the gunman clinging half in, half out of the saddle.

Teet rolled away, but Juniper, Boone, and Birdsong howled on the chase all the way past the Boscomb place.

York climbed to his feet as Esther came running to his side. She threw both arms around him to support him. "Are you all right? Oh, Lord, you're bleeding."

He nodded grimly, rubbing his neck where the shotgun had struck him. The small smear of blood on his hand assured him that he was only scratched. "It's all right."

Teet, too, climbed gamely to his feet and started down the lane.

"Teet!"

Her peremptory call brought him up short. Reassured that her husband was indeed all right, she dropped to her knees and held out her arms. "Teet, come here."

He came and put his head into her hands. "Teet," she crooned. "Good boy. Good old boy. You knew, didn't you? You're the greatest hound. You're the greatest. Good boy." She looked at York for confirmation. "Did you ever see anything like that?"

York shook his head. He had his arms tightly wrapped around his body to try to control his shivering. The sight of those hounds charging past him had shocked him. The bounty hunters had been too terrified even to shoot. "Scary as hell," he agreed.

Esther patted Teet again and then rose. She cupped her hands around her mouth. "Jun-i-per! Bird-song! Boo-oone!" In a minute the hounds came loping back down the road. The men's scent was lost on the air, and the horses had carried the prey out of sight.

"Good boys. Good girl." Esther was beside herself with pride at their hunt. "I can't believe it. I can't believe what they did," she said again. "They didn't even know their prey. But they knew 'take.'"

York stood watching her as they milled around her, panting, their faces turned up to hers, their eyes bright and eager. Four tails wagged violently as she patted them and praised them.

Suddenly, York began to laugh. "They sure scared the hell out of those two guys."

"Not just scared. Teet tore into one of them, didn't you, boy? Another minute and he'd have had him down." She drew a long, shivering breath. Her face went white. "And then I wouldn't have been able to stop him. I had given the command to kill."

His own face hardened. "Don't have a minute's regret." He made a slashing movement with his hand. "When you're up against armed men, you use the best weapons you have. Obviously, those two underestimated the enemy." He patted Teet on the head. "Good boy."

"Do you have any idea who they were?"

"Yes. At least I'm pretty sure. He told me why he was here right from the start."

Esther looked at him expectantly.

York's mouth quirked. "They were looking for your cousins. There's a reward out for Jesse James."

Thirteen

York eased himself between Esther's thighs. As eager as he was, he still supported much of his weight on his arms and knees to take as much as possible off her. While the warmth and scent of him were driving her wild, in one corner of her mind she thanked God for her husband's gentleness, his consideration. Since she had fallen into his life, he had had to rescue her so many times that she had almost lost count. He had become like a rock, the one constant in her life.

She clutched his shoulders. "Please," she begged. "I won't break. I promise to yell if you hurt me. Just do it."

His jaw clenched as he slid into her velvety softness. Staring up into his rapt face, Esther shared his pleasure. Within her the pressure built as his body moved. Then she could look no longer. Her eyes closed; her lips parted as the muscles in her belly tightened.

A guttural groan rasped from him as he thrust hard into her. His tightly self-imposed control snapped. Thrusting harder than ever, he arched his back with the effort. A wordless cry burst from his mouth as his whole body stiffened.

The explosion of male power within her drove Esther over the edge, too. Her own release began not in ripples, but in waves of sensation radiating from the center of her body, through her limbs to the very tips of her fingers and toes. So devastated was she by the succession of shocks, that she could not remain silent. A cry tore out of her throat. And then another.

Even as her body began to relax, she buried her face in his shoulder, experiencing ripples of delight that went on and on. His body replied to those ripples. Within her sheath his shaft still pulsed.

She shyly lifted her mouth to his ear. "You feel so good. Can you feel me the way I feel you?"

"Yes." The shaft leaped within her again. His hands tightened. He shifted her weight until he was lying on his back and she was cradled against his side. His arms held her securely. One hand stroked her shoulder. She pulled up the quilts, enclosing them in a cocoon of warmth.

For a while his breathing was heavy and even. She was sure he was asleep when he started and yawned. "Too bad we can't just stay here forever."

She nodded, her movement barely discernible. "I'm still asleep."

"Oh." He nibbled at her ear and rubbed her back.

"I am." Her eyes remained firmly closed.

"It's morning," he whispered. "I'm afraid I'm going to have to get up, even if you're not."

"What for?"

He whispered in her ear.

"Use the chamber pot," she advised.

Nevertheless, he slid out from under the covers, careful to let in as little chill air as possible.

She watched him don his clothes in quick, efficient motions. The Yankee pants had gone into the stove last night. With his new clothes he no longer looked like the enemy. He was her husband of whom she was glad. This Christmastide, for the first time in a very long time, she had something to be grateful for. She swung her legs out and reached for her robe.

"You can stay until the room gets warm," he offered.

She rose and belted it around her. "Today I have to do something about my daughter."

He looked doubtful. "What are you going to do?"

Esther opened the big walnut wardrobe and stared at her clothing. "I'm going to go get her. For the first time I know that being with my mother is not the best place for her. My daughter called herself a 'female bastard.' And she knew what it meant. She's just a child hearing those slurs and whispers all alone. At least if she were with me, I'd be able to support her."

She pulled out a knee-length black coat and a black wool dress. Both had full skirts made to be worn over crinolines, a style out of fashion since the war. Holding the garments against her, Esther grimaced at herself in the mirror. She was taller than her grandmother had been. Perhaps the skirts would not drag the ground. She looked at her husband inquiringly.

He shrugged. "It'll be fine for what you have to do."

"I think so, too."

"Do you want me to go with you?"

She shook her head. "I have to go alone."

Esther had to lift the heavy black skirts to climb the steps of her mother's church. It was easily the finest building in the county. On top of the knob hill from which the town had gotten its name, the devout had raised a large, rectangular structure of best grade white pine. Atop the rising roof of the sanctuary was perched a bell tower. In the wings on both sides were an office for the minister, Sunday school rooms for the children, and a tiring-room for the choir.

Drawing a deep breath, Esther pulled open the doors and walked down the long center aisle between the carved benches. She had forgotten the view of the mountains and the reason why the church was built where it

was. The church faced east so no rising sun would shine
in the faces of the congregation. Almost the entire western wall at the back was composed of three tall windows
of clear glass. Through them the congregation could con-
template the majestic Ozarks rising behind the altar and
her mother's pulpit.

Esther raised the chancel rail and walked to the windows. How could she have forgotten? Behind the church
was a small courtyard paved with gray slate flagstones.
Trees arched above it, and benches were arranged in a
semicircle underneath it. In the spring the ladies of the
Missionary Society planted flowers.

Esther remembered the first time her mother had married a couple in this courtyard. With the birds singing,
the sun beaming through the leaves, and the mountains
rising behind it all, that wedding had seemed the most
beautiful thing she had ever seen. Her own wedding per-
formed by Preacher with Jesse James's Colt trained on
the groom had marked the end of another of her childhood dreams. She and her husband would never make
their vows before her mother.

Tightening her mouth and thrusting her black-gloved
hands more deeply into her pockets, she faced the door
on the right of the altar. Her mother's offices lay behind
it. Briefly, she reviewed what she planned to say. As she
put her hand on the doorknob, she looked out over the
sanctuary once more. Once she had thought this was
God's house where nothing but goodness and beauty
ever entered. After what Sarah had told her, she could
see it was just a house.

She opened the door and stepped into a short hall
with offices on the left. She walked toward them. Suddenly, the door burst open. Her daughter bolted out and
skidded to a halt. Recognition and then hope disappeared behind a defiant façade. Sarah threw an angry

look over her shoulder before she tore past Esther and out into the sanctuary.

"Sarah Susannah!" Rebecca's preaching voice followed the child and filled the hall.

Daniel appeared in the doorway. He halted at the sight of Esther. His look of hope, too, disappeared. He stood aside to allow his mother to come out.

"Esther."

"Hello, Mother. Daniel."

Rebecca gasped. A guilty expression flickered across her face. She looked quickly to the open door through which her granddaughter had just fled. Obviously disconcerted, she offered the first excuse Esther had ever heard her make. "She's just upset."

"More than that, I think." Esther offered up a silent prayer to whatever angel had brought her into the church at that particular moment. Rebecca could not possibly pretend that Sarah's life was idyllic.

Rebecca knew it. Her eyes met Esther's and fled. When she brought them back it was to look critically at her daughter. "Isn't that your grandmother's coat?"

Esther took the remark for what it was worth, a pathetic attempt to make her uncomfortable. It had the opposite effect. She smiled as if she had received the nicest of compliments and held out the full skirts as if they were the latest Paris style. "You're right. And her dress and bonnet. It's the newest dress I own. My own things were worn out or outgrown years ago. Usually I just put on some of Papa's clothes or whatever stuff Daniel left behind."

Rebecca flinched. Daniel looked away, a slow red creeping up into his cheekbones.

Esther wondered if her mother wished she could take the words back. Probably not. Rebecca believed in plain speaking. It was an admirable trait which the members of her congregation boasted about at Annual Confer-

ence. Their pastor let them know right away where they
stood with the Lord, was the way they put it.

Esther knew beating around the bush wouldn't help.
She took her courage in both hands. "I've come to take
Sarah home with me."

Daniel gasped. His eyes flew to his mother's face.

Rebecca looked as if she had been struck. Her face
turned white; then an unpleasant red stain crept up her
neck. Still she managed to move steadily and gracefully
back to her desk and seat herself behind it. "That's foolish."

Esther followed her and took a seat opposite. She
would have liked to remain standing, but her legs were
shaking so badly she didn't think they would support her.
Moreover, she was afraid she might pass out.

"Sarah Susannah's place is with me, where she can
have a good, decent home—"

"I have a good, decent home," Esther interrupted. "I
have a husband and—"

"A Yankee. One of the James gang."

"He can't be a Yankee and ride with Jesse James."
Esther gave a short laugh. Her mother's look of disap-
proval sobered her instantly. "But that's not the point.
The point is that Sarah would be better off with me."

"That's not true."

Esther leaned forward earnestly to deliver the speech
she had so carefully prepared. She willed her mother to
understand. "Yesterday, my daughter confronted me in
Carolan's store."

Rebecca shot an accusing look at Daniel, who had
taken the chair beside his sister. Unfortunately, he was
staring at his hands clasped between his knees. "She—
er—sometimes wanders down there. I—er—give her a
penny to buy a sack of lemon drops."

"She came looking for me."

"That's a lie." Rebecca's fist clenched. "She doesn't know anything about you. I thought it was best—"

"She does know about me. She knows everything about me because evidently some nasty hypocrites in your church pointed me out to her. And worse than that. She told me she was a female bastard because I didn't marry her father. Those were her exact words."

Rebecca's eyes widened. She sucked in her breath so hard that her nostrils pinched. "You're lying."

"No, Mother." Esther looked across at Daniel. "Did you know this?"

Rebecca looked at him, too. "Of course not. Because it isn't true."

"Did you?"

Daniel clasped his hands tighter. His shoulders heaved.

"Daniel," Rebecca commanded imperiously, "this is not true."

He shook his head. "It is true."

"Daniel!"

"That's why Sarah's so unmanageable, isn't it, Daniel?" Esther was speaking to her brother, but she was watching her mother. Anger, hurt, fear, disgust, all the negative emotions played across Rebecca's features as she looked from one to the other. Clearly, her children were a great trial to her. "Sarah hates being here. She says people whisper behind her back and stare at her and point."

"They wouldn't do such a thing." Rebecca's lips moved stiffly. She sat like a statue, her hands clenched in impotent fists. "Not to an innocent child."

Esther drove her point home. "They took their cue from you, Mother. That's what you did to me, your own daughter. I was an innocent child."

"You were sixteen years old," Rebecca flashed.

"I was innocent. And you didn't stand up for me. You took Daniel away. You turned his back on me, too."

"You had sinned."

"That's what the people in Cutter's Knob believe about me because you told them so. But when you cast stones like that, Mother, they fall on other people besides the ones they were cast at. They fall on the innocent. The congregation believes that somehow Sarah's sinned because you told them so."

Rebecca went absolutely white. She looked to her son, who had finally raised his head and was staring at his sister. "Daniel, tell her none of this is true."

He cleared his throat. "I think that's putting it a little strong, Esther. Mother never—"

Esther held up her hand. "Daniel, don't try to gloss this over. I've come for my child. You told me just two weeks ago that Sarah was a terror."

His face turned red. He threw a shamed look at his mother. "I just meant that she threw temper tantrums sometimes. I didn't mean exactly that she was a terror."

"Now I know why. She thinks she's despised. And she is, Mother. By everyone but you and Daniel." Esther paused, letting her accusations sink in before firing her final shot. "And neither one of you likes her very much because she isn't perfect."

Rebecca shuddered. Then her eyes flashed. She pushed herself up. "Get out."

Esther and Daniel rose at the same time. Daniel moved between the two women.

"Get out!" Rebecca all but screamed. Her pulpit voice thundered. "Get out! You're not welcome here. You've lost all sense of decency of right and wrong. You aren't fit to raise that dear child. She can't be raised in a house of sin."

Esther pushed her brother aside. "And while we're on the subject, Mother. I'm a married woman now and I expect you to call off Elmo Stamford. He isn't to ride by and check on me anymore. He isn't to stop me and York on the way to town and threaten my husband with arrest.

York hasn't done anything except make me very happy. Happier than I've been in five years."

"Get out!"

Daniel threw himself on his sister and hustled her toward the door. "I'll try to get her calmed down. I'll talk to her. I swear I will. This is hard for her to take in."

Out in the hall Esther wrenched herself free. "It's the truth, Daniel. Every word I've said. And you know it."

"I know, but she doesn't. She didn't have any idea what people had said—I didn't either. I didn't have any idea that Sarah had heard— How can people be so cruel?"

Esther shot him a fulminating look.

"I know. I know. It's terrible. Terrible." He was actually shaking; his white, soft hands patted his sister's shoulder when they were not waving helplessly in the air.

Esther captured those hands. She pulled them down between her own, and made him face her. "Daniel, I mean to have Sarah."

His face turned red, and he nodded. "I know you do." He gulped. "And you should."

"Then tell Mother that. Make her understand."

She squeezed his hands hard and pushed them back against his middle. She did not wait for him to answer. They were standing in the sanctuary now, before the beautiful windows, before the altar. Esther couldn't stand the place any longer. She turned and ran down the aisle.

Once outside, she stopped to catch her breath. The first thing she saw was her daughter standing beside Esther's horse. One little hand rubbed Babe's velvety muzzle. The other regarded Esther with frank skepticism.

"I heard what you said," Sarah said.

Esther longed to sweep the child up in her arms and cover her unhappy face with kisses. She wanted to ride away with her and love her so much that Sarah would forget all the terrible things that had been done to her. But this child might not appreciate something like that.

She was a desperately unhappy child, badly wounded by the grownups around her. She had fought them with the only weapons a child could muster, temper tantrums and defiance. Esther didn't know what to say to her. At last, she stammered, "What did you think?"

The child shook her head. She looked sullen. She stopped patting Babe's nose to twist a button on her coat.

Esther went down on her knees in front of the child. "I want you to know that I love you. And I'm doing the best I can to get you to come and live with me." She longed to ask Sarah what the child thought of the idea, but she didn't dare.

Sarah continued to twist the button, never looking at her mother. Esther put out her arms to hug the stiff little body. Sarah dodged back. She dashed up the steps of the church. At the top she spun around. "I hate you," she declared. "I wish you were dead. Like Grandmother said."

York had borrowed one of Esther's horses for the trip up the mountain. While she was away would be a good time to fetch the last personal items from his cabin. He was aware that he rode untroubled through the weak December sunlight. Six weeks ago, he had been carrying misery and confusion with him wherever he went.

He had hidden from the world. He had had to force himself to offer aid to the woman who was now his wife. If he believed in luck or fate, he would be thanking whatever gods might be for that night. Since he believed in neither, he attributed his feeling of well-being to time that had healed his wounds to the extent that he could come close to Esther and allow himself to be drawn into her world.

And a wild world it seemed to be. The outlaw Jesse James and the sheriff Elmo Stamford were surely two of the wildest in it. He had met them and been threatened by them both, but instead of driving him away, they had made him more determined than ever to remain with Esther Woodson.

He came to the curve at Boscomb's place and started up the mountain. The mountain was a combination of dark green pines and stark black skeletons of hardwoods. Beneath them where the sun did not shine directly, patches of snow remained.

He swung the horse's head and spurred the animal to jump the ditch when a shot rang out. The bullet struck the rocks to the left in front of him and spanged away. The horse whinnied and shied. Another shot. Another spurt of dirt and rocks.

He was the target. He reined the horse in a tight circle, sending it running down the road. As it stretched out, he crouched low over its neck, ducking his head into the flying mane. No more shots were fired. As he hit the turn at Boscomb's place, a company of uniformed men spurred their horses across his path. His own mount was among them before he could avoid them. Pistols drawn, they surrounded him. A couple reached out to jerk the reins from his hands.

"Hold it right there, Jayhawk!"

Their leader, a lieutenant, holstered his pistol and surveyed York with satisfaction. Since West Point his work at the garrison in Fort Smith had consisted of sitting at a desk and handling endless papers. His first assignment had come in response to a message for assistance from a local sheriff. He had come to capture the James gang, many of whom were notorious criminals wanted for the burning of Lawrence, Kansas, and the murder of several of its citizens. And now, first drop out of the bucket, he had captured one.

"You're my prisoner, mister. And I'd advise you to come with us quietly. It'll go easier on you."

York surveyed the shavetail calmly. "Lieutenant, you've

made a mistake. I'm not a Jayhawk. I'm a peaceable citizen going about my business on my own land."

The lieutenant scowled. "Tie his hands, Sergeant. We're taking him into town."

York held up one hand mildly. "That won't be necessary. I tell you I'm not a Jayhawk. I'm from—"

He never finished the sentence. The sergeant stuck a gun barrel in his ribs. "Cross them hands over that horn, Reb, and shut your yap. If you don't want to ride into town facedown. Dead's damn near better than alive for Rebs."

Esther saw the bluecoats coming down the road. Her loathing mixed with fear made her turn aside and ride off into a thicket. She wouldn't give them the opportunity to insult her. From time to time soldiers had come through town. Without exception they had leered and poked at every female they saw from girls of ten to grandmothers of seventy.

They had ridden on by before she recognized York in their midst. Her first reaction was wild anger. Had he joined up again? He had deceived her and used her. Perhaps he had come for the express purpose of finding Jesse.

Her second was disappointment. Tears stung her eyes. She had been so taken in by his polite ways and quiet strength that she had welcomed him into her bed. Hardest of all to endure was the sweet memory of her pleasure in their lovemaking.

To find out that he wasn't any better than Clell Miller was hard. He was worse than Clell. At least Clell hadn't deceived her. He hadn't promised her anything. She had expected more, but that was when she was young and foolish. With York she had let herself believe more.

As she stabled Babe, she saw that one of the team was missing. The so-and-so had even stolen one of her horses.

Mechanically, she went about her chores and finally climbed into a cold, lonely bed.

York glared through the bars of the crude cell. "You're making a mistake Lieutenant," he said for the tenth or twelfth time. "I'm not even from around here. I only came here a few weeks ago when I met and married my new wife. Send for her. She'll vouch for everything I say."

"He's a Jayhawk all right." Elmo Stamford rocked back and forth behind his desk. "Tried to arrest him myself the other mornin'. That wife of his jumped me, and some sympathizers held me off so he could get away."

"A woman jumped on you?" Lieutenant Hammer-schild made no special note of this petty fight. He was more concerned with the fact that the man he had delivered to the jail in Cutter's Knob kept maintaining that he was an honorably discharged veteran of the Pennsylvania Cavalry and that he knew absolutely nothing about Jesse James. He told the sheriff as much.

"He's a liar," the sheriff declared. "He's married to one of Jesse's cousins. She's in thick with 'em. I wouldn't be surprised if maybe you ought to arrest her, too."

The lieutenant looked contemptuous. He considered the ignorant, ugly sheriff completely beneath his notice. His job was to lock this man up and keep him locked up until he and his men could return with the rest of the gang. He would then deliver them to the garrison at Fort Smith, where swift justice would be dispensed.

To his eternal frustration, he had graduated West Point too late to fight in the glorious battles of the recent war. Despite exemplary grades, he was condemned to this most miserable outpost west of the Mississippi River where promotion was sure to be slow. He who had dreamed of leading charges against legions was left to capture outlaws and root out the remains of sedition.

On the other hand, if his troop could capture the notorious James gang, he might speed the process up considerably.

The lieutenant drew on his gauntlets. The easy capture of a member of the James gang had encouraged him. Since Jesse had ridden into Oklahoma, he would go after him. If his prisoner suffered at the hands of this sheriff, it was probably no more than he deserved.

"Lieutenant," York called to him from behind the bars. "I'd appreciate just one more minute of your time. I have information that is pertinent to this case."

The lieutenant brightened. He walked over to the bars. "Good. Give me some real information and I promise I'll speak for you at the tribunal."

York pulled himself to strict military attention. "Sir, I have the honor to be Captain York Bradburn, 4th Pennsylvania Cavalry, 64th Volunteers. Retired. If you'll send a telegram to Congressman Neville Bradburn, my father, in Washington, D.C., he'll confirm my identity."

Lieutenant Hammerschild looked the man on the other side of the bars up and down. Then he laughed. "That's good. That's very good. Sounds convincing. The congressman is a nice touch. I've a good mind to take you up on that, but I don't have the time."

He walked back to the sheriff's desk. "I leave it up to you. If you think there's a chance he's telling the truth, you can send the telegram. If you don't believe him, then forget the whole thing. Good day."

Elmo Stamford waited until the lieutenant had ridden out of town. Then he strode ponderously over to the bars. His stomach brushed against them as he delivered his speech on a gust of powerful bad breath. "I don't give a good goddamn whether or not you was tellin' the truth. I knowed you for a yellowleg the minute I saw you. When that fool took you for a Reb, I sure wasn't going to smarten him up. You're in here for a while, fellow. I ain't forgot the first night you and me met. You're a mighty dangerous character. And when you try to escape some dark night, I'm gonna have to shoot you."

York slumped down on the cot. Where was Esther? He hated for her to have to deal with this man. But he needed to speak to her. She would have to send the telegram.

He hated to break the silence to his father. Hated to have to beg for something. Six weeks ago, he probably wouldn't have cared enough to send the telegram. But now he wanted to live.

"He's in jail, Miz Blessing, just like you wanted." Elmo's ugly face had the best smile he could muster. He carried his battered felt hat in his hands. He stood just inside the door of her office, her sanctum.

She smiled at him, her eyes blue, her hair waved over her forehead and arranged in a regal coronet, her hands white and smooth. She gestured to him. "Come in, Sheriff Stamford. Come in. I want to tell you how much I appreciate what you've done for me. And for the people of this county."

He took the chair she indicated and gazed at her. He could have stared at her morning, noon, and night. He would have robbed this one-horse town of everything that wasn't nailed down and carried it across the Missouri border if he hadn't seen her. He could feel the sweat popping out on his forehead. She was so beautiful. "He's telling lies to whoever'll listen," he continued. "But he ain't gettin' outta jail till you say so."

"That's exactly as it should be," Rebecca said softly. "He's no more married to my daughter than—than—Jesse James. When did they marry? Who married them? Ridiculous. She was living in sin. And I won't allow that to go on in this community."

She sensed that Elmo Stamford didn't really care what she said so long as she said it beautifully and smiled at him benignly. He was a rough man, a cruel man even, but he obeyed her without question. And he had power and the will to enforce whatever would bring the best for the many. She thought again that all creatures of God were for the use of God. All could be directed to His glorious work. She smiled again at the sheriff.

"He's been talking about getting a telegram to somebody in Washington, D.C. Claims his paw's a senator or something like that." Elmo scratched his head. "I heard him tell the lieutenant, but I didn't pay no mind, 'cause I wasn't going to send it."

"A waste of money," Rebecca agreed.

They stared at each other in perfect harmony. "Course, Esther might send it for him." Elmo's goggle eyes narrowed. "That is, if she was to get to talk to him."

"Oh, she mustn't talk to him," Rebecca ordered. "She needs to forget him completely. If she doesn't know where he is, it may be days or weeks before she finds out. And perhaps by that time, the army will have picked him up."

She smiled at Elmo again as she opened the drawer of her desk. "I wouldn't want the man to go hungry. Be sure that he has enough to eat and an extra blanket." She took out a dark green enamel cash box and opened its lid. His goggle eyes almost started out of his head at the sight of its contents.

"The church wants mercy and justice for everyone. No one must suffer needlessly." She counted out a sum of money that amounted to half of Elmo's pay for a month and held it out to him. "Sheriff, I know you'll spend this where it will do the most good."

Fourteen

"They tied your husband to his saddle," Bas Boscomb said. "You must've rode right by them. I'm surprised y' didn't see that, Esther girl."

Esther felt decidedly ill. For four days she had kept to herself, mourning, missing him, alternately cursing him and despising herself. She had made no effort to find York when he might be in desperate trouble.

"I heard a couple of shots," Bas told her. "Come out onto the porch with my spyglass. Just curious, like I always am. That's when I seen him. He comes tearing down the road from off of the mountain. Them soldiers was a-waiting right around the bend for him. Figured they must've had a sharpshooter up ahead to turn him around."

"But why?"

Bas scratched his head. "Well, now, I don't rightly know. Guess the fella could have been a deserter."

"That's not possible. The war's over. They wouldn't be hunting deserters five years later." Esther wrapped her arms around her body. "But he hasn't come back. If he didn't want to go with them—if they had to tie him to the saddle—he must not have wanted to go. They must still have him."

From feeling deserted and angry, she now began to feel real fear. What if they had killed him? What if he were taken away and imprisoned somewhere? He was her husband. She had to make every effort to find him.

Once again this true friend of her father's had come forward to help her. She wanted to hug him, but years of shameful isolation had made her shy. All she could manage was to reach out and shake his old hand. "Thank you for telling me. I didn't know where he was and I've been worried sick. I know you've put yourself out, and I appreciate it."

He shook his head. "The walk did me good, Esther. Just you don't worry. He'll turn up. But your worryin' won't do a bit of good."

As he walked away, she began to make her plans. The first thing to do was ask around in town. She should have done that in the first place, instead of moping here. She was going to have to go into town on a regular basis to hear the news rather than sitting out here in the country in fear and shame.

Esther slammed into the sheriff's office. "York, are you all right? Are you hurt?"

Both men sprang to their feet. York gripped the bars of the cell, hope surging through him. She hurried across the office to put her hand around her husband's. Then she strode across the floor to the sheriff's desk. Her eyes flashed with righteous anger. Fury made her voice shake. "What do you mean holding my husband in your jail?"

The sheriff gaped at her and backed up a couple of steps. He had seen her frightened, he had seen her humiliated, but he had never seen her angry before. She turned back to York, her eyes scanned him for any sign that he might have been mistreated.

He smiled at her. Even with a four-day growth of beard and his hair tousled, he looked wonderful. "I'm all right."

The keys lay on the desk top. She snatched them up and thrust them at Stamford. "Open that door."

The sheriff of Benton County managed to close his mouth. With a grunt, he sat back down in his chair. Deliberately, he opened the desk drawer and dropped in the keys. No one was going to barge into his jail and tell him what to do. Much less a woman. Much less this woman. He reared back and stuck his thumbs in his belt. "You better get on out of here unless you want me to arrest you, too."

Esther never faltered. "My mother told you to arrest him. Now I'm telling you to let him out."

He stiffened. His smirk turned to a sneer. "Your mama don't tell me what to do. The U.S. Army brought this man in. He's a member of the James gang."

"If the U.S. Army thought that, then you must have named him. He's a former captain in the army himself." Her anger was mixed with frustration. She had wasted her time coming here. The only person Elmo Stamford would listen to was Rebecca Blessing. She tried once more. "I'll get his mother-in-law over here if I have to."

The sheriff smirked at her threat. "Bring her on. She'll most likely tell me what a fine job I'm doing."

Giving him a look of loathing, Esther stalked back to York's cell. "Is he giving you enough to eat? Have you been cold or hungry?" She raised her voice. "I want to tell my mother if he's hurt you."

York shook his head. He, too, had never seen his wife this determined. The sight boosted his flagging spirits. The time in Stamford's jail had undermined his confidence again. He had had a recurrence of his nightmares. "Just send a telegram for me," he told her softly. "Even the sheriff can't keep me in jail after the answer comes."

Her expression was skeptical. She thought her husband was a great many good things, but she had never believed he was anything but the most ordinary of men. York had been living like a wild man in the woods. He could hardly carry on a conversation when she stumbled into his life. Why would a man with a family—an influential family— hide himself away? If they hadn't been forced by circumstances to remain together for two days, she doubted she would ever have seen him again. She clasped his hands through the bars. "I'll force Mother to get you out."

Something of her doubt must have shown in her face because he tightened his grip until it was almost painful. His expression was one she had never seen before. He was pleading. "Congressman Neville Bradburn in Washington, D.C.," he insisted. He closed his eyes as if the name pained him. Then he raised her hands to his lips and kissed them. "Just send him a telegram."

The touch of York's lips sent shivers through her. Only Stamford's presence kept her from pulling him against the bars and kissing him on the mouth. She was hungry for him. Their eyes spoke a silent language.

"I said," Stamford snarled, "get the hell out of here."

She gently freed her hands. At the door she gave Stamford one last withering look. "I'll be back."

His laughter followed her out into the street.

"I don't know what you expect me to do about this." Rebecca adopted a helpless tone.

For Esther the last vestiges of respect and love for her mother drifted away in the hypocritical air of the sanctuary. In their place came a reaffirmation of her own belief that she had not been at fault five years ago. Her mother was in the wrong. She was the weak one for not standing up to people when her daughter had been raped and forced to bear a child out of wedlock. She was worse than weak. She was mean and petty when she had York Bradburn, an innocent and good man who just happened to be her daughter's husband, thrown into jail to punish Esther.

"I expect you to walk down the hill with me and tell Elmo Stamford that you've made a mistake," Esther said sternly.

"I! I haven't made a mistake," Rebecca argued. "I had nothing to do with any of this."

"Mother, you told me yourself that you had Stamford watching the house."

"Well, certainly." Rebecca managed to look hurt and righteous at the same time. "What loving mother wouldn't make sure that her daughter was safe and sound? Especially when you chose to live out there by yourself."

"Mother, I've only had a choice since the middle of October. Elmo Stamford himself told me that he's been spying on me for years."

Rebecca closed her eyes and clasped her hands in her lap. She didn't actually utter a prayer, but her purpose was clear. The matter was no longer open for discussion.

Esther felt again the impossibility of arguing with religious people. They were absolutely certain that they were right and everyone else was wrong. Anyone who disagreed with them, even in ways that had nothing to do with faith, was wrong. The hot spurt of anger and frustration set Esther to shaking. She wanted to stalk out of the sanctuary and never speak to her mother again. She wanted to sell her land and take her hounds and leave Benton County and the state of Arkansas forever.

But her daughter and now her husband were held hostages by her mother. She made no effort to conceal her anger as she rose. "Elmo Stamford is a bully, Mother. He's dishonest and a disgrace to this town. He terrorizes people and he likes to hurt them. He's your man, Mother. And everybody will know it very soon. What does that make you?"

Rebecca's eyes popped open. The one thing she cared about above all others was how the town perceived her. She frowned, but then her brow smoothed out. "Of course I support him. He's the sheriff. Elmo is strong. Sometimes in the performance of his duty—"

"They'll know, Mother. Because I'll tell them." With that parting shot she stalked out of the sanctuary.

THE HONORABLE NEVILLE BRADBURN REGRETS TO INFORM YOU THAT HE HAS NO SONS.
       BENJAMIN CROWDER,
       SECRETARY TO CONGRESSMAN BRADBURN.

Esther stared down at the message the telegraph operator passed to her.

"Are you sure you got the message correct?" she asked the operator. "Could you possibly have misunderstood?" Even as she asked it, she knew he hadn't made a mistake. York was either a liar or a crazy man who had sent her on a wild goose chase.

Or his father cared no more about him than her mother did her. Both were willing to let their children suffer when they had the power to help them. "Did you send the message that York Bradburn was in jail by mistake?"

The telegraph operator nodded. "I sent just what you wrote down, ma'am. And the answer wasn't long coming." He leaned over the counter to read the reply again as if he had not taken it down letter by letter off the wire. "Looks like you been lied to somewhere."

"Looks like." She folded the telegram and put it in her pocket. Her expression was as bleak as the gray sky of early December.

* * *

Jesse watched from the trees as the lieutenant trotted by at the head of his troop. Hammerschild wasn't the first glory hunter to come after Quantrill's guerrillas. He was merely one in a long string.

"Let 'em go, Jesse," Frank counseled, laying his hand on Jesse's thigh. "They'll get enough of roaming round these hills and head on back to Fort Smith a lot faster if we don't stir 'em up."

Jesse pulled his gun and laid the barrel across his forearm to steady it. He drew a bead on Hammerschild's head, leading the target smoothly, keeping the sight perfectly trained.

"Shoot him," Cole whispered from his other side. "The rest of 'em'll run like rabbits."

The lieutenant led his troop on down the road until the trees hid him from view. Jesse laughed as he eased the hammer down. "That yellowleg don't know how lucky he is. Maybe I'll pay him a visit some night."

Cole Younger laughed. "You'll scare him so bad he'll damn near float outta his blankets."

Frank shook his head. Jesse didn't think about danger the way other people did. He had gone from playing cowboys and Indians to playing Rebs and Yanks. And now he was playing outlaws and lawmen. He was like a spoiled child who wanted more and more attention. Jesse was the one who had made the James gang notorious. He had told everyone his name as if he were Robin Hood. He was the one who refused to wear a mask. Frank shook his head. Sometimes, his little brother scared him.

Esther was so tired and cold she could barely pull the saddle off and throw a blanket over her mare. In full dark she made her way up to the house. More than tired, she was dejected. She would have to go into town tomorrow and show her husband the telegram.

Her first act was to poke the fire and add fresh wood to the big stove. She left the oven door open to warm up the kitchen quickly and set the water to boil for coffee. Then she dropped down in the kitchen chair and closed her eyes. Maybe she really didn't need coffee. She could eat a couple of cold biscuits left over from breakfast and go fall into bed. If she were only sure she would fall into a deep sleep, she would pass up the biscuits.

"M-mother."

Esther tumbled out of the chair. On her hands and knees, she scrambled around to peer into the darkness of the doorway. Her five-year-old daughter was standing there.

Esther felt her heart pound. "Where did you come from?"

The little girl rolled her eyes as if her mother were stupid. In her most sarcastic voice, she delivered her answer. "From the living room. I was asleep. You woke me up when you came in."

Still too stunned to believe her daughter was actually there, Esther sank back on her knees. She closed her eyes for a moment. The darkness of the room must be playing tricks on her eyes. "How did you get here?"

The little girl didn't answer. Instead, she thrust her lower lip out. Her hands balled into fists.

At the sight Esther climbed to her feet and lighted the lamp. She was questioning her daughter when she should be grabbing her and hugging her and telling her how glad she was to see her. She put her hands on the back of the chair she had just fallen out of. "Come and sit down by the fire, Sarah Susannah. This chair is closest."

Her daughter still looked angry. "I told you to call me Sarysue."

"Did you?" Esther pretended surprise. "I thought only people who whispered about you behind your back called you Sarysue. If you really want me to, I will, but it'll take

me a while to get used to that name. I've called you
Sarah in my mind for so long."

While Sarah was deciding, the water came to a boil.
The kettle began to sing. Esther lifted it off the fire. "I
was just getting ready to fix me some hot chocolate. I'll
bet you'd like some, too."

Sarah walked boldly across the room, a three-foot
woman, her defiance pitiful because it was obviously her
only weapon. She climbed up into the chair and held
out her hands to the open oven. "I wasn't cold in the
living room," she informed her mother. "I was covered
up from my head to my toes, and I didn't kick the covers
off a-tall."

"That's good." Esther took down the Baker's chocolate
and began to fix the syrup. "I had a hard time keeping
them on when I was your age."

Sarah watched her mother carefully. Her lip was still
thrust out, her nose bright red and moist. She wiped it
with the back of her hand. "I need a handkerchief."

Esther reached into the linen drawer and pulled out
a napkin. "Will this do?"

Her daughter inspected it. "Don't you have any real
handkerchiefs?"

Esther bowed her head. She could feel the tears starting. Her daughter was sitting within arm's length and
she couldn't think of how to greet her. She couldn't
think what to do or say. She was hopeless and so afraid
she would say the wrong thing that she couldn't say anything.

"Are you crying?" Sarah asked suddenly.

Esther could bear it no longer. She went down on her
knees in front of the little girl's chair. Her face was wet
with tears as she reached for her daughter. "I surely am
crying. I'm going to cry because I'm so happy that you're
here."

Sarah looked at her suspiciously. "You're not supposed to cry if you're happy."

"Sometimes you're so happy you can't help but cry. Please, Sarah Susannah or Sarysue or whatever you want me to call you, please put your arms around me and give me a hug."

The little one looked surprised. Then her chin began to quiver. Hesitantly, she reached out her arms.

Esther leaned forward and gathered her daughter against her. The moment was unbearably sweet. Her daughter was in her arms, her precious child who had been taken away from her before she had ever even seen her. Her daughter's body felt so small, yet hard. Rubbing Sarah's back, Esther could feel the knobs of her spine. Her knees were knobby, too, thrust out into Esther's midriff. Sarah had yet to take a breath.

Esther drew back, still keeping her arms around her daughter. "I'm so glad to see you."

Sarah smiled then. Just a wafer of a grin. "I'm glad to see you, too."

At last Esther stood up. She helped herself to a napkin, and together she and Sarah wiped their eyes. Then she poured the milk into the chocolate syrup. She pulled her chair up beside Sarah's rather than sitting across the table from her. "Your pawpaw used to fix this for me," she told her daughter. "He could make it so well."

Tentatively, Sarah tasted it. "It's good," she acknowledged. "What do you call it?"

Esther blinked. "Hot chocolate. Haven't you ever had it before?"

"I don't think so."

Esther tried to stay calm. Hot chocolate was unimportant. It shouldn't be taken as an example of all Sarah had missed. As a matter of fact, she didn't remember her mother ever fixing it. Perhaps, she didn't know how.

When they had both had a drink, she phrased her question again. "How did you get here?"

Sarah looked at the liquid in the cup. "I rode."

"On a horse? I didn't see—"

"He's just a pony," Sarah said scornfully. "I'm too little for a big horse. At least that's what Uncle Daniel said. He's such a sissy."

Esther choked on her chocolate. Poor Daniel. She had teased him many times when they were children because he wouldn't do the things she did. He was always afraid of being hurt. Now his five-year-old niece thought he was a sissy. "Maybe he just doesn't want you to be hurt."

Sarah rolled her eyes, showing clearly that she didn't believe a word of that. She set the cup down and looked around expectantly. "That was good. Now I'm really hungry."

Esther jumped up. "Of course you are. It'll take me a few minutes to fix us something good. Can you wait or—?"

Sarah slipped down off the chair. "I can help you fix whatever you want. I help Mrs. Hale in the kitchen all the time. She's nice most of the time. It's just when I make her mad that she calls me a bastard."

Esther stooped and took Sarah's face between her hands. "I don't want you to say that again. I don't want you to call yourself that."

Sarah's eyes grew flinty like shards of mica in a forest pool. She thrust out her lower lip. "It's what I am. Nobody can change it." In a defiant singsong voice she repeated to herself. "Nobody can change it. Nobody can change it."

Esther put her hand gently over her daughter's mouth. "Do you know that I got married last month?" She felt the gentle shake of the head. "Yes, I did. I became Mrs. Esther Elizabeth Bradburn. Because I have a husband, you have a father."

The little girl's mouth opened in a sweet round O.

As if she had done it all her life, Esther guided her daughter's head to her shoulder and lifted her child in her arms. "And the very first thing we're going to do is to adopt you."

"What's adopt?"

Esther swore to herself that if York balked at the notion, he would be sorry for the rest of his days. Then she chastised herself for thinking ill of him. Surely, two lost souls could take another unto themselves and make the three whole. "We're going to make you our little girl with York's last name. You'll be Sarah Susannah Bradburn. And you won't be a bastard anymore."

Esther sat down on the chair holding Sarah in her lap, rocking back and forth. After a minute, one little hand crept up and caught at Esther's collar. The gesture was so small, it might have meant nothing, but Esther took it to her heart.

"I've never been in bed with anyone," Sarah objected. Savoring each experience, Esther had fed her daughter a good meal. She had heated water and given her a bath and dressed her in one of Esther's flannel shirts. They had giggled together as Esther had rolled up the sleeves. Then Esther had braided Sarah's fine hair. Secretly, she was appalled at the condition of it. In some places it was only a couple of inches long, but most of it hung down the middle of her back, its ends dead and split.

Despite her resolve to ask no questions that might be taken as criticism, Esther had to find out. "Who takes care of your hair?"

Sarah jerked her head around. Her eyes flashed. "I do. I comb it and cut it. I won't let anyone but me touch me."

After that remark, Esther had been very quiet. If she ever had the chance, she meant to ask Daniel what her

daughter's life had been like. While she had donned her
own gown, Sarah looked at the pictures in the *New England Primer,* the book from which Esther had learned to
read.

When she was dressed, she climbed in beside Sarah.
"Shall I read it to you?"

"I can read it," Sarah said proudly. " 'A is for Apple,
B is for Bull—' "

As Sarah's little tongue recited all the letters in the
alphabet and pointed to each picture in turn, Esther
found herself in tears again. Someone else had taught
her daughter to read. She had missed so many wonderful
things.

As Esther put the book aside and prepared to blow
out the lamp, Sarah slid down on the pillow. "I don't
like to pray."

Esther looked at her daughter, recognizing a test when
she heard one. "All right."

"Aren't you going to ask me why?"

Esther blew out the light. The room would be dark
only until their eyes became accustomed to it, then the
moonlight would enable them to see shapes. She climbed
into bed and turned Sarah to face the edge. She pulled
her daughter into the curve of her body and tucked the
covers around her shoulders. "You should be good and
warm all night. This is the way my brother and I used
to sleep when we were children and the winters were
cold."

But Sarah would not let the matter rest. She lay stiff
as a stick, bristling defiance. "Aren't you going to ask
me why I don't like to pray?"

"All right. Tell me why you don't," Esther murmured.

"Because it doesn't work." Sarah punctuated each
word with a nod of her head. "I prayed and prayed and
prayed. And nothing I ever prayed for was given to me.

It doesn't work, so I'm not ever going to pray anymore."
When she finished, she lay quivering.

Esther knew the child was waiting for some terrible
blow to fall, but she continued to stroke her daughter.
"Let's go to sleep," she whispered. "I'm so tired I can
hardly move. And I'll bet you are, too. We've both had
long rides. I think I may be sore tomorrow."

Sarah let out her breath in a long sigh. "You're right.
I guess I'll go to sleep, too."

In the way of children, she fell instantly into a deep
sleep. When Esther felt her daughter relax, she cuddled
her closer, wetting the pillow with her tears as she struggled to keep her sobs silent.

Rebecca Blessing entered the jail as if it were the most
ordinary place in the world.

Sheriff Stamford leaped to his feet. The chair rolled
away behind him and thudded into the wall. He jerked
the felt hat off his head and smoothed his sparse hair.
"Miz Blessing!" He threw a hasty glance at York, who
was lying on the bunk with his hands locked behind his
head. "Get up there, you. There's a lady here."

York remained where he was. His spirits had risen
when his wife had found him. He had expected she
would send the telegram and wait for the answer. Surely,
Cutter's Knob was within a day's ride of a telegraph office. When she didn't come back in the evening, he became worried. What if she'd met with an accident? What
if her horse had fallen with her? What if she had met
up with Jayhawks or a troop of soldiers?

He should never have told her to send a telegram in
the first place. He should have had more sense. He'd
never have asked his mother or his sister to go out on
such an errand. He'd forgotten how dangerous it was for
a woman to go abroad alone.

"I'd like to speak with your prisoner, Sheriff Stamford," he heard Rebecca say. Rising up on one elbow, he watched the tableau on the other side of the bars.

"Whatever you want, Miz Blessing. He's been pretty quiet since yesterday."

She smiled at the sheriff. "In that case you won't be derelict in your duty if you leave us alone for a few minutes."

Stamford's smile turned to a scowl. Clearly, he didn't want to leave her alone. He was basking in the light of her presence. He wanted her to talk to him, not to his prisoner. York watched the interplay between them with a half smile on his face.

"Why don't you go get yourself some fresh coffee? There's a pot over at the church. Take a walk. Get out in the fresh air before we have another cold spell. I'll be all right. And your prisoner will be safe." She tucked her hand through the sheriff's burly arm and escorted him to the door much as if the jail were hers and he was the guest. Her smile encouraged him, dazzled him.

He bowed out and clapped his hat on his head in the middle of the street. "I'll be back in ten minutes," he promised.

She smiled. "Take your time."

York swung his legs over the edge of the bunk and sat up. Purposefully, he didn't rise and come to the bars as he had with Esther. This woman was not a friend. In fact, she was probably the enemy.

She came to the bars and looked at him. He recognized the expression as the one she had come in wearing. Sympathy was there, but it was false. With the lift of a superior eyebrow, she began, "Mr. York."

"The name is York Bradburn." He hid a smile as he pulled out his family tree. "Bradburn of the Philadelphia Bradburns." While he cared little or nothing for what that phrase implied, he thought perhaps it would further

Esther's cause with her mother. "My mother was a Clymer. Her father signed the Declaration of Independence."

"Ah, yes." She probably didn't believe him. More than likely, she knew nothing about the old families of the original thirteen colonies. Her mouth curled just a little. "You're a long way from Philadelphia. How did you happen into my daughter's life?"

"We met on the mountain." He would answer only the questions that he wanted to answer. Anything that would reflect badly on Esther, such as the fact that she had spent two nights in his cabin, would be turned away.

"I see. And did you know her long before this union that my daughter has told me about?"

"We knew each other," was all he would say.

"I understand you came to my daughter's house with Jesse James."

He rose then. Hanging his thumbs in his belt loops, he took two strides that brought him up against the bars. To her credit she did not step back, even though he was taller. "No, ma'am. I'm from Philadelphia, Pennsylvania, as I told you. The only thing your daughter has against me is that I'm a Yankee. I never rode with Jesse James. From what I've heard about the man, he kills Yankees on sight. He'd never ride with one."

"You were arrested by the soldiers and brought in here," she accused.

York ran his hand around the back of his neck. He looked at her sideways. "Ma'am, you know the truth of that, and so does your crooked sheriff. You sent them after me."

She was shaking her head and looked affronted, but he held up his hand. "Why don't you just say what you have to say and get out? The sheriff's going to be back in a few minutes, and you don't want him in on this."

Respect flickered for a moment in her eyes. Then she dropped her gaze. "You're very forthright."

"Yes, ma'am. It pays."

"I can arrange for you to get out of the jail." She looked at him from under her eyelashes. She might have been an older version of Esther except for the blue eyes. Also her face had a cunning look that Esther's had never had. "I can arrange for a good horse, saddlebags of supplies, a gun, money."

"And a sheriff to shoot me in the back from the top of the ridge and take it all back." York dropped back on the bunk and stretched out. He crossed his legs at the ankles and focused on the ceiling.

She gave an exasperated sigh. The interview had not gone as she had expected. When she spoke again, she had resumed her gentle, reasonable posture. "Not at all, young man. The sheriff would be in the next county running an errand for me."

York pushed himself up on his elbow, but he didn't rise from the bunk. "Why are you so determined to get me out of the state? What's it to you if Esther marries? From what she tells me, you disowned her five years ago."

"My daughter is a foolish child. She doesn't know—"

He couldn't keep himself out of the argument, even though he knew it was futile. "No, Mrs. Blessing. That's not so. Your daughter is a woman grown with a woman's needs."

She cut him off angrily. Her voice rose and fell dramatically. "That's just like a man. You think a woman's needs are what make her grown up."

He stretched out again, lacing his fingers behind his head. "No, ma'am. That's not what makes her grown up. That's just a sign that she is. What makes her grown up is living alone and doing man's work for five years."

"She—she—" Rebecca drew herself up. "I had to make an example of her. It's hard to be a woman preacher. You have to be perfect. Men can do sinful things and their congregations forgive. But if I did something wrong, or anyone in my family, my flock would go somewhere else. They'd think I wasn't strong enough."

Her explanation made a selfish kind of sense. But he'd worked alongside Esther. He had seen the hardscrabble life she lived. He would never cooperate with her tormentor. He studied the ceiling. He'd said his say.

Rebecca regarded him stonily. "I can have Sheriff Stamford take you to the state line and put you over it."

"I'd come back." He sat up again. "Listen, Mrs. Blessing, I—I think the world of your daughter. She did— She's been the best thing that's happened to me in ten years." He had almost told her that he loved Esther. He would have said it. For the first time he realized it was true. But he wanted to say it to Esther first.

Rebecca interrupted his thoughts. Every word was a vicious insult. Her voice carried all the power to condemn him to perdition. "I'm sure you think so. But let me tell you. You're not the best thing that's happened to my daughter. You're just another in a line of catastrophes. If anything, you're worse than the other one. At least he was a nice enough boy before the war. You're a drifter, a yellowleg, probably a deserter from who knows which army. You'd like to settle down and live off her. But you won't do it. I'll see to that."

She panted, in the grip of powerful emotions. As her color faded from red to white, lines stood out prominently. Her face looked strained and old.

He shook his head. Slowly, he rose and walked to the bars. "You sure take the cake, ma'am. You've forgiven that outlaw boy that forced your daughter and got her with child, but you haven't forgiven her. What kind of a church are you running?"

Her breath hissed out in an animalistic snarl, before she spun on her heel and marched out. He watched her go knowing he had made a powerful enemy. She believed. She believed what she did for and to her daughter was right. She would fight anyone who tried to thwart her plans.

Fifteen

Esther stood on the doorstep and drank in the crisp December air. The mountains rose before her, dark evergreens interspersed with the bare branches of majestic hardwoods sleeping through the winter months. Pockets of mist like low-lying clouds dotted the scene. Beyond the kennels, steam rose off the pasture pond as the sun sent its first long rays slanting across her place.

Her place. Her farm. Her home.

She wondered if she should pinch herself to be sure she wasn't dreaming. Instead, she hugged herself with sheer happiness, in the same way she had hugged her daughter against her all night long. She had hardly slept, yet this morning she felt no tiredness—only exhilaration.

She would rear her child here as she had been reared. Sarah would know the simple joys that Esther had known. The love of animals, the security of their unflagging devotion. She would know the warmth of the house where she had been born and her mother before her and her father before her. She would have a sense of family.

York Bradburn.

Guilt nagged at her. She should have ridden into town last night, but she couldn't leave Sarah. As a measure of his importance, she realized that even with her daughter beside her, she missed him terribly. His passion heated her where she stood. She tucked her head and breathed deeply. She would not say she loved him. She didn't love him. Not yet. She loved no one in the world except Sarah. But just maybe the next person she allowed herself to love would be York.

She would see that he was set free to return to her. Whatever it took, she would do it. Her mother and Sheriff Stamford would be made to see reason. York and she would adopt Sarah. They would be a family and Sarah would never be ashamed again.

She took the last drink of her coffee and set the cup back inside on the kitchen table. Drawing on her gloves, she strode out to do the chores. The amount she had to do this morning would have been daunting had she not been buoyed up to hurry, so she could return before Sarah awoke. Without any male help, she was going to have to work extra hard.

And perhaps she would surprise Cousin Jesse with a big hug the next time he came riding up her road.

Stamford had a vicious headache and a stomach that roiled with the least motion. Consequently, he scowled at the tall man whose boot heels clomped across the office floor. Having a prisoner in jail was more trouble than it was worth. For one thing the bunk where the sheriff usually slept off his toots was inside the cell. If Stamford had his way, he would take the Yankee out and shoot him. Then whenever anyone came by and disturbed his nap, he could just send him on his way with a flea in his ear.

The man touched a couple of fingers to his fine handlebar moustache. "Need to speak to your prisoner."

"Who the hell are you?" Stamford grunted.

The man stared at him, grim-faced, his eyes turned hard as flint. His drawl became more pronounced. "You got any problem with me talking to him?"

Stamford felt an itch in the middle of his back. It was

the kind of thing he felt when he knew that something was wrong. He considered letting the fellow speak his piece. After all, he'd be around to hear every word that was said. Then he decided that he didn't like the fellow's attitude.

He dropped his booted feet off the desk and hauled himself to his feet. "Nobody talks to this prisoner unless he's got a gen-u-ine reason. This here is a prisoner of the United States Army. I'm just keeping him locked up for them." He came round the desk and thrust his face into the other man's. "So tell me who you are and I'll let you know."

The man looked the sheriff up and down, in particular noting the bloodshot eyes and the trembling of his hands, evidence of a night's hard drinking. A quick knee to the bottom of that gut and the sheriff would be incapacitated for the rest of the day. He shrugged. "Keep this under your hat."

The sheriff goggled at the card the man pulled out, at the wide-open eye staring up at him from the center. Even though he'd never taken to school, Stamford could read the motto above it. "We Never Sleep."

"Pinkerton?" Stamford breathed.

At the name York pushed himself up on the bunk.

The man restored the card to his pocket. "I need to ask him a couple of questions."

When Stamford would have accompanied him to the bars, the detective glared at him. Stamford halted, then stolidly came on. "This is my jail. Whatever you say to him, I'm gonna hear."

York swung his legs over the edge of the bunk and ran his palm over his unshaven face. Of course, his father must have hired the detective. He had forgotten how cautious, how suspicious, the congressman was. That meant that Esther must have sent the telegram. But where was she? Fear for her safety clutched at his gut.

She must have had a long ride to the telegraph office if a detective had made it to town before she got back.

"York Bradburn?" the detective asked.

"That's right." He rose and came to the front of his cell. He thought about extending his hand through the bars, but the detective's expression was forbidding.

"I was sent here to tell you that you can expect no help from anyone in Washington."

The words hit York squarely in the face. He grasped the bars with both hands and stared at the detective. He shook his head. "What did you say?"

The detective pulled his wallet from his breast pocket and extracted a folded strip of paper. York recognized the Western Union form. The man unfolded it and read it aloud:

"INFORM YORK BRADBURN HE WILL BE GIVEN NO HELP. PRISONER UNKNOWN IN WASHINGTON."

York gripped the bars until his knuckles turned white. Perhaps he should have expected this. Probably the past five years had only hardened his father's anger. He was barely conscious of the detective staring at him without a flicker of emotion, nor the sheriff rocking back on his heels and grinning broadly.

York could have laughed at the irony. Now, when he was healed, when he felt whole enough to be with his family, they no longer wanted him. Dazed, he shook his head.

With the barest of shrugs, the detective brushed by the gawking sheriff and walked out the door.

Stamford followed him out into the street, then watched him climb on his horse and ride away. Then he scratched his head and went back into his office. York had slumped back down on his bunk, his back braced against the wall, his eyes staring at nothing.

"Looks like you didn't have no luck there, Yank," Stamford sneered. "I'm right glad. I ain't had a hanging in this town. It'll shut up that bunch of people that say I don't do my job."

York gave a short bark of ironic laughter. "The army tracked me down and brought me in. I didn't even try to get away. You told them where to find me because Rebecca Blessing told you to. You didn't even send the telegram that brought the detective here. What did you do that's part of your job?"

With a snarl Stamford drew his gun. Stabbing it over and over in the direction of his prisoner, he lumbered over to the cell. "I can shoot you where you sit, yellowleg, and drag your body outta there. How'd you like that? Everybody'd say I was a hero for stopping a jailbreak."

York remained where he was. He could feel the cold sweat break out on his forehead. Like an animal in a cage, he could be shot by this idiot, although the way the man handled his gun, he doubted that he would be killed outright. Probably Stamford was like most men— ignorant of the business of shooting a pistol beyond pointing it and jerking the trigger. Why the bullet went into the floor at his feet or through the roof or right or left of the target was unknown to him.

When the prisoner remained on the bunk, Stamford guessed that the man didn't believe him. His frustration overwhelmed him. This man had beaten him to the punch, thrown his gun away, humiliated him thoroughly. Jesse James or no Jesse James, he was a Yankee. No one in this part of the country would shed a tear for him. "I oughtta kill you," he yelled. "That's what I oughtta do. Just pull this here trigger and blow you all to hell and gone. You went crazy 'cause nobody was going to get you out. You tried to escape."

The sheriff pushed the gun between the bars and brandished it. The barrel swept in a wide circle at the same time it jogged up and down. York dropped off the bunk. Both feet hit the floor, as did his left hand. Thinking his prisoner was going down on his knees to beg, Stamford threw back his head and laughed uproariously.

He never saw the man make his move. York launched himself across the six feet of intervening space. Both hands closed over the sheriff's wrist and twisted upward. At the same time, York reversed his direction. He planted one foot against the bar and threw himself back.

Stamford found himself slammed against the bars. His forehead and nose smacked into iron. The joints in his arm and shoulder sockets cracked loudly under the sudden pressure. He howled in pain. While he was still partially paralyzed, the prisoner twisted his arm under and up.

The gun dropped into York's hand. With the sheriff immobilized by his twisted arm, the prisoner reached outside the bars and found the keys dangling from the man's belt. A twist and they came free, and York stepped back with them in one hand and the sheriff's own gun in the other.

"Sit down." York motioned with the pistol. "Sit *down.*"

Whimpering, Stamford pulled his arm back and cradled it on his chest. "You broke my arm."

"Sit down, I said."

The fat man slid down the bars and hunched over.

York opened the cell door and stepped out.

"You can't do that." Stamford's voice was reedy with pain. "Listen, here."

"Crawl." Again the motion with the gun.

The pain was lessening. Stamford tried to move his arm and found that he could. His glare was poisonous as he hitched himself inside the cell door. "I'm gonna kill you for this," he promised. "Don't make me no difference if you run all the way to Californie, I'm still gonna catch you and kill you."

York locked the cell door and tossed the keys on the scarred desk. "I take it your arm's not broken."

The sheriff snarled again. "God damn you! Get away from there!"

York tucked the gun in his waistband and rummaged through the sheriff's desk for a box of shells. Finding two, he stuffed them both into his coat pockets. From the desk he addressed the sheriff. "If you'll take my advice, you'll go talk to your boss. Tell her I was a captain in the Union Army. And I was never a member of the James gang. Tell her that I'm no murderer or you'd be dead. Tell her I'm not a thief. I'm her daughter's husband. Tell her you think the best thing to do is just forget the whole thing."

"You go to hell."

"Tell her I've been there and that she doesn't want to make war on her own kin. The results are worse than anything she can imagine in her worst sermons." With that York pulled his hat low on his brow and stepped out into the street.

Cutter's Knob looked deserted. On a cold, gray weekday in December, no one had any business. From inside the jail came Stamford's angry howls for help, but no one was about to hear them. York grinned. He wondered how many hours would pass before the sheriff would be found.

Esther's horse must be in the livery stable. Figuring that he would attract more attention to himself if he tried to slip around the back of the buildings, he turned his coat collar up over his cheeks and set off at a brisk walk down the street.

No one stopped him. No one even noticed him. He strode into the dimness of the stable where a boy was raking out the stalls. The boy paid him no attention until he'd finished saddling. "That'll be four bits, mister."

York could have kicked himself. After the army had

left, Stamford had made him turn out his pockets. He should have gotten some of it back from the fat sheriff. He hated to ride out and leave the boy to explain to whoever owned the place.

A ghost of a smile played over his features. "Hold on."

In less than a minute, he opened the door of the jail. Stamford was still howling. Although his cries were hoarser, the curses that punctuated them were more vicious.

At the sight of the prisoner, Stamford broke off. A frightened expression passed over his face. "What'd you come back for?"

York drew his gun and crossed to the bars.

Stamford backed against the wall. "Now listen, Mr. Bradburn, take it easy. You don't want—"

"Turn out your pockets."

Stamford's complexion changed from white to red. He cursed, using an expression that York had not heard anywhere except from the mouth of his sergeant. His jaw set, but York stabbed the pistol directly at his belly.

"I can always shoot you in the gut and take your money before you bleed on it."

"This is robbery." Livid, Stamford pulled out his pockets. From the vest pocket came two one-dollar bills, and from his pants came a handful of change.

York pointed downward. "Put it outside the bars and step back."

Keeping his gun trained on the sheriff, he swept up the money. "Much obliged. I'll let you keep the five you took from me."

The howls redoubled as York closed the door and trotted back to the stable.

Rebecca Blessing's piano-box buggy rolled up in front of Esther's house in the early afternoon. Slowly, Daniel climbed down and hitched the horse. He dreaded what he had come to do. In fact, the entire episode made him sick to his stomach. His mother talked at length about his calling when the time came for her to step down. But the conference was sending her an assistant pastor while he, her own son, had yet to preach his first sermon.

He looked out over the farm. What would he have been like if his father had not been killed? What would he be doing now? He sighed and knocked on the door. From inside he heard an object fall to the floor, a flurry of footsteps. The curtain twitched aside.

"It's Uncle Daniel," Sarah's voice piped. And then, "No. Don't answer the door." The next words were indistinct. Then again Sarah protested. "No-o-o!"

He knocked again, not because he was impatient or even cold. He wanted them both to know that he would not go away.

At length the door opened. Two pairs of brown eyes greeted him. Esther had taken Sarah up in her arms. The little girl had wrapped her arms around her mother's neck until he wondered how his sister could breathe. "Hello," he said quietly. He tried a smile that was a pale copy of his mother's. "Can I come in?"

Silently, Esther walked back into the house. Still holding her daughter, she seated herself in the rocker. Daniel closed the door and came around the settee. His first question surprised them both. "Did you have any trouble making the ride out here, Sarah?"

His niece pulled away from her mother far enough to exchange a look with her. Then she looked suspiciously at Daniel. "No."

"That's good." He sat down on the settee with his hands clasped between his knees. He swallowed, trying to rid his mouth of the foul taste. "I was afraid for you coming all that way alone and you only five. But your grandmother said you'd be fine." He looked meaningfully at his sister. "And she was right, as usual."

Esther shook her head faintly. The import of what he was saying dawned on her. She had thought of many reasons why no one had ridden out after Sarah yesterday, but none she could have thought of was as shocking as the reality. "Do you mean that Rebecca knew she was coming? And let her come?"

He nodded miserably. "Sarah'd been telling everybody she was going to run away and be with you. Rebecca thought it would be a good idea for the two of you to spend the night together."

"I'm not going back," Sarah said suddenly.

"You can't have her back." Esther spoke at the same moment.

Daniel did not move. His sad eyes remained trained on the pair of them. He had never been more certain of anything in his life than that his niece and his sister belonged together. Nevertheless, he spoke the words his mother had told him to say. "Perhaps you could just move into town and then we could all be together."

Esther looked at him appalled. She hugged her daughter and kissed her cheek. "Sarah, would you go in the kitchen and fetch some of the cookies we made? I'm sure Uncle Daniel would like to have some before he starts his ride back."

Obediently, Sarah let herself be set down. "I'll go get the cookies, but I'll listen at the door. I know what you're going to do. You're going to talk about me." Before either of them could deny the accusation, she ran from the room. She banged the kitchen door, and from the other side she shouted. "I'll listen. Just see if I don't."

Brother and sister exchanged looks.

"This was all my mother's plan, wasn't it?"

Daniel nodded. Unable to sit still, he rose and began to pace. "She—she thought that maybe you didn't want

Sarah enough. She thought that because you didn't grab Sarah up on the spot in Carolan's store that you had—" He gulped down a lump in his throat. "—gotten hard and callous."

"And she thought that a hard, callous person was a suitable mother." Esther closed her eyes. All this had been a plan to manipulate her and her daughter. She felt like a raccoon run before the hounds and hunters until it could go nowhere but to its tree. When she opened her eyes, they were hard as steel. "Daniel, is our mother sane?"

He flinched. "Of course."

"Is she? I don't think so." She rose, too, wringing her hands as chill after chill skittered over her skin.

"She's just—" He spread his hands. "She just thinks that she knows what's right for everybody. And in more cases than not, she does."

He couldn't get the words out before Esther was shaking her head. "I've always believed so, but this time it isn't true."

"Esther, please—"

She came across the room and caught his fluttering hands. At the same time she lowered her voice in the hopes that Sarah wouldn't be able to hear. "Daniel, she set her own granddaughter out on a dangerous ride of almost five miles on a pony. With soldiers on the road. Soldiers that for all we know she might have summoned."

"Soldiers?" He looked frightened. "Yankees?"

"Yes!" Esther hissed. "Yankee soldiers. What do you think they would have done if they had passed a little girl riding alone?"

He freed his hand to haul out a handkerchief and mop his brow. "Mother wouldn't send for soldiers. What do we need with soldiers in this country?" He backed away trembling and shaking his head. "Soldiers hanged Papa."

Behind them Sarah opened the kitchen door. So intent were the two adults on their conversation that neither paid any attention as she came into the room.

"I think she'd send for the devil himself if that was the only way to get what she wanted. You've heard her say that everyone is a tool of the Lord. She wanted my husband arrested. Stamford couldn't do it. So she sent for the U.S. Army."

"No. You're wrong." He waved her away.

But Esther wouldn't let her brother go. He had to hear her through to the end and understand what she had come to believe. "She doesn't want me to have a husband or a happy life. She wants me to suffer and suffer for what was never my fault."

"You were a fallen woman."

"Daniel!" In disgust Esther flung his hand away. Turning around, she almost stumbled over her daughter.

Sarah faced her with hands on her hips. "Grandmother says you sinned like Mary." She screwed up her face. "I can't remember which Mary, but because of what you did, I'm a female bastard." Then the dam burst in a flood of heartrending sobs and tears.

Sweeping her daughter up in her arms again, Esther rained kisses on her face.

Daniel covered his face with his hands. "Dear Lord."

"You'd never heard her say that before, had you? Aren't those the most awful words to fall from a baby's innocent lips." Her words seemed to come from a long way off.

"Never." Behind his hands his own voice quivered.

"How long have people been calling you that, Sarah?"

The little girl hid her face against her mother's neck. Her sobs died away to hoarse, snubbing sounds. So long as she could shock people with the phrase and then run away, she could say it and take a certain pleasure in it. But when her mother and her uncle looked at her with such hurt in their eyes, she wished she hadn't. "I don't know. I can't remember."

Daniel sank down on the settee and held his face in his hands. "Mother never knew about any of this."

Esther made a rude sound. "Of course she did. People would let her know what others were saying. You know how the old gossips love to tell the things that hurt the most." Esther could name an even dozen of the town wives whose tongues had lashed her. The first year of her exile, every time she had been forced by absolute necessity to ride into Cutter's Knob, she had ridden home crying. Now she felt the moisture of her own daughter's tears. "Don't cry, sweetheart," she murmured. "It's all right. Mama loves you."

Rising, her brother came to her side. "Sarah," he said softly. "Sarysue."

She kept her head buried.

He put his hands on her shoulders. "Can't you come to Uncle Daniel, Sarysue? He wants to tell you how sorry he is."

With much coaxing she finally allowed herself to be taken into his arms. Immediately, she hid her face in his neck. He stroked her back and crooned to her. "You should have told me the first time someone said anything. I would have stopped it." He looked in agony. "I would have stopped it somehow."

Esther could see the tears shining in his eyes. She put her arms around them both and leaned her forehead against Daniel's. They stood like that for what seemed a long time.

Then Esther stepped back and wiped her eyes. They had wept long enough. Now they had to put regrets aside and plan for the future. At least now Daniel understood. For the first time, she had an ally in her mother's camp. "I think we should all go to the kitchen and have cookies and hot chocolate. What do you say to that?"

Sarah pulled her face out of Daniel's shoulder. It was swollen and red and splotchy, but the eyes were indomitable. "Yes." She looked at her uncle. "Mama puts chocolate in milk. It makes it taste good."

Smiling, Daniel carried Sarah after his sister. "It sure does. I had forgotten about hot chocolate."

Esther leaned forward, her hands extended in supplication. Never had she chosen her words with such care. Her brother had to understand. He had to see that for the sake of Sarah he must take her part against their mother. "Daniel, my daughter came to me of her own free will. She was unhappy. She's told you why herself. She needs to stay with me. York and I will adopt her and change her name. She won't be a bastard any longer."

Daniel looked worried. "That fellow York is the stumbling block in all this."

Esther lifted her cup to her mouth to conceal her irritation behind it. Her brother still didn't understand what had happened. "He's only a stumbling block because Mother made him one. He's a good man, Daniel. Mother just doesn't like him because she didn't select him. He's not the new assistant minister sent by the conference."

Daniel flushed. "I know you're right, but now that he's been arrested, he won't make a very good father."

Esther set the mug down with a thump. She didn't remember her brother being so simple-minded. Taking everything that his mother said as the gospel truth had had a bad effect on him. "Daniel," she explained impatiently, "Mother was the one who had him arrested. She can get him out of jail when she wants to. He's done nothing wrong."

Her brother shook his head. "I think you're wrong. The army rode right into town with—"

The sound of a horse galloping down the road made them look at each other in alarm. Esther scraped back her chair and dashed to the front door in time to see York guiding the wagon horse into the stable. With a cry of joy, she leaped off the porch and ran after him.

In the dim stable, she flung herself into his arms. "You're free." Without thinking she hugged him. His mouth was hot and as eager as hers. His beard scratched her, but she pressed all the closer.

At last he drew back his head and sucked in air. "My God," he whispered. Then, "Easy, there. You'll have me splitting my britches."

Suddenly, she could feel her skin glowing with excitement. At the same time she caught his face between her palms. "You're here. You're free. How did you get here? I was coming to tell you that the telegram from Washington said they didn't know you. I'm so sorry."

"Don't be." He turned his mouth into her palm. "I already know."

"How? What happened?"

Instead of answering he kissed her again. His hands cupped her breasts, slid down over her waist, and pressed her hips against him, hard. She moaned and twisted.

"Oh, Lord, there's no time," he murmured. "I have to go."

She pulled back. Alarm streaked through her, driving the heat and passion before her. Her eyes were enormous, her face white. "Where?"

"Back to the mountain." He stepped back. "Esther, I just broke jail."

"Oh, no." She caught at his arms, searched his face for signs of pain. "Are you hurt? Was anyone hurt?"

He shook his head. His mouth quirked at the corners. He cleared his throat. "Just the sheriff's pride. But that might be the worst thing I could have done. I locked him in his own jail cell."

Esther stared at her husband. His eyelashes veiled his expression, but his mouth twitched. Despite his rumpled appearance, he looked incredibly handsome, especially when she realized he was struggling not to laugh. Then she realized why. She threw her hands up to her mouth. "Oh, no. You locked Elmo Stamford in his own jail cell."

He chuckled. " 'Fraid so."

"Elmo Stamford in his own jail!"

"It gets worse." York turned away, running his hands through his hair. His shoulders heaved. "I didn't have the fifty cents to pay the livery stable, so I went back and made him give it to me."

She staggered back against the manger. "You broke jail and then you went back in and made him give you money." She went into whoops of laughter. "He paid for you to get the horse out of the livery."

York thrust his hands in his pockets and grinned like a boy. "He stole my money. I stole it back."

She caught hold of the side of the stall to keep from falling. "Oh, Lord. I'd give a year off my life to have been there. Was he furious?" She went off into gales again. "Elmo Stamford in his own jail."

York joined her. They collapsed in each other's arms. Then he was kissing her, and she was holding him and kissing him back. When they were both breathless, he propped her back against the stall and stepped away. "I've got to leave. And I think you'd better come with me."

"Me?"

"You told me Stamford's already attacked you once. I've humiliated him by locking him in his own jail. He's going to be dangerous as a mad dog. You'll be the target if he can't find me. He might even lock you up in jail to get me to come back in." He didn't tell her other things Stamford might do to her if he had her in the cell. What she couldn't imagine couldn't give her nightmares. "Come with me so I can take care of you until I can get one of my father's friends to confirm my identity."

Never had she slipped from joy to sadness in the space of a heartbeat. She was a little breathless when she held out her hand. "At least come in the house. You need to know what promises I've made in your name."

One black eyebrow rose. "Uh-oh."

Sixteen

Public humiliation is an unforgivable transgression.

Not that Elmo Stamford would have voiced his anger and frustration in such a way. After hours of yelling and cursing, he was finally able to make someone hear him. And of all people, his rescuer had to be Martha Virginia Ord, spinster and town gossip.

Martha Virginia opened the door of the jail and saw him sitting in his own cell with the door closed. She stared at him open-mouthed. Then her eyes slid round the room seeking some reasonable explanation. Frowning, she stuck one finger in underneath the bun on top of her head and scratched her scalp.

"Martha Virginny—" He swung his legs off the bunk and lunged for the bars. "Just hand me them—" He pointed to the keys on the desk. Too late. She ran screaming down the street.

His luck was all bad because she ran straight to Carolan's Store. People along the way came out of their doors to stare at her. Unfortunately, inside the store were not only the storekeeper and his wife, but also three ladies from the church Missionary Society and the town spit-and-whittle group of old men sitting around the stove. While Martha Virginia led Ed and Bertha Carolan to the jail, their customers had fluttered like geese up and down the street, summoning everyone to come and see their sheriff.

Over a dozen people crowded into his jail to exclaim

and wonder and to hide their smiles behind their hands. By the time Ed Carolan managed to get the right key into the lock and get the door open, Elmo Stamford's face was so red, he looked damn nigh ready to explode. Cursing vividly, he burst out of the cell and plowed through the people in the office. Out in the street, he found practically the whole town of Cutter's Knob waiting, including Rebecca Blessing, who was just coming down the hill from the church.

He wanted to crawl under the boardwalk. To have her hear about the jailbreak would be bad enough. But much more damning was the knowledge that she had witnessed his humiliation and knew he had failed her.

"Are you hurt?" she asked. She didn't touch him. Her face was pale and set. Her usually mobile mouth looked stiff.

"No." He hung his head.

"That's good." She looked around at the congregated citizenry. "We're all glad that you weren't shot or something worse."

No one said a word. No one clapped him on the back or offered up a heartfelt hallelujah that their sheriff had survived one of the dangers of his office. Rebecca looked around her. A faint frown knitted her brow. Was it her imagination, or were some of them looking at her also?

She caught Bertha Carolan's eye. Instantly the storekeeper's wife dropped her gaze. A frightening suspicion took root in Rebecca's mind. She had supported the sheriff, even though he had always been unpopular. This jailbreak would lead many people to believe he was also incompetent. Rebecca's expression chilled.

Stamford saw it. He could have howled even with his throat so sore he could hardly speak. Instead, he rallied gamely. "This yellowleg's got a head start on us, but I'm pretty sure I know where he's headed. Who's with me?"

Ed Carolan rocked back on his heels and looked

around at several of the other men. Drawing support from their silent acquiescence, he confronted the sheriff. "What was he in there for anyway, Elmo? He seemed like a nice enough feller. Him and Esther just got married. They come in last week and bought a big bunch of stuff. Paid cash for it. Bill came to over five dollars."

An awed murmuring made the rounds. Five dollars was more money than most of them saw at any one time.

Stamford bristled. Shoulders squared, he faced the storekeeper whom he outweighed by fifty pounds. "He's one of the James gang. The army brought him in."

"Then let the army go get him," someone else spoke up. "We don't do no favors for the U.S. Army."

"If he's a Yankee, how come he's in with Jesse and the boys?" a woman asked. "Jesse James wouldn't have no truck with a Yankee."

Several muttered in agreement. Their comments swelled. The James gang had supporters all over Missouri and Arkansas.

"I'll catch him!" Stamford yelled hoarsely. "Ain't nobody breaks out of my jail and robs me."

"Did he rob you, too?" Ed Carolan asked innocently. The crowd began to chuckle.

Stamford growled like a timber wolf. The chuckles ceased. By twos and threes the crowd dispersed, walking away to their places of business, to their errands, their heads together, talking as they went. Occasionally the sound of laughter drifted back up the street. Finally, only two people were left in front of the jail.

Stamford looked piteously at Rebecca. "Miz Blessing, I'm sorry as I can be."

"I—er—hope you catch him." She dropped her eyes. Picking up her skirts, she hurried back up the hill and left him standing alone.

* * *

York observed that Daniel Blessing was more than ill at ease. Esther's brother was downright terrified of him. He appeared smaller than Ester, although his shoulders and torso were heavier. His handshake was a limp affair, a mere touch and a quick withdrawal, after which the fellow dropped his eyes.

Not so the little girl. With all the courageous defiance of her mother, she put her hands on her hips. "I'm Sarysue Woodson," she informed him. "When you 'dopt me, I'll be called your name. What is your name?"

He saw his wife tense. His brother-in-law flashed her a quick look before fixing York with an assessing stare.

So this was the promise that Esther had made. York dropped into the kitchen chair and motioned to Sarysue. She looked a little frightened, but she sidled forward courageously. Even though he was unaccustomed to children, he could guess that she was an unusual five-year-old. She talked like an adult. She had faced him squarely, rather than hang back and hide her face. She had mispronounced only one word, and that he could guess was because she had heard it for the first time only a day or so ago. "My name is Bradburn," he told her. He put his hand on her shoulder. "Do you want to be adopted?"

"Mama said I would be. I'm not sure."

"If I adopted you, you'd be my daughter. We'd probably live out here away from town, but you'd still have to go into town to school next year. Would you like that?"

"I wouldn't be a female bastard anymore?" Her bottom lip quivered, but she thrust it out.

"No. You'd be my daughter. You'd be Sarysue Bradburn. Of the Philadelphia Bradburns." He threw in the rest of it not because he wanted to impress her. The first families of Pennsylvania meant nothing in the Ozarks. But it had suddenly occurred to him that he really wanted to make some kind of peace with his father.

Esther's daughter looked steadily into his face. Her

own emotions were clear as crystal, as any child's would be. Disbelief came first when she narrowed her eyes and lifted her chin. Then when he kept his gaze steady, a tiny frown creased the smooth forehead. She lowered her head and toed-in, scuffing her shoes deliberately. "I wouldn't always be good. I'm not perfect, y' know."

"I know. I'm not either."

She looked at her mother, whose face was wet with tears. "I guess it would be all right. Sarah Susannah Bradburn would sound good."

Although she argued fiercely and was hard pressed to keep from crying, Sarah agreed to stay with Daniel and take care of the hounds while Esther rode up onto the mountain with York.

"I'll be back day after tomorrow at the very latest," Esther promised.

Her daughter glanced at York with a disbelieving look on her face.

He put his hand on Esther's shoulder. "You can't come back until we know that Stamford can't keep me in jail. I've got to be able to protect you." He looked to his brother-in-law for support. "She doesn't understand what that crazy sheriff would do to her. I've seen him in action. He's spied on your sister for God knows how long at your mother's instructions. He attacked her on the street in October."

Daniel fluttered his hands at his sister. "I never knew a thing about this. I swear."

York tried to keep his voice neutral, though the man disgusted him. "He's jumped me twice. He stuck his gun through the bars and told me he was going to shoot me where I sat and drag me out in the street and tell people I tried to escape. He's like an animal. He'll get meaner and meaner until he kills someone. Esther can't stay here where he can get his hands on her."

"I've been protecting myself for five years," she snapped.

"Please, Esther." York put his arm around her. "Just until I get my discharge papers that prove who I am."

Letting out her breath in a long sigh, she touched his cheek. Then she went down on her knees to her daughter. "Here's a promise that you can count on. Next spring when the weather is warm and dry, we'll all take a trip up onto the mountain. We'll stay in a real mountain cabin, and you can meet Big Boy."

Sarah lifted her chin. Her mother and father were leaving her. She didn't dare believe they would return. All her protective instincts rose to shield her from hurt. "I probably won't want to go then. Boys are mean and nasty. I don't like boys."

"Big Boy's a cat," Esther explained. "He's the biggest, wildest cat you've ever seen. And he's lonely." She took Sarah by the shoulders and kissed her on her forehead and both cheeks. "I promise. Right now it's cold up there in the mountains, and we're coming up on the shortest day of the year."

"And the darkest." Sarah's eyes got big as she remembered. "It gets dark awful fast."

York leaned down to speak to her, too. He was a little surprised at how strongly he felt that this child should not be deserted. "I have to hide until I get this mess straightened out," he explained. "But it won't take long. Maybe it'll all be settled by Christmas."

Esther hugged her daughter again and rose with her in her arms. "I love you very much, Sarah Susannah. And I'll be back before you know it." She looked to her brother. "You'll take care of everything out here?"

"Everything. I haven't forgotten everything Papa

taught me." He smiled as if he were really glad to take care of the hounds.

Esther kissed her daughter again. "I'll be back quickly. I promise."

York put his arms around them both. "I'll see that she keeps her promise, Sarah."

They didn't gallop out onto the road, but picked their way slowly through the meadows and gradually up the mountain. By doubling back on their tracks and circling, what trail they left would be impossible to follow. In the haze of evening, Esther wondered how she could duplicate the route coming home. Perhaps she should plan to ride down the other side of the mountain and come on by the river.

"My horse isn't up to this," York called back over his shoulder as he swung out of the saddle. As the trail turned precipitous, the old animal had taken to stopping every few yards, head hanging. Its neck and haunches were slick with sweat. "We'll have to walk."

"How much farther?" Esther climbed down, too. It was pitch black. The pines blocked out the moon and stars. She wondered how he could keep from blundering into the bole of a tree.

"Not much." He waited until she caught up with him, then gathered Babe's reins and took Esther's hand. "I hate it that you're here, but I didn't dare leave you."

She squeezed his hand. "I think I would have been all right, but I couldn't let you go up here on your own. I didn't know where you were going or whether you'd be all right. Daniel could stay with Sarah. When I've eased my mind, I'll go back down and take care of her."

They walked on together. The darkness and the cold were pervasive, but she was not depressed. Instead, her heart sang. Despite the fact that she was running from

the law in the depths of the Ozarks, it seemed almost
like a glorious adventure.

"You were wonderful," she told him suddenly. She
leaned her head against his shoulder. "Most men
wouldn't have taken to the idea of adopting another
man's child. Particularly, a female bastard." She choked
on the words.

He put his arm around her. "She's your daughter. I
can only guess at how much you've wanted her with you."
They walked on in silence. "The war's changed a lot of
things in this country. Some things are gone for good—
like slavery. Some things are here for a long, long time,
like Reconstruction. Soldiers ran pretty much wild all
over the South. Soldiers on both sides. Whenever they
got the chance, they probably took advantage of girls like
you. You're not alone. Most of their families have looked
the other way and are raising the baby without making
anything out of it. And that's good. Because being a bastard isn't the baby's fault."

Esther had never felt a kinship for the young women
all over the South who had had the same thing happen
to them. Probably many of them had been raped cruelly
rather than just roughly seduced by some callow boy like
Clell. The way York described everything, she could even
find it in her heart to forgive Clell. He'd been almost as
young as she. And now Jesse said he was dead.

He might never have lived at all except for Sarah.

Esther could feel another piece of the shattered parts
of her life slipping back into place. She lifted her face
and kissed York's cheek.

"Hey!" He kissed her back. Their walk together became punctuated by heated kisses and caresses that drove
the peril of his situation and their own worries to the
back of their minds. Esther drank in the midnight air.
Her whole body was alive with heightened senses. York's

warm hand dropped from her shoulder to her hip, his arm pressed securely across her back.

Moonlight showed through the trees. They stepped out of the dark canopy onto the silver gray of the slate ridge. A frisson slid over Esther's body as the fragile stone crackled under her feet. "I know where we are."

"Careful," he cautioned, hugging her even closer. "I'd just as soon not have to lug you out of there." He turned her in his arms. His hands splayed between her shoulder blades and buttocks, so she was glued to him from knees to chest. The moonlight fell full on her upturned face. He studied her features for a minute. As she looked up at the dark shape, Esther shuddered with wave after wave of desire crashing against her, leaving her knees weak, her head light.

"Don't fight it," he advised softly. "I couldn't stand you right behind me anymore. I had to have you close."

"You mean we could have ridden," she teased him. "You made me walk all this distance."

"It's not much farther." He slid his tongue into her mouth, demonstrating vividly what he intended to do to her when they reached the cabin. He was iron hard, and so insistent that she felt a gush of hot liquid between her legs. Another instant of contact would be too much.

He set her away and groaned. "Come on."

The cabin was just the same, but different. She wanted to cry at the primitiveness, the coldness, the rudeness of the furnishings. They told more clearly than words the nature of his exile. Again she wondered what had brought him to this place. Horror too terrible for her sheltered experiences to imagine.

While she stood bemused, York, too, glanced around. The cabin seemed unlivable now, where less than a month ago, it had been more than he wanted, more than he thought he deserved. Now, he pulled out the single chair. "Madam."

She held out imaginary skirts. "Thank you, kind sir."

The fire in the potbellied stove caught immediately. There was still oil in the lantern. The cistern had filled to overflowing from the snows and rains. "I could get back in the habit if I had to, I guess," he commented as he poured them both mugs of coffee and passed one to her. "But I don't want to."

"No."

He bent above her to kiss her. As their lips met and parted, he shuddered powerfully. A little out of control, heady with the taste of her, he wanted more. The jail had not been an ordeal, certainly nothing in comparison to what he had endured, but marriage had made him weaker, more needy. He felt like a man deprived. He drove his tongue into her mouth, far back into her throat.

She clutched at his shoulders. Her head strained back as her neck arched. She groaned. Instantly, he released her.

"I'm sorry. I didn't mean to be rough." He couldn't believe himself. Knowing what she had been through, he should be more considerate. They both had tender places where they could easily be hurt. He suspected a rough loving would frighten her.

She reached across to him, dropping her gaze to the edge of the table. "You weren't rough. It makes me feel good to know that you want me."

"Want you!" He caught her under the arms and lifted her.

"What? What are you doing?" As if she were a child, he had seated her on the edge of the table.

"What I've wanted to do ever since I met you." His face intense, he kissed her. His hands were busy at the end of her braid. He dropped the leather ribbon on the floor and combed his fingers through her hair. As each twist came apart, static electricity sparked and crackled over his fingers.

While he was busy with it, she kissed his cheeks, the tip of his nose, his chin, his ears. When the hair was a shining curtain about her shoulders, he stood back. "Open your shirt for me." His eyes were black wells. His husky voice sent chills down her spine. "I want to kiss your breasts."

"Only if you take off your pants for me."

He shuddered, his teeth set to stifle a groan of primal desire.

Her hands trembled as she opened the first button on her blouse. "Now you."

A flush burned on his cheekbones. It thrilled her. She knew a dark joy that he was as excited as she was. Her words had excited him almost as much as her eyes did when they slid from his face down the column of his throat to his belt buckle. While she watched he undid it, his hands only a little clumsy.

He emerged engorged and hard as oak before she was naked to the waist. He put his mouth on one breast while he cupped the other with his hands. She closed her hands around him, breathing hard. Barely conscious of what she did, she stroked upward, drawing shuddering groans of pleasure from him.

Then he dropped to his knees, pulling himself out of her hands. "Lean down," he begged. "Lean down."

The intensity of pleasure was a shock. He was kissing and caressing her breasts while they hung pendulous above him. The downward pull started an ache in her belly. She clutched at his shoulders and moaned.

The wetness and heat between her legs forced her to shift her hips uncontrollably. He had her pants unbuttoned and down to the table before she knew. "Lift your hips," he whispered.

She couldn't do anything but obey him. She ached too much, wanted him too much. Without a murmur, she braced her arms back against the table and arched up. Her pants slipped down, and his mouth closed over her mound.

She shrieked with the shock of it. Still unsure about a man's mouth on her most private part, she tried to be embarrassed, but all she could feel was pleasure as he pushed her back and parted her. His tongue touched her. She screamed again, this time in release.

It went on and on. She felt pinned to the table, wondering how and why no one had ever even hinted at this pleasure before. She would have to think about it when she could think.

Her back relaxed against the bleached wood; her head sank back until it hung over the edge. She heard the rustle of clothing. And then he was between her legs, pressing himself into the liquid warmth, creating more of the same sensations when she thought no more were possible. She gasped for breath as he closed one hand on her hipbone and the other on her shoulder.

He was holding her in a frighteningly practical fashion. Like a vise he clamped her body while he drove into her with long, torturous strokes.

She opened her eyes to the sight of his face in the lantern light. His eyes were half-closed, glazed. His teeth were set. His muscles and tendons corded in his jaw. She had never known a man could be beautiful. Especially not one with wild hair and a week's growth of beard. Her man was angelic, spiritual, godlike.

"York," she called, a hoarse gasp. "Oh, York, please take your pleasure. Please, York, please."

His answer was a terrible groan.

The speed of his strokes increased. They should have hurt, but somehow her body accommodated itself to him. In the grip of pleasure that gave him preternatural strength, he lifted her off the table. Hot liquid gushed into her, and she exploded again.

As they slumped across the table together, she wondered how Sarah would welcome a baby brother or sister.

Lieutenant Hammerschild was having a bad dream. For several days now he had dreamed all night long of riding. In the morning he awoke to find himself as tired as when he went to bed. He had ridden miles through the Ozarks. He had probably crossed and recrossed his own trail, but he was confused. Moreover, he had not seen any sign of Jesse James.

Native Arkansans or Missourians or Kansans—he no longer knew which state he was in—told him that Jesse had just been there, or that they had heard that he was somewhere else. At first, he had led his troop at a gallop, but lately his abused rear had become so sore that he could manage no more than a walk.

Now, he dreamed that he had fallen asleep across the saddle. Its horn was poking him in the stomach. He frowned and tried to get off it, but it poked him again.

"Wake up," a voice insisted close in his ear. "Wake up, Yankee."

His eyes opened, blinked, focused. Pain stabbed his belly again. He was lying on his side. Just enough light came through the open door of a lantern to see a man's grinning face no more than a foot away.

"I hear y'all are looking for me."

"Who are you?" Hammerschild's lips were stiff.

His visitor laughed softly. "You must have real bad reward posters. How'd you ever recognize me if you was to come up on me?"

Hammerschild made a move to throw back the covers.

"Just take it easy," he was advised. "This here Navy Colt's got a hair trigger."

He began to sweat. "You wouldn't shoot a man while he's asleep."

The grin widened. The eyes danced like the very devil was in them. "That's the best way to go. He don't never know what hit him."

"Are you Jesse J-James?"

"Go to the head of the class, yellowleg." Jesse pulled his gun back a couple of inches. "I just dropped by to find out why y'all are looking for me."

Hammerschild tried to remember what had started him out on this road. "You robbed a bank."

His visitor shrugged. "I've done it before. I'll do it again. What's the U.S. Army care about a few dollars in Missouri?"

"You terrorized a town here in Arkansas. The minister sent word by the sheriff that they needed help." Hammerschild frowned. That all seemed a long time ago.

Jesse reared back. His eyes widened. "What town?"

"Er—Cutler's—Cutter's—"

"Cutter's Knob," Jesse supplied.

"That's right." Hammerschild remembered it all. "We arrested one of your gang right there on the spot."

Jesse was grinning again. "That so. Who'd you get? Brother Frank or Cousin Cole?"

Hammerschild looked disgusted. "Nobody important. Some fellow who claimed he was from Pennsylvania." He scratched his head. "York. That was his name. York."

Jesse sobered. "You arrested York Bradburn?"

Hammerschild looked pleased. "Good friend of yours?"

"Not particularly. But he's married to the minister's daughter. I'll bet your commanding officer'll just love that when he gets wind of it."

"The minister's daughter! But—But— " The muzzle of Jessie's Navy Colt yawned in Hammerschild's face. He looked cross-eyed at it.

It didn't go away as Jesse rose. "Listen, yellowleg. You ain't going to catch me unless I want you to. I'd kill you right now, but I want you to do a job for me."

Hammerschild gulped again. He could feel his sweat soaking the sheets.

"Go on back to Fort Smith, but on your way through Bentonville, send a messenger over there to let York Bradburn go. You've got the wrong man in jail." Jesse closed the door on the lantern. In the pitch blackness he vanished.

York brought in another jug of whiskey. He poured himself a tot and added a drop to Esther's coffee. Then he sat down and tasted it. His eyebrows rose, and he swallowed gingerly. A minute passed, and then he smiled. "Smooth as satin. I'll have to find someplace else for the still. I make this stuff too good to give it up."

She shook her head. Somehow she would have to keep that from her mother above all things. Rebecca was hell on whiskey drinking. She would never speak to York if she found out he operated a still. "I don't know what to compare it with, but it tastes pretty good in coffee."

He laughed. They sat together in companionable silence. He finished the mug and put it down. "I suppose I should tell you something about myself."

She regarded him in mock-seriousness. "Apart from being a Yankee jailbreaker, what else is there to know?"

He turned the mug in his hand, transferred it from one hand to the other, and finally set it down. A muscle jumped in his jaw. Tendons strutted in his neck. "I was in the army, during the war."

She reached across the table and covered his hand. "You don't have to tell me anything you'd rather keep a secret. You're my husband. But you had a life before we met."

"I don't think you'll condemn me for this." His voice dropped lower and lower as if he were terrified that others might hear. "But if you do, I'll understand. God knows, my father and mother—" He shook his head. Putting his elbow on the table, he rubbed his forehead between his eyes. "My sister—"

She waited. He was determined to tell this. She must listen with all her heart and mind. She said a little prayer, not to God, but to Rebecca Blessing for understanding.

"I was in the 4th Pennsylvania Cavalry. We were the 64th Volunteers. John Childe was our colonel. He was a gentleman; therefore, my father approved of him. Did I tell you my father is a United States Congressman?" His face darkened, the nostrils pinched. He closed his eyes.

"We saw a lot of action in Virginia and Tennessee. All along the Shenandoah and the Blue Ridge. We generally charged into battle against foot soldiers. We'd yell and swing our sabers and run right through them. They'd jump out of the way and a few of them would fall down. A few of us would be wounded or fall. Most of the time everybody was standing when the dust cleared. It was more like a game than anything else." He looked at her with haunted eyes. "No one I knew or cared anything about got so much as a scratch."

Rising, she pulled the cob out of the jug and poured each of them a tot of whiskey straight. He stared at it, then drank it down like water.

"My mother's from Virginia. I don't guess I told you that. She was born on a tobacco plantation on the North Carolina border. Her people were slave owners. Of course, she'd lived in Philadelphia for twenty years. But my brother Edmond had spent a lot of time in the South. He believed in states' rights. States' rights." York repeated the words like a curse.

Esther couldn't remember whether she had ever heard the term before. She shifted in her chair. Her husband's

superior education made her feel inferior. Here in the
Ozarks what happened on the other side of the Mississippi River didn't affect folks much.

"Edmond was a captain, too. Mother told me. She had
a terrible time when he joined up. She told me she had
visions of us aiming guns at each other. I told her not
to worry. It would never happen. Edmond couldn't even
ride a horse. He was born with something wrong with
his hip. He'd always walked with a limp. Father and I
were sure Edmond would be adjutant to some general
back in Richmond."

The anguish grew in his voice as he begged her to
understand. Sweat popped out on his forehead. The
knuckles showed white where his fist gripped the mug.
Then his haunted eyes no longer saw the dim room, no
longer saw her, though she took both his hands in her
own. They looked into another time.

"We flanked them. They had their guns trained on
the infantry regiment with their big flags. Colonel Childe
had read some military tactics, and he'd been waiting to
use them. He gave the order and we charged. Right down
the line. God! It was a slaughter. The only thing they
had to use against us was their commander's swords. The
gunners didn't even have side arms. And they didn't surrender."

He looked at her then as if she were the Angel of
Judgment. "The gallant idiots swung at us with their
rammers and swabs while the rest of the crew touched
off the powder. I'd led my troop to the end of the line
and started back again when a man came running out
of the smoke at me. He had an officer's sword, and he
was swinging it at me. My horse reared and went down.
I got off him before he could roll. The smoke was so
thick. I couldn't see. There was yelling all around me.
The infantry was charging. They broke through with
bayonets. I couldn't see who I was fighting. I couldn't

see." He began to cry. Great wracking sobs tore out of his throat.

"I believe you, York. I believe you." Esther pried the mug from his sweaty, icy hand and put her arms around him. "I believe you."

"I couldn't see!" he yelled. "I couldn't see. He was charging at me, swinging the sword. I cut him down. Cut him right across the knees. I had to kill them. Had to put out the guns."

"Yes. Yes. I see. It's all right." She pushed the table aside and pressed his head against her breast. "I see."

"I got knocked down again." He dropped his voice until it was only a whisper. "I got right back up. I did. My troop had gone on. I didn't know how far I was from the end of the line. How far back in we'd gone. I started to run and then I tripped."

He wrapped his arms around her body and hid his head. He was holding her so tightly his teeth grazed her breast through the layers of clothing.

"I fell on my brother," he whispered. "He was sprawled on the gun. He was alive, but the blood was everywhere. Spouting. I tried to stop it. But my arm wouldn't work right."

He fell silent. She knew he was still crying because she could feel the copious tears soaking through her clothing. The minutes passed. His breath rasped in his throat.

When she thought he had finished, she tried to straighten to ease her cramped position.

He clutched her tighter still. "He tried to kill me."

The words were uttered so softly that she almost said, "What?"

"I tried to tie off a tourniquet. I'd cut an artery in his leg. It was spouting. And he swung at me with his sword." He began to cry again.

"He didn't know it was you." Instantly, Esther gave him the words he needed to hear. She drove her fingers into York's thick, black hair and pulled his head back. His face was a mask of torment, wet and stained with tears. His mouth was open in a silent scream of such agony as the human spirit should not have to endure.

"He didn't know it was you," she repeated. "He didn't recognize you. You were a Yankee officer on a horse. He tried to cut you down. He could just as easily be the one here crying."

"I didn't try to stop him," York protested. "I ducked. And—"

"He died," she finished for him.

"No. Not then. But he never regained consciousness. There were nurses. I started yelling right then. I yelled and I yelled. I held his hand and yelled for help. And when I wasn't yelling for help, I was yelling that I loved him."

"He heard you," Esther said positively.

He looked at her with some intelligence in his eyes. "What?"

"He heard you. He heard you. He knew."

He lumbered up and headed for the door, but she caught him and brought him back. Shaking his head, he tried to fight her, but she ducked under his flailing arms. "I killed my brother," he sobbed. "I killed him!"

"The war killed him!" she yelled. "The war! The war!"

He struck at her again. She knocked his arm aside and slapped his face. "York! York Bradburn!"

"Esther." He blinked. "Esther." He swiped an arm across his face. Then a hand across the lower part of his face. The guns were still echoing in his ears. His eyes still stung with the smoke of battle. His brother's blood still stained his hands. "Esther?"

"Let's lie down." She took his arm. Obediently, he let her help him stretch out on the narrow bunk. She removed his boots and covered him. She added more logs to the stove and turned off the lantern. Then she climbed in beside him.

He hid his face against her like a child would against its mother. She gathered him in her arms. "Let's go to sleep," she whispered. "Sleep, sleep, sleep."

He lay a long time, stiff with remembered agony. At last he spoke. "Why did you say he heard me? You weren't there."

She stroked his hair and kissed his forehead. "Because all the old folks know that the hearing is the last to go. That's why you must never say anything unkind or unhopeful at a deathbed. They can still hear you. They haven't left their bodies yet. They can't open their eyes any longer to see or their mouths to speak, but their ears are open. Carrying messages to their brains."

"Folk tales," he scoffed, though with a note of uncertainty.

"Maybe so, but think about how many times your ears have waked you out of a sound sleep. We can close off everything else, but not our ears. The last link with our loved ones is their voices." Her own voice faltered. She believed this with all her heart. She wanted desperately to make her husband believe it for the measure of comfort it would give him.

He sighed. "You can't know that."

She kissed his eyelids. "Go to sleep and dream of it."

In a minute his breathing evened. She held him while she wept for him and his brother and their family. For her own daughter and brother. For the loss of their father hanged so brutally and needlessly. Of all the things that had ever happened in this country, certainly the war was the worst.

Seventeen

Her arm went dead beneath his weight.

Four squares of bright winter sun crept across the floor. She could imagine the hounds rising and stretching, moving from their houses to a favored spot where its rays would strike them. Daniel would wake Sarah and slice some of the pumpkin bread Esther had left, cut an apple into quarters, pour milk. Then they would go together to the kennels. She regretted that she was not there to see Sarah's eyes grow wide when Teet put his inquisitive nose to work on her.

She listened to the even breathing of the man who rested against her. He had trusted her implicitly with the darkest secret of his life. The war had cost him his brother and the sanctuary of his family. He knew she had lost almost the same things—her father and the love of her family. With everything lost to them, the two alone had found each other.

She consigned her enemy to the dust. York Bradburn was no longer her enemy. The war was over. He had lost as much as she had. Risking pursuit, he had come back to her house to take her out of danger. He could have fled to the mountain or left the county altogether and never been seen again. She had heard tales of women and girls who had married soldiers and then never seen them again. He was her husband for the rest of their lives. She'd be beside him when he woke up. And she prayed they would be together when one of them closed his eyes for the last time.

Just when she thought her cramped muscles would compel her to disturb him, he grunted softly. She could hear him clear his throat, feel his jaw move against her collarbone. A moment later he lifted his head. "Thank you, Lord," he whispered fervently.

"Good morning."

He sat up, holding his head in his hands. "I feel as if I've been beaten and dragged."

She winced as she surreptitiously tried to get the blood flowing back into her arm. "I'm not surprised."

He pulled himself up in bed until his shoulders were braced against the wall. Smoothing her hair back from her forehead, he guided her head over into his lap. "Pretty bad time last night. I shouldn't have dropped all that on you."

"You needed to tell it. It explains so much."

"I'm sorry. Once I got started, I couldn't seem to stop." He closed his eyes, then looked down at her, searching her face with eyes full of shadows. "Even though I didn't even have much to drink, a lot of what I said is kind of hazy." He shook his head. "I told you about Edmond?"

Catching his hand and carrying it to her lips, she nodded.

"I think I told you more than I've told everybody put together. I'm sorry I dumped it all on you." While he talked, he continued to stroke her hair. "Thank you for listening."

The tears welled up in her eyes. Such a simple thing as listening shouldn't require thanks. She kissed the hand that stroked her. He bent to kiss her on the lips, his long length slid down beside her, warm, tender—

A peremptory meow came from outside.

They looked at each other. A slow smile spread on her face. He looked resigned. "I'm surprised he's still around."

"Cats don't like to move," she told him. "Haven't you ever heard the stories of cats being taken to a different town and showing up at their old homeplaces weeks later."

"I must have missed that one. The Ozarks are like a different country from Philadelphia." He kissed her again, using his tongue and hands.

This time the yowl was louder, more demanding.

York sighed. "He's not going to give up." He slid from under the covers and padded across the cold floor. Esther rolled over on her stomach and watched him open the door. "Come in."

The black cat looked up at the man with such disdain that Esther giggled. York couldn't keep the smile from his face either. The massive head rotated slowly, surveying the cabin. The green eyes slid over the humans with unblinking scrutiny. Last, the tom lifted his nose and sniffed the air.

"Come in," York repeated. "It's cold enough in here without letting in the whole outdoors."

Stiffly, Big Boy rose. His winter coat fluffed out around his head and shoulders like a lion's mane, he paced into the room. Less wary than usual he did not immediately follow York to the stove, but strolled in toward the bed. Esther propped herself up on her elbows. "Good morning, your majesty."

The muscular black shape stopped, one paw poised in midair. His ears flicked forward. Then he settled back on his haunches. Esther stared back. The cat didn't move. York added wood to the stove and set the coffeepot on to boil. Still the animal regarded Esther.

"I think he remembers me," she said at last.

"He'd be a fool not to." With a lazy smile on his face he crossed the cabin and lifted the quilts.

"What are you doing?"

"Getting back in bed. The cabin's still cold."

"York!" She jumped and squealed when he burrowed under the layers of clothing. His cold hands closed over her bare breasts. She shivered so hard she had to set her teeth, but her response had nothing to do with cold.

"York." He took her nipple between his teeth, nipping gently. She arched against him and caught double handfuls of hair. Instead of pulling, she hung on while he pushed her pants down around her ankles and grasped her with his thumb and fingers.

"York!" Her cry of delight mingled with shyness and trepidation. It brought him up on his knees. Opening his own clothing, he freed himself and followed where his fingers led the way.

"Husband." He thrust himself into her as far as he could reach. She threw her head back, the crown of her head almost touching the pillow. Every muscle in her body concentrated on holding him within her, making the ecstasy last. The pressure, the heat, the moisture overwhelmed him. He pulled back, felt the dam burst within him, and pushed forward.

A hoarse shout of pleasure burst from his throat, mingling with her gasps and sighs.

Big Boy regarded them with an unblinking stare. When they both stopped moving, he yawned and stalked away to curl up behind the stove.

"The closest telegraph is in Bentonville," Esther complained. "It's half a day's ride from here." She had never felt so content. After nothing but coffee and some hard bread brought from home, she only wanted to snuggle down on the bunk and let her hands roam where they would.

He looked at her in mock disgust. "I have to get up

and get my own breakfast, I offer to take you to town, and all you want to do is stay in bed. Have I married a slacker?"

She slid her hands inside his shirt and gently scratched his ribs with her short-clipped nails. "Could be. I know I've always wanted to be one."

He laughed.

The black cat darted out from under the stove and sprang to the top of the table. He arched his back and spat. Ears laid flat back on his head, fangs bared, his eyes blazed at the door.

"What is it?"

York covered her mouth with his hand and shook his head. Throwing back the quilt, he reached for his boots. Esther scrambled out after him and began fastening her clothing. He put his finger to his lips before crossing the cabin and kneeling beside the stove. With the poker he pried up a board. His arms delved inside the opening where they moved aside the saddlebags. From beneath them he took a long object wrapped in an army "gum" blanket.

Big Boy hissed again. His claws dug into the table, and he leaped to the top of the pie safe.

York let the poncho fall away from a Henry repeater. From the drawer of the pie safe, he took a square box. While Esther watched openmouthed, he loaded twelve rimfire cartridges into the magazine and then levered one into the chamber. She shuddered. The enemy was back in his face if only a replica of how he must have looked then.

Face grim, jaw set, he motioned her to crouch down behind the stove.

A shadow broke the light beneath the door. A board creaked. York lifted the weapon to his shoulder. The cat growled low in his throat, the sound heavy with warning, with menace. Esther glanced upward. Somehow, Big

Boy's presence was reassuring. York was not alone with the small panther above him, crouched to spring.

Heavy metal thudded against the door. Esther clapped her hands to her mouth. Again. The door shuddered. The hinges creaked. The door wasn't locked. Why didn't they come in? "Bradburn!"

The word was followed by a flurry of movement as if the man had ducked back against the cabin wall. They were afraid of York. From what she had seen, they were right to be.

Stupid. One corner of York's mouth flicked upward in a smile. *The door's the same thickness as the wall.* He dropped down on one knee, boxing Esther into a corner behind the stove and his own body. She put her hand on his shoulder. He could feel it warm and steady.

"Bradburn! Come on outta there. Make it easy on yerself!"

Easy to kill.

Another flurry of movement. A shadow broke the light. The door creaked open. A click and skitter of nails on the weathered boards. The cat hissed again and spat. Another skitter and a huge black-and-tan bloodhound appeared in the doorway. The creature weighed fully a hundred pounds, nearly twice the size of Teet or Juniper. As the scents of the two people crouching inside filled its nostrils, it threw up its muzzle and howled. The bounty hunter slipped its chain.

"Take it! Take!" he yelled.

The bloodhound charged.

Before York could pull the trigger, a frightful yowl raised the hair on the back of his neck. A black shape sprang from the pie safe, Big Boy launching his body onto the bloodhound's head. Ten needle sabers slashed into the loose skin and tore it to ribbons. Ears, eyes, nose, the most sensitive parts of the dog's anatomy, the senses by which it hunted and found its prey, were put out of commission with one blow.

Its howl broke off in a poignant yelp. It swung its head back and forth, but the big tom hung on, clawing. To keep his hold, he sank his teeth into the base of the drooping ear. His hind feet ripped the dewlaps in great slashing swathes. His front claws tore at the eyes.

Yelping in panic and pain, the bloodhound backed out of the cabin. Shaking its head from side to side, it fell off the porch and galloped yelping into the woods. Its murderous rider clung like a burr.

"Shit!" came the querulous complaint. "What in the hell was that?"

"That was a damn cat," a second voice suggested. "Maybe there's nobody home."

"Just go on in if you're so all-fired anxious."

Esther squeezed her husband's shoulder. The bounty hunters hadn't given up. York nodded. They were amateurs giving away their positions by their voices. He took careful aim at the wall beside the door. Before he could pull the trigger, the man dropped back off the porch.

From the woods came the bloodhound's howl of agony.

Closer at hand, the crackle of frozen brush traced their steps as they moved away. He could almost see them planning their next move, arguing and whining between themselves.

"Hey, Bradburn! Bradburn, listen. We've got you. You've got to come through that door. You can come through easy and surrender. Or we can burn you out and take you in over the saddle."

Esther smothered a cry of distress as she clutched at his shoulder. He covered her hand reassuringly.

"Come on, Bradburn," the second man whined. "We're freezing our asses off out here."

York rose. Keeping low, he motioned to Esther to keep back. They were amateurs, but their cartridges were as good as anything he had. Probably they were ex-soldiers with Spencer repeaters. Surprise was his weapon, and quick movement. He took a deep breath and launched himself through the door. He hit the porch on his hip and rolled.

"Get 'im!"

"Shoot 'im!"

The bounty hunters yelled instructions to each other simultaneously rather than fire their own weapons. The idiots must have lowered their rifles while they were waiting for him to surrender.

He hit the ground on his knees, flipped over and hugged the wall as he ran for the trees. He heard them following him. A shot spanged into a stone several yards ahead of him. He ducked around the back of the cabin. The distance of only some twenty steps separated him from a thicket. Twenty steps in the open.

Thrusting the Henry around the side of the cabin, he fired one round. He jerked back and ran. With every step he set his teeth and arched his back, anticipating the killing blow of a bullet. Two yards to go. One. He dashed among the trees and dived for the thicket. He had made it.

A rifle boomed, and a blow struck his left arm. With the force of a pile driver, it slammed him through the thin branches onto the hard ground beneath.

Stunned, he had to make himself roll over and climb to his feet. Hot blood flowed down his arm inside his shirt. Before he had taken half a dozen steps, it sluiced over his fingers in a scarlet flood. But he felt no pain. For the time being, he could put the wound out of his mind and concentrate on losing himself in the pines and hardwoods.

"Got 'im!" a voice howled triumphantly.

"Where'd he go?"

"We'll find him easy. He's leaving a trail."

A big pine loomed in front of him. He ducked behind

it and peered around. One of them stood bent over, staring at the ground. York levered a fresh round into the chamber. Sighting along the barrel, he squeezed the trigger. The bounty hunter clutched his shoulder and toppled over.

Instantly, York moved off to the right. If he could circle the cabin and get to the horses—

"Help me!" the wounded man yelled for his partner. "Goddamn son-of-a-bitch shot me. Oh, lord-ee. I'm bleedin'. Help!"

Frantically, Esther searched the hole beneath the floor. In the saddlebags she found an oilskin packet of money and papers, but no more weapons. She clenched her fists and prayed with all her heart. The noise of battle was agony. Her only course was to hide. Unarmed, she could not help York against the bounty hunters. If she got in the way, she might put him in danger.

Then the gunshots ceased and a man began to scream.

The first words told her it was not York and raised her hopes. While one helped the other, she and her husband might be able to escape. However, they couldn't escape if she didn't get out of the cabin.

The papers and money lay in the hole. Her first impulse was to fit the board back in place, leaving them concealed. Her second was to take them with her. The bounty hunters had already threatened to burn the place down. Furthermore, if they had found this place, others would, too. She snatched up the packet and dropped it down the back of her clothing. It slid into the hollow at the back of her waist. Through four layers no one would notice it.

The man kept calling for help. Perhaps his partner was dead. She knew a moment's mercy for a suffering human being. Should she go to his aid? The thought died quickly. They would have captured York and taken him back to be hanged, even though he wasn't guilty. They might even have killed him and taken in his body.

She needed to get to the trees where she and York could find each other and leave. Taking the butcher knife from the drawer, she tiptoed to the door. The man's cries had lapsed into sobs of pain and fear. Remembering how York had gone out low, she dropped to her hands and knees and peeked around the corner.

York couldn't believe his luck. Instead of their own horses unsaddled and hobbled, he stumbled across the mounts of the bounty hunters. Before he remembered he jerked the reins free.

Pain streaked through his shoulder. Terrifying weakness and nausea swept over him. Black spots threatened to overwhelm his vision. Swallowing convulsively, he leaned against a tree and felt for his wound. He had a hole in the sleeve of his shirt just below the armpit—and another in the back. His mind told him this was good. The bullet had gone straight through, but how deep. He made a fist and doubled his arm.

The blood flowed faster, but at least his arm was not broken. Now was the time to move. He climbed into the saddle of a rangy bay. Lying along the neck, he walked both horses through the trees, ever circling to the right.

"Bradburn!"

He ignored the call.

"Bradburn! Come on in. I've got this gal of yourn."

The words sent a flood of ice water through his veins. He cursed vividly but made no sound. And he kept the horse moving. He wouldn't surrender his gun until he was sure there was no other way to save her life. He kept the horse moving, slowly, through the trees.

"Help!" the wounded man begged. His words came out between wracking sobs. "I'm bleedin' bad."

York ducked and craned his neck. The sight through the trees almost brought him tumbling off his horse. The bounty hunter had dragged Esther out of the cabin and thrown her down. In the middle of the yard, he straddled her, his rifle inches from her face.

From his hiding place, York knew he could drop the man with one shot, but could he kill him instantly before he could squeeze a shot off? He had to be sure—and he couldn't be sure.

Off to the left, he heard thrashing and whimpering. The bloodhound had blundered into a bush. It backed out, yelping.

"Bradburn." York recognized the man as the one whom Teet had savaged. "I'm not kiddin'. Woman or no woman, you get yourself down here or she's dead."

Esther had pushed herself up on her elbows. As York watched, she pulled her leg up slowly. *Lie still. Lie still,* he commanded silently. *It's too dangerous.*

Whimpering, the bloodhound limped into the clearing. One ear was chewed half off. Reeling and staggering from side to side, it headed toward the voice of the man. Every couple of steps it stopped to paw at its face.

"Bradburn. I'm tellin' you—"

"Don't, York! Don't!" Esther screamed.

"Shut up." Her captor jabbed at her face, forcing her head back to the ground.

York lifted the Henry to his shoulder. His left bicep was a flaming mass of pain. Stoically, he forced the muscle to obey. His finger was on the trigger.

The bloodhound limped on, whining. It yelped as it blundered into a tree stump. Big Boy's claws must have blinded it. York managed a half grin. "You took out your share, Big Boy," he whispered. "Now it's my turn."

The bounty hunter heard the dog, too. Pivoting to face the sound, he brought the muzzle of the rifle up.

Between his legs, Esther brought her knee up to her chest.

The bloodhound stumbled out into the clearing. When the light hit it, it swung its head from side to side, then staggered sidewise and fell.

York squeezed the trigger.

Esther drove her boot into the bounty hunter's groin the instant before he caught York's shot. What should have drilled him dead center in the chest went through the top of his shoulder. The man dropped his weapon and grabbed his crotch.

Esther clawed the rifle and scrambled to her feet. Running as fast as ever she followed her hounds, she dashed for the woods.

York reined the bay around and rode to meet her. "Esther," he yelled. "Esther!"

She never broke stride. Nor did her foot touch the stirrup. She vaulted into the saddle. He pitched her the reins and they were off, clinging to the necks of their horses, ducking their heads as pines slashed at their faces and threatened to scrape them off.

They were almost down the mountain when he signalled a halt. The bleeding had stopped of its own accord, but he was trembling with weakness. His arm had hurt like sin for the last couple of miles. Even though the air was chilly, the sun was hot on his bare head. He twisted in the saddle. As the darkness closed in on all sides, he aimed his stare at his wife.

"Sorry, Esther. You'll have to take it from here." He slid sideways, caught at the horn with his good arm, and kept himself from falling until she could catch up.

Esther had never felt so desperate in her life. With her leg and York's crushed between the two horses, she held him in the saddle and headed them down the mountain westward. The only trouble was she didn't know where westward was. York had led them twisting and turning, down draws, through rough country, over ridges. His purpose was to thoroughly lose their pursuers. He had succeeded in thoroughly losing themselves.

Worse, they had no food or water. What kind of bounty hunters went out without canteens on their saddles? Dumb ones, she supposed.

She checked the wound on York's arm. So far as she could tell it was no longer bleeding. No fresh blood stained either of the holes. It was the very best thing in the world, she reasoned. Everyone knew a wounded deer, shot through the body, would get up and run—and live to run another day.

Suddenly, she sat up alertly. Woodsmoke. She could not be mistaken. Woodsmoke meant a fire very possibly in a cabin. The sun was setting low in the west. They needed a place to spend the night. York needed to rest and regain his strength. They both needed water badly and food.

And for herself, she was sure her rear and the insides of her thighs must be a solid blister. She had to get out of the saddle soon, or she would start crying. She kicked her heels in the sides of the tired horse.

"Where are we?" York whispered.

"We're safe. In a bed," Esther whispered. She lay perfectly still on her stomach, her body stiff and throbbing. Unused to horseback riding for longer than an hour or two once a week, she was in awful shape. And she had it all to do over again tomorrow.

"Where?"

"A friend." Esther lifted her hips, trying to find a more comfortable position for tendons so strained they were like red-hot ropes. "In fact, she's a very distant cousin.

I was lost when we came down the mountain, but we ended up on the road to Bentonville. This farm belongs to a relative of mine—Aunt Hester Diehl. There's water in the pitcher beside you."

He looked around. By the last rays of day fading through a lace curtain, he saw a large white pitcher. Sitting up gingerly, he filled the glass beside it to drink and drink again. Then he settled back. "How long have we been here?"

"A couple of hours." She buried her face in the pillow. Her hurts were painful and so embarrassing. Aunt Hester had suggested warm saltwater, which had set the burst blisters on fire.

"The bounty hunters?"

"No sign of them."

He drank again, then lay back. She lifted her head and caught him rubbing his bandaged arm. "How bad is it?" he asked.

"Practically healed. The reason why it bled so much is because it was a crease. Aunt Hester said it didn't even need stitching."

He flexed it and found it true. "I need to get to the telegraph office."

"Too late. The operator's already gone home." She allowed her head to drift back onto the pillow. "And I—can't—move."

Amos Wilford scratched his head. "Bradburn. Bradburn. There was a woman in here yesterday late looking for you."

Esther caught York's arm. "Was she older? Blond?"

The telegraph operator shook his head. He looked over his spectacles at her, then at him. "No, can't say she was older. And she sure weren't blond." He studied

York. "Looked a lot like you, young feller. Strong family resemblance, I'd say."

York gasped. He clutched Esther's hand. "Did she give her name?"

"No, can't say as how she did. She just wanted to know if this was the office that sent the telegram to Washington, D.C., last week."

"Where did she go?" York looked around the office as if the woman might suddenly appear.

Wilford shrugged. "I guess she went to the hotel. It was too late to leave town. It was about dark."

York caught Esther's hands. "Where's the hotel?"

York knocked on the door of the hotel room. "Felicity," he called. "Felicity."

"York?" A cry of excitement and a flurry of footsteps. The door was flung open. "York!" A beautiful young woman flung herself into York's arms, bowling him across the hall. "Baby brother!" She threw her arms around his neck, knocking his hat off. Then she began to kiss him.

He laughed aloud as he kissed her and swung her so high that her skirts flew shoulder high revealing her petticoats and pantalettes frothed with lace. "Felicity. Felicity."

With tears in her eyes, Esther watched their reunion. The telegraph operator had been right. No one looking at them together or apart could doubt they were brother and sister. York's handsome features were softened and transmuted into an exquisite woman.

Felicity Bradburn Rush had masses of wavy black hair styled in the latest fashion. Her eyes were the same dark brown as York's with the same long, curling lashes. Where his fine-grained skin was tanned, hers was as creamy and satiny as a magnolia petal. Her nose was long and straight, her lips full. The forest green velvet and plaid taffeta dress she wore was so stylish that Esther Woodson from Cutter's Knob had never seen anything like it.

In short she made Esther frighteningly aware of the difference in York's status and her own. Folding her arms across her chest, Esther leaned against the doorjamb and watched while the two hugged and kissed and wiped each other's tears.

"How did you get out of jail?" Felicity asked when she could speak coherently. "The telegram said you were jailed by mistake. It asked someone to confirm your identity."

York looked to his wife. "I broke out. The sheriff had a cell that wasn't good for much but holding an occasional drunk. And the town was so sleepy, it didn't even know I was missing for hours."

Felicity laughed and clapped her hands. "You're a terrible person. But you sound like your old self. You really do. I'm so glad."

"You're right. I guess I can forgive myself after all these years. And I owe it all to my wife." York held out his hand.

Smiling hesitantly, Esther put her hand in his. He drew her into the circle of his arm. "Esther, I'd like you to meet my ferocious older sister, Felicity Rush. Felicity, this is my outlaw wife, Esther. For your information, sister, Esther just kicked a man in the crotch and got me safely away from a pair of bounty hunters."

Esther couldn't believe her ears. She poked York in the ribs and tried to make excuses.

"Kicked a man in the crotch?" Felicity exclaimed. "Did it work? I've always wanted to do that. I hear it causes great damage."

Esther gasped. If her mother knew that she had kicked a man in the crotch, she would pray for Esther's soul. York's introduction of his sister as ferocious took on new meaning. She smiled a little proudly. "He didn't get up and chase us."

"Were you being chased, York?" Felicity expressed less tender concern and more lively interest.

He nodded, grinning as if it were the most fun in the world. Esther was getting a little disgusted with them both. "It seems I've been mistaken for a member of the James gang," he chortled.

"Jesse James. Jesse and Frank James." Felicity clapped her hands again. "But that's wonderful. You've been robbing banks for the last five years. Here Mother and I had been worried that you might have committed suicide. And you've been leading the life of a Rebel Robin Hood."

Remembering where she had found him, Esther wondered if there were times when her husband might have been close to suicide. She wondered whether this beautiful creature would clap her hands if she knew York had almost left Esther in a ravine in freezing cold temperatures rather than touch her.

"How long have you been married?" Felicity put out her hand to Esther and drew her onto the settee. York closed the door.

"Just a few days," Esther told her honestly. "We—er— That is, we—"

"What Esther is making such a bad job of telling you is that we were married by a preacher in Jesse James's gang." York was grinning from ear to ear. Esther had been embarrassed before. Now she was turning red.

Felicity shook her finger at her brother. "That was a terrible thing to tell me. Esther, you be sure you keep in practice with that kick to the crotch. You may need it from time to time." She looked serious. "York, are you sure this is a legal marriage? I mean, shouldn't you have it done over by someone who's ordained?" She squeezed Esther's hand. "He has political aspirations you know.

He can't have some mudslinger dig up something like that and distress the voters."

Esther's head was spinning. No talk of sin and shame. No worries for her immortal soul. Merely concern about some mudslinging politician. What sort of family had she married into?

York put his hand on her shoulder. "I think my political aspirations are a thing of the past. Besides, the fact that Esther and I are friends of Jesse James counts more *for* my election in Arkansas or Missouri than it counts *against.*"

His statement sent Felicity off into another discussion about political campaigns won despite scandal and those destroyed by the silliest things. It was all very lively and largely incomprehensible to Esther. It depressed her dreadfully. How long could she expect York to be happy with her in the little town of Cutter's Knob if he had these kinds of relatives and these kinds of ambitions? The word "money" caught her attention.

"Did you bring some with you?" York was asking.

"Not with me," came the quick reply. "We'll have to apply to the Western Union office."

Esther sat up. "I have your money."

He stared at her in amazement. "You do?"

"I'd forgotten I had it or I would have given it to you." She pulled the packet out of her clothes. "I was afraid they might find it, or burn the cabin after we left."

He pulled her to her feet and kissed her soundly and long. Without a care that his sister watched, his kiss turned passionate. He held her tight. When he broke the kiss, he kept his arm around her. "She's the best thing that's ever happened to me," he told his sister truthfully. "She found me and brought me out of the woods. I was living like a wild animal." His face twisted in remembered pain. "She says I can forgive myself."

Felicity faltered. Her own pain ravaged the exquisite features. "You have to, York."

"Father will never forgive me."

"Because he can't forgive *himself* either. He saw the war coming. He knows he should have ordered Edmond home months before Fort Sumter." Felicity rose and came to stand beside them. Her arms went round them both. She touched her forehead to Esther's. "This family has suffered the tortures of the damned for seven years. Thanks to you, York has been made whole. Maybe now, he can reason with Father."

They stood together for a long minute. Esther's eyes were wet with tears. How she wished her mother and she and Daniel could stand as they were doing.

Then Felicity pulled away. "I'm hungry," she said practically. "Let's go down to breakfast. You'll be so delighted, York. I brought you Blue Devil."

Eighteen

Blue Devil was the most magnificent horse Esther had ever seen. Even though she was unfamiliar with blooded horses, she could recognize his quality. A steeldust roan, sixteen hands high, built on the lines of a foxhunter, from nose to tail he was perfection. Stunned with emotion, York put his arms around the horse's neck and laid his cheek against the black velvet muzzle.

The women watched in silence as the horse and man renewed their acquaintance. At last York stepped away and wiped his eyes. It was another minute before he could smile at his sister. "How did you get him here so fast, Felicity? I don't see how either you or the horse made it from Washington in less than a week."

The daughter of Congressman Neville Bradburn and the wife of a grandson of a signer of the Declaration of Independence tossed her exquisite head. "Oh, here a word, there a word." She nodded mischievously to her sister-in-law. "Actually, Crowder—you remember father's secretary, York. The old stick—"

Esther remembered the name on the telegram.

"—he felt awful about what Father told him to write. He showed me Esther's message. I was going to send a telegram myself, but I thought that two telegrams with conflicting messages might cause more problems than they solved.

"An army train bound for Kansas City was delighted

to add another car. Then we just switched it over and down I came." She looked around her with some disdain at the primitive stable and the dirt street beyond the door. "Although I can't say exactly where I came to."

"This is Bentonville, Arkansas," Esther told her. "And it's not a place you want to spend your life in, unless you're a farmer."

Felicity shuddered delicately. "When will you take her away from all this, York? You have your own place in Philadelphia."

Esther tensed, waiting for the answer that would spell the end of their marriage.

York glanced at his wife. Her face was in shadows. He could not read the expression in her eyes, but he could well imagine. "I can't talk about that right now." He stroked Blue Devil's noble head and straightened his forelock. The horse stretched forward and nuzzled his master's pocket. York drew out a small chunk of sugar that he had pared off the lump at breakfast. "You haven't forgotten where the sugar is, have you, boy?"

"Enough of this stable," Felicity announced. "People will think we're crazy talking to the livestock. I suggest we go back to the hotel and find a good place to catch up on our lives." She looked at Esther with frank curiosity. "And get to know each other."

Esther looked from one to the other. "I'd love to, but I have to get home. You all go back to the hotel and have a nice visit." To Felicity she said, "You're more than welcome to come to Cutter's Knob. We'd be delighted to have you. The place isn't fancy, but the beds are comfortable and the food's good."

York frowned. "You can't. What are you talking about? You can't start for Cutter's Knob by yourself."

Esther raised one eyebrow. "Of course I can. I'll take the bay that you rode yesterday. He's got an easier gait than—"

"You can't ride off through the Ozarks alone," York interrupted. "It's dangerous."

Esther stiffened. Her daughter's disbelief, the pitiful acceptance on her face as she watched them ride off together leaving her behind, made Esther cringe inside. She had promised Sarah she would be back in a couple of days. It was already getting on toward evening of the second day.

"York," Felicity warned.

"I rode over here and back in one day to send the telegram to get you out of jail." Esther had trouble keeping her voice under control to conceal her irritation. She'd been riding around these hills for five years completely alone. Had he forgotten who brought him down the mountain yesterday?

He shook his head. "You should never have done it. When I asked you to do it, I didn't know you had to ride so far. There's no sense in you taking a chance if you don't have to. We'll go home together. Felicity and I will make plans."

He put his arm around her and led her over to his sister. Together the three of them walked back to the hotel. Felicity glanced once or twice in her sister-in-law's direction, but Esther kept her expression blank. Inside, she was seething. She thought of her daughter deserted by the mother she had just discovered. She thought of her brother gallantly assuming the responsibilities of the kennel and his niece, so his sister could ride off into the mountains with her husband of a few days.

Long years of dealing with her mother had taught her the futility of arguing with someone who had made up his mind. No, she wasn't going to argue. She let her breath out slowly as they walked up the steps of the hotel. She wouldn't argue.

In Felicity's suite, the best and only suite in the hotel, they sat in the parlor. The talk at first was about their mother and father. Esther learned that her mother-in-law was subject to palpitations when something did not suit her. Both brother and sister laughed heartily over her miraculous recoveries when people gathered around her and accommodated her.

Their father was another matter. "He's the voice of reason in the House of Representatives. So calm. So statesmanlike. He rallies the party to the issue. He meets with house members individually and lends them strength to do the right thing. There's talk that he may be Speaker of the House if he keeps on. He's like another person when he's on the floor. Then he comes home, and Mother says he locks himself in his study," Felicity told her brother gravely. "I don't understand any of it. And I don't understand how Mother can stand much more."

Esther had lived through the separation of her own family. She deeply sympathized. "Guilt could very well be making him too ashamed to face her," she suggested. "He's a man of power, but he didn't have the power to save his own son."

The pair exchanged glances. "Listen to her," York advised. "She's very wise."

The compliment poured over Esther like liquid gold. She bowed her head beneath York's smile of approval. Now was the time to leave them. She rose. "If you'll excuse me for a few minutes, I'll go over to the telegraph office. I just thought that I can hire someone to carry a message to Cutter's Knob, telling Daniel where I am so he won't worry."

Felicity looked at her shrewdly, but York was all affability. "That's a fine idea." He pulled the packet from his breast pocket and handed her money. "Hire the best horse in town."

"I will."

* * *

The rangy bay that York had stolen from the bounty hunters ate up the miles. Esther bent low over his neck and urged him to his best speed. She needed to get far ahead. When York discovered she was gone, he might come after her. In which case the big steeldust would catch her easily if she took the first miles slowly.

She hated to leave, but her daughter had become uppermost in her mind. From having no family at all, she had suddenly come to having almost too much family. Suddenly, everyone wanted her time and her presence.

Elmo Stamford had tried two mornings in a row to talk with Rebecca. The first morning, she was just getting her things together to go visiting the ones who had failed to make an appearance at church on Sunday morning. The second, she was working on her sermon.

He had gone away, his teeth set, a muscle in his jaw jumping. People in town were laughing at him—behind his back, to be sure—but they were laughing. They would stop laughing if she told them to. He was a good lawman. He had had a member of the James gang in his jail. Everybody knew how desperate that bunch of outlaws was. They robbed banks and broke jail.

Stamford had thought about the jailbreak until he had it all worked out in his mind. He was lucky that he hadn't put up more of a fight. He'd figured Jesse and Frank were out on the edge of town just waiting to ride in and rescue Bradburn. He'd saved the town from a raid like the one that they'd made on Lawrence, Kansas.

When he thought about it, he was a hero. He'd tried to tell that to Ed Carolan. The storekeeper had looked at him as if he was crazy and then had walked away laughing. The sheriff knew Carolan had laughed, even though he hadn't heard him. They were all laughing at him.

He had to see Rebecca and make her understand what

had happened. If she told his side of it, say at the end
of her sermon on Sunday morning, everyone would
know it was the truth. They'd know he was a hero and
things would be the way they were before, only better.

His pard had died right where the son-of-a-bitch had
dropped him. By the time he'd gotten his own shoulder
patched up and gone over to check on the other bounty
hunter, he was barely breathing. There was blood all over
the ground to show where he'd about bled to death.

About that time the dog had come blundering over to
him all chewed to pieces. He'd shot him to put him out
of his misery. Then he'd gone in and looked around the
empty cabin, but he didn't find a damn thing. He was
mad enough to spit nails. All this time and money spent
and nothing to show for it.

Damn! He was mad. He'd ride back down to that place
with them dogs. This time that gal wouldn't get a chance
to kick him in the crotch. He'd fix her wagon but good,
and then he'd haul Bradburn's ass off to jail.

The only good thing he could think of coming out of
this mess was that he wouldn't have to split the reward
with anybody.

York had forgotten so much or put so much out of his
mind that when Felicity began to relate the stories of old
friends and events that had happened in Philadelphia, he
became totally engrossed. Now that he could accept himself, he began to believe that he could accept society again.
Forgotten were the people who had scorned him as his
brother's killer, the ones who had patted him on the shoulder and told him to buck up and put aside his grief, the
ones who had thought he was crazy because he could still

hear the guns and the screams. He'd forgotten them. And if he'd forgotten them, they'd probably forgotten him, too.

He was swept with a wave of homesickness. Moreover, he longed to return to the City of Brotherly Love, where he could introduce his wife—

He looked around him and started to his feet. "Esther."

Felicity sat back in her chair. "I imagine that she's long gone."

"What?" He started for the door, but his sister called him back.

"York, she needed to get back to her daughter."

At the mention of the daughter, York stopped. "I would have taken her back tomorrow," he said sheepishly. "She shouldn't be riding around the countryside by herself."

"Then you should have taken her home when she asked to go."

"Whose side are you on?" He clenched his fists. The idea of Esther calmly riding off without him angered him. She could get hurt. She didn't need to act like a man anymore. She had a man of her own. He expected her to act like a woman. He said as much to his sister.

"She acted like a good mother," Felicity reminded him. "She was thinking of her daughter. Your daughter."

"You're here," he insisted stubbornly.

Felicity took his hands and smoothed out his clenched fists. "My children are much older, York. I have a tutor and a governess, a house full of servants who spoil them rotten."

Her words brought back a host of memories and an ache at the poverty and hardship of Esther's life. She was all Sarah had. In a sense, she was really all he had.

He pressed the heels of his hands to his temples. "I've forgotten so much. I didn't even remember how to carry on a conversation when she found me," he groaned. He came to his sister's side. "Come to Cutter's Knob with me. We can visit on the way and you can see the place. It's a good place. Esther's been doing all the work on it for five years. That's a story that'll take at least the trip over there, if not the trip back."

Felicity kissed him on both cheeks. "I have to return to Washington. Even while I was employing the voice of sweet reason, I was remembering my children. I don't want them to think for one minute that they don't need their mother. I'll tell Father what I've done and what has happened to you. With any luck, he'll relent right away. Otherwise, he'll relent when he hears about his grandchild."

York bounded to his feet. "What? What's this? What did she tell you?"

"Nothing. Nothing. I only meant that undoubtedly some time in the near future you will wish to have children." Felicity took a long time getting him calmed down. So long as she kept him talking, Esther could get farther away and closer to Cutter's Knob. Felicity knew her brother. York was perfectly capable of dragging his wife back to Bentonville from the outskirts of her destination.

She insisted that he take the extra money she had brought with her. He gave her a power of attorney to arrange for the transfer of his funds in Philadelphia to the bank in Bentonville. It all took a distressingly short time.

Then she went with him while he saddled the steeldust and hung on to him for a long time while she tried to hide her tears. Her baby brother had been restored to life, but not to her. Whether with his new wife in their place in the Ozarks or somewhere else, unless she was very much mistaken, he had found a new life.

* * *

"Daniel, you're being foolish. What more reason can you need to pack up and move your niece back to her home? The first time that outlaw beckoned, Esther was off to the hills with him. You can't seriously believe she'd be a good mother to Sarah." Rebecca held forth in the middle of Esther's kitchen.

"Sarah." Daniel put his arm around his niece and bent to whisper in her ear. The little girl kept her gaze fixed on her lunch, untouched on her plate. "Why don't you go give each of the hounds a piece of jerky?"

His niece reproached him with her eyes. "Grandmother's going to talk about me. I want to hear."

Rebecca smiled sweetly. "All I'm going to say, Sarah, is to tell Uncle Daniel that you want to go back to town with me. Out here in the woods, you'd be lonely. There aren't any children for you to play with."

"Nobody ever plays with me in town." Sarah stuck out her lip mutinously. "Out here at least I've got Teet and Juniper."

Rebecca's mouth tightened. "You're entirely too young to be allowed near those vicious beasts. You don't know what they can do. They're killers, every one of them."

Sarah's eyes got big and round. "Killers?"

"They're trained to run through the woods and kill little rabbits and squirrels."

"Stop it, Mother." Daniel plucked Sarah up from the table and bundled her into her coat and muffler. "Go." He patted her little rear and sent her out the door.

When he came back, his mother was smiling. "You do that so well. Maybe we should find you a wife. I'd thought we ought to wait another year or two until you got a little more mature."

Rebecca just couldn't help herself, Daniel realized. She saw everyone in the world as helpless children who needed her direction. They needed her to tell them when to marry, and whom. They needed her advice and supervision in the rearing of their children, even though she had done a poor job of raising her own. They waited for her to decide what jobs they were to have and when they were old enough to take them over. He was twenty years old and had never kissed a woman. He was very close to a decision himself.

"Mother, I'm thinking about leaving Cutter's Knob."

She stared at him. Her face lost a bit of color, but her smile scarcely faltered. She sat down at the table and folded her hands. "Well, of course you are, dear. And I agree that you should. A year at the seminary in Shreveport would be perfect. Then you'd be ready—"

"Mother. I'm thinking of going to California." He had no such intention before he started the conversation. He still had no such intention, but the state that was the farthest from his mother's influence seemed the best thing for him. Perhaps a good shock was what Rebecca needed. He saw her knuckles whiten. Her smile disappeared.

"Don't be ridiculous. What would you do in California? Always supposing you had sense enough to get there."

He was surprised only at how much it hurt to hear her belittle and insult him. He might have been the same age as Sarah. In another minute she would be telling him that all Californians were killers who ran through the woods hunting little rabbits. He supposed he had always known that she regarded him as a child. "Work. Get a job. That's what most men do."

She laughed, but her laughter faded. "You can't be serious."

He regarded her steadily until she dropped her eyes. "At least I'll never take your place in the pulpit," he said softly. "You can preach your sermons and care for your flock without worrying that I'm going to take your place."

Both of them heard the horse galloping up the road. A moment later the hooves were drowned by the bay of the hounds. High above the deep, chopping barks of welcome came Sarah's squeal of joy. "Mother!"

Rebecca shot to her feet and started for the door. "Now see what you've done," she scolded as if he were the one at fault. "It would have been so much easier if we had been gone."

Daniel rose, too. "Wait. Don't go out there."

"I most certainly will."

He cut her off from the door. "This is their moment. Let them have it."

"Mother!" Sarah came running, arms outstretched, face alight with joy.

Esther swung down and fell to her knees, holding out her arms as well. A thrill of delight went through her when Sarah flung herself against her. Her daughter's arms closed round her neck. Esther toppled over into the dry grass.

Sarah was giggling with delight as she and her mother rolled around. She had never in all her life rolled on the ground before. She kicked her heels and crowed for joy.

Esther covered her face with kisses. Tears of happiness flowed down her cheeks. "I'm sorry, Sarah. I'm so sorry I was late getting back, but you mustn't ever worry. I'll always come back to you. I promise."

"Uncle Daniel and I took care of everything so good," Sarah informed her when she had her mother on the bottom and herself sitting on top. "You have good dogs. I 'specially like Teet."

"He's my favorite dog, too," Esther agreed. The ground chill was seeping through her clothing, but she could have lain there forever so long as Sarah was bouncing delightedly and telling her things. "He's the best one I've got. He's like a teacher to the young ones."

"Uncle Daniel and I made hot chocolate every night. I showed him how to make it, and then he could do it." Another bounce and Esther grunted in mock pain. Sarah beamed, enjoying the novelty of sitting on a grown-up.

"Where's my new father?" was Sarah's next question. She looked down with a worried frown. "When will he be coming back? He promised to 'dopt me."

Esther was a little worried herself. She hoped York wasn't too angry. If he only thought about it, he would see that she had done the very best thing for the both of them. He could stay as long as he wanted to visit with his sister. To Sarah she said, "I imagine he'll be along before too long. I don't know just when. We had an adventure, and then your father's sister met us in Bentonville. She's your Aunt Felicity and she's—"

Suddenly, Sarah surged to her feet. Esther sat up and looked over her shoulder. Her brother and mother were coming down the lawn toward them. She felt a chill that had nothing to do with the ground on which she sat. Then she shrugged and climbed to her feet. She held out her hand. Sarah wrapped both of hers around it.

"Daniel. I'm back. Sarah said you took care of everything 'so good.' Mother, how nice to see you."

Daniel gave her a welcoming hug. The gesture surprised and pleased her. She recognized it as a show of strength. His smile said, *I'm on your side.*

Rebecca did not hug her. Instead, she looked disapprovingly at her daughter and granddaughter. "I learn from Daniel that you've been riding all over the country with that outlaw. I'm sure the marriage isn't legal. And I assume he's left you."

Esther glanced down at Sarah's frightened face. "He's in Bentonville, with his sister."

Rebecca sniffed. "I doubt the woman was his sister."

Esther picked her daughter up in her arms and marched off toward the house.

"Esther Elizabeth—"

"The wind's cold, Mother. I don't want Sarah to get an earache."

Daniel bowed. "Let's go in, Mother. Unless you think you'd better be getting on back to town. It's late and—"

Rebecca threw him a warning look calculated to turn his blood to ice. He merely shrugged and followed in her wake.

Instead of setting Sarah down inside the kitchen door, Esther carried her on into the living room. There she took her place in the rocking chair, keeping her daughter in her arms. The memories of her grandparents and her father felt strongest there. She could face the fight that was to come.

"I suppose you're going to send me to the bedroom," Sarah whispered, her face solemn.

Esther considered. This child had heard the world call her a female bastard. Where some children were willows in the wind, Sarah was a rock in a stream. "Not unless you want to go."

"I don't want to go now." Sarah looked down at her small feet. She huddled against her mother, her hands clasped tightly together. "But I may later."

Rebecca came in and surveyed them. The anger and frustration had smoothed out of her face. She had adopted her forebearing countenance, the loving mother whose children tried her sorely. "I only want what is best for you both," she began.

Neither of the rocking chair's occupants said a word.

"I thought that Sarah's coming here would be a sort of test for you both." She waited again. "But, Esther, your care of her was not what it should have been. Obviously, you're thinking only of self or at least of your husband. Perhaps the flush of new love clouded your judgment, but isn't it true that you deserted her? That was terribly wrong. And with a young child sacrifices have to be made."

She pursed her lips. "I think of all the sacrifices I made for you and your brother. I'm sure you remember."

Esther thought briefly. She could not remember a single sacrifice her mother had made for her. She had always been called upon to make sacrifices. Her mother had never read and studied with her. That had been her father's responsibility. When Esther was old enough, she had kept the house, done the cooking and the washing and the ironing. Her mother had been dedicated to the word and work of God. "I remember you were always writing your sermons and studying your Bible."

Rebecca's eyebrows rose. "Well, of course. That's exactly what I meant. You do remember. I had to make sacrifices. The time I wanted to spend with you and Daniel had to be spent for doing work for others. I sacrificed and sacrificed. I didn't get to play with you, or any of that."

Daniel came in and leaned against the mantel. His face was strained. As he listened in silence to his mother, his lips curved cynically.

Rebecca went on and on, warming to her work. Her voice rose and fell as she preached. Her vision of her life led her for almost ten minutes. Then as she began to draw her conclusions, she faltered.

Three pairs of eyes regarded her without blinking.

In the silence that followed, Esther gave Sarah a little hug. "Mother, your own speech condemns you."

Rebecca was outraged. "It does not. How can you say such a thing?"

"You aren't any different today than you were twenty years ago when you got the calling. You left me to Papa then. And as soon as Daniel was born, you left him, too. And now you've left Sarah to whoever will rear her. She doesn't have any friends. She's scorned and name-called by the citizens of Cutter's Knob."

"Well, she should have told me about that." Rebecca fairly radiated indignation. "I'm sure I didn't have any idea that they would do such a thing. I'm sure it was just one or two."

"Uh-uh," Sarah said softly. "It was a lot of 'em."

The hands in the elegant black gloves clenched. "Children should be seen and not heard."

Another horse could be heard galloping up the road. Esther inclined her head to look at Sarah. "I wouldn't be surprised if that's not your father coming home."

Sarah immediately slid down and dashed to the front door. Out on the porch she skidded to a halt. "Mother," she cried. "It's Sheriff Mo."

Coming out behind her, Esther felt a twinge of fear. "Get back in the house, Sarah. Go straight to Uncle Daniel."

The little girl for once did not argue. She scurried back inside. "Uncle Daniel! Uncle Daniel! It's Sheriff Mo."

Elmo Stamford had ridden into the yard. Seeing his quarry on the porch, he swung down in front of her. "I've come to arrest you, Esther Woodson."

"Me!" She couldn't believe her ears. Elmo had gone crazy. "I haven't done anything."

Elmo grinned nastily. "If I've got you in my jail, then your husband or whatever he is will come in and give himself up. And I'll be right with the U.S. Army."

"You're going to be right with the army anyway. York has a letter from—"

He drew his gun.

"Put that thing away," she said faintly.

Rebecca came out on the porch. She took in the burly sheriff. "I think your idea seems sound, Sheriff Stamford."

"Did you plan this, Mother? Did you order him to come out here and do this? You did, didn't you?"

"I assure you the sheriff is acting on his own and his plan seems sound to me."

"Arresting an innocent person and throwing her in jail seems sound to you?"

"Your husband is a member of the James gang."

Esther stamped her foot in utter frustration. "My husband is a Bradburn of the Philadelphia Bradburns. His sister is married to the grandson of Benjamin Rush, who signed the Declaration of Independence. He could not possibly be a member of the James gang. And, Mother, your hired man has a loaded gun pointed at me."

Rebecca had the grace to drop her eyes. Her mouth thinned.

Stamford grinned as he mounted the porch. He pulled a length of rope from his pocket. "I ain't got no fancy handcuffs like they do in the big towns."

At that point Rebecca murmured, "Surely, that isn't necessary."

Obviously, Stamford was enjoying himself. He made a big show of gathering Esther's wrists in one ham hand and throwing the slipknot loop over them. When he jerked it tight, he looked into her face, hoping to see some sign that he had hurt her or frightened her. When she didn't wince, he glowered. "Yes, ma'am, it is. Maybe she didn't help him break jail, but she rode off with him when he was escaping. She's guilty as he is."

"York isn't guilty."

But he paid no attention. While her mother stood there on the porch, Stamford pulled on the rope. "Come on."

Both women looked horrified. Rebecca cleared her throat. "You'll have to get her horse."

"It ain't far to town." Stamford chuckled as he swung

up on his mount and snubbed the end of the rope around the horn.

Rebecca came to the edge of the porch to stare at her daughter. Her eyes spoke a silent message, demanding, commanding, willing. Suddenly, Esther knew exactly what her mother was waiting for. Pleas for mercy, for intervention, possibly tears. She was waiting for Esther to break down in panic. To be so afraid and so ashamed of being dragged off to jail that she would fall on her knees and promise to do whatever Rebecca wanted her to do. The sheriff was acting on Rebecca's orders to bring her daughter back under her thumb.

Her mother had become utterly ruthless. So sure was she that she was right, she could not allow anyone to take a different path. Whatever Esther might have been—fallen woman, miserable sinner—she was now Mrs. York Bradburn. He would be coming back to Cutter's Knob to set the record straight. When he came, Elmo Stamford would be through. Esther turned her back on her mother.

She heard Rebecca's quick intake of breath. Then Stamford slapped the reins across the horse's neck and took off at a trot. Esther was jerked forward, so she had to run to keep up.

Sarah shook her head and held to her Uncle Daniel's leg. "I can't go back. I help Daniel take care of the hounds. There's a lot of work."

On the point of screaming, Rebecca held out her hands to her recalcitrant granddaughter. "You have to come back to town. You've had a nice visit, but now I need you in town. How could I get on without my little helper?"

"Grandmother, you know I don't help you." Sarah's

reply was mutinous. "You just say that 'cause I don't have anybody to play with."

Rebecca bit her lip. She looked at Daniel. She had never seen such an angry expression on his face. Quickly, she dropped her eyes. "You must come, Sarah. Daniel is coming, too. We're all going back to town together."

"Not me," her son snarled. "Someone's got to take care of Esther's place since she can't take care of it herself."

"I'm sure we can send someone out from town," Rebecca began. Those hounds again. When her husband was hanged, she should have taken a gun and shot every last one of them. They had never been anything but a pack of noisy, panting monsters.

"I'll take care of them, Mother. Sarah can help me."

"No!" Rebecca bristled. Red mottling stained her perfect ivory complexion. Her voice rose shrilly. "Sarah isn't staying in this house one minute longer. I made a mistake in letting her come out here at all."

"I came out here by myself," Sarah declared. "You didn't let me do anything."

"You did no such thing. I knew you were coming. I always know what you're doing." Rebecca caught hold of the little girl's hand and jerked hard.

"No. No. No." Sarah screamed and held on tighter.

Rebecca looked to her son for help. His eyes were closed, his face red, his lips pressed together in a thin line. He swayed with each jerk of his body. Rebecca had the sense that the last remnants of her control over him kept him from actively opposing her.

"Sarah," she said firmly. "You will stop this immediately. I'm not going to argue anymore. You're a child. You'll do as I say."

"I won't." Sarah twisted and tried to pull out of her grandmother's grasp.

"Mother," Daniel protested. "You've gone too far."

"Get her things and yours."

"No. This isn't right. You're going to be sorry for this."
Daniel had never felt so ineffectual. He couldn't bring
himself to lay hands on his mother. Still protesting, he
followed her out as she dragged Sarah away.

Rebecca's face was red and she was panting. Sarah was
protesting and hanging back. When Rebecca bent to lift
Sarah into the buggy, her granddaughter doubled up her
fist.

Rebecca turned white. "You wouldn't hurt your grandmother, would you?" she said in a quavery voice.

Sarah froze, brought to heel by the force of her love.

Rebecca kissed her cheek and lifted her into the buggy.
"We'll go home and you can have some tea."

"I want hot chocolate."

The uneasy truce prevailed only until Sarah saw her
mother being dragged behind Stamford's horse. The little girl screamed and almost jumped from the buggy.
Rebecca had all she could do to hold her granddaughter
on the seat beside her and whip up the horse.

In the cloud of dust that rolled up behind the buggy,
Esther's face was white. Stamford reined his mount and
turned around in the saddle. "Looks like she done took
that baby back. And a good thing, too. A jailbird for a
maw ain't no way to raise a child."

"You're through in this town," Esther promised.
"When my husband hears about this, he'll make sure
that you lose your job."

Stamford looked murderous. If that army lieutenant
didn't get back here to take the man away, he wouldn't
be surprised if she was right. "When I catch sight of him,
he won't make sure of nothing. He'll be pushing up dai-
sies the next minute."

With that he slammed his heels into his mount's sides and slapped the reins across its withers. "Giddy-up!"

The jerk pulled Esther off her feet. Twisting and spinning at the end of the rope, she was dragged down the road by her wrists.

Nineteen

"I'm so glad we've found each other again," Felicity told her brother for the tenth time. The northbound train had whistled from the top of the hill above Bentonville. The time for parting was very near. "Please come soon. Mother doesn't deserve to have lost you both. And neither does Father."

As it chugged into the station, York embraced her again. The switch engine pushed the private car off the siding; the train backed up. There was the jolt as it coupled on. York felt an agony of parting. He had always loved his sister. Then he had been dead to love. Now he was alive again and he was hurting. He wanted all his family together as they had been in Philadelphia. He wanted to show Esther to his mother to be entertained and treated fondly. He wanted his mother to get to know his wife and love her as he did. He wanted his sister to see the noble hounds and the house at the foot of the mountains. He wanted her to look around the valley that sheltered Cutter's Knob and see that he was living in a beautiful place. He wanted—

"Board! All aboard!" the conductor's deep voice called as York helped his sister on board. The train whistled again. Its big bell tolled.

"You'd better go," Felicity said through her tears. "Otherwise, you'll have to jump. Esther doesn't need a cripple around there."

"No." He held her hand until the last minute. Walking then jogging, beside the train to the end of the platform. From there he waved it out of sight.

He sighed as he dropped his hand. Then he mounted Blue Devil and guided him across the railroad tracks. Pulling his hat down on his brow, he gave the horse his head.

"Merciful heavens! Elmo Stamford done lost his mind." Bertha Carolan's cry brought her husband from behind the counter and all their customers crowding to the door.

"It's Esther Woodson," one woman said aloud. "My land, he's got her tied to his horse. Oh, the poor thing's bleeding."

Ed Carolan turned to the boy he paid to sweep out the store after school. "You run up that hill as fast as you can and tell Miz Blessing she needs to come quick."

The boy took off running past Esther and Elmo. As he dashed on up the hill, he kept throwing amazed glances over his shoulder. Elmo was grinning from ear to ear as more and more people came out on the street. Esther was a sorry sight. Her wrists were bleeding as well as her cheek and her chin. Her hair and her face were caked with red clay. Her clothing was ripped down the front and off one shoulder from being dragged.

She tried to straighten and carry herself with dignity, but her shoulders were burning from the jerking and jolting. She wondered dimly if the left one were dislocated. She had felt something give beneath her shoulder blade. She could feel the blood dripping off her chin.

The townspeople were muttering among themselves when Bertha Carolan, of all people, suddenly charged down off the boardwalk and ran down the street. "Shame on you! Shame! Shame! You let her go!" she cried. She ran up beside Elmo Stamford's horse and shook her finger in the sheriff's face. "You let that girl go this instant!"

Stamford only grinned. Women were soft anyway. They didn't like to see things hurt. He'd been to hangings in Fort Smith a couple of times, and he'd noticed that they usually looked the other way. Sometimes they even left long before the hangman sprang the trapdoor.

"You let her go, Mo Stamford." Another woman, her face red with outrage, joined Bertha. On the other side of his horse, his old maid schoolteacher brandished her walking stick at him. "Let her go. You've no call to treat a woman like that. The very idea."

"Elmo Stamford, you let her go."

"Yes!"

"Let her go!"

"You've gone plumb crazy. Let her go."

He had to halt his horse. His way was barred by several townsmen.

"I'spect that's about far enough." Ed Carolan stepped up to the saddle. Before Stamford knew what was happening, the storekeeper had opened out his pocket knife and sawed through the rope. When the sheriff started to dismount, the schoolteacher kept him in the saddle by waving her walking stick under his nose.

Esther's arms dropped down in front of her body. She staggered back and barely managed to muffle a cry of pain.

When Martha Virginia Ord tried to put her arm around Esther's shoulders, she winced away. Shaky with exhaustion and shock, she lost her balance and fell to her knees. "No, don't touch me!"

"Where's that dang boy?" Ed yelled.

Red-faced, Stamford tumbled off his horse on the right side and tried to push his way through the crowd to his prisoner. "You all get the hell outta my way."

The storekeeper stepped in front of the sheriff. "Stamford, you have purely lost your mind arresting Miz Blessing's daughter. What the hell for? First, you put her husband in jail and now her. She sure ain't a member of the James gang."

The speech crystalized the feelings of the townspeople, who nodded and muttered angrily. Stamford shook his head like a bull. "Her husband's wanted by the U.S. Army. She helped him escape. She's just as guilty as he is."

"Since when do you work for the U.S. Army, Elmo?" the schoolteacher wanted to know. She had taught the children in Cutter's Knob for nearly thirty years. Esther and her brother Daniel had both been her students as had more than half of the people standing shoulder to shoulder with her. Stamford, who had been a dunce and a bully, had not finished the third grade. "We don't do the Yankees' dirty work for them. If the U.S. Army wants him, I say let them catch him. You don't have any call to drag poor Esther Elizabeth all the way to town. Mrs. Blessing'll have your job."

The sheriff spun around. "Who do you think sent me out to get her? Miz Blessing, that's who." At the shocked gasp he realized he had said too much. "I mean, she just went out there to get her granddaughter and I—"

The boy came running back down the hill. "Miz Blessing says she's real busy. She'll come down later," he reported, then volunteered other information. "She's watching from the window."

Another gasp went up, followed by a loud buzz of discussion. Several of the women glanced in the direction of the church.

"Well, Lord o' mercy," Bertha Carolan sighed. She looked around her at the other ladies of the Missionary Society. "Lord o' mercy."

"If that don't beat all."

"Her own daughter."

One after another they turned to stare at the church. Rebecca Blessing was their leader, their moral voice. They trusted her always to do the right thing, to explain God's word and will, to offer comfort, to guide, and when the occasion warranted to chastise them for their transgressions. This time they waited in vain for her to appear and set things right.

Stamford pushed the storekeeper aside and caught Esther under the arm. She cried out as he lifted her to her feet.

"Come on, dang you." He dragged her through the crowd which parted reluctantly, protesting mildly, begging him to wait until Mrs. Blessing got there. Shoving her inside the jail, he faced the crowd while he blocked the door with his bulky body. "Now you all clear the street. Go on! Get on about your rat-killin'. You're interfering with a law officer doing his duty."

With that he slammed the door and slid the bolt into place.

In the sanctuary Rebecca Blessing clutched the windowsill. She had been surprised by the boy from Ed's store. When he had burst into the church, she had just quieted her mutinous granddaughter and was sitting perfectly still holding the little girl's hand and calming them both. So she had sent him away. Of course, she had not lied to him. She was very busy, but she had certainly put him off.

Sarah pulled her hand out of her grandmother's. Twisting off the pew, she put her fists on her hips. "If that old Sheriff Mo hurts my mother, my father will smite him."

"Children should be seen and not heard," Rebecca scolded. "I swear. A few days away from my instruction and you behave like a heathen savage."

"My father—"

"Be quiet! You don't have a father. You never have had one." At the sight of her granddaughter's stricken expression, Rebecca stifled her tirade. Calming her voice, she put on her most beneficent face. "It's unfortunate, but don't forget you are still a child of God. Now, I want you to go to your room right this minute and pray for God to show you the way back to love and goodness. Don't say another word. Stay there and ask him to forgive you for your unthoughtful words."

Sarah thrust her lower lip out and delivered her best hate-filled expression before she stomped off.

Rebecca sank back against the pew. Stamford had really created a problem for her. He had lost the support of her congregation. As soon as this affair was finished and Esther had been taught a lesson, the ministry would have to disavow him publicly. He would probably be angry, but he would have to go.

"Just get on in there and don't open your trap!" Stamford unlocked the cell and pulled the door open. He shoved Esther through with the sole of his boot on her rear. She fell sprawling onto the bunk.

Her hands were still tied in front of her, but he figured she could get the knot loose with her teeth. Or if she couldn't that was her tough luck. That damned storekeeper! He should've arrested him, too, for trying to aid a prisoner to escape. And his old schoolteacher. He should've arrested her for swinging her walking stick at him. He'd always hated her anyway. She'd kept him after school and tried to make him learn arithmetic.

While Stamford paced his office muttering to himself and clenching his fists, Esther pulled herself around on the bunk and stared down at her hands. Her fingertips were blue from lack of circulation. Her left thumb was bleeding sluggishly.

Bad as they looked, they were nothing in comparison to the condition of her wrists. The cotton and hemp rope was stained with blood and caked with dirt. She made herself a little sick imagining the condition of the wounds underneath. She glanced in the direction of her captor.

Stamford seemed to be winding down. He paced more slowly now; his steps dragged more. At last he halted with his hands thrust into the hip pockets of his overalls. He swung his heavy head in her direction. "You better pray your Yankee gets here pretty soon. 'Cause that's the only way I'm letting you out of there."

She didn't answer. She knew instinctively that she would have to get the rope off by herself. Stamford was a bully who would want her to beg and plead with him so he could have the pleasure of refusing her whatever she needed.

At least the townspeople knew where she was. Surely, someone would come to her aid before too much longer if to do nothing other than bring her some water and food. She hiked herself up on the bunk so her back was against the wall and gingerly lowered her bound hands to her lap. She was exhausted from the five-mile run and then drag to town.

To Stamford's disappointment, she closed her eyes and fell asleep while he watched her.

The soldiers hadn't seen hide nor hair of Jesse James.

Of course, none of them knew that a man claiming to be Jesse James had sneaked into Lieutenant Hammerschild's tent and held their commander at gunpoint. His men might be demoralized if they knew that the man they were hunting was so daring and dangerous. So Hammerschild had reasoned and consequently had told no one. After the outlaw had left, he had dressed and walked around the entire perimeter of the camp, checking with his sentries. Though he had questioned them carefully, they hadn't seen or heard anything. As far as they were concerned, not a mouse could slip through their cordon.

Now Hammerschild had almost convinced himself that they had it right. The whole visitation had taken on the aura of a dream. He had been overtired. He had had the outlaw on the brain. Still, the thing had been very vivid while it was taking place.

Since the "dream," he had wondered about the man he had locked up in Cutter's Knob. For two cents he wouldn't bother going back to that dismal little town at all. The sheriff had probably let the prisoner out before the troop's dust had settled in the road. Hammerschild had found relatives of Jesse James in almost every town he had visited. Moreover, the whole of Northern Arkansas was a hotbed of Confederate sympathizers. He had decided to ride back to Fort Smith and report that he had run Jesse into the Indian Territory.

He and his men had been riding south from the Missouri border all morning. After a while he had begun to look for the bird with the three-note whistle that had called repeatedly from the rocks and trees along their way. For miles he had had vague, uneasy feelings. Several times he had swung round in his saddle sure that something or someone was observing them close at hand. Once he had even seen the back end of a horse disappearing into a grove of trees at the bend of the road ahead.

Although the day was cold, sweat ran down Hammerschild's uniform. When he led his men down the streets of Bentonville in their bluecoats, he was sure he wasn't imagining the overwhelming hostility emanating from every single person on the street. His men guided their horses in tighter together and closed up ranks. They all wanted out of these mountains fast. Just north of the courthouse, a crossroad wound east to Cutter's Knob. The troop halted. The lieutenant stared longingly to the south.

The men's tack jingled. The three-note whistle sounded. Once. Twice. A whole flock of invisible birds made their nests in Bentonville.

As he stared uneasily around him, an acute prickling sensation centered itself between his shoulder blades. He was a target. He knew it. He whirled around in the saddle, scanning the street and the buildings on both sides. He could see nothing out of the ordinary. He wanted nothing so much as to clap spurs to his horse's flanks. But he didn't dare. The sensation was still in his back.

Like a man hypnotized, he signalled to his troop and led them across the railroad track toward the east.

"Damn, Jess, but you sure do know how to make a man tuck his tail between his legs." Cole shook his head in admiration as his cousin lowered the rifle and leaned back against the wall of the hotel balcony.

"Some men are too dumb to live," Jesse agreed. "And some are too scared to die. That greenhorn lieutenant just bought himself a little while longer."

"Where to now?"

"I think we'll just follow him back to Cutter's Knob." Jesse stood up and stretched. He climbed back in through the window into the arms of a smiling woman in a peach satin wrapper. Her lavish breasts brushed against his chest as she leaned his rifle against the wall beside the bed. As he allowed her to unbutton his shirt, he spoke over his shoulder to his cousin. "Just not too close. I got me a date tonight with a bottle of whiskey and Baby Flo here."

* * *

At Daniel's urging and against his best judgment, York followed his brother-in-law down the church aisle. Murderous thoughts roiled through his brain. If Elmo Stamford had harmed Esther, he was a dead man. York had sworn it in language so vile that Daniel Woodson had turned a little pale.

His first thought had been to kick in the door of the sheriff's tin can jail and get his wife out. Only by catching hold of Blue Devil's bridle and risk being dragged had Daniel been able to stop him.

"I'll go in first and talk to Mother," his brother-in-law was saying in a hushed voice. He led the way past the altar and through the door into the church office area.

"I'll talk to her myself," York growled, catching up to him and putting his hand on Daniel's shoulder. "You tried to talk to her before. You didn't do any good. Now which is Her Majesty's office?"

Daniel started to protest, then bowed his head. He had never felt less able to cope with people. Perhaps he had never been able to. With a stab of insight that wounded even as it illuminated, he realized that his whole life had been lived with people telling him what to do. His only comfort was that he was only twenty years old. He had time to change. Numbly, he pointed to the first door on the left.

York knocked sharply and then opened the door without waiting for an answer. His mother-in-law had a book open in front of her. A half dozen long strides brought him up to her desk.

Rebecca's head shot up from the big leather-bound Bible. Her eyes widened. The hand she raised to her throat trembled slightly. "Get out." The words came out in a voiceless wheeze. She swallowed and tried again. "Just who do you think you are? Get out of here!"

York shook his head. "I'll get out, but you'll come with me."

"I'll do no such thing."

"P-Papa?"

He started and whirled around. Esther's daughter—his daughter—was seated in a high-backed chair facing the desk. He had walked right past without seeing her. "Sarah."

Her feet dangled six inches off the floor. She clutched the padded leather arms. Her little face was a mixture of worry and pleading. "Is Mama all right?"

He dropped down in front of the chair and held out his arms. "That's what we're all going to find out. You want to come, too?"

She nodded vigorously and started to wiggle out of the seat.

"You'll do no such thing." Behind them Rebecca rose from her chair. "Stay where you are, Sarah Susannah." She caught sight of her son standing in the doorway. "Go get the sheriff, Daniel."

"Let's all go get him," was the stilted reply.

If a rattler had suddenly coiled to strike, she could not have looked more appalled or frightened. "Daniel!"

York straightened with Sarah in his arms. The little girl put her arms around his neck and shot her grandmother a look of malevolent triumph. "Let's go get that old Mo. He hurt my mother. He had her tied up and was dragging her along behind his horse."

"Good Lord," York whispered. He glared at Rebecca. "What kind of mother are you? And what kind of preacher?"

Ignoring his question, Rebecca clutched the Bible in front of her. "Put that child down. Daniel David Blessing, don't just stand there like a statue. Get the sheriff."

York walked back to the desk. "We're all going down to see the sheriff, Mrs. Blessing. I hope you'll come with me of your own free will. We'll make a perfect family group walking down the hill."

"I'll do no such thing. You'll be sorry for this."

Sarah tucked her head into her father's neck. "She's right. She always makes everybody feel sorry."

"Not this time," York said positively. Still holding Sarah, he stepped closer to the desk. Compared with the delicate woman, he was tall and imposing. In his long blue army coat and campaign hat, his air of authority, of command, was unmistakable. The lean, dark face with the dark eyes brooked no argument. "One way or the other, Mrs. Blessing, you're going to be coming down that hill. You'll tell your hired man to open that jail door and let my wife out. And you might as well know this. If he doesn't do as you tell him, then he's in for big trouble."

For the first time in her life, Rebecca Blessing could think of nothing to say. Never before in her ministry had she faced a person who did not defer to her. This was all her daughter's fault, she reasoned. Acutely, she felt the undermining of her moral authority. If Esther had not been so stubborn, she would never have been arrested. If she had only asked for forgiveness—

York kept his hard gaze directed at her while he gave Sarah an extra squeeze. "Where's your coat, baby doll?"

"In the closet."

He set her down. "Run and get it."

Sarah clattered out of the office. They could all hear her footsteps racing down the hall. Rebecca raised her Bible in front of her as if it were a shield.

Daniel walked to the coat tree. "Mother, let me help you into your coat."

She threw him a furious glance. "You'll live to regret this. You've let your mother be bullied and insulted. This church is God's house."

A door slammed, followed by running footsteps. York cut off Rebecca's scolding. "Let's go, Mrs. Blessing.

Sarah's back." He came round the desk and took the woman by the elbow.

She balked, but he pressed her forward until she had to take a step or lose her balance. "Daniel." She tried one more time in her most despairing voice. "How can you let him do this to me?"

Her son held out her coat. "Mother, how could you let Elmo Stamford take Esther away?"

Through the store window Bertha Carolan spotted the procession first. "Lord o' mercy."

Her husband came from behind the counter where he was entering accounts in his ledger. He adjusted his glasses, then took them off entirely. He put his hand over his mouth.

Customers came to the window, then trooped out onto the sidewalk. From other buildings others came out, just as they had the day before when Esther had been dragged into town at the end of a rope. This time the mutterings were softer, awed whispers, an occasional smothered exclamation. The women stared with appalled faces; the men shook their heads.

The tall Yankee in his blue coat and hat had a firm grip on Rebecca Blessing's arm. He was tight-lipped, his eyes straight ahead. A muscle flickered in his jaw. His free hand held Sarah.

The little girl looked around her at the townspeople, her face alight with a proud, defiant smile. Every three or four steps, she had to skip to make up for the difference in the length of her father's stride. Daniel walked on her other side, his face grave and white.

Their minister's face was white to the lips except for spots of color blazing on her cheekbones. Her fist was crushed against her heart. Bertha Carolan remembered that she had never seen Rebecca Blessing's hands without her gloves on outside of church.

In front of the jail, they halted. By that time more than two dozen people had gathered around them. York let go of his mother-in-law's elbow and bent to speak to Sarah. "Stay close to Uncle Daniel, baby doll."

She reached up to catch him around the neck. Quick as a butterfly, she kissed his cheek. "Yes, Papa."

He hugged her and exchanged a meaningful glance with Daniel before he turned to his mother-in-law. "Do you want to call him out, or shall I?"

"I don't have anything to say to an officer in the performance of his duty." An instant later she regretted her remark. A gasp of outrage went up from the listening crowd, and the buzz of voices rose.

"Well, I never."

"Her own daughter."

"—never did anything to be arrested for."

"Elmo Stamford's got too big fer his britches."

York shrugged. Then he vaulted up the steps. In a smooth, businesslike motion, he pulled his pistol from under his coat and struck the door with the butt. "Open up that cell, Stamford!"

Behind him Daniel Blessing added his voice. "Bring my sister out, Stamford. You've made your mistake worse by arresting her. You had the wrong man locked up in the first place."

"York!" Esther's voice came through the door.

"Shut up!" Stamford yelled.

"That's my husband. He's come for me. Let me out!"

"Shut up! Damn you!" Something heavy thudded to the floor. Esther cried out.

"Son-of-a-bitch! Don't you hurt her!" York lost his temper completely. He kicked at the door. Then he whirled and motioned to Daniel. "Come on up here. Help me break the damn thing in."

With a proud smile Sarah looked up at Bertha and Ed Carolan. "My papa uses the awfulest words when he's mad."

The ladies in the crowd looked disapproving of the "female bastard and town's shame and embarrassment" being so outspoken, but a few of the men chuckled.

The sheriff's office and jail had walls nearly a foot thick made of natural stone and mortar. It boasted a door of solid oak and two small windows with iron bars.

"Perhaps Mother could call to him," Daniel suggested.

York was fast losing patience with them all. He sprang down from the sidewalk in front of Rebecca. "Call him."

"I don't stand in the street and yell," she replied haughtily. Behind her the townspeople muttered and gossiped. She hunched her shoulders as if she could hide behind them. "It isn't the thing a lady does."

"Not even if her daughter's unjustly locked in a jail cell?"

York's sarcastic question made her wince. Again Rebecca felt a rush of anger. Her daughter was to blame for this whole terrible thing. She should never have been running around on the mountain to begin with. She had brought this rude, crude Yankee into their midst. Now the whole town was witness to what was essentially a family disagreement.

"Come on," York said to Daniel. They started up the steps.

"Better not." Stamford's voice came through the door. "I'm sitting here with my gun trained on this outlaw woman. First one through the door gets shot, and no telling where the second shot might hit. Bullets do bounce around off these here rock walls."

"Oh, Lord," someone in the crowd exclaimed. "Is that the sheriff talking?"

"He's always been real mean to Esther," Bertha Carolan told her ladies of the Missionary Society. "Looks like we're going to have to take a long look at him."

"Give it up, Stamford," York called. He felt sick to his stomach at the thought of his wife trapped in a cage with no protection from the sheriff's vicious attacks. Based on his own experience, he had no doubt that the man would shoot her out of pure meanness. Striving to control his anger and speak with sweet reason, he leaned closer to the door. "You've made a mistake, Stamford. No one's going to blame you for that. That shavetail lieutenant told you to lock me up. You did what he told you. Just open the door and let her out, and we'll call it quits."

From inside the jail, Stamford laughed. "No one comes in here and takes a prisoner out of my jail."

York would have liked to remind Stamford that he had broken out of the jail with almost no trouble. Instead, he came back down the steps and caught his mother-in-law by the elbow. "Up on the porch."

"I will not. No! How dare you!"

Even as she protested, he pulled her up on the porch and pushed her in front of the barred window. "Look here," he called to Stamford. "Here's your boss."

Again the townspeople gasped. If Rebecca had had a gun, she would have shot York Bradburn. He was destroying her reputation and her usefulness. Her only hope was to refuse steadfastly to speak to Stamford. If she did speak, he would probably do what she said, and then people would believe she had been responsible for putting her own daughter in jail. "I have nothing to do with him," she muttered. "Elmo Stamford is an officer of the law. He performs his duties as he's supposed to without any influence from anyone."

"Uh-huh," York grunted. "That's why he's been snooping around out at my wife's place."

Again the people muttered. They were looking closely at their minister now.

Rebecca flushed. "I merely asked him to protect her."

"And is this how he does it?" York used the gunbutt again, cracking the window glass in the process.

Stamford howled in protest.

York pushed Rebecca to the bars. "Now you won't have to yell in the streets. Tell him in a ladylike voice to let her out."

"Go ahead, Miz Blessing," someone called from the street. "Darn shame to have a nice girl like Esther locked up in jail."

"That's right."

"Go ahead."

Rebecca looked through the window. Stamford was standing sideways to the cell. The gun in his hand was pointed in her daughter's general direction. He had lost his mind to take this thing so far. She swallowed. Esther was not always a good child, but she was her daughter. "Please let her out, Sheriff Stamford."

"Miz Blessing." He gaped at her. "Damn it. I got her in here and I gotta have somebody. That lieutenant told me—"

"It's all over," York called to him. "I've got letters of identification here from a senator and two congressmen in Washington, D.C. I've got my U.S. Army record. I was honorably discharged nearly six years ago. I've never been a member of the James gang."

A silence ensued. The crowd held its breath. Sarah would have climbed the porch, but Daniel pulled her back. At last the door opened a crack. Stamford's florid face appeared. "You've got papers?"

Silently, York passed the packet over.

"What good is it going to do for him to look at those papers?" the old schoolteacher asked loudly. "He can't read 'cat.'"

The crowd burst into excited laughter as the remark broke the tension.

Stamford's face turned puce. "The hell with you!" He flung the papers on the porch and fired his pistol into the street. "The hell with you all!"

People scattered, screaming and shouting. One man clutched the top of his shoulder where Stamford's shot had grazed him. Stamford slammed the door and bolted it.

Daniel swept Sarah up in his arms and raced into Carolan's store. York caught his mother-in-law around the waist and leaped off the porch with her. "What the hell kind of man have you got working for you?" he snarled in her ear as he pressed her against the building, covering her with his body.

She was shaking so hard, she wouldn't have been able to answer if she could have thought of something to say. All she could see was Stamford's contorted face as he fired into a crowd of innocent citizens, her congregation.

"He's gone plumb crazy."

"He's lost his mind!"

"I'm bleedin' like a stuck hog! Help me, Cleo."

The citizens of Cutter's Knob crouched down behind the rain barrels and horse troughs or retreated to the relative safety of their buildings.

At that moment Lieutenant Hammerschild and his troop came riding down the street.

Twenty

With his gun shaking in his hand, Stamford stumbled back against his desk. He couldn't understand what he'd done. They'd made him so mad. He'd clenched his fists, and the gun had just gone off on its own. He hadn't even known he'd squeezed the trigger. Cold air poured in through the broken pane, but his own sweat stung his eyes. He wiped at them and stumbled over to the window.

The street was empty. At least he'd cleared them out. They shouldn't have gathered around like that anyway. Like a pack of dogs growling at him. He shook his head. He needed time to think.

"Let me go," Esther called to him from the cell. "You haven't hurt anyone. You'll be all right. Everything will be all right."

"Shut up!"

Everything wasn't all right. She didn't know about the person he'd shot. He hoped it was that old schoolmarm. He hated her. It was all her fault that he'd fired anyway. She'd told them all that he couldn't read. He promised himself right then and there that when he got this all over with, he'd run her out of town.

"You heard my mother." Esther's voice seemed to come from far away. "She told you to let me go."

He shook his head. His goggle eyes rolled. Sweat trickled into them. Growling deep in his throat, he stalked to the cell.

Esther held out her bruised and swollen hands. "Everything will be all right, Elmo," she said. Her voice was shaking, and tears were making paths through the dirt on her cheeks. He really had gone crazy. "Please, Elmo. Let me out of here. Then everybody will go away."

"Shut up!" He brandished the pistol at her, careful not to let the barrel through the bars. He'd never make that mistake again. "Shut up and stay shut up!"

When she cowered away from the gun. He puffed out his chest. "Now just set yourself down on that bunk and keep your trap shut."

Not until she had dropped down on the bunk cradling her sore arm did he walk away. At least he got respect in his own jail. She looked scared to death. And that was good enough for her. She was a bad girl. She'd had one bastard by one of the James gang. She was probably pregnant by that other one. Her mother hadn't said so, but Miz Blessing was too much a lady to know about bad stuff like that.

He made his way over to the desk and dropped down in his chair to think things over. He was sorry that Miz Blessing had had to see him shoot somebody, but whoever he'd shot had asked for it. She'd forgive him. He was sure of that. She forgave everybody. To tell the truth, she forgave too many people. He scowled at his prisoner. She was bad clean through. No doubt about it.

"Sheriff Stamford!"

A man's voice hailed him from the street. He didn't recognize the voice. Nobody important. He opened the lowest drawer in his desk and pulled out his whiskey.

"He's holed up in there with my wife as his prisoner." York's wrath blasted Hammerschild's ears. "When the commander for this sector hears about this—and he will—you'll be busted back to second lieutenant."

"He dragged that poor little woman into town at the end of a rope. And she's the preacher's daughter. He won't let her go." Hammerschild's face had turned from red to white as the storekeeper, Ed Carolan, recounted the whole story, emphasizing how the people had tried to reason with him.

"I can't help—" Hammerschild began. "That is, I came back to take care of this." He found he couldn't meet York's angry eyes. He looked at the jail, inwardly cursing the crazy jackleg sheriff, the town of Cutter's Knob, the county, and the whole damn state of Arkansas where a man could be awakened in the middle of the night with Jesse James poking him in the belly.

"Talk to him," York continued. "Get up on that porch and talk to him. Tell him that you made a mistake."

Hammerschild's eyes flickered. He hated to admit anything like that, especially when his men were gathered around trying to look serious but with their mouths twitching at the corners. He tried another tack. "How do I know you're who you say you are? You still could be a member of the James gang. I don't—"

York slammed the oilskin packet into his hand. "Read them through, Lieutenant. And while you're reading them, remember that my wife had to ride to Bentonville and back by herself to send the telegram to get this information. Something you should have sent a man to do. Your commandant's going to know about that, too."

"I told that sheriff to do it." Hammerschild reluctantly unfolded the papers. He did not have to read them. The congressional letterheads and the signatures blasted his eyes. He could feel sweat pop out on his forehead. That senator in particular could effectively put an end to his career if the lieutenant's name ever came to his attention. Carefully, he folded the letters and passed them back. "I'll talk to him."

* * *

"What do you suppose is going on down there?"

Frank James pulled his spyglass from his saddlebag and sighted down into the main street of Cutter's Knob. "Can't tell. But it looks like that shavetail lieutenant's in the big middle of it."

Cole Younger laughed. "You should've shot him, Jesse. Just plugged him right through the middle. Nobody'd given a damn."

Jesse reached over and took the spyglass from his brother. Casually, he let it roam the faces and figures congregated there. Soldiers on horseback made up the outside ring. Civilians, both men and women, crowded around the lieutenant and a tall man, whom Jesse recognized as the Yankee, York Bradburn. He looked at the women again. He couldn't find his cousin Esther, but he did recognize Esther's holier-than-thou mother, Rebecca Blessing.

He lowered the spyglass. "Let's step down a spell, boys. We'll watch and see what happens."

"We're wasting time," Cole objected.

"Maybe so, maybe not." Jesse threw his leg over the saddle horn and slid to the ground. "Anyway, we've got a show going on down there. Might as well enjoy it."

Hammerschild was trembling and sweating when he mounted the steps. A crazy man with a gun who had already shot one man waited behind the door. He looked over his shoulder at the crowd waiting down the street. Even the ladies had come back out and were craning their necks to get a look.

"Er—Sheriff Stamford—"

No answer.

"Sheriff Stamford!" Hammerschild swallowed as he

lifted his fist. Standing behind the rock wall rather than the oak door, he knocked. "Sheriff Stamford. Open up."

"Go to hell!"

"Sheriff Stamford. It's Lieutenant Hammerschild. I've come to tell you to release your prisoner. You've made a mistake." His palm was drenched with sweat. He flexed his fingers and knocked again. "Bring her on out."

"No!"

Hammerschild did not try again. He ducked off the porch and hurried back down the street. "He won't bring her out. I've tried." He appealed to Captain York Phillip Bradburn (Retired). "What do you want me to do? My troops could open fire."

York's scowl withered him in his boots. "With my wife in the jail. Who do you think he'd hide behind, Lieutenant, always supposing she wasn't killed by the first bullet? Get back up there and tell him you'll protect him when he comes out."

"Protect him! Now just a minute."

From the jail a shot rang out, followed by a scream. York drew his own revolver and raced up the steps. "Esther! Esther!"

Her voice was breathless and high-pitched. Clearly she was terrified. "I'm all right, York. I'm all right."

He slumped against the wall. "What happened in there?"

"I just planted a bullet right next to your wife's head," Stamford yelled. "I figured that'd get everybody's attention."

York cursed viciously. Hammerschild remained in the street, out of the line of the sheriff's sight.

"Tell that army lieutenant that if he wants to catch Jesse James, just to hang around. I've got his cousin locked up in my jail. He'll be along pretty soon to break her out. And I'll get the re-ward." Stamford's words were slurred.

"Are you drinking?" York demanded.

"What's it to you if I am?" Stamford fired another shot. Another scream. "That one was next to her foot. I can hit anything I aim at."

Jesse stood and stretched. Purple shadows had slipped down into the streets of the town. Late afternoon had given way to evening. "I think I'll mosey on down there and find out what's happening."

"Have you lost your mind?" Frank sprang up and slammed his hat onto the ground. "You're going to get yourself killed."

Other members of the gang sat up, looking at each other and at the James brothers.

"Naw! People see who they want to see. A stranger rides into town. They won't think a thing about it, let alone figure out who I am." Jesse's white teeth flashed. His eyes were blinking fast. He tightened his mount's girth and swung up. "I'll signal if I need you all to come running."

Before anyone could say another word, he had disappeared in the increasing gloom.

"Crazy as a coot," Cole opined from beneath his hat. He remained stretched out on his blanket, his legs crossed at the ankles. The rest of the gang followed his example and settled back down, leaving Frank to pace and mutter.

No one noticed the stranger in their midst. The ladies had gone home to fix supper and take care of their children. Only the men remained in the streets. Bertha Carolan had taken Rebecca Blessing and her granddaughter into her store, where she had fixed them tea and toast. Then she had lighted the lanterns and kept the store open for the troopers to come in to buy tobacco and canned foods and hard candies to eat.

Jesse had gotten the whole story from a grizzled sergeant named Tompkins. Hammerschild was green as grass to begin with and probably a jackass from the word go. The jackleg sheriff was crazy and drunk to boot. They didn't know anything about the woman except that she was married to the captain who had threatened to shoot Hammerschild if he rode away without getting her out of there. So they were stuck in the street with a cold night coming on and the whole town mad as fire at them.

Nobody had heard from the sheriff in more than an hour.

"Maybe he's passed out," Jesse suggested.

The sergeant gave him a hard stare, but the outlaw smiled innocently and moved on.

"Got any ideas?" Jesse's voice resonated in York's ear.

His cousin-in-law spun around and gaped incredulously. Then he frowned. Without a word, he put an arm around Jesse's shoulder and led him into the darkest shadows beyond the light spill from Carolan's store.

"There's a lieutenant here hunting you," York told him. "You're in danger."

Jesse's white teeth flashed in the darkness. "Well, now, thank you kindly, Cousin York. I'll remember you cared to warn me. But he's the one in danger. I've been tailing him for about a month now. I even paid him a visit one night. That's why he wants to get out of here."

"You paid him a visit?" York exclaimed. "And you're here? Are you crazy?"

"Maybe." Jesse laughed a little. "Hell, I do what I want to do and go where I want to go. That's why it's fun to be an outlaw. Otherwise, I'd be a dirt farmer. I'm Jesse James, and people are going to remember my name."

York shook his head. Not for the first time he wondered what kind of family he had married into. His wife ran through the woods in the dead of night. His daughter fought everything in sight. His mother-in-law preached love and charity but didn't practice it. His cousin-in-law thought being an outlaw was fun.

"How's Esther?"

York heaved a sigh. "She's alive. She's talked to me a couple of times, but I don't know what condition she's in. The bastard dragged her into town at the end of a rope right past Sarah. That little girl is tough as they come, but she's seen more than any child ought to have. And now, just when she's found her mother, this has to happen. That stupid son-of-a-bitch."

Jesse struck a match and lighted a cigar. Its end glowed in the dark before he spoke. "We could pull that jail down."

York felt a chill run down his spine. "How?"

"Leave it to me. Jailbreaking and bank robbing are my specialties. Why don't you send that Yankee lieutenant on his way?" Jesse continued. "I'll signal the gang."

York hesitated. Esther would be in danger.

"Go on," Jesse said softly. "Get rid of the lieutenant."

Hammerschild didn't question his good fortune. The minute York had suggested that this was a town problem, the lieutenant had rousted his men out and ridden off with indecent haste. Jesse set a boy to swinging a lantern up in front of the church at the top of the hill. Ed Carolan offered to supply the rope.

York couldn't believe the way the people in Cutter's Knob accepted the young outlaw. He might have been a white knight riding to save the fair maiden the way the people jumped when Jesse flashed his smile at them. Privately, York doubted that any other man in the country could have gotten more respect and admiration.

"Are you really my cousin?" Sarah Susannah cocked

her head to one side and studied Jesse with skeptical eyes. "I didn't know I had any cousins."

"I sure am," came the reply. "We come from the same family. My grandfather was your great grandfather."

"I never met him," Sarah said candidly. "I didn't know I had any family except my mama and grandmother and Uncle Daniel because I'm a female bastard."

In the light of the lantern Jesse's face hardened. Two spots of color magically stained his cheekbones. For the first and only time, York caught a glimpse behind the grinning devil's mask Jesse habitually wore. The man hunkered down until he and Sarah were face-to-face. "Who called you that?"

She thrust out her lip. "Everybody."

Rebecca had drawn close. Jesse exchanged a defiant stare with her. Then he put his hands on Sarah's shoulders. "What do you do when they call you that?"

Sarah looked over her shoulder at her grandmother; then she looked into the piercing eyes level with her own. "I hate 'em."

Jesse gave a bark of laughter and hugged her hard. "Good for you. Come on over here with me and meet your cousin Frank." He rose with her in the crook of his arm. Jesse James, the son and stepson of Methodist preachers, froze Rebecca when she would have interfered. "You're going to be just fine, Sarah Susannah. The Bible says to hate those who do evil."

Halfway down the road into the next valley, Sergeant Tompkins caught up with the troop commander. "How about splitting some of that money you got, Lieutenant?" he suggested loudly enough for the rest of the men to hear. "It's share and share alike in this man's army."

Hammerschild drew his horse to a halt. "What the hell are you talking about, Sergeant?"

The veteran of Stones River, Shiloh, and Vicksburg spat a stream of tobacco into the night air. "I mean how much money did that feller give you to ride on off."

"He didn't give me a damn thing," Hammerschild snarled. "He told me the town could handle their crazy sheriff on their own. I didn't argue with him. Somebody was going to get killed, and I saw the chance to keep one or all of us from being shot."

"Uh-huh!" The sergeant shifted the plug of tobacco to the other side of his jaw. "You got a wad of money to lead us off. Don't say you didn't."

"Who in hell would I have gotten money from?"

Tompkins threw back his head and laughed. "Damn if I don't half believe you. I knew you was dumb as dirt, but I didn't know how dumb. That feller that rode into town just before you pulled us outta there. That was Jesse James."

York had to admit that the James gang worked together as well as any men he had ever seen. Not surprisingly, they seemed to be experts at tearing down jails. Brother Jim and Cole crawled up on the porch and fastened the ropes to the bars. Not just one bar, but all four had a rope looped around them just above the crosspiece.

"He's snoring like a hog in a waller," Jim reported.

"Why don't I just go back and plug the son-of-a-bitch?" Cole wanted to know. "It'd save us all a lot of trouble."

"He's the sheriff. The people are disgusted with him, but they don't have any reason to want him killed. Leave him alone. They'll take care of him." *Or I will*, York finished silently. If anything had happened to Esther, Elmo Stamford would have to get out of town or die.

"You don't know these dirt farmers," Cole told him. "They hired him because he was mean as a rattler. Shooting's the only thing that'll mark paid on this deal."

With that Cole walked away to his horse. The others, except Jesse, were already mounted. While York had come to accept, grudgingly, the other members of the gang and even to like Jesse, he loathed Cole Younger. The man was devoid of feeling or morals. York was sure that Jesse's cousin would shoot anything that moved for no more reason than it displeased him.

"Ready, cousin." Jesse pulled his hat down tight.

"Ready."

Keeping low, the two men mounted the porch and stationed themselves on either side of the barred window. The long ropes lay like four dark snakes between them. Through the broken pane York could hear Stamford's snoring. He drew his gun. The four horsemen spread in a fan shape along the street. Jesse raised his hand. They leaned forward in their saddles.

Jesse dropped his hand.

"Hyaah!"

"Eeee-haw!"

Four horses sprang forward. They were at a dead run when the slack ran out. The entire grate, bars and frame and the glass behind it, spanged outward from the wall. In one horrendous crash it hit the edge of the porch and went thundering down the street.

From the porch in front of Carolan's store went up a general cheer from the men who had hung around to see the sight.

York was the first through the window with Jesse right behind him. They could have taken their time. The noise had wakened the sheriff out of an alcoholic sleep. He had lost his balance and fallen from his chair. He was on his hands and knees trying to figure out what happened when Jesse pistol-whipped him into unconsciousness.

York took longer to light the lamp and find the keys.

When he opened the cell door, Esther fell into his arms. "Are you all right?" he asked.

"Yes. Are you?" Her voice was a hoarse whisper.

"Yes." He squeezed her tightly enough to crack her ribs, then lifted her into his arms. "Are you sure?"

She tucked her head underneath his chin. "Just get me out of here and let me have a drink of water. Please."

Jesse took the keys from the cell door and opened the jail. York carried her out into the street. When they had broken into the jail, the town had been in profound darkness. Now in every building lamps were being lighted. People brought lanterns out into the street.

The soft murmurs of the townspeople were all around them. People wondered and marvelled at the ruthless efficiency of the James gang. Nobody seemed surprised. After all, they were all Ozark boys with plenty of get-up-and-go. More important, Esther was free without a shot being fired. Some of them looked curiously at the jail, but mostly they gathered around the preacher's daughter and her Yankee husband.

"Bring her into the store. We can take care of her." Bertha Carolan motioned to York from the steps.

"No, you can bring her up to the boardinghouse," a man offered. "My wife's got a clean bed all turned down for her. She can fix up a good meal quick as a wink."

"She'll come up to the parsonage." Rebecca's firm tones cleared a path for her as she came through the people gathered in the street, some in their nightclothes.

York hesitated. The logical place for him to take Esther would be to her mother. If the mother were a loving one. He seriously doubted whether Rebecca Blessing was capable of being kind.

His wife's body was exhausted and starved. Her mind and nerves would be in even worse shape. No one could go through what she had for almost forty-eight hours and not be in desperate condition. He could attest personally to the fact that the human mind suffered as much or even more than the body did. "I think—"

She clutched at his collar. "The boardinghouse."

The hoarse whisper reached the ears of those standing closest. Immediately they repeated it, sending it murmuring back to the edges of the throng.

The James gang had thrown the ropes off their saddle horns and abandoned the window halfway up the hill. They had walked their horses back down to the edge of the circle in time to hear Esther's plea. Frank shook his head a bit sadly. Cole merely chuckled.

The flickering lamplight masked the flush of embarrassment on Rebecca's face, but did not hide the angry tightening of her lips. She closed her hand over her son-in-law's wrist. "Sarah won't go to sleep without her."

Jesse James had stepped down off the porch and come to stand at his cousin's shoulder. His wild devil's grin flashed. "Now, there's not a bit of reason in the world to put yourself out, Aunt Becky. I'll just go get Cousin Sarah and bring her on down to her mama."

Rebecca's control snapped. "Mind your own business, Jesse James. You're not needed here any longer. And I'm not your Aunt Becky. I'm no kin to you at all."

Jesse grinned even wider. He swept off his hat in a mockery of a gallant bow. "No, ma'am. And I'm glad you reminded me of that fact."

"Please get me out of here," Esther whispered.

York could feel her tears on his neck. While these people insulted each other, his wife needed to rest. The Yankee made his decision. "I'd be obliged if you'd go get Sarah, Jesse. And you, sir. I don't know your name, but my wife needs a hot bath, food, and medical attention. Lead the way to your boardinghouse."

"Roseberry's the name. Folks call me Rosey. Right this way." The proprietor cleared the way for York to carry his wife.

Rebecca was left standing in the street in a little pool of emptiness. Her people. Her congregation drew back from her. She clasped her hands together before her and stepped in front of Jesse James.

Outlaw and preacher faced each other. Malice arced between them like lightning in a winter storm. The townspeople pressed closer, but what the two would have said to each other was interrupted by the galloping of horses coming fast down the hill.

"Better hit the trail, Jess," Preacher White called. "Looks like that lieutenant caught on to who we was."

"Hell!" Jesse touched his hat. "Sorry to leave unfinished business, Aunt Becky. Again. But I'm sure you understand."

Frank brought Jesse's horse out of the alley. The outlaw sprang into the saddle.

"And by the way, Clell didn't mean any harm," Jesse added.

Rebecca followed him. She pointed her finger at him. "Hell is where you're bound for, Jesse James. Don't you ever come back here again and bother my family."

A laugh was his only reply, and it trailed away into the dark as the horses tore up the hill past the church.

At that moment, Elmo Stamford staggered out of the door of his jail, brandishing his pistol. He was weaving and cussing a blue streak. Blood trickled down from a pumpknot on his temple.

"Sheriff Stamford," Rebecca murmured his name before she picked up her skirts and fled. The rest of the onlookers scattered like chickens, dousing their lanterns as they dashed away.

"Come back here!" Stamford pointed his gun at the sky and fired.

As the troopers galloped into town toward a dozen lights, suddenly the lights were gone and somebody was shooting at them.

Lieutenant Hammerschild knew he had found Jesse James. He drew his sword. "Charge!"

"What the hell—?" Stamford staggered in a circle in the middle of the street. The cavalry galloped toward him, their pistols drawn. He fired point-blank at them and missed.

Sergeant Tompkins's horse knocked him down. The horses coming behind stepped on him. He screamed and squealed. More hooves struck him. They tumbled and rolled him as they galloped over him. His body ended up bleeding and barely conscious in the mud beside the horse trough.

In the boardinghouse York held water for Esther to drink while Dr. Redner washed her wrists in dilute carbolic acid and Mrs. Roseberry heated water for a bath. The wounds were not too serious, the doctor opined. He had seen much worse that had healed with no scarring or any crippling.

York felt his gut twist at the sight of the raw and half-scabbed wounds, still crusted with dirt. Like two hideous bracelets, they circled Esther's wrists at the crest of puffy red skin swollen up on either side. The sheriff hadn't even given her water to drink, let alone wash in. York promised himself that when he could get his wife and daughter home and safe, he would run the jackleg sheriff out of town.

When at last the wounds were cleaned to the doctor's satisfaction, he bandaged them in strips of clean linen. "Just leave those in place for the next couple of days. If they don't swell up on you and turn putrid, you can take them off and go on about your business." He ran his hands up her arms and around her elbows. "Any particularly sharp pains anywhere along here?"

Esther shook her head. "My shoulders are sore and stiff."

Redner rotated them in their sockets. She gasped and groaned, but he nodded. "I think that could be considered normal under the circumstances."

She finished the glass of water, and York poured her another one.

"Let's put a little 'soothing syrup' in that." The doctor pulled out a small bottle and suited action to words, although his dose looked more like a splash than a couple of drops. He smiled beneficently as he passed the solution of laudanum back to York. "No sense hurting if you don't have to."

York held it to her lips. It contained so much "soothing syrup" that she grimaced and pulled away. He looked at it suspiciously, but Dr. Redner merely smiled and nodded. Adding a little more water, York tried again. This time Esther was too thirsty to protest and drank it right down.

"That's the way. That's the way." The doctor closed his bag. "Drink plenty of water; eat nourishing food. Mrs. Roseberry makes a real tasty rabbit stew. I recommend it."

York was shaking the man's hand when gunfire erupted in the street. They exchanged glances. "Sounds like you finished here just in time."

Redner took off his glasses and cleaned them with a sigh. "This has been a busy day for me. I thought the war was over, but I guess not."

"What do I owe you?" York followed him to the door.

"I'll send you a bill." He nodded to them each in turn and left.

York gave her a bath.

Esther had never thought of such a thing in her life.

When the Roseberrys brought in the tub and the buckets of hot water and left, she realized that she was going to have a problem, but York quickly solved that.

He began with a kiss. With his mouth on hers he stood her on her feet and began to unbutton her blouse. Esther could have protested. A hot blush rose in her cheeks. She promised herself she would protest as soon as he stopped kissing her, only he never stopped. The kiss went on and on, as her garments one after another were skinned off her body. Finally, when she was standing in the middle of her clothing, he lifted her and set her on the edge of the bed again.

"Lift your foot."

The laudanum was making her a little woozy. She blinked lazily. "I can't—"

He put his big hand under her heel and lifted it for her. When her shoes and socks were gone, he helped her to her feet again. "Get in."

The room was too chilly for her to think of protesting. With his support she stepped into the tub and sat down.

"Put your arms outside."

Dreamily, she obeyed, leaning back, her head lolling, her hands palm up on the floor. He poured the water over her, tipping the bucket under her chin, so the steam rose in her face. She shuddered in the grip of sensuous delight. Hot, but not too hot, sluicing over her chilled skin, rising around her hips, slipping into the secret places of her body. And her husband was doing it, looking down at her, seeing her nipples, her navel, the shadow of hair between her legs. She shuddered again at her thoughts.

The dirt and blood and fear were being washed away by the man she loved. With a bar of soap and a washcloth he began to touch the spots he had looked at. She stirred in embarrassment when he slid his fingers between her legs, but the "soothing syrup" relaxed her thighs.

His jaw set, he washed every inch of her except her hair. "At this time of night, I'm afraid to get it wet," he muttered hoarsely. "There's too much of it. You're too tired to sit up while I dry it."

She merely rolled her head on the edge of the tub. The warm water and his soothing hands were hypnotizing her. She couldn't think. All she felt was good. The pain in her wrists and shoulder was far, far away.

As he would a child, York stood her up in the bathtub and poured more warm, clear water over her. It covered her like the warm sun. It felt like satin sliding over her skin. She sighed and swayed.

He tucked a towel around her waist and threw another around her shoulders. "Time to get you out and into bed." His breath caressed the lobe of her ear. "Step out. That's right. Good girl. Now a couple of steps."

"—dizzy."

"You should be. Your body and mind have been abused until you need to sleep for a week. Then the doctor gave you enough laudanum to put a horse down."

At the bed he pulled the covers back and seated her on the edge. When she was dry, even between her toes, he slid her beneath the covers.

"Ooo-oo-oh! It's cold." She huddled between the sheets. Her eyes wide, their pupils slightly dilated.

"Can't have that." He stripped to the buff and climbed into the tub. A quick soaping, a rinse, and he was out, drying himself with his shirt. "Are you still cold?"

She cleared her throat. Her eyes were glassy, her lips moist. "Your body is beautiful."

Her words stopped him in his tracks. His scarred shoulder twitched. He half raised his hand to cover the wrinkled twisted skin.

"You're so beautiful. So tall and long-legged and your hair is so black. Black. Black. 'Black is the color of my true love's hair.' " Sing-song words came from between her lips. She held out her bandaged hand to him.

She's hurt. She's drugged. She doesn't know what she's saying.

"I feel so-o-oh sorry for the other women in this town." She sighed. "In this state. They don't have you. With your long legs and your big shoulders and your hands. I love your hands." She stretched her body and pushed at the covers. "Your hands feel so good."

He wanted to climb in bed with her and kiss her all over, but he also wanted to hear what else she had to say. He knew he was like an eavesdropper hearing secret thoughts, but he couldn't move. Like a statue he stood, feeling a silly grin twitch up the corners of his mouth.

"Your thighs," she whispered. Her eyelids drooped over the glistening eyes. "I wouldn't dare tell you how much I want to kiss your thighs. Women aren't supposed to want their men like that. But I do. I do. I want to kiss you everywhere you kiss me."

Her words trailed away. Her eyelids closed, rose once, then settled. Her tongue flicked across her lower lip. She nestled into the pillow.

He looked down at his body. He was hard, throbbing. His organ was like a separate being. Both of them wanted her.

The cold air swirled round him, but he was steaming. He sucked in his breath. She was his wife. She wanted him. He wanted her.

He lifted his clenched fists to the ceiling, then climbed into bed and took her in his arms.

She opened her eyes. A smile lighted her face as she slid her thigh up over his hip opening her body to him. He slid into her hot, welcoming sheath.

They held each other tightly. Neither moved, but their other selves deep inside them moved, tightened, swelled, and exploded.

She opened her eyes wide. He wondered what she was

seeing. Her pupils were dilated until the iris was no more than a ring. "York."

"What is it, sweetheart?"

"I love you," she said simply. "Do you love me?"

He didn't hesitate. He had found his home and his life with her. "With all my heart, I love you."

Twenty-one

The charge of Lieutenant Hammerschild's troopers tumbled and bruised Elmo Stamford. Where the steel-shod hooves grazed him, he was torn and smashed. When they passed, he climbed to his feet and staggered away, clutching at his head and dripping blood. He shook his fist after the riders, cursing them in a voice so strong that everyone still on the street heard every word. Only by the grace of God had he escaped being brained, but he seemed oblivious to his condition.

He had lost his gun, and three of his fingers on his right hand were broken. But the worst damage was to his face. A chunk of flesh had been sliced away from the curve of his jawbone on the left side. His ear was half gone. Blood poured down his shirt.

Still he went lumbering up the street the way the soldiers had gone. In a stentorian voice he cursed them, threatened them, dared them to stay and fight. "Jesse James!" he thundered. "Jesse James!"

The people inside Carolan's store shook their heads. The unspoken thought was that the quicker Cutter's Knob could get rid of their crazy sheriff, the better off they would be. Rebecca Blessing gathered her granddaughter in her arms. "I'll be going back to the church now. My granddaughter has fallen asleep. She's been up entirely too late. She should have been in bed long ago."

Bertha Carolan looked doubtful. "Rebecca, I don't

think you ought to go out in the street tonight. It's not safe out there. Jesse and his boys could double back. I'll make you all a pallet on the floor here by the stove."

"That crazy Yankee lieutenant might come back after him, too. If he's smart enough to figure it out," Ed added. "You and little Sarysue can stay here. We've got plenty of room."

The idea of a pallet on the floor when her own bed was only a couple of minutes away was supremely unattractive. Moreover, Rebecca remembered how the Carolans had seemed to favor Esther and York. She hugged her granddaughter more tightly and put on her most benign face. "God bless you both for your charity, but I think it best if I tuck this child into her own bed. Things have quieted down out there now. I can slip out the back door and up the hill before you can get things made up here."

She brushed aside the separating curtain and was waiting by the back door when Ed came after her to let her out. Tucking her head, she hurried away into the dark.

"Are you awake, Mrs. Bradburn?" Esther lay on her stomach. The covers were pulled up over her ears; her head was half-buried under a pillow. York uncovered her cheek and softly kissed it.

She moaned. A headache pounded her temples. Her mouth and throat felt as if they were coated with sand. "No, Mr. Bradburn," she managed to whisper. "I'm dying." She opened her eyes, carefully. The room was dim. "Why are you waking me up? It's not daylight yet."

"It's dark all over again. You've slept all night and all day."

She groaned. "I feel so awful."

He set the cup of steaming coffee down on the bedside table and gently turned her over. "That's the trouble with 'soothing syrup.' Once its effects have worn off, you have to have some more to feel half-decent." He cradled her against his chest while she whimpered plaintively. "Here. Have some coffee. It'll do a lot to put you right. And then I'll feed you."

"Please." She turned her head away. "Don't mention food."

He put his hand on her breast and squeezed it.

Instantly, her eyes popped open. "What are you doing?"

He laughed. "Getting you to drink your coffee."

She sat straight up, ignoring the drumbeats inside her skull. "Are you the kind of man who would take advantage of his sick wife?"

"Yes, ma'am. Any chance I get I'll take advantage of." He let his eyes run over her. She was beautiful, even with dark shadows in the hollows of her face. He could feel himself hardening. He would like to roll her over in the welter of pillows and blankets and make love until they both passed out from pleasure, but she had slept until late afternoon. She needed to be awake and about. She needed to drink a pitcher of water and a pot of coffee while she ate a good meal. They needed to collect Sarah and get back to the farm. He caressed her shoulder and pulled her back against him. Settling her head beneath his chin, he said, "But I don't think I will right now. The next time I make love to you, I want it to be in our own bed."

She relaxed against him with a sigh.

"I woke you up to take you home," he whispered. "It's time to go home."

She looked up at him. "Is it your home, too?"

"I believe it is." He kissed her again. "Do you remember what I said last night?"

She smiled. "I might have been drugged, but not that drugged. I remember."

"Then it's not necessary for me to say it again."

"Oh, no." She put her hand on his cheek. "Say it again. And again. And again."

"I love you." He kissed her. "I love you." This was going to lead to disaster. He moved out from under her. "Here now. Drink your coffee. We'll get dressed and go get Sarah. Then we'll go home."

Many of the congregation were already in their pews when Esther and York entered the church. A pianist was softly playing "Away in a Manger." The altar was draped with white and green cloth. The windows were garlanded in greenery. Behind them, lanterns mounted and swinging between tall poles lighted the darkness. Esther halted, her hands clasped to her bosom. "I had forgotten. Oh, how could I have forgotten?" she whispered. "It's Christmas Eve."

"Christmas." York looked around him. He shook his head. So long had he been hiding out on the mountain that he was going to have a whole new world to remember. "I'd forgotten, too." Then, "I didn't get you a present."

Esther choked and pressed her fist hard against her mouth. She hadn't remembered a Christmas present for her daughter either. "We'll have to plan for presents next year for all three of us."

He put his arm around her. "What's wrong?"

"I haven't thought about Christmas in five years. Oh, that's not true. I thought about it. I cried and cried and felt sorry for myself." She slipped her arm around his waist and hugged him against her side. "I think I'm going to cry again. It's going to be so wonderful. Now I can let myself plan for Christmas next year."

The pianist switched to "While Shepherds Watched Their Flocks By Night." As Handel's music filled the church, York dropped a quick kiss on his wife's brow. "For five years there hasn't been any Christmas for me either. Next year we'll have it."

"Oh, look." She pointed.

Daniel led Sarah Susannah out from behind the altar to the first pew next to the podium. The little girl was dressed in the sort of garments that Rebecca afforded for herself. She wore forest green velvet. Her hair had been washed and curled and was tied up in a matching green velvet bow. Daniel seated her and held up his finger in warning. Sarah folded her arms across her chest and thrust her lower lip out.

"Shall I get her?" York asked.

"No." Esther put her hand on his arm. "Let's just sit quietly here in the corner. We can see and hear the service."

"We could go and sit with Sarah."

Esther looked down at her garments. Even Mrs. Roseberry's best efforts with needle and soap and water had not been able to make them presentable. They looked as if she had been wearing them when someone had dragged her down a rough road behind a horse. "I won't embarrass everyone that way."

York guided her to the farthest pew from the front. "You're nicer than I am. They all deserve to see how you've been treated."

At that moment one of the Missionary Society ladies turned around to see who was whispering. She gasped at the sight of York and Esther and immediately leaned forward to tell the woman in front of her. Within minutes everyone in the congregation had contrived to look over his shoulder to locate the couple. Some smiled a little warily in welcome. Some pretended they were looking at the decorations. Some lifted their noses and turned around, shifting angrily to let the Bradburns know that as far as they were concerned all was not forgiven.

The pianist began the marching beat of "O Come, All Ye Faithful." Singing the ancient hymn, the choir entered two by two in flowing white robes. The congregation joined in.

The sanctuary doors closed behind them. Only those people in the last pews heard the sounds of voices raised in argument. York looked at Esther. "Something's happening out there."

"Mother and Daniel should have come in last," she agreed. "They always bring up the rear in the procession."

The choir had split before the altar and wended their way onto the benches on either side of the chancel.

A hoarse male voice shouted something. A body thudded against the wall. Esther caught York's hand. "That sounds like a fight."

Her husband was already on his feet. The choir sang "Amen," and the pianist lifted her hands from the keyboard. The buzz of inquiring voices passed through the church. Everyone turned to look back down the aisle in time to see Esther's Yankee husband open one of the double doors. While it was open, those with the right angle could see Daniel Blessing picking himself up off the floor of the entry. Then the door swung to.

"You can't treat me that way, Miz Blessing. I always did just like you told me."

York could not conceal his shock at the sight of Sheriff Elmo Stamford. The man's face was hideously swollen. The doctor must not have found him, for the wounds on his face and ear were uncovered and only partially scabbed. Under ordinary circumstances the pain would have been terrible, but Stamford smelled like a still. York could well imagine he had spent the day drinking to render the pain bearable. Now he reeled on his feet.

He had knocked Daniel Blessing against the wall. Blood dripped from the young man's nose and the corner of his mouth. He was having a hard time climbing to his feet. He looked immeasurably relieved at the sight of his brother-in-law.

Stamford loomed over Rebecca Blessing, whom he had backed into a corner. "I'm sorry," he was saying. "God, I'm sorry as I can be 'bout Jesse gettin' away. I knowed you wanted me to get him, but they was too many. They come racing them horses down the street last night. Wouldn't pay no attention to me." He swung his head from side to side and groaned. A trickle of blood slid down his bulging neck.

Over his shoulder Rebecca caught sight of York. She put her hand on Stamford's arm. "You've got to sit down and rest, Sheriff Stamford. In fact, you should be in bed. You've been wounded." She kept her voice low and gentle. "Why don't you let—er—Captain Bradburn help you back into my office? I have a couch in there. You can lie down."

Stamford's shoulders hunched. Like a bull he tossed his head and rocked on unsteady feet.

"You'll be glad to do that, won't you, Captain Bradburn?"

She motioned to her son-in-law. York had to hand it to her. Cool as any seasoned commander in the forefront of battle, she gave the orders while she smiled comfortingly at the miserable hulk swaying above her.

Daniel pushed himself to his feet and leaned against the wall. His blood spattered the front of his robe, standing out vividly against the white. He wiped his hand across his mouth. When it came away stained with red, Daniel closed his eyes and bent from the waist. He was about to be sick.

Esther came through the door and froze. "Dear Lord."

In the sanctuary, the choir began "Silent Night."

Elmo Stamford pivoted drunkenly. His bleary eyes tried to focus. From the dilation of the left pupil, York guessed he had sustained a concussion. He doubted that the sheriff recognized either of them. He stumbled into an excuse. "I come for the service, just like I always do."

Rebecca put her hand under his elbow. "Just go with Captain Bradburn. He'll take you where you can hear the service in comfort."

Suddenly, Stamford realized whom she was giving him to. He jerked his elbow away from her. Swinging his arms wildly, he backed away. "No! No! God damn it! No!"

"Easy, fellow." York started for him with arms spread.

"No. I ain't going nowhere with that bastard!" Drunk with pain and whiskey, he bawled the words at the top of his lungs.

Rebecca ducked under his flailing arms and dashed past York to the door of her sanctuary. "Keep him out," she commanded. "For heaven's sake, keep him out."

"Miz Blessing—" Stamford reeled after her.

She opened the sanctuary door and slipped through, closing it behind her. Daniel, his blood still dripping on his white robe, blocked Stamford's way. "Brother Stamford, you're hurt. Let's get the doctor for you."

"No." The burly Stamford swept the smaller man aside with a blow to the side of the head. "I'm going—"

York grabbed the drunken law officer from behind. Wrapping one elbow in a hammerlock, he managed to turn the man around. Esther pushed the outer door open, and York wrestled him out onto the stone steps.

"You're under arrest!" Stamford shouted. "Both of you. Goddam—"

"Calm down, Sheriff," York growled in his ear. "You're making a fool of yourself."

Suddenly, the man turned maudlin. His voice became choked with tears. "I'm going to church. This is America.

I'm going to church. Everybody's got the right to go to church."

York tightened his grip until the man squealed. "Take a deep breath. You're too drunk to sit there with decent people. You need help. You're bleeding."

The fight seemed to go out of Stamford. His body collapsed. York eased him down onto the steps, where he sat with head bowed, sobbing noisily. The church door opened behind them. Daniel brought Dr. Redner. Behind them came the voices of the choir and congregation singing "O Little Town of Bethlehem."

"I gotta right to go to church," Stamford insisted doggedly.

Redner lifted the man's face. The lights of the flickering lamps made the swollen, bloody wreck into a hideous gargoyle mask. Esther gasped and stepped back. Redner's eyes widened. "How long ago did this happen?"

For a minute no one answered. Stamford blinked, then swiped a filthy hand at his tears. "Damn Jesse James done run me down."

"Jesse didn't do this," York contradicted him.

The doctor raised his hand for silence. "We need to get you over to my office, Sheriff. I can't tell what's been done, but you probably need stitches."

"Go to church." Stamford rolled his head on his bull neck.

"Help me get him down the hill." The doctor took Stamford's arm. As he raised it, the light revealed its swollen, twisted fingers. He whistled softly. "I've got to hand it to him," he murmured to the others. "He's tough as an old bull."

Both Daniel and York were required to get the injured man down to the doctor's office. He staggered ponderously between them, occasionally snuffling and hiccupping, but all the fight seemed to have gone out of him. Only their strength got him onto the examination table so he could stretch out. By the light of Dr. Redner's lamps they could see his severe injuries. His day as sheriff of Cutter's Knob was probably over.

"I'll take care of him from now on," the doctor waved them away. "Go on back and enjoy the rest of the service."

Outside in the chill night air, they listened. The church on the hill was a beacon of light, and the singing of the choir and the congregation drifted softly over them.

"What are you going to do?" Daniel asked.

Once York would have taken offense at his brother-in-law's question. He saw it as an effort on the younger man's part to try to come to his own decision. Christmas was a time for renewal, for soul-searching. "Take Esther and Sarah back to the farm. Teach them both how to trust again at the same time I learn myself. We'll be a family. Folks will forget."

"Folks around here have long memories," Daniel said bleakly.

"The whole country's got too much to forget and get over to spend long on Esther's little stumble. Most of the men have already let it pass. The ladies felt sorry for her when Stamford dragged her into town. He probably did her a favor." York put his hand on Daniel's shoulder. "We'd better hurry. She'll be worried about us."

Rebecca's story of the Christ child seemed to take on new meaning to Esther. Barred from her mother's church for so long, she had closed her mind to the glories of Christmas and the birth of the Savior come to give sinners a chance for Heaven.

Tears trickled unchecked down her cheeks as the story was told, as the choir sang "It Came Upon a Midnight Clear" with its promise of "—rest beside the weary road, and hear the angels sing." York slipped into the pew beside her and put his arms around her. If only Sarah were between them, this would be the most glorious Christmas of her life.

Rebecca's sermon was remarkably subdued. She spoke of forgiveness and love and the unity of families. Esther tried to harden her heart, but no one could preach with more light and grace than Rebecca Blessing. She truly and with all her heart believed everything she said. Esther hid her face against her husband's broad shoulder and prayed for strength to do what was right for the three of them.

For the benediction Rebecca came to the chancel rail before the altar. She raised her arms, blessing them all, commending them all to Christ as they went to their homes.

"My God! Lookee there!" a man's voice rang out.

As one the congregation raised their heads in time to see a pole of lanterns come crashing through one of the tall windows. Glass showered over Rebecca as well as the choir and some of the parishioners in the front pews. Kerosene from the smashed lanterns splashed the greenery and altar cloth, the choir robes.

The quiet congregation, their heads bowed with thoughts of peace and good will toward men, became a screaming, fleeing bedlam.

"Sarah!" Esther screamed. "We have to get to her."

The second pole followed the first, crashing through the second window, bringing tongues of fire that leaped and danced on the altar. Blue flames ran across the floor toward the chancel rail. The swags of greenery blazed up with the speed of an explosion. Smoke filled the sanctuary.

The aisles were suddenly jammed with people, screaming and clawing, trying to reach the double doors. In their panic they overturned the pews and tripped and fell. Their bodies blocked the escape of their friends and neighbors. Behind them another great crash signalled the fall of the third pole of lanterns.

As the first parishioners burst out of the sanctuary, the building became a cavern with two outlets. The fire fed on icy wind sucked in through the windows and raced to follow it out toward the doors. The blast extinguished all the candles. The only light was the unholy flames of kerosene splashed wood.

"Sarah!" Esther screamed again. Then, "Mother!"

York pushed his wife toward the end of the pew. "Get out. I'll get them."

"You can't." She threw her long leg over the pew in front of her. At that moment, it toppled backward, barely missing her foot. She flung herself over it and started over the next one. York set his boot against the edge of their pew and sent it slamming back into the wall and clearing the way to the door.

The crowd fanned out, still pushing, still screaming. Through the thickening smoke, he saw his wife fighting valiantly to reach the front of the church.

Halfway down the sanctuary, York realized the aisle was almost clear. The only people in it were men who had recovered themselves and had come back to help the fallen. He vaulted over a pew and skidded into the aisle. From there his long legs carried him down to the front of the church to arrive at the same time as Esther made it over the last pew.

"Sarah! Sarah!"

"Sarah!" he bellowed, adding his voice to his wife's.

They heard her at the same time. She could scarcely get the words out for coughing. "Mama. Mama."

She had crouched behind the end of the choir pew, but she came out in a rush. Esther swept her up in her arms. "Baby."

"Come on." York tore off his coat and threw it over their heads. The smoke blinded them. Flames had found the swags of greenery along the walls and now shot along them to the back of the church. The heat was deadly. If not for the open windows, York knew they would have lost consciousness. The entire place would be an inferno in seconds. He put his arms around them both and started to lead them up the aisle.

Then they heard the scream.

"Mother!"

"Grandmother!"

Both his women fought to get out from under the coat. He tightened his grip on Esther's shoulders. "Don't stop. You've got to get Sarah out of here."

The little girl was struggling valiantly to get down. The screams became panicky cries for help.

"Grandmother! Grandmother!"

"I'll get her, Sarah," he yelled. "Let your mother take you out."

Esther hesitated for a heartbeat.

"Go on," he yelled. "Otherwise, I'll have to take you both."

Another instant and then she began to run toward the door. Two steps and she had vanished in the smoke. He spun. Ducking low, he covered his face with his arm and ran toward the voice.

He blundered into the chancel rail and almost fell on his face. Instead of straightening up, he tumbled over it and began to crawl. The air was breathable close to the floor. Icy air pouring through the windows dropped below the fire and smoke. He was able to crawl with his eyes open, crawl toward the screams.

Heavy cloth brushed across his face. Rebecca must have lost her way in the blinding smoke. He caught her skirts with both hands and tugged. She fell screaming upon him.

She was burning. The silk robes of her Christmas vestment wrapped her upper body in flames. He yelled him-

self as the fire attacked his hands and arms as he tried
to hold her down. His own clothing began to smoulder.
She fought him like a tiger, screaming and pushing at
him, calling upon God, trying to tear the robe away.

His coat had gone with Esther and Sarah. His shirt was
nothing. He had nothing to put out the fire. Her only
hope was for him to carry her out. He took a deep breath
of the cold air on the floor and rose. In the same motion
he tossed the screaming woman up over his shoulder
and started for the door.

Through the smoke and the flames, he would later
swear he heard the cannons. He knew he heard his
brother's voice. Rebecca's screams became the screams
of the rebel gunners trying to load their weapons and
fend off charging cavalry with swabs and rams.

Somewhere before him was the chancel rail. It caught
him just above the knee and toppled him over. He
breathed again and struggled up. The woman over his
shoulder was no longer screaming and fighting. Her body
hung limp. With a terrible certainty in his heart, he lumbered for the door. Midway up the aisle, another figure
met him. Esther.

Esther!

He began to cry. The cannons were silenced. His
brother's screams and the screams of the others died
away. Only the creaking and groaning of the dying
church, the hissing of the fire, and the roaring of the
wind followed them out into the cool night air.

When he dropped to his knees, strong arms relieved
him of his burden, lifted him, carried him farther from
the holocaust as the steeple toppled into the blazing
sanctuary, sending flames and sparks hundreds of feet
into the night sky.

Someone threw a blanket around his shoulders. He
was surprised at how much it hurt. He must have been
burned, but he didn't remember. He bent over coughing,

his head swimming from lack of air. Figures were shadows, their features only partially visible in the firelight. A group gathered a short distance from him.

Somewhere a woman wailed. Another joined her. He heard a child crying.

"She's dead," someone said.

"If she ain't, she don't have long," a man's voice opined sadly. "Lordy-lord."

York straightened. His job wasn't over. "Esther," he called. "Where are you?"

The group gave way. She reached out for him. "York. Oh, York, she's so badly burned."

His legs were stiff, but he managed to totter to her. He put his hands on her shoulders and leaned above her. The earthly form of Rebecca Ruth Blessing lay on the ground before them unrecognizable. Her hair, eyebrows, and eyelashes had all been burned away. To say that she was blistered was to misspeak. Her skin looked crisped as if it had been fried.

Her clothing above the waist was charred, leaving no doubt of the condition of the skin beneath. She lay without moving, her face turned to one side. One hand still clutched the Bible to her chest. It rose ever so slightly.

"She's not dead," he whispered. And then he wished it were not so. Nothing could save her. And the few short hours that remained to her held nothing but hideous pain. He had seen men burned before. He could remember their screams, their pleas for death.

Dr. Redner looked up from his knees on her other side. "You're wrong," he said positively. His eyes looked deep into York's own. "She's dead."

A great wailing arose as one after another the word passed among the congregation.

Behind them, the church itself had burned down until nothing remained except a smoking ruin. The flames carried by a north wind attacked the wings.

"Help me get her body down to my office," Redner instructed. "Pick her up carefully." He and four others lifted her and bore her away. York helped Esther to her feet, and she kept pace with them down the hill.

Mrs. Carolan offered to take Sarah to her home. The little girl was too shocked to protest. Limp as a rag doll, she allowed the storekeeper's wife to carry her away.

"Someone set the church afire deliberately," Daniel said fiercely. "Somebody tried to burn us all to death." His voice was high, almost hysterical, quivering with emotion. For his grief he was substituting anger.

"He's right," one of the church elders chimed in instantly. "Those lanterns went over like one, two, three. Some lowlife skunk had to've pushed them."

"Jesse James!" somebody yelled.

"That Yankee lieutenant!" yelled another.

"No!" York had been hunted and jailed for something he didn't do. He didn't want the wrong person blamed. "Jesse wouldn't do that. He may be an outlaw, but he wouldn't burn a church."

"Tell that to the folks in Lawrence!" someone yelled.

But Daniel raised his voice to kill that idea before it went any farther. "No. He's right. Cousin Jesse wouldn't do anything like that. His own father was a minister. And his stepfather. His little brother got burned to death by a Yankee fire bomb. He wouldn't do anything like that."

Still the crowd muttered.

"Where's the sheriff?" somebody wanted to know.

"Yeah. Where is he? Never around when we need him."

Before York could stop him, Daniel stepped forward. In a voice haunted by horror, he related what had happened at the beginning of the service. "He tried to break into the church. He attacked Mother and me."

"We left him at the doctor's office," York reminded him.

"Still and all, maybe we ought to ask him some questions."

"I been thinking he's gone plumb crazy ever since he dragged poor Esther into town the way he did," the boardinghouse owner declared. "Let's go find him."

York caught up to his brother-in-law. "This could be bad if Elmo Stamford didn't have anything to do with this."

Daniel was shaking with reaction and pain. His mother's death had left him bereft. She had been his rock and his guide. He had never made any decisions, never even taken care of himself. "If the sheriff did it," he snarled, "it'll be even worse."

Twenty-two

A thick, gray haze hung over the valley that Christmas morning. Ground mist rising among the trees smelled like smoke.

Alone, York rode Blue Devil down the lane past Bas Boscomb's place. Esther and Sarah still lay in exhausted sleep at Mrs. Roseberry's. He didn't feel too well himself. His burns smarted, and his chest ached from coughing; but the hounds had to be fed.

Sarah had cried herself to sleep in her mother's arms when he and Esther had told her that her grandmother was dead. Esther had wept, too, partly for her mother's death, and partly because the time was gone forever to make peace between them. Both had clung to him as their strength in time of need. It was a great responsibility.

Before she fell into a sleep so deep that it was almost a coma, Esther's last fleeting thought had been for the hounds. Helpless, loyal creatures locked in their pens starving for water and food. "Wake me, York. I have to go feed them."

This morning he'd kissed Esther's forehead and tucked Sarah's hand back under the covers. His whole life now turned around his girls. From a virtual hermit, he had become a man of many parts. Husband, father, brother-in-law, town counselor, hero, friend of outlaws, and now farmer. He smiled to himself. Despite the fire, the time in jail, and the threats from the James gang, he considered when he had found the courage to rescue Esther from the ravine the turning point of his life. Inexorably, she had drawn him back into the world. She had drawn him back to love.

Arriving at the farm, he galloped the steeldust straight to the kennels. At his arrival Teet let loose with a bugling call. Immediately, the others answered with a thunderous chorus. At the noise so close, Blue Devil reared and fought the bit. Only by main force of hand, thighs, and voice could York bring him down.

He tied the horse securely and went into the shed for the wheelbarrow. Food and water only. The kennels might be a bit rank, but the hounds would be fine. He had to be back at the boardinghouse before his girls woke up. They would still be devastated by the tragedy. He wanted to be there to comfort them both.

He had learned the names of all the hounds, and as he tossed them treats, he spoke to each in turn. They caught the jerky in the air before it could hit the food dish. When he dished up their regular food, they wolfed it in four or five great gulps and sniffed around for more. The water splashed on their heads because they were so thirsty they couldn't wait to drink. He filled each of their bowls twice and came back with more.

At Juniper's run, York filled the water bowl for the last time. He heard the squeak of leather shoes and the thud of heavy heels. Spinning around, he found himself staring into the muzzle of a frighteningly familiar pistol.

Elmo Stamford's mutilated face looked even more hideous in the full light of day. More than thirty-six hours had passed since he had been trampled. His whole head looked fearfully swollen. One side was stained a deep purple from crown to collar. Dr. Redner's bandage seemed a puny effort for so great a wound.

Moreover, Stamford must be very ill and crazy with the

pain. His bulging eyes glittered and rolled feverishly. The hand that held the gun trembled.

With the fatalism of a cavalry captain, York braced himself to take the round. Inwardly, he cursed himself that he had left his own pistol back in the boardinghouse. Even with Stamford still at large, he had not thought to strap it on to go take care of the animals.

York frowned. Why had the hounds set up an alarm when he rode in on Blue Devil, but made no sound at the sheriff's approach?

Stamford seemed to read his mind. "Them dogs know me pretty good, don't they?" he whispered hoarsely. "I took care to bring 'em some meat a couple of times. They don't pay me no mind."

That the sheriff was talking was a good sign. Very few men could keep a gun pointed straight at their targets for more than a few minutes. The weight of the weapon plus the ammunition dragged the arm down inexorably. If York could lull the sick man into complacency, he might be able to slap the gun aside and knock his adversary off his feet. He pretended concern. "What happened to your voice?"

Stamford shifted uneasily. He refused to meet the Yankee's steady gaze. "Caught me a cold." He gestured with the pistol. "It don't stop me none. I come to arrest you again. You're going back to jail where you belong."

York started. Either the man was insane, or he had no idea what he had caused last night. Never once did York doubt that Stamford had set the fires. He edged a cautious half step to the right and pretended to lean against Juniper's fence. "You've got more important things to do than arrest me. You've got a murderer to find."

Stamford's eyes goggled. The bruised mouth dropped open. "What the hell you talking about?"

York shook his head sadly. "That fire last night. You

know it burned down the church. You know about that, don't you?"

"I was over at Doc's." The gun sagged. Stamford lifted his broken hand to wipe at the perspiration stippling his forehead. The fingers were swollen like sausages. They must have pained him because he lowered his hand gingerly without touching himself.

"That's funny. Nobody saw you when it was all over and they brought the people back." York watched him closely. "It was terrible. Terrible tragedy. The whole town was in that church. Lot of people hurt. Burned and trampled mostly."

Eyes rolling wildly, Stamford looked everywhere but at York. He shook his head like a beleaguered bull and growled something like, "—accident—"

"No. It wasn't an accident." York shifted his grip on the water bucket. Too bad it was empty. He could use all the weight he could swing. "It was murder. We were all in the church when we saw the poles with the lanterns through the windows. Not a breath of air stirring. And those things crashed right through the glass one right after another. No, someone big and strong lifted them right out of their holes and threw them through the windows. It was murder."

The gun muzzle slipped lower. York had kept the sheriff talking long enough, but perverse curiosity kept the bucket swinging at his side. The man did not know what he had done. York wanted to be absolutely certain. The sheriff's reaction would tell it all.

"Horrible thing." He shook his head sadly. "Horrible. Awful way to die. Burned to death. She was standing right in front of those windows. Kerosene from the lanterns splashed all over her."

Stamford ceased his muttering. His face twisted. "Who?"

"The minister. Rebecca Ruth Blessing."

For the space of a heartbeat, Stamford froze. "No," he whispered. He had no voice. The word came out in an expellation of air. "No," louder this time, his mouth opened wider. The teeth champed, biting nothing. Tears flooded the goggle eyes. "NO! You're lying."

York felt no pity. "When I got to her, she was still on her feet; but her white silk robe had caught, and she was burning like a torch."

"NO!" He looked around him wildly. His mouth worked. His chest heaved.

The hounds leaped to their feet, whining, excited, thrusting their noses through the wire mesh, drinking in the air, as Stamford's panic communicated itself to them.

"When I carried her out," York continued, raising his voice to penetrate the man's panic, "if we hadn't known who it was, we wouldn't have recognized her. Her whole head was burned."

Stamford reeled. The gunsight dropped. York lunged at him, bringing the bucket up in a wide arc that connected with the side of the sheriff's head. If it had contained water, the fight would have been over, but Stamford was so distraught he scarcely seemed to feel it. Howling, he swung the gun back toward York, who caught his wrist and grappled with him.

Juniper began the chopping bark he used when the quarry was treed. He leaped at the fence, his forepaws catching in the mesh near the top. His hind paws caught. He tried to climb, but fell back. At the other end of the path, Teet answered, with all the hounds in between joining, too.

In the midst of the din, the two men grappled. Stamford waded forward, pushing his girth into York, trying to encircle the smaller man with his arms. If the sheriff managed to get his arms locked around York's back, his greater bulk could break it. York retreated, dragging the sheriff with him, squeezing and twisting at the gun arm.

Down the aisle between the runs they fought, the hounds leaping and snapping at them on both sides. Chopping barks filled the air, punctuated by occasional howls. Reeling from side to side, Stamford pressed his weight and still York gave ground. In front of Teet's run, Stamford caught his adversary. His hideous visage only inches from York's, the sheriff slammed the lighter man back against the fence. The mesh gave, a pole snapped and they tumbled into the kennel with the great black-and-tan.

Teet scrambled back as the two men flailed their arms. York landed on top, but he had lost his grip on Stamford's wrist. The sheriff cracked York a glancing blow with the pistol. York tumbled off, and Stamford scrambled up and flung himself belly down on his opponent's chest. His elbow jabbed into York's groin. The blow would have been paralyzing if York had not already been dazed. Even clumsy from his wound, Stamford could kill a man with his bare hands.

When York shook the cobwebs from his brain, Stamford's gun was aimed at his forehead.

The two men stared at each other, gasping for breath. The struggle had opened up the wounds beneath the bandage on Stamford's face. Bright red stains began to seep through.

Likewise, York could feel blood trickling down from his temple. Teet crouched at his side, growling ominously. Every muscle in the hound's body quivered.

"Put your hand through that dog's collar, or I'll shoot him," Stamford grated.

Obediently, York dropped his arm around the animal.

"Now, tell me the truth. Don't tell me no more lies." Stamford's teeth champed again. He shook his head. Blood trickled down his unshaven cheek and dripped onto his filthy shirt.

"I haven't told you a lie." York heaved an exhausted

sigh. "I wish I had. The whole town is in mourning. Mrs.
Blessing is dead. Dr. Redner said she breathed in the fire
and it burned her lungs. She went quick because of it.
Never regained consciousness."

He started to stand up, but Stamford waved him back
down.

"It was a mercy that she died. She was so badly burned
that the pain would have been unbearable. At least she
didn't feel that."

Stamford's eyes filled with tears. His face contorted.
"She was so good. So pretty. I never seen a more beautiful woman. Never in my whole life. She was always so
polite to me. She said I was the Lord's tool. She used to
let me come and talk to her."

"Why'd you do it?" York wanted to know.

Stamford stiffened. "I didn't do it. What the hell you
talking about? Jesse James did it. Hell, you did it yourself.
You're one of the gang."

York shook his head. "Nobody'll ever believe that. The
whole town was in the streets when Jesse and his boys
left. You picked a fight with Daniel just as the service
was starting. We took you over to Doc Redner's but after
he left you and came back to the service, you had plenty
of time to knock those poles over. I just don't see why.
Why'd you do it?"

"I was drunk," Stamford wept. "You know how drunk
I was."

York said nothing. Teet growled. Saliva dripped from
his canines.

The sheriff turned sullen. "She wouldn't let me come
in the church."

York cursed the sheriff. "Of course she wouldn't, man.
You were falling down drunk and beating up on her
son."

Stamford shook his head violently. Blood splattered
into the sawdust and pine straw. "I figured they weren't

any better than I was. If I couldn't sit in church, they couldn't either. That's why I knocked the lanterns over. Nobody was supposed to get hurt. They was all sitting back on them benches."

"All except Mrs. Blessing," York said softly. "She was behind the chancel rail. The burning kerosene and glass shattered over her. You burned her to death."

"Don't say that." Stamford stabbed the gun at him. Despite himself York ducked.

"It's the truth."

"Jesse James," Stamford insisted, lumbering to his feet. Teet's growls rose in volume. The sheriff swung the gun from man to hound and back again, but it was never more than an inch or two off a target.

"Jesse and his whole gang had already made it into the Indian Territory," York said positively. He rolled half over. One arm was under him, tensed to lever him up. He planted his foot on the ground. "You killed her. Burned her alive in her own church."

"Damn you!" Stamford screamed. "Damn you to hell!"

He jabbed the pistol wildly. His finger twitched on the trigger.

York pulled his arm off the hound. "Take him!" he yelled. "Take! Teet! Take!"

Slavering, the big black-and-tan sprang. Stamford cursed and fired. The bullet tugged at York's sleeve. Sixty pounds of primal killer hit the sheriff in the chest. Stamford screamed. His arms flailed wildly, knocking the hound off before the jaws could fasten on his throat.

Still on his knees, York lunged for the sheriff's gun, but missed as the fat man rolled away. With astonishing speed, he began to crawl down the path between the kennels. On either side of him, the hounds began to chop. Terrified, he pulled himself up hand over hand in the mesh and ran.

Teet bayed once, then tore after his quarry. York sprang to his feet and followed.

Behind the stable Stamford made a grab for his horse. The frightened animal reared and sidestepped. Stamford missed the stirrup.

With a growl Teet sprang at his back.

By the time York caught hold of the hound's collar, the great jaws had done their work. As swiftly as they had rid the Ozarks of wild varmints, they tore the throat out of Elmo Stamford.

Teet pointed his bloody muzzle at the skies and howled his triumph, and the pack in their kennels answered him.

York needed all of his strength to wrestle the bloody, maddened hound into the stable and bolt the door. He leaned against it thinking fast. A dog that killed a man would likely be shot, no matter how laudable the act was. The loss of Teet would grind Esther down, when she had suffered enough.

Grimly, he wrapped the sheriff's remains in a tarpaulin. Attaching a rope to Blue Devil's saddle horn, he dragged the body deep into the forest and buried it. Then he stripped the sheriff's horse and buried the saddle and bridle, too. Finally, he led the animal down the back side of the mountain and released it not far from a crossroads near Bentonville. From there the animal would stand no chance of wandering back to Cutter's Knob and raising questions.

At mid-afternoon he arrived back at the farm. So weary he could barely move, he nevertheless went straight to the stable. When he entered, the hound looked at him with reproachful eyes. "You saved me, old boy." York knelt and ruffled the black-and-tan's ears. "Saved my life and did your duty by Esther, too. Don't you worry. I'll see that she knows all about it."

With warm water he bathed the blood of battle from Teet. He dried the animal with soft towels and caressed the noble head.

The dog crooned and whined softly.

"I don't know, old boy." York shook his head. The valuable hunting animal might be ruined forever. "I don't know whether she can ever order you to take again. You've hunted down the wrong game. You might never trail a raccoon or a fox again. But I promise you, you'll live in luxury for as long as you live."

The citizens of Cutter's Knob were in agreement that the sheriff had burned down the church, killed the minister, and then run for his life. Wanted posters were printed and distributed. A reward of one hundred dollars was offered by the town council. The Church Conference offered another hundred, but it was never collected.

The grief with which Esther and her family buried Rebecca Blessing did much to disperse the remnants of prejudice against her. Esther stood beside her mother's grave, dressed in her grandmother's old black dress, and holding her daughter's hand. Her brother and husband supported her on either side, and Esther's tears moved the congregation. Afterward, without exception, the entire town came up to pay their respects.

"You must come to the farm with us," Esther told Daniel. "It belongs to the Woodsons. You're a Woodson. It's part of your heritage."

He shook his head. "I'm packing my bags and heading for California."

"California?"

"One of the last things I told Mother was that I was leaving right after Christmas. I didn't know whether I'd be able to go or not. Now there's nothing to keep me."

Esther would have protested, but York put one hand

on her shoulder. The other he held out to his brother-in-law. They grasped hands.

Daniel grinned. "The first thing I'm going to do when I get out of this valley is kiss a girl. I want to find out what I've been missing."

While York and Sarah sat in the wagon, Esther walked to her mother's grave once more. They had buried her in the garden behind the ruins of the church. When it was rebuilt and the new minister brought in, her grave would be a part of it. In a sense she would never leave it.

Dry-eyed, Esther stared down at the wilted and shattered flowers. Late in the night, York had repeated Stamford's confession and told her what Teet had done. Without speaking, they both knew that Rebecca had raised an ignorant bully to a position of power because he would do her bidding. She had called him the Lord's tool, but he had been her tool. Then in one violent moment, she had lost control of him and paid with her life.

Esther closed her eyes. Bible verses tumbled through her mind. Verses about vengeance, about retribution, about forgiveness. But they were all confused. She could not put one together to repeat above her mother's grave. In utter misery, she opened her eyes. And there before her was the stark and eternal beauty of the mountains.

A chill wind ruffled her skirts. Perhaps later she would be able to say the right words.

She hurried back to the wagon. Taking Sarah into her lap, she huddled against her husband. He turned the horses around and trotted them back down the hill toward home.

Epilogue

With Sarah running ahead of them, York and Esther climbed the ridge to his cabin. With mixed feelings Esther approached. She had promised Sarah this trip. As a result, the five-year-old had reminded her of the promise almost daily and requested endless stories of what they would see and do.

"Oh, look. Look. There it is! Oh, it's just like you said. It's so small. Like Red Riding Hood's grandmother's house. Will there be a wolf?" Sarah laughed delightedly. In the past three months, Esther had read her all of Mother Goose and the Brothers Grimm. Now the girl saw the weathered shack as a place of magic.

York called to her. "Sarah, better wait for me. There might be some kind of varmint in there."

Obediently, the little girl waited, dancing on one foot and then the other and sighing at the slow pace of her parents.

The cabin door stood open, a grim reminder to the adults that bounty hunters had rousted them out not so long ago. Esther shuddered. The very spot where Sarah was standing was the spot where she had lain on her back with a gun barrel inches from her face.

While Esther held Sarah's hand, York walked into the dimness. In a minute he called to them. "All clear. Come on in."

"Yahoo!" Sarah yelled. She sprang up the steps like a

shot. Until she came to live with her parents, she had never been allowed to yell. Now she did quite a lot of yelling.

"Whoa, there. You'll fall down and break your crown." Her father caught her around the waist as she sprinted through the door.

"Like Jack and Jill. Not me." She squealed in delight as he swung her up in his arms.

He put her down and let her explore while he walked to each of the pieces of furniture in turn, touching each lightly, staring at everything with new eyes. At length, he paused in the middle of the cabin floor with his hands on his hips. "How did I ever live like this?"

Esther came and put her arms around his waist and nibbled his earlobe. "You didn't want to leave here," she reminded him softly. "You had to struggle with yourself to come down and have Thanksgiving dinner with me."

"I was crazier than I thought." He ran his hand through his hair. "What did we come here for?"

Esther laughed. And Sarah came to his side and tugged on his sleeve. "Please show me where you fished, Papa."

"Right away, sweetheart." He grinned down at her. "I remember now," he said to Esther.

Three days later, they were ready to leave. A new hand had been hired to help at the kennel so they could take Sarah on this trip. York was already planning to hire him to do the chores for a month in the fall while they travelled to Philadelphia to visit his family.

"This'll make a good hunting cabin," York mused. "We can leave everything as it is, except for this." He pulled a tin can out of the top shelf of the pie safe.

Opening it, he drew out a handful of crumpled bills. Esther peered at them suspiciously. He had had money under the floorboard as well. Why were they separate?

He thumbed through them. They were U.S. dollars, all small bills—ones and an occasional five. Once he thumbed up a ten. "That represents my earnings," he explained. "Two years of making whiskey."

She raised an eyebrow. "It hardly seems worthwhile."

He rolled the bills back up neatly and put them in his vest pocket. "It had its moments. I guess it kept me busy in mind and body." He put his arms around her and kissed her with lips and tongue and hands. She was trembling when he patted her sweet little rear. "Now we're both ready to get back to our own room again." She nodded, her breath coming faster.

"Hey, Sarah," he called. "Let's show your mother the still."

For herself Esther was unimpressed with her husband's construction, and Sarah soon wandered off to explore some magical cracks in the rocks where dwarves might hide the entrance to their mines. On the other hand, York was as proud as a boy of his work.

He drew her attention to the way he had concealed it beside the artesian spring that bubbled from the rocks. "The water disappears in the ground another hundred feet down the ridge," he explained, "so no one can follow the stream back up here."

She hugged him. "You don't care about that anymore, do you?"

He had to stop his tour to kiss her. She was glad Sarah had gotten so used to their hugging and kissing that she didn't pay attention anymore. She wondered what was going to happen next year when Sarah went to school and perhaps learned that some children's mothers and fathers did not hug and kiss from morning till night.

With great pride York pointed out the furnace, the still itself, the relay, the heater box, and the thumper. "This is a fifty gallon rig," he informed her. "Of course, I never made fifty gallons. Once I made thirty gallons, but I didn't like the taste. After that I just made small batches."

"I think you do brandy best," Esther murmured.

He kissed her again and squeezed her hip. "I just kept busy while I waited for you to come along and save me."

She watched Sarah paddle in the artesian spring while he shut the still down. "We won't throw anything away." He winked at her. "We'll want to come back and make some more for Christmas presents for Jesse and the boys."

She rolled her eyes. "I don't expect to see Jesse again for a long time, but you never know."

"No, you never know about Jesse James." He drew off the whiskey. "I've got two gallons here. You carry one jug and I'll carry the other. No sense wasting it. We might not get any more for a long time."

With Sarah between them, they walked back to the cabin. "I'll just close the front door," York told her.

As Esther breathed in the delicious scents of the quiet spring woods, a black shape detached itself from the trees and paced with majestic solemnity toward them. A yard from the bottom step, he stopped and sat, his four paws precisely placed together.

"Look, Mama," Sarah crooned ecstatically. "It's Big Boy."

"Son-of-a-gun." York came out of the cabin. "I thought for sure he was a goner when he hadn't shown up."

Esther bent forward and extended a hand. "Hello, big fellow. We almost missed you. How've you been? Lonesome, I'll bet."

York's throat worked. He went down on one knee beside Esther. He, too, extended his hand. "I'm surely glad to see him. He probably saved my life just like Teet. He was brave as a lion, Sarah. A real hero."

The little girl's eyes were huge and shining. "Brave as a lion," she crooned.

The big male regarded them with unblinking green eyes, staring reproachfully at the closed door and at the three people.

Shaking his head regretfully, York rose and dusted off his pant leg. "He'll never come home with us. He's never even let me pick him up."

"Maybe he will this time." Esther crouched, holding out her hands. "Come on, Big Boy," she called. "Come on, big kitty."

"Come on, Big Boy," Sarah crooned.

"It's time to come down out of the mountains." She looked over her shoulder at York while the cat made up his mind. "You'll have to carry both gallon jugs of whiskey."

York nodded. "I can manage." He stared at the cat, who shifted his gaze, looking around the clearing as if taking stock. "Come on, old fellow. You're welcome to come with us. Believe me. It's the land of milk and honey. You never had it so good."

Esther wiggled her fingers invitingly to the cat. "Come on, big kitty."

"Come on, big kitty." Sarah imitated her mother.

Deliberately, he rose, stretching his length fore and aft. He yawned, displaying his glistening fangs and rough pink tongue. Then with an air of quiet serenity he stalked forward and bent his head under Esther's hand.

With tears in her eyes, she stroked the thick, black fur on the arched neck. A deep, growling purr broke from his throat. Her other hand stroked along his side and under his belly. Beneath the thick pelt, she could feel the hidden scars. "Will you let me pick you up, Big Boy?" she murmured. "Will you let me carry you?"

Gingerly, she got her hands under him and gathered

him in against her. His deep purring never stopped as he rubbed his neck against her breast.

"I'll be damned," York murmured as he steadied her to her feet.

She looked up at him, all the love in the world in her eyes. "He's ready to come down, too."

Together the four of them headed down into the valley.